PRAISE FOR ALAN DEAN FOSTER

"Rip-roaring action sequences and the mystery of Madrenga's curious powers propel the story through a series of consistently surprising twists and turns."

—*Publishers Weekly*

"Alan Dean Foster is the modern day Renaissance writer, as his abilities seem to have no genre boundaries."

—*Bookbrowser*

"One of the most consistently inventive and fertile writers of science-fiction and fantasy."

—*The Times* (London)

MADRENGA

MADRENGA

ALAN DEAN FOSTER

WFP
WordFire Press

MADRENGA
Copyright © 2020 Alan Dean Foster

EBook ISBN: 978-1-68057-143-1
Trade Paperback ISBN: 978-1-68057-143-1
Hardcover ISBN: 978-1-68057-145-5

Cover design by Alexandre Rito

Kevin J. Anderson, Art Director
Published by
WordFire Press, LLC
PO Box 1840
Monument CO 80132
Kevin J. Anderson & Rebecca Moesta, Publishers

WordFire Press eBook Edition 2020
WordFire Press Trade Paperback Edition 2020
WordFire Press Hardcover Edition 2020
Printed in the USA
Join our WordFire Press Readers Group for
sneak previews, updates, new projects, and giveaways.
Sign up at wordfirepress.com

CHAPTER ONE

BOTH THE MORNING AND HER MAJESTY QUEEN ALYRIATA OF Harup-taw-shet dawned gray and overcast. It was not that she was in a foul mood as much as she was dubious. While the crimson-lacquered nails of her left hand reached up and back to idly stroke the whispering cantwet that perched on her silk-clad shoulder, the fingers of the other thoughtfully cradled a chin that, while still sharply defined, had seen better times. Nowadays her face, like the kingdom's politics, required regular applications of cosmetics.

The matter of the moment demanded that she defer to the advice of Chief Counselor Natoum. Used to relying on her own judgment in all things from menus to misters, she was reluctant as always to grant the power of decision to another. But then, she told herself as she leaned slightly forward on the throne that had been carved from a single gutted aquamarine, of what use is a Chief Counselor if one never accepted his counsel? Not in bed, surely, though Natoum would have leaped at the chance. She smiled ever so slightly to herself. The sometime wizard was master of many realms, but not the one that lay between the covers.

"He's just a boy," she finally opined.

Smiling confidently behind long whiskers that were in dire

ALAN DEAN FOSTER

need of salvation, Natoum stepped sideways to put a hand on the
shoulder of the slim youth who stood nervously facing the Queen.

"He's not just a boy, your Majesty. He is Madrenga."

Alyriata of Harup-taw-shet continued to caress the cantwet.
Alternately purring and whistling softly on her shoulder, it tucked
the nearest of its heads behind an ear that dripped pearls the color
of ghosted canaries.

"So that's his name—Madrenga?"

Distinctly uncomfortable beneath the razor-sharp royal scrutiny, the youth cut his eyes imploringly at the Counselor. A helpful
Natoum answered for him.

"Indeed that is his name, your Majesty. Madrenga is what
he is."

"I don't like riddles, Natoum. Or poor grammar. I don't have
time for either. With the King off fighting the Balatians, the affairs
of state fall to me. Or more properly, on me. For this one small
thing we speak of today, I make time for myself." Her head came
up and her chin flicked accusingly at the slender youth standing
head down before her. "What makes you think this callow
stripling is up to such a task?" She sniffed. "I could break him
myself."

If the subject of the insult was offended, he showed no sign of
it. From a Queen one suffers much. From a Queen such as Alyriata one suffers anything.

Unlike his young charge, the Counselor was not intimidated.
"I assure your Majesty that he is ideal for the task you have in
mind."

"Hmph." She leaned back in the throne and rested the side of
her head against her left fist. As she reclined, the cantwet fluttered
its gold and silver wings as it struggled to retain its perch on her
left shoulder. "Well, the motley business of empire yammers in the
corridors. It rings in my ears when all I want is a quiet day and a
hot bath. While my husband defends, I must make amends. To
such ends does this mission incur and infer." The fingers of her
right hand began to tap-tap on the arm of the aquamarine throne.

2

"If he has a name but is also a thing you call Madrenga, then I suppose that will serve him well enough." She studied the would-be courier grudgingly. "Boy, Natoum shows a confidence in you I do not see. Will you undertake an errand for me?" *As if he was in a position to refuse,* she mused.

When no response was forthcoming, the Counselor dropped his hand from the youth's shoulder to his back and gave him a gentle but firm nudge. The reassuring smile that accompanied the gesture was more helpful than the shove in persuading the boy to take a step forward. His voice was halting but the response audible.

"Y-yes, your Majesty. With thanks and pleasure." He hesitated, plainly wishing to say something else but unable to give movement to the words.

Alyriata raised a hand and gestured impatiently. "Come, come, boy—Madrenga. You heard me. My time is more precious than the throne upon which I sit. If you have something to say, puke it up!"

The youth swallowed. "I have no family, Majesty. Only two companions. Small things they are, but they are all I have. I would not abandon them, not even for a royal mission."

"Oh, for the love of Saringar! Are you speaking of pets, boy?"

He nodded timidly. "A small dog, your Majesty, and a pony."

The Queen rolled her eyes. Unlike her hair and much of the rest of her, the fire in them had not aged one whit, and their color was still a match for that of the throne.

"By all means," she told him with mock gravity, "take them with you. Who can say but that they might prove useful on your journey? For example, if attacked by ravenous beasts you will have something to place between them and yourself while you attempt to make your escape."

At this bloodthirsty image the youth winced perceptibly, but held his tongue.

Rising, Alyriata came forward and descended the three steps from the dais on which sat the throne of Harup-taw-shet. Natoum bowed his head, whacked his charge on the back to remind the youth to do the same, and stepped aside. Striding to a twisting table of caramel-colored eletak wood that seemed rooted to rather than placed on the floor, she opened a box fashioned of the most precious pietra dura. From within she withdrew a prepared scroll of very thin rolled gold over which the court scribe had labored for much of a day. Re-reading the words to reassure herself of their content, she silently pronounced herself pleased. Securing the scroll with a red ribbon, she slid the thick foil into the engraved corium cylinder that had been fashioned to hold it. The container boasted fine artwork on its exterior but no official markings, the better to mask the royal origin of what was contained within.

Pivoting, she walked over to her Chief Counselor and his protégé. "This is to be delivered to Zhelerasjju, Queen of all the Darians and the lands to the farthest east. It is both a matter of state and a personal matter. I require that this be done with all speed and security. None are to read the contents of the scroll contained herein. Look at me, boy!" His head snapped up. Eyes that were like shards of the throne itself bored into his own. "That includes you. Especially you."

Seeing that his charge was starting to tremble and beginning to wither beneath that royal glare, Natoum took a hasty step forward. "That will not be an issue, your Majesty. The Madrenga— Madrenga, he cannot read."

Alyriata grunted softly and moved back. "Strong neither in body nor in mind. I hope you know what you are doing, Natoum. If my communication fails to reach Daria, I will have the cost of trying again deducted from your annual recompense."

"Your Majesty must have trust in my judgment."

She nodded tersely. "It is not your judgment I question, Natoum, but the muscles of your messenger. Unlike your usually sound counsel, they are nowhere to be found." She waved a diffident hand. As she did so, the cantwet on her shoulder relieved itself of a flute-like melody. "I can spend no more time on this.

Moneymen and honest citizens await the decisions that fall to me. Damn all husbands and their propensity to go to war! I miss him so." With a last circumspect glance at the Counselor and his chosen youth she turned away and headed briskly for the throne room's exit, a fast-moving cloud of lavender and lace. Her voice floated back to them.

"See that this Madrenga is properly kitted out, Natoum, and send him on his way. Why should I worry? It will all proceed as you say. Nothing can go wrong. After all, he will have the aid of a puppy and a pony."

The silence in the throne room was magnified by its vastness. Banners like silken beards and as high as a three-story window looked down upon the two men, one as old as the other was young. Natoum turned to the newly-anointed messenger.

"That went well, I think."

Madrenga spoke up, his voice a little clearer now that the overwhelming presence of the Queen had left them. "She has no confidence in me, Natoum."

Once again, a hand came down on the youth's shoulder. "She expected someone twice your size, boy, clad in glistening graven armor and trailing a sword half his own height."

The youth let out a soft exhalation. "And instead, she got me." He eyed the Counselor. "What makes you think I can do this?"

"Because you are a Madrenga, boy. Perhaps the only one in the capital, I'd wager. You know nothing of your parents, of your origin, of your background or heritage." There was a twinkle in the old man's eye. "But I do."

"And how do you know such things, old man? If I myself do not know them about me, how can you?"

Natoum shrugged. "The signs of your heritage are there. The markings, the motions, the subtle movements. I'd wager strong you are of the family Madrenga. I *am* wagering strong that you are of the family Madrenga. And I had best be right." He shook his head. "No telling what the replacement cost is of that scroll you now carry. Not to mention the damage to my reputation if you fail to deliver it."

"I've never been to Daria, sir. How will I find the way?"

"I will provide you with directions. And along the way, if you are a true Madrenga, you will muster any help you require. The journey will be long and arduous."

The youth made a disparaging sound. "Aren't all such journeys?"

"I wouldn't know. Never been beyond the borders of Haruptaw-shet myself." He patted his charge on the arm. "But you'll do fine, boy, you'll do fine. When you need it, help will find you— one way or another, I am hoping. Now let's get your kit together so you can be on your way at first light."

"Directions or no directions, I wish you were coming with me, Natoum."

The old man's eyes widened slightly as he regarded the youth. "I couldn't possibly, young Madrenga! I am the Queen's Chief Counselor. My services are all the more necessary with the King off at war. They cannot possibly be dispensed with. Besides, the journey is far too dangerous for someone of my advanced years to undertake."

"But not for someone of my inexperienced ones," the youth shot back tightly.

"Oh, you'll be fine, you'll be fine. In a difficult spot you can run whereas I could only mumble hopeful imprecations. Now let's fit you out. You'll want a solid meal and a good night's rest before setting out in the morning."

"We also need to see to Orania and Bit."

"What? Oh, yes, your pets."

"They are not my pets," the youth countered a bit stiffly. "They're my companions."

"They're a pony and a pup, but however it suits you to call them so may it be. I can't believe you really intend to embark on this trek with them. Looking after them and attending to their needs can only slow you down."

"Friends never slow one down," Madrenga countered.

Natoum pursed his lips and nodded sagely. "Perhaps you're not so much the fool as our great queen thinks. Certainly I must believe otherwise or I would not have been compelled to recruit you for this singular honor." He wagged a long, aged finger in the youth's direction. A ring of mystic power glinted on the furrowed digit. Both were badly in need of a cleaning. "Take care, do well, deliver the scroll, and it may be the making of you. So the old books say about all the family Madrenga."

"*If* I truly am one of the kind of which you speak, old man, and if in a moment of need I can indeed find the help of which you speak."

Natoum shook his head. "You will not find the help. It will find you." Natoum spoke reassuringly as they began to make their way out of the throne room, striding in the queen's wake.

"And if it does not? How will I know it if it does?" the youth asked him thoughtfully.

"When the time comes, you'll know it. Or you will die."

Though he was offered a mount from the royal stables, Madrenga declined. Two horses would be too much for him to look after. "Besides," he declared in explaining his refusal, "Orania can carry what little I need."

As the sounds and smells of the stables swirled around them, Natoum eyed the pony dubiously. Lean of body and lanky of leg, it looked barely capable of keeping itself upright, let alone carrying packed supplies.

"You'll need more than good spirits to keep you fed and healthy. Money for expenses I've already given you." He nodded in the direction of Madrenga's waist, where a snap-sealed leather purse formed a counterweight to the scroll container slung on the other side. "But there will be places, times, occasions, when you may not be able to buy what you need."

"I've always heard that he who travels light travels fast." The youth looked slightly embarrassed. "Besides, I wouldn't know what to do with a royal horse."

He smiled at the pony, the runt half of a pair of foals. The owner having only wished to keep the larger, healthier one, Madrenga had requested and received permission to take her sickly twin, though the owner's wife had wanted her for the stewpot. Dark russet splotched with white, her mane clipped short, Orania barely came up to his waist. She quietly cropped hay as a stable boy carefully cinched tight the lightweight leather pack that had been draped across her back. Nearby, Bit noisily gnawed on a bone he had salvaged from the depths of the stables. It was old, filthy, and stank of decay. No wonder the pup found it so tasty. Madrenga turned back to Natoum.

"Didn't you say yourself, Chief Counselor, that the reason you chose me for this task was because a force of armored and armed men would make too much commotion while traveling and suggest a tempting target to bandits? Whereas I might pass through unnoticed, as one not worth troubling with?"

Natoum nodded. "That is so, boy." *Also, every soldier worth his steel was off fighting beside the King.* "You have the knife I gave you?"

Madrenga indicated where the blade was scabbarded at his hip, not far from the precious cylinder that contained the Queen's important message to her counterpart in Daria. It was a modest weapon. Not much defense against any serious trouble he might encounter. But the Counselor had predicated the entire journey on the premise that one as insignificant as Madrenga would not draw attention to himself, and that he would not be worth the trouble it would take to kill him.

Still, the youth thought, he would rather have had a sword. A real sword. Not that he possessed any clue on how to wield such a weapon, but he could envision the sight of one such giving pause to leery brigands. He gave a mental shrug. He would just have to make do with the knife.

Or, he thought as he smiled down at the coal-black pup chewing energetically on his scavenged prize, he could always sic his dog on them.

"Come on, bone-crusher." Bit looked up. "It's time we were on our way. As the good Counselor says, it's a long way to Daria." Taking up the reins that hung from Orania's simple bridle, he gave a tug to urge her away from the hay.

Once clear of the stables Natoum accompanied them as far as the inner city gate. Barkers, buskers, housewives, entertainers, merchants and more would have roughly and unapologetically shoved the much younger Madrenga aside. But they respectfully made way for the Chief Counsel.

"Tell me, sir," the youth asked, "do you know nothing of what is written on the golden scroll I carry?"

"Nothing." Natoum shook his head, his whiskers swaying.

"Are you not curious?"

"Of course I'm curious! I'm seriously, maddeningly curious." He clutched his staff of office with both hands. "But I prefer continuing the flow of blood to my head to satisfying my curiosity. Peering at the Queen's private correspondence would offer a fast track to decapitation."

Madrenga looked around. The crowd was dense, dusty, and noisy, the citizens of which it was comprised intent on minding their own business. No one was watching the old counselor and his young companion.

"We could look at it now, sir. No one would know."

Disgust colored Natoum's response. "You are young, healthy, and stupid. Why those three qualities must always be linked I do not know. Wiser men than I have tried to make sense of such things. Do you not understand that one of the ways a crown keeps its power is by always knowing what its happy people are about? To facilitate that they employ a raft of agents to be their eyes and ears. These men and women lurk everywhere. Their job is to vacuum up bits and pieces of suspected sedition and report them to the palace. A wary populace is a peaceful populace." He took a step back and gestured with an open hand. "But if you want to try and read what is on the scroll, go right ahead! Surely no one is watching, as you say."

Madrenga hesitated. The corium cylinder dangling from his new belt was heavy with import. If the Counselor was to be believed, there was nothing keeping him from opening the container, removing the precious coil of metal it held, and perusing the contents. Except for the small fact that he did not know how to read, and that even if he tried an unseen eye might observe his actions.

What kind of royal courier are you? he admonished himself. He, a poor nothing with no family, had been entrusted with the property of the Queen herself. A bad job he would make of it if he betrayed her trust and privacy even before he was a single day outward bound. He lowered his head, unable to meet the Counselor's reproving gaze.

"I am ashamed of myself. I will think no more of such things."

"That's good. That's smart." Reaching over, Natoum gave the youth a paternal pat on the head. "Hew to such beliefs and perhaps you will retain a while longer the organ that allows you to think. Now be off with you. Onward to far Daria, where you and that which you carry will be accorded the welcome they surely deserve! Luck to you, young Madrenga. May you find your way as well as the way." With that he turned and, in a flurry of robes and thrust of staff, was swallowed up by the crowd.

It did not trouble Madrenga to find himself alone. It was the condition in which he had spent all of his life, and he was no stranger to it. Wrapping himself in the isolation that was his near constant companion, he gave Orania's reins a chuck and started for the outer gate. A peripatetic brown blur, Bit flanked pony and then master, occasionally darting beneath Orania's spindly legs with complete disregard for either his safety or hers.

Equivalent energy marked Madrenga's stride. He was embarked on a great adventure (or at least a great delivery) with money in his purse and the manqué of Queen Alyriata on his person. Why the Chief Counselor had selected him for such a task the youth still was not certain. He knew only that one did not look a gift horse in the mouth lest it bite off your nose.

Alas, when Natoum had explained to him that the kingdom maintained a network of informants outside the place, the Counselor had not thought to add that there were others who did the opposite.

"He don't look like much to me."

From where he stood in the alley, Varpan the Morose watched the young man pass by. Shielded by the striped awning that shaded a vendor of melons bright and succulent, the bandit frowned as their prey strode obliviously onward.

"It ain't him we want." Shorter and more lithe than his thickset associate, Ginore was studying every piece of the youth's kit, from what might be causing a bulge in his left boot to the innocuous pack bobbing on the scrawny pony's back. "Sanmal assured me the boy's carrying something of value." Small black eyes turned on the muscle looming beside him. "Don't you see, you great fool? Whatever it is, the royals are trying to sneak it out of the city. Why engage a company of swordsmen when a clever ruse is worth a hundred blades?"

Varpan's frown deepened. "I don't know much about such strategies, but he still don't look like much to me."

Ginore sighed. "Which is the point, ox-butt. That all such as ourselves should look upon this youth and see someone of no consequence who is obviously transporting nothing of value."

A massive hand rose and a thick finger screwed into a dirty coal pit of an ear. "Then why are we bothering."

Raising his gaze to the heavens, the smaller man gave up trying to explain. "Just grab him when I tell you to, all right?"

Simple instructions Varpan could understand. He nodded vigorously.

The sprawling market that occupied the space between the

city's inner and outer ramparts was undisciplined, chaotic, loud, and wonderful. Madrenga knew it well. He could never afford to buy outright any of the thousands upon thousands of wares displayed by its vendors, but he had often worked for some of them. Not for pretty toys, but for food and shelter for him and his animals. Poor he might be, and without relatives, but he was no thief. Better to die an honest man, he had vowed, than to risk one's honor for a bauble. What more valuable possession does a homeless man have than his honor? When he had spoken of this determination, those few friends he had among the street folk had laughed at him. Just as they had taunted and teased him when he had taken in first the weakling foal and later the abandoned pup.

"You have not enough food for yourself," they would chide him. "You would do better to eat the foal and sell the dog. What good are they to you?"

"They give me love, and companionship," he would reply tightly.

"The first is always for sale, cheap, and second overrated. Better a full belly."

He disagreed, and his friends would leave him, chuckling and shaking their heads as they departed, amused at his naïveté. A pleasant enough fellow, all were agreed, companionable and earnest and well-meaning, and probably not long for this world.

If they could see him now, he thought with pride. With money in hand and embarked on a mission for the Queen herself! No failure he; only a victim of unfortunate circumstance in life. Now that he had at last been given a chance, he was determined to make the most of it. When presented with opportunity unexpected, it behooves one to take advantage.

The two brigands who jumped him and quickly wrestled him into the shadowy alley felt exactly the same way.

While the much bigger Varpan held the struggling youth's arms behind his back, Ginore looked him up and down with a practiced, speculative eye.

"This don't seem right," the thief muttered. "What fool would assign anything of importance to such a callow stripling? Why, he's barely of age and virtually unarmed."

"Hardly worth breaking his back," rumbled Varpan. He nodded in the direction of the diminutive but game Bit, who was barking furiously. Repeatedly the pup would charge Ginore's booted feet, then beat a hasty retreat. The bandit ignored the diminutive canine. Common as they were in the alleys and byways of the outer marketplace, barking or even fighting dogs would draw no attention from the crowd of vendors and shoppers. As for the pony, she stood nearby shivering slightly and waiting for whatever the outcome might be.

Ginore sighed. "Nothing for it but to get on with it, I suppose." Taking a step forward, he locked eyes with the imprisoned youth. "You're carrying something valuable. I would relieve you of the burden."

"I—I don't have any such thing," Madrenga stammered. "Do I look like someone who would be carrying anything valuable?"

"No, you don't. But the inside source who says you do has always been reliable." He smiled, showing yellowed, broken teeth. "Now, you can tell us where it is, or we can simply take everything you own, down to your codpiece."

"I'm not wearing a codpiece." Thinking furiously but to no end, Madrenga tried to stall.

Ginore's brows rose slightly but he was not to be distracted. "We can begin by removing your clothing." He nodded at the bigger man who was holding the youth's arms fast. "Or I can have Varpan start by removing your head. It's all the same to me." His eyes abruptly focused on the snapshut leather sack hanging from the young man's belt. "Ah—no need for such unpleasantness, I see. Unless I miss my guess, that would be a purse. It may not be the special thing of value you carry, but it will be a fine beginning." He reached for the leather container.

"NO!" Madrenga shouted. Whereupon several things happened at once, none of them any more explicable in retrospect than they were at the moment when they occurred.

Leaping into the air, Bit brought his jaws down on the back of Varpan's right hand. That the pup could make such a vertical jump was astonishing in itself. More remarkably, he held on tight despite the cursing brigand's furious attempts to shake the dog loose.

"Bastard off a bitch teat!" Forgetting for a moment their prey's purse, Ginore drew his knife and stepped forward, aiming the tip of the blade at the dog's spine. And then he too was describing a vertical leap—over the growling Bit, over a startled Varpan's right shoulder, and toward the rear of the alley. Facing him hindquarters first was the gangly-limbed form of Orania. With the two-legged kick the pony had demonstrated a strength in her rear legs that Madrenga did not imagine she possessed.

Sputtering fury, Varpan flung aside the youth he had been holding. With his left hand he reached for the small dog that was fastened like a large brown staple to his other hand. One grab, one quick twist, would break the pup's neck and rid the big man of the momentary irritation.

Whether panic or fear for Bit's life prompted him to draw his own blade Madrenga could not have said. He remembered only that he threw himself at the much bigger man with as much force as he could muster. The battle cry he uttered was as high-pitched as the rest of his not yet matured voice, but there was nothing adolescent about the knife he plunged into Varpan's back.

The big man blinked and turned, forgetting the snarling canine blot that continued to cling leech-like to his right hand. His gaze came to rest on his unexpected assailant, who even now was standing in shock and wonder at what he had done. With his left hand Varpan slapped at his right, sending a yelping Bit flying free to bounce off the nearby stone wall. Eyes narrowed as they focused on the youth who had stabbed him. This was no longer a matter of a simple heist. It had moved beyond that. Propriety demanded that instead of breaking the dog's neck, he now snap the boy's. Heavy hands, one bleeding profusely, reached for the youth.

Something, Madrenga knew not what (instinct?) made him fall prone to the dry cobblestone paving. "Please sir, don't …!"

A shape passed over him as Ginore lunged forward with his sword, intending to drive the blade into the youth's back. At the same time Orania backed up and delivered a second unexpectedly powerful kick to the big man's lower back, her hooves striking the place where Madrenga's knife had penetrated. Letting out a roar of pain, Varpan stumbled forward. His belly met the blade of his companion as it thrust from the opposite direction.

Ginore could only gape in astonishment as his partner in felony stumbled to his right, large hands gripping the haft of the sword as Varpan's weight wrenched it from its owner's grasp. In lieu of words, bubbles of saliva foamed from the big man's twitching lips. A dark stain appeared on his jerkin and spread rapidly. It had covered a plate-sized area by the time its owner fell to the ground.

Scrambling to his feet, the blood-stained knife still gripped in his right hand, Madrenga sized up the situation as a head-shaking Bit recovered his footing and a snorting, neighing Orania began to advance from the left. Armed now only with a knife himself, a stunned Ginore found his way blocked by a boy, a pony, and a puppy. The dog was barking, the pony pawing the cobblestones, and the boy—the boy was wild-eyed.

Little in the way of formal education had forced its cognitive tentacles into Ginore's brain, but he was no fool. Something peculiar was happening here. Something more than met the eye. A glance to his left showed the fleshy motionless mass of Varpan the Morose lying on his side against the alley wall, hands clutching futilely at the haft of the sword that protruded from his midsection. Ginore's gaze returned to those who were advancing toward him. His eyes narrowed, then widened as he detected the changes. Though barely noticeable, they were no less real for their seeming insignificance. They were changes as impossible as they were slight.

That was enough for him. Purse or no purse, valuables or no valuables, he sensed that his continuing health depended on him removing himself as expeditiously as possible from his present circumstances. Whirling, he ran as if all the Devils of Thanandu themselves were after him, scrambled up a back wall, and vanished into the darkness and stinks of the most distant corner of the alley. There were no devils, of course. Only a boy, a dog, and a pony.

Sort of.

CHAPTER TWO

LEFT BEHIND AND UNHARMED SAVE FOR THE ACHING IN HIS arms where the now motionless Varpan had gripped them, Madrenga continued to stare down the alley toward the place where his surviving attacker had disappeared. Lowering his gaze, he eyed the bloody knife. Turning slowly, he contemplated the still, lifeless shape of the brigand who had been but a moment from putting an end to Bit. Then he carefully wiped the knife against his right leg, resheathed the crudely cleaned weapon, walked over to the wall opposite the dead body, leaned against the stones, and threw up. Looking on, Bit whined with concern. Orania shook out her close-cropped mane and turned away. Nostrils flexing as she lowered her head, she began searching the crevices between the cobblestones for anything that might prove edible.

Lucky. He'd been lucky, he knew. If he had not fallen to the ground to beg for his life when the smaller brigand had executed his sword thrust, the lethal blade would have gone through him instead of over his head. If at the same time Orania had not kicked the bigger man in the back and caused him to stumble forward, he would not have met his death at the point of that very same blade.

It struck Madrenga that this was an odd coincidence.

No, not coincidence, he told himself. Luck. Some long-gone, unknown ancestors had been watching over him. Had there been three bandits, or four, the outcome might have been very different. Turning, he looked toward the busy marketplace beyond the alley. No one had noticed the altercation that had taken place within. Or if they had, they had chosen to ignore it. What would have been surprising was if anyone had bothered to intervene. As for members of the cityforce, they were doubtless busy shaking down some poor fruit merchant. When it came to simple matters like assault, ordinary citizens like Madrenga were on their own. But he was used to that.

What he was not used to was the kind of formidable intercession that had been shown by his companions. Picking up Bit in both hands, he grinned at the pup and brought him close. A pink canine tongue too big for its mouth flopped out to slather the youth's nose with cheery saliva while the rest of the dog hung loosely in his master's grasp like a brown sack of wet sand. A glance behind him showed that Orania had given up her futile attempt to graze the cobblestones in favor of nuzzling the back of his legs. Setting the pup down, Madrenga wiped his nose and gave the pony a hug. She whinnied softly in delight as Bit, barking furiously, ran excited circles around them both.

"Bit's bite I understand, Orania, but what made you kick like that? You're not a dog, much less a mule." As the uncomprehending pony looked at him sideways the youth wondered what he was doing, standing in an alley talking to a horse. It wasn't as if there was going to be a response. "No matter. I'm just glad that you did." Frowning, he eyed her more closely.

"I must be dazed. Your mane looks longer and I know I had it cut not more than a couple of fortnights ago." Dropping into a crouch, he scrutinized her legs. "Bedamned if I don't think you've grown these last weeks more than I'd noticed. Bit seems a bit bigger, too." He straightened and shrugged. "I need to pay more attention to the both of you. When most of one's waking hours are devoted to just getting enough for everyone to eat, I suppose one tends to overlook such things." His attention turned once more to the bustling, seamy marketplace. Lying in repose nearby, the hulking mass of the slain bandit was beginning to weigh on his thoughts.

"Let's get out of here before someone comes looking for this dead stench. Daria isn't getting any closer."

No one so much as glanced in their direction as the youth and his animals emerged from the alleyway entrance. Slipping smoothly into the ebb and flow of the market, its energy quickly swept them along. Nor did anyone, either interested authorities or friends of the demolished, materialize in pursuit as Madrenga made his way outside the city proper and started up the main road heading east.

That evening he made camp among a loosely organized crowd of fellow travelers. Reluctant to start spending the money Natoum had given him so early in the journey, he foreswore the comfort promised by a nearby travelers' inn. The small waterproof tent that comprised part of the supplies packed on Orania's back would serve his needs perfectly well. Wrapping himself in the single blanket that had been provided, he lay on his side with a snuffling Bit pressing tight against him. Outside the tent Orania stood quietly, head down and occasionally shuffling her feet. There was no need to tether her. Madrenga knew she would not run off.

Small as she was, though, that did not mean someone would be averse to taking her.

Horse theft had not been a problem in the city. Even as a foal her markings had been distinctive. Taken, she could have been found. Stealing is always more difficult in the presence of witnesses.

Late that night there were no witnesses save the moon, whose opinion everyone seeks but which is immune to subpoena. The man who in the darkness silently approached the untied pony was elderly but not decrepit, clever if not intelligent. He was also very hungry and in mind of preparing a mess of horse jerky, some of which he could also make available for sale. While the pony's owner had chosen a sleeping site somewhat isolated from the other travelers, the angular chef-thief still approached with caution. Though quite ready to fight for the animal, stealing off with it quietly was much the preferred course of action.

Within the tent Madrenga slept soundly. It would have been a tiring first day even without the stressful encounter with the two would-be muggers. He was exhausted and his body demanded rest.

Not so with the four-legged lump cuddling against his chest. Bit's head came up nose-first as he sampled the air. As every dog knows, malice smells just like shit, and the pup was instantly on alert. Alert, but not yet certain of either the stink's source or intent. Sniffing energetically, he padded away from his master and outside the simple round tent.

The elderly horse-eater was already reaching for the reins that hung from Orania's bridle. Clutching them, he gave a firm, no-nonsense tug. As far as he was concerned the horse was already his. His tongue smacked against his palate. With one this young the meat would be tender. There would be steaks and stew meat.

Roused by the pull on the reins, the prospective stew meat opened her eyes and regarded her would-be abductor. He saw something, or thought he saw something, within them that was not horse. Whatever it was it was enough to cause him to scream softly.

Flinging away the reins the old man stumbled backward. As he did so something small, brown, and pudgy leaped for his throat. This caused the incipient horsenapper to scream again. Flailing wildly at his canine assailant with both hands, the old man turned and ran.

Sleepy voices began to rise from suddenly awakened travelers. Some were irritated, others concerned. They were joined by Madrenga. He emerged from the tent gripping his knife. But there was nothing to be seen. A voice called to him through the darkness, inquiring if the young traveler was alright.

"I'm fine!" he yelled back. "Everything is well. Go back to bed, friends."

Concern was replaced by muttering as, one by one, the other campers returned to their own tents or blankets. Still holding the knife, a puzzled Madrenga regarded his two companions. Orania shook her head while Bit sat down on his backside and gazed up at his puzzled master, tongue lolling out of one side of his mouth.

"You two—if it's going to be like this all the way to Daria I'll never get any sleep." Turning, he bent low to re-enter the tent.

Orania had certainly grown, he told himself as he slid back beneath the blanket and pulled it up to his neck. How had he failed to notice such a recent growth spurt? The warm body that wriggled in to rejoin him was also larger than he remembered it. Was there something wrong with his memory, he wondered? Or was it his eyes? Reaching around, he scratched Bit's side and back. Squirming beneath the blanket, the pup whimpered with delight. Much bigger, for certain, a confused Madrenga told himself. Surely too much bigger to casually overlook. Yet that was what he had done. It was a puzzlement for certain, and more than a bit of a mystery.

Too tired to marvel further, he fell asleep with one hand resting on Bit's butt. Had he been less exhausted he might well have reflected on the realization that his open palm could no longer fully encompass the dog's backside. Also, unlike when he had originally retired, the blanket was no longer long enough to completely cover his own feet.

Morning dawned bright and cheerful as a baby's giggle. Some relaxed bargaining bought him a ride in the back of a wagon bound for Bariele. The hokounut merchant with whom he had struck an agreement for transportation did not even mind that his paying passenger brought his pup on board with him.

"If he pees on one of the barrels," the happy-go-lucky businessman told Madrenga, "just try to make sure he sprays evenly and not all in one place." When he winked, one huge bushy eyebrow descended over an eye like a caterpillar protectively screening the next leaf on its menu.

Nor was Orania a problem. Loosely tethered to the fold-down rear door that doubled as a loading ramp, she trotted along behind the barrel-filled wagon. As it bumped along the increasingly rough road Madrenga marveled at how in only a couple of days her legs seemed to have lengthened and strengthened. As had, for that matter, Bit's—and his own.

An illusion, he told himself. A consequence of for the first time in his life emerging from the cosseted confines of Harup-taw-shet and striking out into the vast country beyond. Or perhaps it was the result of some undeclared parting magic on the part of his sponsor, the wily Natoum, that was designed to facilitate the carrying out of his mission.

If that were so, though, why not announce the intention to enchant prior to his departure from the city, Madrenga found himself wondering. What was there to be gained by withholding such information and leaving the recipient to swim in his own bemusement? He shrugged. It was not for him to fathom the motivations of Counselors to the royal court any more than it was to wonder at the contents of the scroll he carried. That scroll—a quick peek, surely, could do no harm, would cause no empires to tremble. Even if he couldn't read it, there might be images and symbols he could recognize.

Reaching to his waist, as he habitually did several times a day, he found the corium cylinder still secured to his belt. The cap was closed with red sealing wax, true, but it was nothing he could not repair. He could remove the contents, at least have a look at what lay therein, and reseal it with any flame. No one, least of all Alyriata of Harup-taw-shet or Zhelerasjju of the Darians, would be any the less for the experience.

But would he? That was the imponderable he could not ignore. What if the scroll contained some horrible protective spell laid upon it by Natoum or some other court sorcerer? A spell designed to inflict horrors upon any not qualified to peruse the contents engraved on the gold foil? Merely glancing at an illustrative image or words he could not understand might turn him into a smear on the road, or a toad, or a road toad, or …

Stop tormenting yourself, he thought firmly. Put it out of your mind. You are a delivery boy, nothing more. And as such, the perusal of palace poetry is beyond your purview. Do your job and shut your thoughts.

"Damn it all to Calequa!"

The curse and the wagon came to a halt at the same time. Wondering at such atypical vehemence from the driver, Madrenga climbed out to see what was the matter. It was only recently that he would have had to gently carry Bit out with him and set the pup on the ground. Bigger and stronger through means that continued to baffle his owner, the dog simply hopped out by himself, sniffed at the nearest wheel, and waited for his master to join him. At least the pup's dripping tongue, the youth reflected, seemed to have changed in proportion to the rest of the dog's body.

While Bit accompanied him around to the front of the wagon, Orania turned to her left and began quietly cropping at the grass and weeds that crowded the side of the dirt track.

The hokounut merchant's wagon was not the only one drawn up on the near side of the river. A dozen other vehicles crowded nearby, having pulled off onto a level flat clearing by the side of the road. Their interiors lined with velvet and down, a couple of large wheeled ovals were passenger transports. One such was dominated by a crooked upside-down funnel from which emerged puffs of smoke. This was suffused with the rich, earthy aroma of smoking meat.

The source of the merchant's curse, his sudden halt, the impromptu assembly of eclectic transports, and the downcast babble of voices from the nearby clearing was one and the same. Flowing from north to south, the river that now blocked travel to the east was in near flood, its surface as much white as blue. Having fallen on the remnants of the winter snowpack, recent warm rains had rapidly melted any snow lying at lower elevations and sent it tumbling and crashing toward the distant sea. None of which would have mattered to those stalled on its western shore had not the earth beneath the bridge support pylons on that same riverbank been undermined and given way, sending that end of the bridge crashing into the water below.

Having trod a careful path down to the river, a couple of dozen men and women stood surveying the damage. Several burly individuals were wrestling with the ropes attached to one of the pylons, trying to drag it ashore.

It was plain to see that while the various components of the bridge remained intact, putting them back in place and restoring them to service was going to take some time. Most likely, word would have to be sent all the way back to Harup-taw-shet. An engineering and construction team would be assembled and marched to the site. Rebuilding would take days or possibly even weeks. Meanwhile, merchants and travelers stuck on the west bank would have the option of taking a long, long way around, southward to the next bridge. Or they could hire a dragon to ferry them and their goods across.

Madrenga smiled to himself. *That* was likely. There were no such things as dragons. Only rumors and stories, tall tales spun by old men who had traveled far and wide, if only in their own imaginations.

He couldn't wait days and weeks. He was on a royal mission. Having been plucked from obscurity and handed a singular and unexpected opportunity he was not about to squander it through delay. He turned to the merchant of hokounuts.

"Thank you, Pymar, for the kindness you have shown to a lone traveler."

The rotund trader grunted. "You paid. No kindness was involved."

"Nevertheless, I thank you."

While the merchant looked on, his young passenger walked to the back of the wagon, only to return a moment later with his small pack-laden horse in tow. When he gave every sign of proceeding onward instead of joining the rest of the stalled travelers, Pymar pushed his cap back on his wide forehead and called out.

"Now where might you think you're going, lad?"

Madrenga paused to look back. "I'm going to cross the river."

The merchant indicated the youth's companions. "With them?"

"With them." Madrenga nodded.

"Well then, say hello to Death for me when you meet him. I've myself always been curious as to his actual appearance, though more percipient folk than I say it's best to avoid the meeting as long as possible. You, it would appear, are of a different mind."

"We'll get across." Madrenga spoke with an assurance he did not feel. But he knew he had to try. At worst, perhaps, he would be swept downriver, later to crawl out cold and drenched and, with luck, on the far shore.

"You will entertain, is what you will do. I will watch, and inform the others, so that at least your demise may be the source of some healthy betting. Though I fear the contesting will suffer from a dearth of those willing to wager any money on your survival." He shook his head. "Always a pity when someone dies before they have had a chance to live."

Finding the merchant's commentary more than a little depressing, Madrenga resumed heading downslope toward the river.

"You will gain nothing from this adventure, lad, save a lesson! And a lesson that cannot be used is worse than a continuation of ignorance."

"Not so," Madrenga shouted back. "I will for certain gain something, as all this blather of yours is making me thirsty!"

His bravado shrank in proportion to his proximity to the river. By the time he reached the rocky western shore the true force of the snowmelt was fully apparent. White water was everywhere as the power of the current raged over hidden boulders and pinned against them entire trees that had been washed down from the high mountains. If he lost his footing out in the current and was pushed beneath a log, he would be trapped and drowned. If he stepped in a hole he would be swept away and drowned. If a piece of fast-floating debris struck him he might be knocked unconscious and drowned. But if he turned back now, Pymar and the others would laugh at him and call him coward.

There are fates worse than drowning. Fashioning a leash from a length of leather, he placed Bit on top of the pack on Orania's back, jabbed a finger at the pup, and yelled above the roar of the river, "Stay!" Wrapped in slipskin to protect against damage from rain, the contents of the leather pack should remain dry. Whether they would remain intact remained to be seen.

He took a long pause to study the foaming torrent. From what he knew, water raced most furious where it flowed most shallow. Those were the dangerous places where the chances of being swept away were greater. But quieter water would be deeper, likely over his head. Still, better where possible to swim than to fight. Before leaving Harup-taw-shet he might not have considered what he was about to try. But he felt stronger now than ever he had in his life, as if he had grown and matured in a matter of days. Feeling he had seen similar changes, inexplicable though they might be, in his animals, he saw no reason why the mysterious maturation should not have extended to himself. Gripping Orania's reins tightly in his right hand, he stepped into the water and began wading across, angling for the less contorted, less angry stretches of stream. The pony followed without hesitation.

No doubt those on shore, alerted by the merchant Pymar (who doubtless had taken charge of any betting pool), were watching. Doubtless they were also yelling encouragement or expectations of disaster according to their individual temperaments. If so, he could hear none of it, so loud was the roaring of the river in his ears. Feeling his feet lose any semblance of grip on the bottom, he started swimming, still gripping Orania's reins.

It was more than passing strange. Instead of growing weaker with the effort his body demanded simply to stay in place, he felt himself becoming stronger. This be an illusion for sure, he thought. But if so, a useful one. His right arm dug at the water, pulling him forward. The only thing he could hear above the thundering rapids was Bit's nonstop barking. There then came a moment of fear when the reins went slack in his hand. Whirling in the current, he expected to see that the bridle had come loose from Orania's jaws and that she was being swept downstream. Neither proved true.

Having redoubled her own efforts, the young horse was catching up to and passing him. As her light brown flank slid past, Bit turned atop the pack to bark furious encouragement at his master. Facing his dog and confronted with his horse's hindquarters, Madrenga kicked harder still. Noting Orania's unexpected progress he felt confident enough to let go of the reins altogether, which restored the use of his left arm for swimming.

Eventually all three of them emerged on the far shore. Cold, drenched, and dripping, he found a smooth sun-warmed boulder and laid down upon it, soaking up the drying, warming rays of the sun. Turning his head to his right, he could see excited spectators high up on the far side of the river gesticulating in his direction, though he could not hear what they were saying. No doubt the most enthusiastic, he told himself, were those few who had bet on his survival and now stood to collect their winnings from the enterprising Pymar. Breathing hard, he closed his eyes against the sun. He too had laid a bet, and had won bigger than any of the travelers and traders he had left behind.

The snowmelt-swollen river had presented a challenge. He had accepted it and had prevailed. Through determination and luck he had defeated a force of Nature much as he and his companions had overcome the pair of brigands back in the city. Someone, perhaps his mother (of whom only the vaguest images occasionally teased his memories) had once told him that every victory over adversity makes one stronger. The aphorism was at the forefront of his thoughts as he rose and looked down at himself. He had never had occasion to believe the parable should be taken literally.

This time there was no mistaking what he saw. Not only had his legs grown perceptibly longer; the muscles of his thighs and calves had thickened as well. Even his feet appeared to have widened and lengthened. What's more, his attire had stretched to compliment his increased size. Squinting, he leaned forward. Was that a hint of armor that had appeared, out of nowhere, to cover both his shins? What manner of magic was this, to manifest itself in the wilderness shy of the presence of any apparent architect? Astonishment overcame his exhaustion as he slid off the rock and stood. Bending forward, he examined his legs, running tentative fingers downward from his knees. The metal shining there felt familiarly cold and hard to the touch.

Metal like steel it was, but different. Light but strong, not unlike the cylinder that protected the royal scroll. Whence had it come to him, and why? When initially he had marked its appearance, he had been bewildered. Now he was scared.

His fright and uncertainty deepened when he again took a moment to consider his companions. Kneeling beside a complaisant Orania, he marveled at the gleaming breastplate that now shielded her chest. Fashioned of the same exotic material that had appeared over his shins, it was attached by woven metal strands to a saddle that ...

Saddle? Where had a saddle come from?

Utterly baffled, he straightened. It was only when he did so that he realized how much the pony had grown. As if in response to their clash with the swift river current, her legs had lengthened anew and strengthened even more. Though not yet the height of a full-grown horse, she was now far too big to be considered a mere pony. Pushed to the rear by the inexplicable appearance of the saddle, his simple pack now lay behind it, still firmly secured in place. The pack itself appeared unchanged.

It wasn't much of a saddle, he saw. Plain leather straps for stirrups, a raw wooden pommel, and an unpadded seat. Even so, between its appearance and Orania's increased size, the way forward to Daria suddenly appeared more manageable ... assuming that she would let him sit on her back. Lightweight as he was (or had been until recently), he had never tried riding the pony, even in jest. Would she tolerate his presence and his weight atop her spine, or would she buck him off? Only one way to find out, he told himself.

Putting his right foot in the thin stirrup strap, he threw his left leg over her back and plonked himself down in the saddle. She started and her head came up sharply. There was a penetrating whinny, she reared up on her hind legs (though not enough to throw him), and then she relaxed.

"Good girl, Orania." Leaning forward, he patted her on the side of her neck, then stroked it repeatedly. "Good girl!"

So far so good, he told himself. There remained the awkward fact that though she seemed willing to carry him, he had never learned how to ride. Fair enough, he told himself. She had never learned how to carry. They would have to learn together.

Giving a light chuck on the reins induced no forward motion. Repeating the action while accompanying it with a soft kick of one heel into her right side caused her to start forward. As she was still far from a fully-grown animal his feet swayed perilously close to the ground. But the strange new sensations of riding and being ridden quickly became comfortable for both of them, and his feet hosannaed their thanks.

Bit trotted alongside, occasionally wandering off to sniff at a bush or rock on the side of the rough road. As Orania had somehow blossomed into a small horse, so had Madrenga's puppy swollen into a semblance of a dog. The street mutt was starting to take on the appearance of an identifiable breed, though the specifics eluded the perplexed youth. No sleek hunting dog was Bit. No fluffy household pet, either. His hair stayed short and had grown darker. It was jet black now, the lightly jouncing Madrenga decided, though when the sunlight struck it at a certain angle the dog's color took on a peculiar purplish sheen, as though the fur was momentarily infused with amethyst. He shook his head wonderingly. Considering everything else that had happened to him and his animals since embarking on the undertaking, why should he be surprised by the abrupt transformation of a puppy into a partially purple dog?

Bit's head had grown larger, too. Enough that it seemed slightly too large in proportion to the rest of his body. A longer tail might have served as a visual counterbalance, but that appendage remained stubbornly short and thick. Then there was the troubling change in the dog's teeth. Sharp canines were to be expected in a growing dog, but Bit's were unusually pointed. As were the rest of his teeth, as if his mouth was filling up with nothing *but* canines. If that did not change it might present a problem, Madrenga decided. How could a dog chew if his jaws were filled with nothing but canines?

It was too much to think about all at once. Mulling the many mysteries of the morning could wait for another time. What was important was that he was safely across the river. If forces unknown had chosen to gift him with shin armor and his pony— his horse, he corrected himself—with a handsome breastplate and related tack made of similar material, who was he to question the Fates' interest in boys and horses? Regarding what had happened to his own body, his longer legs would make easier the crossing of future streams and crevasses. Feeling better about himself and his circumstances, if no less confused, he tilted back his head and contemplated the sky.

"I thank whoever or whatever is responsible for these mystifying gifts and abase myself before such power." He paused, thinking, and added tentatively, "I could use some fresh food, too."

Nothing fell from the sky in response to his request. No loaves of warm bread, no chilled fruits, no dried and salted meats. A pollu bird did pass by and leave behind a gift, but it was one the youth did not request and could have done without. The removing of it did, however, serve to take his mind off unsolvable mysteries and return him from a place of expectation to a state of humbleness. It might well be, he reflected, that he had received everything in the manner of unrequested intervention that he was going to receive, and should be both grateful and content with as much as had come his way.

So it was, that days later his thoughts turned to more immediate matters of sustenance and shelter by the time he entered the outskirts of the hill town called Hamuldar.

CHAPTER THREE

WHY ARE YOU LOOKING FOR AN EMPTY FIELD IN WHICH TO PITCH A tent?

Why indeed, he wondered? To say that he had been sparing of the expense money Counselor Natoum had given him was beyond understatement. To date he had spent only on food to supplement the dried stores he had brought with him. Now he found himself in a bustling crossroads town crowded with taverns and inns. Should he not avail himself of travelers' hospitality? After his desperate crossing of the roaring river did he not deserve a night's rest in a real bed, a hot bath, and a meal at a proper table? Setting his own wants and needs aside, did not after all her patient trekking, swimming, and hauling, Orania not deserve a night in a clean dry stall surrounded by fresh hay, and faithful Bit something tasty to chew on?

That decided it. Simply because he was relentlessly parsimonious did not mean that he had the right to deny the occasional indulgence to his devoted traveling companions.

"Thank you, Bit. Thank you, Orania. You have decided for me." The dog eyed him quizzically while the small steed who was maturing with unaccountable speed did not bother to look back at her rider.

Situated at the nexus of major north-south and east-west roads, Hamuldar boasted a plethora of places to spend the night. Multi-storied inns built of cut stone and finished lumber featured upper-floor rooms that flaunted wide balconies. Less prepossessing establishments huddled at the dark ends of short closes as if embarrassed to be seen on the main cobblestone streets. Many private dwellings offered rooms for rent. Shops, now closed for the day, sold all manner of necessities for travelers on their way through to the country known as Elsewhere.

Having no knowledge of the town, Madrenga had no idea which hostelry to choose. The larger facilities all looked inviting, but would doubtless prove correspondingly costly. Unable to make up his mind, he found himself advancing further and further toward the center of town, until the rising commotion he had been hearing for some time finally exploded around him in a burst of noise and color.

The central town square was alive with a fair. Acrobats tossed one another back and forth, dancers in exotic costume gyrated, harlequins teased visitors, and Hamuldar's night watch was alert for pickpockets and snatch thieves. Flames leaped from the lubricated lips of firebreathers and the iron grills of food vendors. Raucous laughter, excited shouts, and drunken accusations competed for ear time with the melodies of instruments whose appearance as well as sounds were entirely new to Madrenga. His eyes were wide as he guided Orania around pandemonium's periphery. Outer Market Day at Harup-taw-shet seemed tame by comparison.

Then Bit began barking accusingly as a trio of men blocked Orania's path. Well-trained as she was, she halted rather than attempt to push past them. The three had clearly been drinking, but not yet to excess. They confronted the youth on the small horse forcefully, but their smiles were genuine.

"Now here's one to cast a wager upon! Look at him, seated straight and proud upon this handsome little steed of his!"

"Aye," rumbled a man equally parts fat and faux fury, "thinks he's too good to join in, does he?" Liquor tinged eyes fixed on the uncertain youth. "Or do you?"

"Uh, actually I've come quite a distance, and was hoping to find a place to get something to eat, and then have a sleep."

"Eat? Sleep?" The third man looked askance at his partying companions. "This is Strove End-Month! Time to drink, not to eat." A hand reached for the wary Madrenga, pawing at his shirt. "Come now, lad. Do we then look so like thieves that you'd refuse even our company?"

It had to be admitted, Madrenga mused, that this trio bore scant resemblance to the malicious pair who had threatened to gut him in the alley back in Harup-taw-shet.

"It's not that," he argued. "It's only that I'm very tired and ..."

Another hand was tugging on his shirt. Orania backed slightly but otherwise held her ground. "Join us then, lad! We're buying." A florid, sun-creased face lurched close to Madrenga's as he was set upon by warm breath redolent of recently deceased hops. "A better offer you'll not have this night!"

Maybe the best way to extricate himself from the confrontation was to briefly embrace it, Madrenga decided. Disengaging feet from stirrups, he dropped to the ground.

"Well enough, then. One drink, and then I really must find a bed before the ground finds me."

A hand clapped him on the back. Before starting his journey, such a blow would have knocked him off balance. This night, strangely, it felt only like the brotherly slap it was meant to be. Finding a hitching rail, he secured the uncomplaining Orania between a pair of full-grown pack horses. In the flickering, chiaroscuro light she looked very small alongside them. But not, he reflected in confusion, as small as she once had been. Placing Bit atop the saddle, which he fully expected to vanish one morning as mysteriously as it had appeared, he commanded the dog to stay, and then allowed himself to be drawn toward the center of the laughter-infused maelstrom.

The closer he and his new companions drew to the middle of

the square, the louder and more frenetic grew the action around them. Boys chased one another, girls toyed with sugared air, men argued, women primped, one couple fornicated beneath a wagon piled high with windwheels for sale. The proprietor paid them no mind. Perhaps, a gaping Madrenga thought, the presence of the copulating couple was good for business. It certainly caught the eye of a certain unsophisticated young visitor.

Something said to him earlier returned to the forefront of his thoughts and he addressed the first man who had spoken to him. "What did you mean when you said, 'Here's one to cast a wager upon'?"

"I could tell you." The townsman winked. "But better to show you."

Amid the surging, rollicking crowd and beneath tall torches and magpie-oil lanterns was a small paved clearing. Near the back, surrounded by admiring men, doe-eyed women, and wide-eyed children, stood a giant of man. Broad of shoulder and thick of chest, he sported a wicked downthrusting blonde mustache that tapered sharply to a point at each end. His hair was cut into two brush-like strips, one running across either side of his skull.

On the smooth stones before him rested a pair of pumpkin-sized crystal globes connected together by a glass tube. Softly lit from within, each crystal sphere as well as the connector was filled with darting fish. Gold-colored, red-striped, black-faced, they meandered through the unique aquarium from one globe to another, using the linking tube as a highway.

Standing before giant and object, an elderly barker held a vase-sized crystalline megaphone to his lips and addressed the crowd.

"Who here dares to try and match the strength of the great Langan of Jithros? Who can claim to be his equal?" From a pouch at his waist the elder withdrew a small golden statue studded with gems that caught the lamplight and threw it back. At the sight of this bejeweled artifact the crowd dutifully oohed and aahed.

"This irreplaceable treasure, this golden statue from an ancient time, goes to whomever can match the power of Langan! Who will risk a silver piece and try?" Crowd noise bubbled around and behind the spectators, but from those ringing the clearing there came only a hesitant murmuring.

"Come, come!" The barker chided the reluctant onlookers. "Are there no men in Hamuldar? None passing through on Fair day?" He made a rude sound. "Perhaps Langan and I were wrong to stop here. If it was women we wished to deal with we would have stopped at the first whorehouse!"

Anger underlined some of the tentativeness in the crowd, but none responded either to the challenge or to the insult. Then a stocky drover, dressed for the fair into fresh cotton and brushed leather, stepped forward.

"Ah, I was wrong." The old man gracefully accepted the ribbed coin the drover handed him. Stepping back, he made a sweeping gesture in the direction of the double-globed aquarium. "Your effort at your leisure, honored sir. Once over your head, if you please. And if you can."

While his friends cheered him on, the drover took up a shoulder-width stance behind the glass connecting tube. Wiping his large, rough hands against his pants, he leaned forward, bent his knees, and took a firm grip on the bar. Teeth clenched, head up, eyes squinting, he let out a bellow that drew the attention of those in the crowd who were merely nearby and not watching. Through his shirt, thick muscles could be seen straining. Slowly, the twin globes and their connecting tube rose off the ground. About a hand's breadth, Madrenga estimated.

The crowd groaned as the drover set the apparatus back down. It made a clinking sound as it struck the paving stones. The thick crystal survived the short drop without so much as a scratch.

"Another?" the old man prompted. "What? No more challengers?"

"It's the weight of the water, not the fish and the crystal," someone shouted from the crowd.

"Yeah, let's see the 'great Langan' lift it!" challenged another.

"You doubt his strength?" The oldster replied with mock

outrage. "Very well then. An irrefutable confirmation you shall have." Moving aside, he made room for his partner.

Stepping right up to the glass tube, the massive Langan let out a derisive snort. Without hesitation or preparation, he bent his knees, grabbed the aquarium in both fists, and in one motion raised it over his head. The crowd gasped. Men blinked, women near swooned, and children squealed in amazement and delight. Several times Langan proceeded to press the aquarium from chest to arm's length before setting it gently back down on the pavement. As a rush of applause and cheers rose from the crowd, the elderly barker redoubled his blandishments.

"See how the mighty Langan effortlessly moves up and down the bar of the Twin Seas! Yet to win the statue a challenger need do so only once! Surely there is more than one man among all of Hamuldar and its visitors! Come, don't be shy. There is no shame in matching yourself against a master, and much to be gained if you succeed!"

Tempted by ego or urged on by sweethearts, others tried. The best of them could not raise the aquarium higher than his knees. Much encouragement and cheering from the crowd drove the challengers to try.

"You spoke of me being one to wager upon." Madrenga regarded his companions. "Surely you did not mean for me to take up this challenge?"

"Ah no, 'twas a jest only, lad," declared one of the men.

"Clearly you could not lift one end of the object off the ground," insisted another.

Though slight, the insult was sufficient at which to take umbrage. "I might could do more than lift one end—if the performance were not a trick."

This assertion quieted but did not silence his hosts. "A trick?" echoed the third of the group. "How so a trick?"

What prompted him to continue speaking, nor whence came the words he spoke, Madrenga could not at that moment have said. He knew only that he was listening to himself but somehow hearing the opinion of another.

"The two large crystal spheres that are filled with decorative fish? They are lit from within."

As one, his companions turned to consider the apparatus. "They still are. What of it?" wondered the first speaker.

Madrenga plunged onward. "Did you not notice the change?"

The third man frowned. "Change? What change, lad?"

"When the challengers try to lift and when the object simply rests, the illumination that arises from within is constant. But when 'the mighty Langan' picks it up, the glow is muted slightly. It is not just a lighting spell that shows to best advantage the sea life that dwells within, but a lighten spell that allows the lifter to show such 'strength'. When he lifts, the weight is somehow reduced together with the internal illumination."

"Magic!" muttered the second speaker. The expression on the man beside him darkened.

"It's a cheat, then! For all the absence of cards and dice, a deception nonetheless!"

"What is a cheat?"

The trio abruptly went silent. Having overheard, the old barker had come up on them too quickly for any of the three to flee. Or Madrenga as well. Eyes that had seen much narrowed as they met the youth's own.

"Was it your voice I heard? Yes," he decided without waiting for confirmation, "it was you … boy. Unusual to encounter such a wild observation in one so young." Reaching out, he grabbed Madrenga's right wrist and drew him forward into the clearing. As he tugged, he raised his voice.

"Another challenger! A bold youth, nominated to be a shining example to the reluctant adolescents of Hamuldar!" The fresh roar that rose from the crowd contained as much laughter as encouragement. The old barker swung Madrenga around. Why he allowed himself to be so led the youth did not know. Though there was surprising strength in the old man's grasp, he still could have broken free easily.

Yet here he was, standing before the twin spheres and the goggle-eyed seafood they held, unable to escape the glare of lamplight or the attention of amused onlookers. His three "friends" had taken the opportunity to melt into the crowd lest the oldster next drag them forward into similar embarrassment. Looming nearby, Langan of Jithros favored the latest challenger with his most intimidating sneer.

Yells of encouragement flavored with ridicule rained down on him.

"Go on, give it a try … boy!"

"It's a trick you said, so twirl it over your head!"

"Show your muscles, lad … if you have any!"

"A gold piece says he pees his pants!"

Anger surged up inside Madrenga. Why had he opened his mouth? Why had he spoken so audibly? He could have slipped quietly away, back to his animals. Now he found himself the subject of scorn and derision.

"Go on, boy. Have a try." The old man spoke in lowered, amused tones. "I know you can't lift it. But I'll cut you a deal despite your thoughtless insult. If you can push it along the ground the length of your prick, I'll give you the golden statue anyway." His eyes crinkled with delight at the humiliation he was inflicting on his young victim. "That means you'll only have to move it an inch." When Madrenga still failed to step up to the glass tube, the elder moved back and nodded at his partner. The youth felt a heavy hand come down on his shoulder as Langan of Jithros roughly shoved him forward.

Lamplight made him blink. Torchlight caused his eyes to water. He looked down at the slender glass cylinder that connected the two water-and-fish-filled crystal globes. What was he doing here? He had come into this town intent on finding a place to eat and to sleep only to be waylaid by a trio of forceful but friendly locals. Because of a casual opinion carelessly voiced he now found himself the subject of derisive stares, scathing comments, and mocking gestures. Like his eyes, his ears began to burn. Insults heaped on him like night-soil on a potato patch.

Bending, he grasped the glass tube with both hands and pushed as hard as he could. To his surprise the transparent cylinder moved. Not only moved, but came up in his hands, rose to his waist, and thence to his chin. Ignorant of what he was doing and how he was doing it, he thrust it overhead. Glowing brightly, the two crystal globes filled with water and fish ascended with it and in tandem.

There was a moment of shocked silence during which the shouts and laughs of more distant fairgoers filled the small square like an echo. A few of the onlookers gasped. Then every member of the crowd burst into wild cheers and shouts, their contempt transformed into feverish adoration as swiftly as a hot kettle turned dead leaves and water into tea.

Stunned but unwilling to fully countenance what he had just seen, the aged barker rushed forward to confront Madrenga as soon as the youth set the apparatus down. The old man stood so close to the young man that Madrenga could count his missing teeth.

"You accuse us of cheating, yet it is clear enough for anyone to see that it is you who are the trickster! I don't know how you did that, but plainly it was not through the use of those floppy appendages you call arms!" Stepping back, he looked behind Madrenga, at his boots and legs. "Where is the device you used? Where is the unnatural booster?" One arm crossed over his chest as the weighty sculpted and bejeweled golden burden swung from a cord. "The statue of the ancients is not for swindlers such as you!"

Feeling light-headed, not to mention possessed by a giddy optimism that was totally unsupported by reality, Madrenga smiled blithely at his accuser. "Okay, then I'll do it again."

And he did, somehow raising the spheres containing the miniature twin seas a second time over his head. Having by now suspended anything resembling disbelief, the astounded crowd roared its approval. Lowering the apparatus to his thighs, he let it hang there as he regarded the old man.

"I claim the statue. I have won fair and true. Give to me that which I deserve."

"So we shall!" Rushing forward, Langan of Jithros grabbed the glass tube on either side of Madrenga's hands and shoved. The startled youth went backward and down with both the glass bar and the much bigger man on top of him. Grinning, his face not far from that of the pained youth, Langan pressed hard. The weight of the tube, crystal globes, and his tormentor pinned Madrenga forcefully to the ground. He let out a groan of pain.

Sides in the crowd having switched, a couple of men took steps forward while others muttered angrily among themselves, wondering whether to interfere. A couple of women yelled for someone to call the night guard. Looking up, a glare from Langan caused the would-be righteous to hesitate.

"Keep clear of this, peddlers and fishmongers. This is not your quarrel. You will want to go home to your wives and children with all your limbs intact."

"Let the lad up," demanded one of the men even as he halted his advance.

"'Tis no fair contest, this," mumbled another. "If this keeps up, he'll kill the boy!"

"And what is that to you?" Stepping between the crowd and the pair of combatants on the ground, the old barker glowered at them, one hand gripping the ivory hilt of the kris that was scabbarded at his waist. "Is he one of you, then? Related to someone here?" The agitated murmuring continued, but no one would confront the old man directly. He smirked at the wall of reluctant men and women. "Then why risk your blood for one who is not of your own?" He looked back to where Langan was all but lying atop the pinioned youth. "We'll settle this quickly enough!" He spared a backward glance and his mouth tightened. Indeed, it would all be over soon. Though he would in truth have gladly given over the statue, fashioned as it was of gilded lead and paste jewels and not ancient but recently made, to know how the odd youth had managed the seemingly impossible lift.

Weighing twice as much as Madrenga, Langan of Jithros continued to lean his weight against the glass tube. "They say it takes a cheat to know one, boy," he whispered tautly. "While I admit to nothing, my senior partner and I would be pleased to know by what means *you* managed the trick." His grin spread. "After all, one's last words should always be useful."

Strain as he might, Madrenga couldn't so much as twitch. Between the weight of the man lying atop him and that of the water-filled lifting apparatus he couldn't move. His face turned red and his breathing labored.

It was all over. Consummation of his royal mission, the hopes for the future that rested upon it—everything. All because he had allowed himself to be detoured from his path. His vision began to blur as his system reacted to the lack of oxygen. With so much mass pressing down on his chest he could hardly breathe. Unable to think straight, he could not have responded positively to Langan's demand even had he wished to do so. If only he could get his breath....

The giant Langan drew back abruptly. Had that been a flash in the boy's eyes? Just a trick of the torchlight, he told himself as he leaned back down. Or more likely, a sign that the stupid youth was on the verge of passing out. Too bad if he failed to divulge how he had come by a means of mastering the lightening spell. If the magic could not be squeezed out of him, then Langan would settle for taking his life. It was not a choice that troubled him.

Madrenga inhaled sharply ... and pushed.

Slowly his arms straightened. Like the clothing that enclosed them, they suddenly seemed to have thickened and grown more muscular. A stupefied Langan found himself rising into the air as the glass tube pressed forcefully upward against his own chest. Trying to resume the downward pressure, he felt as if he was pushing against a breaching whale. When the youth beneath him had risen to a forty-five-degree angle, the giant found himself on his feet and stumbling backwards. The antagonism in his visage had been replaced by fear.

An initial cry of encouragement from the crowd faded as Madrenga rose to his feet, holding the glass tube against his chest and the twin crystal globes off the ground. When the light emanating from the spheres began to intensify, a few nervous mutters could be heard among the onlookers. Soon the lights were too bright to look at directly. The fish within the globes were now swimming in faster and faster circles. As if desperate to get out, some bumped wildly against the curving transparent walls.

"You asked for my last words," the youth could be heard to intone. "Here they are. *Leave me alone!*"

With that, he threw the apparatus at the giant.

The glass tube struck Langan of Jithros square in the chest. The wince-inducing *crack* of splintering bone could be heard over the steady susurration of the crowd. A woman among the onlookers fainted.

Bouncing off the giant's chest as the dead man fell backward, the tube that now connected two globes of fire dropped to the ground. There came a shattering as if every piece of glass in the town had suddenly imploded in sympathy. Accompanying the crystalline disintegration of the twin spheres was a high-pitched scream that had nothing to do with glass, town, or anything human.

No less stunned by what he had done, Madrenga took a couple of steps backward, staring blankly as the lights that had illuminated the globes went out. Freed from its twin prisons, water splashed and flowed over and around his feet. Likewise liberated were the sea creatures who had dwelled within. Spilling out onto the pavement, they flopped and twisted spasmodically. Until their tiny feet appeared. And their small but sharp teeth. And their horns, and barbed tails, and wild, angry eyes.

The flow of liberated water spread quickly among the crowd, but not as fast as the panic. Men, women, and children fled in terror as the creatures that had been released from the imprisoning spheres spread out and filtered in among them. Some snapped ferociously at feet and legs while others simply sought escape, scampering wildly toward freedom on two, four, or six legs. Deprived of water, they now effortlessly breathed air. Some exhaled smoke. The scent of sulphur filled the square.

Alarm diffused rapidly through the rest of the fairgoers. Though ignorant of its source, they were quick to partake of the rapidly expanding panic, a germ that spreads faster and is more contagious than the common cold.

Recovering somewhat, a shocked Madrenga walked over to the fallen Langan of Jithros. The giant lay on his back, arms akimbo, one leg drawn up and bent unnaturally beneath him. The glass tube lay across the ankle of his outthrust right leg. His eyes were closed. His chest had been caved in. Blood had pooled in his open mouth and was running down both sides of his face.

"I'm sorry—I didn't mean ..." Reaching down with his right hand, the youth picked up the glass tube. It snapped in half between his fingers. Bits of broken glass snowflaked to the ground.

Mouth agape, the old barker was staring and backing away. "He has broken the light. He has *broken the light*. No one can break light!" A hand rose and pointed. *"Demon!"*

Frowning, Madrenga turned to face the oldster. "Now wait a minute...."

He was not given more than seconds as the already terrified crowd took up the refrain. Cries of "Demon! ... Monster ...!" filled the night air. Madrenga continued to protest, to no avail. Having seen something they could neither explain nor understand, those onlookers who had been witness to the confrontation were all too easily swayed by an explanation that, if not fair, fit neatly into the always available socket of ignorance in their heads. The mob that had been against him, then with him, now railed against him once more.

Realizing that logic and reason would make no further headway this night, Madrenga turned and bolted for the place where he had left his companions. He was not accompanied by his sozzled trio of casual friends. They had joined much of the rest of the crowd in its mad desire to escape from the interloper's presence. His animals, Madrenga feared, were in imminent danger of being seriously spooked by the spreading panic. Those in the crowd who did not get out of his way fast enough he shoved aside. So worried was he about Orania and Bit that it did not occur to him that he had suddenly and inexplicably become big and strong enough to push grown adults out of his way. Nor, given his concern, did the terror in their eyes register upon him.

"Bit! Orania! Be calm—I'm coming!"

Bolder and stronger than the rest, a few of the men in the surging, swirling throng reached out to try and restrain him. When one managed to slow the intruder down, others took courage and joined in. Despite his most strenuous exertions, Madrenga found his progress first inhibited, then halted.

"To the gaol with him!" one man shouted excitedly.

"Yes, yes, give him to the night watch and the magistrates!" another bawled, while a third muttered ominously, "This is proud Hamuldar, and we burn demons here!"

Their increasingly murderous enthusiasm was cut off by a growl that, appropriately enough, seemed to come from the depths of Hell itself. Everyone stopped where they were. Startled by the sound, even Madrenga ceased struggling.

It was unmistakably a dog-growl, but one the tone and tenor of which had never before been heard in Hamuldar. Or possibly anywhere else. It emerged from the throat of a four-legged cylinder of meat and bone the size of a full-grown boar. Beneath taut skin and short black fur, rippling muscles wrapped around the stocky shape. Staring at them, Madrenga was reminded of roots at the base of a tree. Squirming like pythons awakening from a deep sleep, they threatened to burst free from the skeleton to which they were attached. The canine head was wide and heavy, the eyes burning with deep-seated lupine fury. The dog-thing growled again. As it did so, it opened its mouth.

ALAN DEAN FOSTER

Such teeth, a wondering Madrenga thought, belonged in the jaws of a dragon, not a dog.

"Hi, Bit."

A tongue emerged; long, red, and pointed. The dog began to pant. Taking heart from the sudden display of canine affection, one of the men drew a sword and thrust. Growling anew, Bit dodged slightly to one side as the point of the blade flashed past him. Then he swung his head around and bit down on the metal. It was not the finest steel, but neither was the blade made of base antimony. That did not stop the dog from biting it in half.

Drawing back the haft of the sword, its owner gaped at the couple of inches of metal that remained, looked again at the dog. It was advancing on him slowly and deliberately. Flinging the now useless remnant of the weapon aside, he let out a gargled cry, whirled, and fled. Those still holding tight to the youth in their midst were not far behind.

Swaying uncertainly, Madrenga looked down at his dog. In the course of the preceding days he had seen but chosen to largely ignore the changes that had come over his companion. As Bit advanced on him, the wide mouth with its dragon teeth agape, it struck him that he ought to have paid more attention. Then the alien red tongue emerged again. Kneeling, the youth tentatively opened his arms. What sorceral invocation ought he to employ in the face of this astonishing transformation? What mystic phraseology, what profound bewitched words would be most appropriate to defuse a potentially deadly confrontation?

"Here, boy," was all he could think of to say.

Suitably enchanted or not, it proved to be enough. Bit leaped in his arms, the red tongue lashing out to slather the youth's face with a surfeit of saliva that smelled faintly of ozone and sulphur, but felt no less gooey for all its aberrant aroma. Pushing the solid mass of muscle off his thighs, Madrenga rose and wiped his nose and cheeks. Faces in the crowd regarded him and his dog with a mix of wonderment, interest, and unabashed terror. He had no time to try and explain. Any such attempt was in any event

46

doomed to failure, since he could not explain to himself what had just transpired. He knew only that for him there was now no warm bed and hot meal to be had in this town. Moving on was all that was left to him. Moving on, and some deep thinking.

If he was shocked by what he had done to Langan of Jithros and the change that had come over his endearing and companionable pup Bit, it was as nothing compared to the transformation that had overtaken his pet pony. Ever since their departure from Harup-taw-shet, Orania had unaccountably matured from scarcely foal-sized into a stout young horse. As he neared the place where he had left her, he saw that in the course of the single chaotic evening she had, like Bit, grown explosively to become something else. Something more.

"Orania, what has happened to ...?"

She did not give him time to finish his bewildered query. At the sound of his voice she turned. In doing so she wrenched free of the earth the hitching rail to which her reins had been tied as well as the two stout poles to which the rail had been attached. This required no especial exertion on her part because she had, in the course of the single frantic, frenzied evening grown completely into her legs. Though she retained the lines of a racing horse, her withers were higher than Madrenga's eyes. She came toward him, bobbing her head and neighing softly, while the two horses that had been tied on opposite sides of her fought frantically to free themselves from the hitch rail that was being dragged along the ground. First one, then the other, worked themselves loose and fled, fleeing from her presence much as the townsfolk had fled from her master's.

"By the golden hooves of Escarius," Madrenga murmured as he reached up to stroke her forehead, "what a miracle of horseflesh you have become!" No one who had seen the often-sickly foal Orania had been could have envisioned the hulking yet elegant four-legged form that now stood before him. As he fought to free her from the wooden railing to which she was still tied he noticed that his supplies appeared to have increased in size as well. Though her back was now far broader, the pack still sloped over both flanks behind the saddle and forward of her hips.

There were more secrets at play here than any one man should be expected to fathom, he thought to himself. Later he would ponder on it. Right now he needed to get out of town as fast as possible.

The leather strap that served as a stirrup was gone. It its place was a beautiful piece of finely worked tack inlaid with silver. In the feeble light of distant lamps. he was forced to squint. No, not silver, he corrected himself. The stirrup was ornamented with same the peculiar shiny gray armor that now protected his shins. Arabesques and whorls scrolled across the surface. These framed more realistic designs, including some that resembled faces, but in the dim light and in a considerable hurry he did not take them time to examine them more closely.

Sitting in the saddle of his mysteriously matured mount caused him to suck in air sharply. It was now a long way from Orania's spine to the ground below. The new stirrups helped to steady him, as did the enhanced pommel. That horn seemed to glow in the darkness with an unearthly internal fire, as if a persistent ember had been implanted deep within the rounded shape. Behind him he could hear the sounds of a mob growing and coming his way. Bed or no bed, meal or no meal, it was time to go. Leaning forward he reached for the reins, but the distance had grown too great even for his longer arms.

It was not a problem. Taking the end of the reins between her teeth, Orania obediently turned her head and handed them to him. Man eyes meet equine gaze. There was nothing more there than there had ever been, Madrenga told himself. Orania was a horse. A mysteriously altered horse, it was true, but still only a horse. Familiarity led her to pass him the reins; that was all. Giving them a flick and adding a terse, "Hup!" he pushed his legs out to the sides, intending to give her a gentle kick in the flanks.

It wasn't necessary. In response to his command she fairly erupted off the ground. Had there been a ditch thrice her length in front of her she would have cleared it effortlessly with that initial leap. It was only when they left the hitching area near the fair square and turned down the main road that led out of Hamuldar that a sudden realization caused him to cast a frantic look backward.

"Bit! We left him behind and …!"

Maybe he had left Bit behind, but the dog had not left him. Stout, muscular legs an impossible blur, Bit was racing along beside the horse, his tongue lolling, a canine smile on his face. Staring, Madrenga could not imagine how the dog was keeping up, but keeping up he was. Another happening with no explanation. Holding the reins lightly in his teeth and relying on his mount to keep going in a straight line the youth extended both arms outward toward the dog.

"Come on, boy—jump! Give it a try!"

It was a request he could never have made of the puppy he had rescued years ago, nor even to the dog it had become outside Hamuldar. But the broad-chested, dragon-toothed creature running alongside the horse was no longer an ordinary dog. Nothing was ordinary anymore, a baffled Madrenga told himself.

In any event, Bit complied with the command. Instead of leaping into his master's waiting arms, however, the dog landed in the center of the pack that was slung across Orania's back. More cat- than dog-like, Bit's claws dug in and gave him a firm grip. The added weight neither startled Orania nor caused her to slow her stride.

Behind them, distant but not out of sight, a growing collection of lights showed that the bolder among the townsfolk had made the decision to give chase.

CHAPTER FOUR

As he galloped eastward through the mountains Madrenga had much on which to brood. So many things had happened, so much had changed, in such a short period of time. Only necromancy of some kind could explain the physical transformations that had overcome his companions and himself. But what unknown mage was interfering in his life? Did it have something to do with the obligation he had taken on, or were the continuing transmogrifications affecting both him and his animals due to something separate and apart from his task? What force had rendered him progressively bigger and stronger, turned Orania into a mount fit for a king, and fashioned Bit into the puppy from Hell?

More importantly, why?

Counselor Natoum might know the answers. But Counselor Natoum was not here. Furthermore, Madrenga wasn't sure he knew the questions. Certainly if the strange phenomenon that had overtaken him and his companions persisted, he would vigorously confront the senior court advisor upon returning from Daria. For now, though, he could only press on. And quickly, since the rippling glow of torchlight behind him showed no sign of abating. Having acquired courage from numbers, had their strength supplemented by members of Hamuldar's night watch, and doubt-less egged on by Langan's furious elderly partner, a mass of angry townsfolk was still in pursuit. Had he known of the night watch's lack of enthusiasm for the chase, the youth might have relaxed. Like so many of their compatriots elsewhere, they were charged with pursuing—not necessarily with catching.

Trundling down the narrow road at a modest pace, the double-decker wagon blocking the road ahead showed dim lights in its upper story. Smoke curled from the crooked stovepipe that jutted through the tough canvas roof. A team of six catarox yoked three abreast trudged methodically forward, alternately bellowing and meowing gruffly. A familiar sight from home and from childhood, the sight of the powerful dray animals moved the fleeing Madrenga to near tears. Poverty and lack of family notwithstanding, he suddenly found himself wishing he was back home in Harup-taw-shet. At least there he knew well his surroundings, which of his acquaintances could be counted as friends and which as enemies, and what his boot size would be when he woke up each morning.

On the other hand, he mused as he considered his strength-ened arms, more powerful legs, and broadened chest, there were compensations to traveling under the dark cloud of an interposi-tioning thamaturgy he did not understand.

Given the speed at which he was moving, his fear of being overtaken was gradually beginning to subside. Orania, enchanted, all but flew along the winding dirt road, the tips of her extended mane occasionally reaching back far enough to tickle his face. Seemingly now made of solid, polished obsidian, her enlarged hooves seemed to skim rather than touch the ground. For all he knew, that was the case. He was not about to lean over and down far enough to find out for certain lest his deeply inclined torso intercept a passing rock or tree. It was enough that she was keeping well ahead of the ongoing chase, if not actually putting much distance between him and his pursuers.

His concern was that sooner or later she would begin to tire, whereas any organized pursuit might have brought along spare mounts. It was therefore imperative that he leave the ill-intentioned citizens of Hamuldar far behind, or else find a place to hide.

That one should so suddenly and unexpectedly be presented to him was a boon even magic seemed hard-pressed to explain.

As he prepared to send Orania dashing around the right side of the ambling, rumbling, two-story wagon, the back end of the lower floor dropped open, crashing to the ground where its leading edge began to kick up dirt and gravel. Standing in the opening to the storage area thus revealed was a woman Madrenga guessed to be on the verge of embarking on her fourth decade. Her black hair was secured in a silk neckerchief. Clad in a simple skirt and brightly embroidered blouse, she gestured anxiously to him with a hand that had seen much hard labor.

Her gesturing fingers and the look in her eyes combined to create an invitation that was unmistakable. Accepting without a word, he directed Orania forward. The clack-clack of her hooves as she strode up the wooden ramp told him that her feet were indeed touching the ground.

As soon as horse, rider, and dog were inside, the woman pulled a lever set into one wall. Counterweights plunged and the ramp was pulled up, once more forming a solid back to the wagon. Turning, she shouted forward. Responding to urgent commands from the unseen driver, the two teams of catarox swung slowly to their left. The jouncing beneath Madrenga's feet intensified as he dismounted, suggesting that they had turned off onto a side road. Seeing the look of fear that had suddenly appeared on the woman's face at the sight of Bit, the youth hastened to reassure her.

"That's just Bit. He won't hurt you." Hearing his name, the dog opened his mouth and let his tongue loll freely. The fact that it hit the floor did not reassure the woman. Nor did the sight of the stocky, muscular canine's outrageously deformed dentition. "He only bites those he thinks are threatening me."

"Remind me never to threaten you, then."

It struck Madrenga that the woman was looking up at him. This was odd, because judging by her height they ought to have been nearly eye to eye. With a shock he realized that he had grown even more since the near-fatal encounter in Hamuldar's square. Miraculously, his clothing had stretched and lengthened to accommodate his increased size. In addition to the argent armor that had appeared over his shins, matching plates now adorned his sleeves. So preoccupied had he been with the events of the past few hours, that he had failed to notice the transformation in both his attire and himself. A glance showed that Bit's leather collar had acquired metal studs while the enigmatic breastplate that had affixed itself to Orania's tack had expanded to cover the rest of her chest and her upper legs as well.

The woman was watching him uncertainly. "Are you all right, noble sir? You have the look of one forced to stand too long on the deck of a heaving vessel."

He shook his head. "I'm all right—I guess."

"You guess?"

Still attractive despite her relatively simple garb and lack of jewelry or cosmetics, he found himself thinking that she would have been a raging beauty not ten years or so ago. A hard life had sandpapered her looks. The eyes, though, still flashed. Under different circumstances she might have been vivacious. Now she appeared tired—and concerned.

"I have been under some strain lately," he told her by way of explanation. "I have been suffering from a condition for which I have neither explanation nor remedy."

"You look healthy enough." Her gaze moved from his chest to his arms, which by this time had expanded far beyond what any impartial observer would have described as youthful. It was the body not just of a healthy young man, but of a warrior. Though he had readily noted the changes in his animal companions, Madrenga had remained somewhat oblivious to his own physical transformation because he was, in the truest sense, too close to it.

It is one thing to observe sorcery at work; quite another to inhabit it.

"Something else. You called me 'noble sir'. I am no noble, but only a humble delivery boy."

This admission caused her to grin. She patted him on the chest. "I will acquit you humble, then, but of your claimed delivery I know nothing. I do know that you are no boy." Her expression turned serious again. "Were that the observed case I would not have offered you concealment from those who hunt."

His expression narrowed. "How did you know I was being pursued?"

"I inferred it from the look on your face and the speed at which you were riding." Her eyes met his. "Was I wrong?"

He hesitated, then replied honestly. Many things could he sense filling this mobile household, but neither malice nor duplicity was among them.

"No. I was involved in an altercation in Hamuldar. A number of the townsfolk have chosen to judge the outcome in an unkind manner, and so I was forced to depart in haste." Gazing past her, he regarded the back wall-cum-ramp that formed the rear of the wagon's lower floor. "I would have expected to hear them by now, if only in passing."

"Doubtless their anger and single-mindedness have propelled them further along the main road. We turned off it a little while ago."

He nodded. "Would it be overmuch to trouble you for something to eat? For my mount and dog as well, if you can manage it. I can pay." He sighed heavily. "I intended to do so in Hamuldar, so the money might as well go to you."

She shook her head and smiled. "We will gladly share with you, traveler, and take no coin. Seeing your satisfaction will be payment enough. I am Elenna."

"I am called Madrenga."

For what reason he could not imagine, this revelation visibly took her aback, though she recovered quickly. "Madrenga. I am

—pleased, I suppose." Brushing past him, she lifted a hanging cloth divider, looked back, and beckoned for him to follow. "First we will provide some fodder for your magnificence of a horse, then find something for the dog with the steel-trap jaws to chew upon. I regret we have no gryphon bone, for such I think he would make short work of. Then you and I can sup, and have a talk."

"What about your driver?" While tired and confused, the youth was ever polite.

"My husband has already eaten, though he will be pleased to share talk with us. Come—Madrenga."

Why his name should prompt such evident hesitation on her part he did not know. As it usually did, however, the promise of food easily overrode any inclination to engage in extended philosophical speculation.

Shared on the first floor, covered bench at the front of the wagon, the meal was not only filling but excellent. Everything about Elenna and her husband Bieracol hinted at a monied existence that belied their current circumstances. The more they talked, the more he came to know them, the greater the refinement he detected in their speech and mannerisms. A merchant family fallen on hard times, he thought, or perhaps the last of a line of debased nobility. Curious though he was, he did not pry. They would explain their situation to him of their own free will or he would be content to remain in courteous ignorance.

Elenna did elucidate, but the words were not those he was anticipating. "My husband and I once traded in gems and precious metals. Gold, silver, loose stones, corium ..." She gestured at his right arm. "Like that which guards your lower legs and forearms."

So that was what the magically materialized metal was, Madrenga mused. Corium. The same material of which the scroll container he carried was forged. "My dear Bieracol made some unwise investments and we lost everything save this wagon and its humble contents." To the youth's surprise and unease, she looked as if she was about to burst into tears. Much to his relief, she collected her emotions and continued calmly. "Now it seems we have also lost that which is most precious to us."

"Jewelry?" Madrenga wondered aloud. "Family treasure?"

"Family treasure for certain." She sniffled but managed to keep her emotions under control. "Our daughter Elenacol has been taken from us." Anger replaced sorrow in her face and voice. "Stolen away while my husband and I were engaged in a business transaction of some import. When we returned to our wagon, we found only a note she managed to scribble in her own blood." Turning and reaching back into the wagon proper, she brought forth a small chest. From its interior she removed a piece of paper that had been crumpled and then smoothed back out. As she showed it to Madrenga he started to recoil, then relaxed when he saw that the words originally scribed in blood had dried to a soot-like black. The image this conjured continued to make him a little queasy.

He stared at the missive. The hastily scrawled script on the paper flowed from a feminine hand, but it would not have mattered had it been written in large block letters. His tone was apologetic.

"I am ashamed to say that I cannot read, Elenna."

She eyed him in surprise. "One as old and clearly experienced as yourself?"

He looked down, feeling even less than his actual age. "I am neither as old nor as experienced as my present appearance may lead you to believe."

Her brows drew together. On the other side of the platform her husband held firm to the reins as he guided the double team of catarox onward through the night. Though Bieracol was letting his wife do all the talking, Madrenga felt certain the older man missed nothing. His profound silence was a reflection of his spouse's intensity.

"The name of her kidnapper is Kakran-mul. We made inquiries in Hamuldar. He is well known in this region as a merchant of skill and cunning who is as ruthless in his personal affairs as he is in commerce. In the course of doing business in the town we had a brief exchange with him of what we thought were pleasantries. No trade was carried out and no money changed hands." She took a deep breath. "Little did we know, how could we guess, that all the time he was speaking to us of metal prices what he was actually coveting was our daughter."

"Is there no way he will agree to return her to you?" Having never known his true parents, Madrenga could scarce imagine what it must be like to have them only to be stolen away.

Elenna shook her head and the black hair that fell to her waist rippled like a waterfall made of liquefied coal. "Through an intermediary we immediately offered to ransom her. We said that despite our reduced circumstances we would find the means to pay whatever he requested. Kakran-mul replied that he had enough money but not enough wives." The woman's lips tightened. "Utterly disregarding our anguish and despair he chose to mock us." Looking past their passenger, she nodded toward her still silent husband. "Bieracol threatened to steal into his dwelling and blind him, but he only laughed. 'Come and try', he said." She spread her hands in a gesture of helplessness.

"We are merchants, traders. Peaceful folk, not warriors. Even so, we were informed that he caused to be placed around his residence a newly purchased spell especially composed to keep out any relations or even close friends of our daughter." She met his gaze. "You, Madrenga, are neither. You are a stranger to both Elenacol and to Kakran-mul. You can stroll into his compound and the restraining spell will not affect you."

"Perhaps," Madrenga conceded. "The question that follows naturally is, would I be able to walk out again?"

In front of them, the middle of the lead three catarox let out an agitated bawl and nipped at the one on her left. The big male hissed and snapped back. As he jerked on a pair of heavy leather reins Bieracol shouted something that echoed through the night. The catarox returned to their plodding. Elenacol nodded in the direction of her passenger's waist.

"With your youth, size, strength, and mighty sword, you could rescue our daughter. She is but a wisp of a thing whom you could easily carry to freedom while simultaneously wielding your weapon."

"What mighty sword?" Madrenga protested. "I don't have a …" A glance at his waist cut short his insistence. Like Bit, like Orania, like himself and his clothing, his knife had also been transformed. It was now indeed a prodigious blade nearly as long as his arm. Open-mouthed with surprise he reached down and pulled it part way from its scabbard. Even in the moonlight the double-sided blade glistened. It felt surprisingly light in his grasp.

"Corium?" He marveled at the transformation that had over-taken his modest childhood weapon.

She eyed it appraisingly. "No, that's steel. Very fine steel by the looks of it. Where did you get it? A present from some Lord?"

"N-no … I don't know where I got it. I don't know *how* I got it. To me it was only a knife. An old friend of a small blade that has somehow now become something else."

"You are a strange youth, Madrenga."

"More and more I find myself agreeing with that," he replied fervently.

Elenna's voice was effervescent with eagerness. "Then you will try to rescue our daughter?"

Looking away, he let his gaze reach out beyond the lead catarox, into the dead of night. "I cannot. I am on a royal mission. I have no time for detours. I thank you for hiding me from the misguided townsfolk of Hamuldar, and for the food, and the ride, but I cannot change course. There is too much at stake for me."

"Our daughter's future is at stake." Elenna spoke softly. "I cannot compel you, Madrenga. We can only pay, and I can only beg." The waterfall of black hair seemed to rise up behind her to frame her dark face. When he said nothing, she added, "We saved your life."

"Perhaps," he argued. "With my 'mighty sword' I might have

been able to fight off my pursuers, had they managed to catch up to me."

"That is the thing of saving a life," she told him. "When it fails, the loser is often unaware of what has happened." Bowing her head, she reached forward to place a hand on each of his knees. "I said I would beg. I am doing so now. Do this thing for us, and then go wherever your mission or desire takes you. Leave this family whole again."

He swallowed. He was embarrassed and unsettled. His had been a lifetime of begging. Having someone else beg him for something was profoundly unnerving. Reaching down, he gently took her hands in his and placed them back in her lap.

"Good Elenna, I have no experience at this sort of thing. No matter what you think and how I presently appear, I possess not the knowledge that would enable me to carry out such a rescue."

Raising her head, her gaze once more met his. "You have youth, and strength, and energy. However you came by that sword, such weaponry does not find its way to those who are reluctant to make use of it."

"I can use a knife," he admitted.

"Then do so!" Her voice rose until it seemed to envelope him, the wagon, the heaving catarox, and the few scudding clouds overhead. "Use it like a knife, if you must, but employ it to save our daughter!"

For long moments it was silent save for the creaking of the wheels and the snuffling of the catarox. "You're sure this spell is designed only to keep out friends and relatives?"

She shrugged. "If not, then you will be prevented from entering the compound. No harm done then, and Bieracol and I will be forced to try something else."

"If I *did* manage to get inside … I don't want to kill anyone."

"We are asking you to liberate, not kill. Not even, for all his evil, Kakran-mul. Any such decisions remain ultimately with you." She smiled encouragingly. "You may not be able to read, but you are good with words. Mayhap you can talk to him."

Sure, the youth thought. Like he had talked to Langan of Jithros and his manager back in Hamuldar. His talking had led to his having to flee, and thence to the discomforting situation in which he presently found himself.

But perhaps the distraught mother was right. As a rank outsider maybe he *could* talk to this Kakran-mul. It wouldn't constitute much of a diversion, he rationalized. A few minutes chat. Then he could return to the bereaved parents and declare himself the perpetrator of an honorable failure before continuing on his way clear of conscience.

"Very well. I will try to talk with this Kakran-mul."

"Yes, yes, reason with him! Promise him anything, but return our daughter to us!" Unable to restrain her emotions any longer, a relieved Elenna threw her arms around the youth and began to sob openly. Not knowing what to do with his hands, a flustered Madrenga could do no better than hold them down at his sides.

What, he wondered, had he gone and gotten himself into now? What if this Kakran-mul, who sounded like a much tougher character than even Langan of Jithros, was not in the mood for polite conversation? The partial armor that Madrenga had somehow acquired was far from extensive enough to protect his vital regions. "Reason with him," the agitated mother had suggested. Reason would not stop a line of spears or a flight of arrows.

Too late now, he told himself. He had surrendered his better judgment to sympathy. Nothing for it now but to follow through. As for the mighty sword slung at his belt, he had a sinking feeling that if words failed, he would not know how to make proper use of it.

Better learn fast, a voice in his head declared.

CHAPTER FIVE

EVEN ON A WINDLESS NIGHT LIT BY HALF A RELUCTANT MOON that hung in the sky like the tip of an invisible candle, a nervous Madrenga could see that the residence of Kakran-mul was much less than a castle and considerably more than a home. The high stone walls of the compound were topped with plate-sized shards of broken glass that threw back fragments of shattered moonlight. His ears conveyed only silence. At this hour of the night that was not surprising.

A few evergreen trees stood sentry before the walls, but they were shorter and sparser of branch than those that filled the mountain forests through which he had recently passed. Brush was more common here, rising in rounded goblin shapes on both sides of the approach road. Somewhere an unknown bird called querulously, and occasionally a bat or batringa would interpose its ghostly membranous shape between the world and the moon.

I am not afraid, he told himself. Alone for as long as he could remember, he had never feared the dark. Night was a comforting companion that had shielded him from marauding perverts, unscrupulous slavers, and corrupt officials. It had been his friend and companion. He hoped it would be so now.

The heavy double door that barred entry to the inner courtyard was wide enough to admit large wagons and strong enough to hold off a battering ram wielded by bandits. Set within the door on the left side was a smaller, man-sized pedestrian entry. In Harup-taw-shet, he would have had to rise on tiptoes to stand at eye level with it. The unexplained changes that had transformed his body in the course of his journey now required him to bend slightly at the knees. A weathered brass bell hung from an iron spike off to one side. Tugging on the attached cord produced a jangle that was unmissable without being too loud. When nothing responded, he yanked on the cord a second time.

This louder clang caused the wooden panel that blocked the barred eyeport to be drawn aside. All he could see of the man's face on the other side consisted of blue eyes, bushy brows, and sun-crumpled skin. These were accompanied by a voice that was irritable and impatient.

"State your business, night-muck."

Swallowing, Madrenga tried to sound older than he was. His voice had not changed as much as his body. "I represent, uh, the grain guild, of Hamuldar, and have a message from them for your master."

The heavy brows drew together. "Do you think me daft, whoever you are?" As the man stepped back Madrenga could see his entire face while the guard addressed a companion. At least two to deal with, then. "He says he's on business from the grain guild." Both men shared a chuckle, then the eyes and brows once again filled the narrow opening. "I don't know who you are or what you're playing at, but we can settle your gonads tomorrow. Kakran-mul does not receive visitors at this hour. Not for all the oats in Opulchungu. Even if he did, I wouldn't let you in."

"Why not?" Madrenga asked automatically.

"I don't like your looks, night-muck. Go sleep in a rathan sump somewhere and rethink your strategy." With that the wooden shutter behind the bars was slammed shut.

Madrenga leaned near to the now closed opening and raised

his voice slightly. "It will only take a minute of your master's time." He hesitated. "I will pay you to let me in."

He could hear laughter behind the gate. A glance at the sky confirmed the time. While new at this sort of thing, he knew he did not want to wait for daylight. With the coming of the dawn the entire household would be awake, including far more armed men. He needed to get inside, and he needed to do it before the sun made his task all the more difficult. Turning, he beckoned to the patiently waiting Orania.

"Bit, get out of the way." He waved at the now massive dog, which obediently backed up. The black head cocked sideways as he eyed his master curiously, the tip of that absurdly lengthened tongue barely clearing the ground. Using firm hands and soft commands, Madrenga turned his mount around and positioned her.

"Easy there, girl—that's it. Just a little farther." When he had backed her to within an arm's length of the pedestrian entryway, he stepped to one side and raised his left hand. At the same time as he brought it down sharply on her rump, he yelled, "Kick!"

Orania's startled snort was followed by an explosion of dust and splinters. His intention was to simply draw the attention of the gate guards. What he got was something more.

Waving a hand to brush the settling dust away from his face he saw that the pedestrian gate was now open. No, he corrected himself as he stepped through the gap: it wasn't open—it was gone. On his left a pair of heavy cast-iron metal hinges twice the diameter of his spread palm hung from the thick wood of the larger gate. On his right, a vee-shaped gap in the wood showed where the smaller gate had once bolted to the large one. Of the pedestrian gate itself, with its small barred opening for exchanging looks and conversation, there was no sign.

He located it clear across a courtyard paved with head-sized, rounded stones set in a circular pattern around a central fountain. The noise from the fast-flowing fountain, which splashed and bubbled energetically, had served to mask first the concussion from

Orania's vigorous kick and then the sound of the pedestrian gate hitting the wall on the opposite side of the courtyard. The only sign of the two guards was a hand sticking out from behind the violently displaced wooden barrier. That, and the blood that was seeping from beneath the bottom edge of the wood. The door itself and the two guards who had the misfortune to have been standing behind it when Orania had responded to her master's slap and command were still behind the door, but now firmly embedded in the stone wall.

He looked around anxiously. Except for the excited burbling of the big fountain and the basso panting of the dog sitting at his feet, the lamp-lit courtyard remained empty and quiet. Some heavy sleepers dwelled here, he decided. It probably wasn't unusual for loud sounds to occasionally reverberate through what was plainly a busy place. Or maybe he was just lucky. He'd had the benefit of a lot of luck, lately. Hopefully it would hold.

He found the watchman dozing at his post outside a central two-story structure that dominated the rest of the walled complex. In a lord's compound such a structure would likely be a meeting hall, Madrenga knew. Here, in a rich man's private surroundings, it was reasonable to assume it served as the dwelling place of the owner. He had to be certain. He could hardly go stalking about waking half the inhabitants in his attempt to locate Kakran-mul. It would be much better if he could find the man on the first try.

Bending over and reaching down, he firmly grasped the watchman's shoulder and shook gently. "Pardon me, but you have to wake up." He shook again. "Wake up, sir."

Eyelids fluttered, focused, snapped wide open. As they did so the burly guard's right hand reached for the double-bladed pike leaning against the nearby wall. With a soft growl, Bit closed his jaws around the man's arm just below the elbow. The look of terror that spread across the watchman's face was perfectly under-standable.

"Keep your composure if you want to keep your arm," Madrenga murmured to him.

Trembling slightly, the man nodded his understanding. "What manner of monstrous beast is that, sir?"

"I don't know Bit's breed, and in fact it seems to be changing by the day, but he's my puppy and he'll do as I say, so mind your voice."

"That's a puppy?"

Madrenga leaned closer and did his best to both sound and look intimidating. It appeared to work. "I did not come here to discuss dog breeding. Where is your master?" When the man didn't answer, the youth nodded at Bit. The dog's massive jaws tightened slightly and dragon teeth began to bite.

"Surrender, sir, I surrender! Call off your fiend!"

Madrenga nodded at Bit again and smiled. Visibly disappointed, the dog relaxed its jaws and eased the pressure.

"I won't ask a third time." As he drew his sword Madrenga was surprised at the increasing depth of his own voice. "Where is Kakran-mul?"

"The master loves his food and never goes to bed without a late meal." Carefully, the watchman turned his head to his right and nodded once. "If he has not yet retired you should find him alone in the main dining hall. Entryway will be on your left." He eyed the hopeful Bit and pleaded. "Please, may I have my arm back now?"

Madrenga nodded and stepped aside. "Bit, leave it." Complying reluctantly the dog backed away, freeing the watchman from those crushing jaws. The guard's relief was short-lived as Madrenga brought the butt end of his sword down against the side of the man's head. Intending only to knock him out, he looked on in shock as the body went flying sideways and came to rest on the pavement in a twisted mass of arms and legs. A hurried check revealed that the cooperative watchman was not dead. Madrenga had only inadvertently broken his jaw.

He would have to watch his inexplicable new strength, the stunned youth told himself. Like everything else about and around him, that too seemed to be changing from day to day.

The empty corridor was longer than he had guessed. Paintings, sculptures, and sideboard furniture of fine quality ornamented both walls. Elenna's talk of her nemesis's wealth had not been an exaggeration. Madrenga's mouth tightened. He knew of many people like this, who not only thought but expected that their money could and would buy them anything. Including protection from the vested authorities should they choose to step outside the boundaries of law and decency by engaging in everything from fraud to murder. Or in the case of this Kakran-mul, kidnapping.

The dining hall itself was splendid; high-vaulted, with enough decorative pennants and banners and hanging crystal to suggest that the master of this manse desired to at least imitate the trappings of a nobility he did not possess through natural descent. Oil-lamps of filigree and gold illuminated the great room while the profusion of precious objects far exceeded what he had encountered in the hallway. It was an ostentatious display of wealth that bordered on the obscene. Seated amid such vulgar surroundings, their owner proved something of a disappointment.

The grilled envo fowl leg he was holding was bigger than his own forearm. Very much shorter and slimmer than Madrenga had expected, Kakran-mul needed a chair with an unusually high seat in order to be able to sit at the head of the long and otherwise empty dining table. A matched pewter flagon and goblet stood close by his left hand while the pewter plate before him was piled high with roasted pink potatoes and steamed vegetables. Madrenga could smell the garlic. Grease ran down the man's left cheek. An unruly thicket of brown hair was bound up in a single gold band at the back of his head. The white silk shirt was heavily food-stained but otherwise unadorned. No embroidery emboldened collar or cuffs, nor the plain cotton pants or suede boots.

It was not often, Madrenga reflected as he advanced into the high-ceilinged room, that one encountered evil with such simple personal tastes. A money-hoarder, he told himself. Probably there was a storeroom behind a secret door or hidden in a cellar where coins and jewels and other valuable objects were kept so that when he so desired their owner could gaze upon them in safety and silence. As someone who had more than once gone long without food, Madrenga harbored a deep-seated dislike for hoarders. Stockpiled money made a poor tombstone for a man.

Big as Madrenga had become, even one as preoccupied with his food as Kakran-mul could hardly fail to acknowledge the youth's entrance. Turning to face the entryway, the merchant's greeting was as straightforward as his meal.

"Who are you and what in the name of Wortrun's anus do you want?"

"I am here to …" Madrenga began as firmly as he could.

Having put forth his questions, the master merchant gave the intruder no time to respond. Rising to his feet, he shoved the high-backed wooden chair away from the table.

"How did you get in here? Who allowed you to pass?" The furious Kakran-mul leaned forward over table and food as he strained to see past the youth and into the hall beyond. "I am going to make drinking cups of some skulls tonight!"

Since the merchant was manifestly a man who favored direct-ness, Madrenga decided to respond in kind.

"I came for the girl Elenacol."

"Oh. For the girl Elenacol. Did you now? Her misbegotten parents sent you, I suppose." Seeing no harm in admitting to the obvious, Madrenga nodded tersely. "I stand before you amazed. Amazed that they could find someone as big, gullible, and stupid as yourself to sacrifice himself on behalf of such a futile endeavor." With that he sat back down and resumed his predatory gnawing of the chunky avian leg bone. "I am tired and find myself in an atypi-cally generous mood. Possibly it is your youth that softens me. Get out, and I will account this intrusion an entertainment rather than an affront."

Madrenga took several steps into the dining hall. "I came for the girl. I intend to leave with the girl."

"I see. Impertinence is the reward, then, for my generosity and compassion." Leaning back, Kakran-mul put both booted feet up on the intricately carved wooden table and crossed his legs. His speech he continued to conduct with the leg bone. "You will make an interesting addition to my collection."

"Collection?" Madrenga echoed before he could catch himself.

"Yes." Bone and greasy sinew-strewn bird flesh gestured toward the hallway from which the young intruder had emerged. "You saw some of my artwork, some of my fine furniture?"

"I did. Very nice things. All the more reason why you don't need to hold one girl against her will."

"But my boy, where is the pleasure in not holding them against their will? Surely you are not so young and naïve to speak of something like love? The collection I speak of is far more valuable to me precisely because it does not consist of such common objects as pictures and sculptures, gold and silver. Any dullard with money or inheritance can accumulate such things. Whereas I have applied myself to the mastery of certain arts known only to a few."

Madrenga tensed. "I was not told you were a necromancer."

"Because I am not. I am merely a practitioner of a single simple art which I have studied long and hard so that I might accumulate my collection." Kakran-mul smiled, and it reminded Madrenga of some of the groping hands he had avoided as a child. "Gold, silver—these are not the measure of a man. That must be valued in terms of what he has learned." With a sigh he rose from his seat a second time. On this occasion he chose to forgo the remnants of his meal. Instead of reaching for food, he raised a knife. Though the blade was intended for dissecting a roast and not a visitor, Madrenga was immediately on guard.

But the merchant was not looking in his direction, far less threatening him with the comparatively insignificant blade. Having turned to face the far wall, he began to chant. This would have been more intimidating, Madrenga decided, had Kakran-mul been a larger man, with a deeper voice.

His eyes widened as the carved wooden panels that lined the far side of the dining hall swung open. They grew wider still as what lay behind them began to emerge. Still holding the knife high like the wand it was not, the merchant looked back at his youthful visitor and offered up a twisted grin.

"Behold, transgressor of a quiet meal, my cabinet of curiosities!"

Collection of horrors was more like it, a shocked Madrenga thought. Where the merchant had gathered, or purchased, or stolen the fantastical mélange of monstrosities the youth could not imagine. Each was different from its neighbor, each plucked whole and original from a separate nightmare.

As they came shambling around the dining table and toward the tall intruder Madrenga found himself unable to move. Dread had rooted him to the spot. At carnival time in Harup-taw-shet he and his fellow street urchins had seen one or two such abominations: poor misshapen beings consigned to a life of being gawked at with revulsion and disgust by those who paid to gape at such sights. While his friends had laughed and pointed and made rude noises in tandem with the rest of the crowd, Madrenga had found them more deserving of pity than contempt.

Unlike them, however, the atrocities that had begun to file around the table and lurch toward him were heavily armed. The merchant's "curiosities" carried war-axes and swords, clubs and maces. They made sounds that were not words but nonetheless conveyed their intent. Sitting back down in his seat, a contemptuous Kakran-mul resumed his interrupted meal as though nothing untoward was amiss. This was not the first time he had unleashed his collection on someone who displeased him, and he knew well the preordained outcome.

Fight! a voice shouted in Madrenga's head. *Draw your sword— fight!* Though he heard the voice and recognized its import and urgency, Madrenga remained paralyzed. Taller, stronger, better equipped than had been the adolescent who had left Harup-taw-shet, inside his head he was still the slender inexperienced youth whom Counselor Natoum had plucked from the streets of the city. When threatened in Hamuldar he had reflexively defended himself, but he still did not know how he had managed the feat.

Besides, it had consisted of little more than an instinctive reaction to a single opponent. Now he found himself confronted by more than a dozen foes armed and inhuman.

A stout dark green figure with a single vertical eye where its nose should have been raised a club that ended in an iron square large enough to crush a man's skull. As it advanced toward Madrenga with the intention of doing exactly that, something big, black, and snarling shot past the youth's shoulder as if flung from a catapult. More leonine than canine, Bit's roar echoed through the room as he slammed both jaws shut on the green assailant's arm, twisted with the weight of his whole body, and wrenched the limb free. Puzzled by the sudden loss of a major appendage, its owner eyed the vacant socket in confusion. Madrenga's shock was compounded as he stared: there was no blood.

Kakran-mul had looked up and was grinning. "Nice dog you have there, but he can't kill any of my collection. Neither can you. You see, they're already dead, and become animated only when I demand it of them. Why not surrender sensibly to the inevitable? It will go easier on you." He gestured with his knife. "And on your dog."

Responding to Bit's intervention, a trio of lumbering, rotting simian shapes had formed a semi-circle in front of the dog and were backing him into a corner. The snarling canine still had the green monster's dismembered arm clamped tight in his jaws. Two of the advancing ape-like creatures were raising clubs not unlike the one wielded by the now one-armed monstrosity confronting Madrenga. One chunk of cold iron was lined with short, thick spikes.

"Bit!" His four-legged friend was in trouble: that broke the spell, or paralysis, or whatever emotional lock had been holding Madrenga back. Drawing his sword, he rushed toward his dog. As he did so, the one-armed green thing brought its battleaxe around in a sweeping arc, the blade aimed at the intruder's neck. Without thinking, Madrenga struck out blindly in defense with his sword. The blade cut clean through the axe's thick ironwood handle,

sending the axe-head flying wildly. It was stopped by the chest of a slavering frog-thing that had chosen an inopportune moment to charge the tall youth. As the flying axe-head struck it in the upper portion of its body, the frog-beast was knocked backward. The head of the mace it was swinging went wild and struck a bat-eared lump of half-formed yellowish protoplasm on the side of its head. Green-thing, frog-beast, and lump all went down more or less simultaneously.

The remainder of his meal now forgotten, a suddenly troubled Kakran-mul rose from where he had been sitting.

True to the merchant's description of his collection, none of the heavily armed things shed blood when they were cut, cleaved, lopped, or otherwise battered by Madrenga's whirling sword. As long as they remained on their feet or pseudopods they continued to come at him. The dining chamber was filled with flying limbs and other body parts as an anxious Madrenga, hardly aware of the carnage he was wreaking, hacked his way toward his cornered pet. Dead they might already be, or undead while functioning under the merchant's inimical influence, but they were not invulnerable, and hardly immune to the youth's raging blade.

Bit did not relax while his master worked. Leaping to and fro, bouncing off walls and ceiling to avoid the thrusts of swords and swings of clubs, the dog busied himself ripping off hands, arms, and heads. When such prominent targets grew in short supply, he switched to eviscerating one attacker after another. One barrel-shaped multi-tentacled gray amphibian found itself wrapped and bound in the intestines of another creature as Bit ran circles around the water-dweller with one end of the second monstrosity's digestive system held firmly in his mouth.

Early in the clash, a party of armed men had appeared at the rear entrance to the dining hall. When a three-eyed decapitated head came flying at them they retreated as fast as they could back through the same doorway.

When finally the last grotesque skull had bounced off the dining table or one of the enclosing walls and the final body had been hewed beyond the capacity to deliver harm, Madrenga sheathed his sword and resumed his advance on the now distressed merchant. Stepping over severed limbs that still twitched and quivered in a horrible parody of life, he had to pause to kick the occasional grasping hand or tentacle out of the way. Disembodied heads snapped at his feet. Legs that had been divorced from their torsos tried to kick or trip him. He avoided all such attempts easily.

Kakran-mul did not wait for Madrenga to reach the table. Turning, he bolted for the rear door but only got a couple of steps. Abruptly reversing course, he began backing toward the table.

"Easy there now—nice dog. Nice doggy."

The furious clash having energized yet another mysterious boost to Bit's anatomy, the black dog's muzzle was now at chest level with the merchant. Bit's teeth had become scimitars and the embers that burned deep behind his eyes resembled the lakes of lava that surge and boil in the throats of volcanoes. Like steel petals, the spikes on his collar had grown until they were each longer than a man's index finger. Formerly blunted at the ends, they were now sharp as cactus spines. The growl that emerged from deep within the broad black chest and muscular throat would have chilled the blood of the bravest man.

It was a description for which Kakran-mul was ill-suited. He was no coward, but confronted by the eyes and jaws of a creature that was pure fiend in canine form, the merchant's legs grew weak. Momentarily distracted, Bit looked down and picked something off the floor. Still wrapped in rotting material, it was recognizable as the upper leg bone of one of his undead simian attackers. Jaws came together and the sound of thigh splintering filled the room.

"Bit loves bones." Madrenga found he was not even breathing hard. Once again he marveled at the transformation that had come over him. Lowering his gaze, he looked meaningfully at the merchant's nether extremities, comparing them to the bagatelle on which Bit was presently munching. Kakran-mul's response was not what the youth expected.

"Come work for me."

Madrenga blinked. The merchant might be a thug and a kidnapper and a bit of a coward, but he had presence of mind. "What?"

"Come work for me. Whatever those foggy old fools who hired you are paying, I will double it. Triple it! Never have I seen such a warrior who was at first so underestimated and who subsequently turned out to be so powerful!" He made a sweeping gesture. "You have destroyed my collection. I forgive you that."

"You forgive …?" A gaping Madrenga marveled at the man's audacity. "I am not a warrior," he protested. "I am a courier."

Kakran-mul did not hear him, so immersed was he in his anticipated glory to be. "I will take the cost of restoration and repair out of your salary, which I assure you will be commensurate with your skills. You and your dog will become my personal bodyguard. I can already see the faces of the guild chairmen when I walk into a meeting with the both of you at my side! They will grant any concessions I ask, lest in the course of the usual negotiations I lose my temper. Oh, it will be a marvelous thing to see!"

"No, it won't." Madrenga had had just about enough of this self-important, self-delusional popinjay. "Because in order to see, one must have eyes."

As he moved nearer a newly nervous Kakran-mul tried to retreat. Once again, a warning growl stopped him in his tracks. Reaching out and down, for he was now considerably taller than the merchant, Madrenga put the thumbs of each hand over the man's eyes while his fingers wrapped around the sides of the head.

"Tell me where the girl Elenacol is and I won't crush your skull."

Madrenga would never have dispatched even as vicious a creature as the merchant in so brutal a manner. Inside, he was still the boy from the warrens and alleys of Harup-taw-shet. But Kakran-mul didn't know that. Just as the youth's thumbs began to press inward, the merchant jerked violently away and fell back in his chair, gazing up in fear at the young intruder while doing his best to shrink back into the carved wood.

"All right, all right, enough! You can have the bitch!"

Relieved he had not been forced to carry out even a portion of his threat, Madrenga stepped back. "Where is she?"

"After all," the merchant mumbled to himself, "what's one girl more or less? Not worth this trouble, not worth it at all." His attention having come to rest on the slaughter that now paved the floor of the dining hall, he seemed to have forgotten the young man who towered over him. "My beautiful curiosities! Look what you've done to them. Restoring them will cost …"

"Will cost you your head if you don't shut up." Madrenga's patience was wearing thin. He was also concerned that the merchant's mercenaries, who had fled earlier, might be regrouping their forces and stiffening their backbones for a fresh assault on the dining hall. "The girl. Where?"

"Hmm? Oh yes, the girl." A distracted Kakran-mul raised a hand and pointed. "There."

Frowning, the youth turned to look in the indicated direction. There was no one to be seen in the space the merchant had singled out. Only some furniture: a sideboard of hand-milled nortenwood flanked by a pair of matching chairs and a five-shelf bookcase filled with leather-bound tomes, small sculptures and other bric-a-brac. On the top shelf a pair of tall candlesticks in silver holders flanked half a dozen bottles of colored glass, each a different size and shape.

"Bit," he said tightly.

Advancing on the seated merchant, the dog clamped his jaws around the man's lower left leg. Bit did so gently, but with an understated implication that was almost as terrifying as an actual bite. Terror underscored Kakran-mul's frantic response.

"She's there, right there!" he stammered as he stared wide-eyed down at the pair of massive jaws that were attached to the canine at his feet. "The bottles contain spirits. Gantone whiskey, parmalla wine, essence of collay, essence of girl…."

Striving to convey a sophistication he did not possess, a bemused Madrenga walked over to the shelves. "Fourth bottle?" he asked hesitantly.

Without taking his eyes off the dog-thing locked on his leg, Kakran-mul nodded violently. "Fourth bottle. You may get a small shock when you pick it up. The candlesticks are linked by a spell of force that restrains anything within the bottles. I take as much care to protect my liquor as I do my women."

"Not your woman." Madrenga reached for the bottle. He did indeed feel a tremor run through his hand as it interrupted the force that invisibly linked the two candlesticks, but it was little more than a tingle. The glass of which the bottle was blown was thick, red, and opaque. He stared at it, still not quite believing in what he might be holding. "She's in this?"

"Yes, yes." Kakran-mul swallowed hard. "Now call off your dog."

"Bit—off."

Misinterpreting the young man's words, the merchant closed his eyes and went stiff, expecting the worst. But the dog released his leg, the slashing teeth tearing only the fabric of the pants as they withdrew. Turning away from the relieved trader, Bit rummaged through the piles of undead body parts until he found one that was suitable, or tasty, or both, and set to chewing. With each crack of bone a still uneasy Kakran-mul winced visibly.

"How do I get her out?"

"Just remove the stopper. It's not spelled," the merchant added as he saw Madrenga continue to hesitate. "None of my people would dare to touch any of the bottles. Thirsty though they might be they would fear opening the wrong one."

What did the remaining two bottles contain, then? Madrenga wondered. The implication was unnerving. No matter. Reaching down, he twisted and tugged on the stopper of the red bottle until it came loose. Immediately a dark vapor began to emerge from the interior. Startled, he dropped the bottle and stepped back as the thick haze coiled upward in front of him.

"You lied to me! It is an evil apparition!"

With Bit having removed himself from his leg the merchant had regained some of his former bravado. "Kakran-mul of Mulereer does not lie. Deceive, trick, dupe or occasionally swindle perhaps, but he does not lie." He shook his head regretfully. "To be bested by one so young and ignorant is shaming. My soul is flogged."

Even Bit looked up from his chunk of half-gnawed shoulder as the swirling mist in front of his master continued to rise and condense. Emerging from the depths of the tepid fog, smaller extensions of itself began to twist and coil on their own. A rush of glitter flashed through the churning darkness as if it had been suddenly strewn with mica; a sparkling tornado seen in slow-motion.

Vaporish gloom gave way to a pale red that shifted and surged until it became the color and consistency of dark flesh. Out of the haze, hollows and protrusions slowly took shape and became familiar. Too familiar. Madrenga knew he should avert his eyes, but he could not. No man could.

A thousand tiny vapor trails hardened into waist-length strands of black hair. Profuse though they were, they were insufficient in density and location to appropriately cover the female form that now stood upright before the wonderstruck young man. He was not so stunned, however, that he failed to remember certain words that had been spoken to him by this woman's mother.

"She's just a wisp of a thing," Elenna had told him. More true than he could have imagined, he now realized. He finally found his voice.

"You're a smoke sprite!"

"I see that I have been drawn forth by a man of brilliance and penetrating insight." Elenacol's gaze narrowed as she appraised her rescuer. "Or a very large boy."

Madrenga straightened to the maximum degree his unaccountably enhanced stature would allow. "I am a man!" In the presence of the remaining vapor he then sneezed, an action which somehow mitigated his declaration.

"We'll see." Looking down at herself, she spread her arms wide. "You are correct that I am a smoke sprite. I am also a naked smoke sprite."

"What? Oh—I hadn't noticed."

"A liar as well."

Hastily removing his outer shirt, he draped it carefully around the young woman's shoulders. As she pulled it around her he reflected that he would now be cold when they ventured outside, but no matter the pre-dawn temperature he resolved not to admit to any discomfort.

"I've come to take you back to your parents. They're worried about you."

"Obviously, or you wouldn't be here." She sighed. "I suppose saving excuses staring." Her gaze wandered past him to the seated figure of Kakran-mul. "Sir, my wish would be for one day to be your personal chef, so that I might make a fine ragout of your own testicles and watch you eat them."

Kakran-mul stiffened slightly. "And I had fine plans for you that also involved some grilling. Is it possible for one to put a brand on smoke? Now I will never know." He nodded at Madrenga. "I insulted this youthful intruder and it cost me. I underestimated him and it cost me. You would be wise to do neither."

Uncertain how to respond to compliments from such an unexpected source, Madrenga made no comment. Unbeknownst to him, it was the mature thing to do.

"Let's be away from this place." The young man put an arm around the sprite's now covered shoulders. As he led her from the dining hall, she finally noticed that portions of it had been recarpeted with body parts. Her gaze rose to his face.

"You did this?"

He nodded. "And my dog." Bit had trotted up to accompany

them. Pacing alongside his master, the dog proudly carried an entire severed arm in his jaws. Madrenga eyed it distastefully.

"Bit, drop it! That's disgusting!"

"He's a dog," she said matter-of-factly. "In my experience the only time 'disgusting' can be used in an affectionate manner is when referring to a dog."

"You have a dog?" They were outside now, heading for the courtyard.

"No. I have dust bunnies."

At her first sight of his mount she stopped and stared. "Is that —your horse?"

He nodded. "Orania's gotten a little bigger since we left home. So has Bit. So have I. It is something I do not understand, and do not have time to ponder more than occasionally." As they drew closer the mare looked back and snorted softly.

There plainly being no way the perfectly formed but modestly statured Elenacol was going to be able to get a foot up to the high stirrup, Madrenga gave her a boost into the saddle. Being unacquainted with such gallant maneuvers, his hand slipped from her foot to more curvaceous regions north. Expecting a curse or other reprimand, he was surprised when she smiled down at him.

"You have saved me. Be not so diffident. How old are you, anyway? And what is your name?"

"I am called Madrenga." He mounted up behind her, there being ample room in the great saddle to accommodate both of them. Without having to be told, Bit leaped to his now familiar perch on the backpack that straddled the horse's hindquarters.

The same mica sparkle he had seen earlier now turned her black eyes to ornaments. "Ah. That explains much."

Not to him it didn't. But there was no time to press the matter. Shouts and cries were rising from deeper within the merchant's compound. Whether they represented the humiliated Kakran-mul attempting to rally his household fighters, the screams of servants summoned to clean up the corpse-laden dining hall, or something else, Madrenga had no inclination to linger and learn the explanation. Nudging Orania, he sent the now partially armored horse bolting forward. Neither the guards at the gate nor the gate itself having yet been replaced, there was still a welcoming opening where the pedestrian entrance had been.

"Lower yourself!" Madrenga told the girl. She bent as far forward as she could, bringing her head below the level of Orania's mane. He did likewise. This pressed his upper body into her back which, despite the two shirts that separated them, felt like anything but smoke.

Excited shouts and a couple of arrows followed them as they raced clear of the compound, indications that Kakran-mul's fighters were recovering their courage. This did not extend to their mounting a formal pursuit. In any event Madrenga doubted there was a horse alive that could catch what Orania had become. The yelling quickly faded behind them.

Elenacol straightened in the saddle, his heavy outer shirt tenting around her. While there was room for the two of them, it was a tight fit when she sat back, one made all the tighter by the unavoidable bumping and jouncing of Orania's swift gait. Whereas this increasing proximity did not seem to trouble her at all, it unsettled him more than a little. But not in a manner that troubled him.

As they rode on through the night, the promise of an approaching dawn was not the only wish that found itself fulfilled.

CHAPTER SIX

FOR THE FIRST TIME SINCE HE HAD AGREED TO TRY AND HELP the bereaved couple, Madrenga heard Bieracol speak. Behind a great silvery froth of a beard, behind sheepdog-like eyebrows sufficiently wooly they threatened to block his vision, the husband of Elenna and father of Elenacol expressed his gratitude.

"When my wife told me what she had learned of you, I thought you had little chance of success, given your self-evident youth and professed inexperience in such matters. Kakran-mul is a turd in the catbox of life from which the smell cannot be erased." A beaming smile emerged from behind the cloud of whiskers. "I am pleased to see how wrong I was about you, and your abilities. Clearly you are accomplished beyond your years." Before the lavishly praised Madrenga could reply the old man opened his arms to embrace his daughter. "I feared you might be lost to us forever, my dear one!"

Dissolving into a swirl of silver-flecked smoke, Elenacol did not so much embrace her father as envelop him. It was an all-encompassing hug the likes of which no human could duplicate. She was not just in his arms, but in all of him. Despite having previously witnessed the girl's transformation from smoke into flesh, Madrenga was no less enthralled to observe the reverse. He smiled to himself. Surely whoever had coined the phrase "where there's smoke there's fire" must have had a delicious creature like Elenacol in mind. The ride back from Kakran-mul's compound had provided ample proof of that particular truism.

Turning away from her father, the column of slowly spinning vapor drifted toward Elenna. Having already battled the undead in order to rescue an enchantment, Madrenga was less astonished than he otherwise might have been when the mother now dissolved into a cold mist. Mother and daughter were both smoke sprites.

They twisted and twined about one another in a sooty ballet that bespoke spells and sorcery unknown. Their physical manifestations notwithstanding, there was nothing of the dark arts about their reunion. Theirs was not the smokiness of burnt offerings, of sacrifices unwilling, or ruined homes, or forest-ravaging fires. It was the domesticated smoke that rises from flames that warm hearth and home, that adds savory to fine meats or puffs contentedly from well-worn, hand-rubbed pipes. As they whirled past, spinning and dancing about one another, suddenly there were four of them. He blinked.

No, not four. It was the same two, mother and daughter. The illusion arose from the transformation of the father, one which to Madrenga's amazed eyes was more striking than that which had overtaken the two women.

Where Bieracol had sat on the front seat of the tall wagon there now stood a vaguely humanoid figure that appeared to be sheathed in reflective glory. It took Madrenga a moment or two to analyze and discard all possibilities save the most obvious. Mother and daughter were born of smoke. Father Bieracol, on the other hand, was a mirror sprite. The second pair of women he thought he had glimpsed were reflections of wife and daughter not just in the father's eye, but in his whole torso.

This family was not, then, members of some debased nobility.

It made perfect sense that such beings would be successful dealers in precious metals, as Elenna had told him when first she had taken him into her confidence. They dealt, as it was, in what they were.

Eventually the family's unreserved joy at their successful reunion began to subside. Elenna and her daughter resumed their human form and, upon reflection, Bieracol did likewise.

"We owe you more than we can say." Bowing slightly in Madrenga's direction, Elenna lowered her eyes, as did her husband and daughter. His embarrassment at this display of deference was equally unrestrained.

"Is there nothing we can give you?" Accomplishing the seemingly impossible, Elenacol managed to be both solemn and coquettish as she spoke these words. If any further confirmation of what she was suggesting was necessary, the look in her eyes provided eloquent punctuation.

"I ..." He swallowed, uncertain how exactly to respond. "I have everything I need. Food, enough money to help me over any rough patches, and my companions. Though I was reluctant at first, I'm glad now that I was able to help you. Having no family of my own, I think I understand better than most how important it is to keep one together if you are fortunate enough to have one."

"In truth," Bieracol murmured, "you are not as young as you claim."

Madrenga looked away, discomfited by the praise in the man's voice and expression. "Sometimes circumstances force one to grow up faster than one would wish."

"You must take *something*." Elenna was insistent. "Even if only a small memento, so that you will not forget us."

"*We* certainly will not forget *you*." This time Elenacol's eyes were challenging as well as offering. Did she realize, he wondered, that despite his size he was younger than her? It was a scary notion. Did the age difference not matter to her? That was an even more frightening thought. It was as much to escape her burning stare as to please her mother that he allowed Elenna to lead him into the interior of the wagon. Despite his apparent compliance he had no intention of taking anything more than a trifle.

We lost everything save this wagon and its poor contents, the mother had informed him yesterday. What he had told her just now was the truth. He felt that he did have everything he needed. Willingly offered memento or not, he was not about to impose on this impoverished family.

As it developed, her interpretation of "poor" differed somewhat from his. But then, he managed to tell himself through his shock as he gaped at the previously covered bottom portion of the wagon's interior, it was to be expected that a human's definition of certain things might differ to some degree from that of a family of sprites.

When, riding hard to escape the pursuing citizens of Hamuldar and he had first come up on the wagon in the darkness, he had wondered idly how such a tall vehicle kept from toppling over. He imagined it must contain in its lowermost compartments a certain amount of stone or lead ballast. Ballast there was in abundance, but it was not composed of river rock or lead ingots.

Gold coin stamped with images and insignia from lands whose names he knew not gleamed from openings in heavy cloth bags designed to keep their contents from spilling. Wide-mouthed buckets overflowed with cut gems: diamond and ruby, sapphire and crysoberyl, emerald and opal and dragoneye. Keeping it all from shifting, the bags and pans were held in place by lengths of metal siding fashioned from alloyed gold. The bolts that held the siding together were made of dropped platinum. Elenna's words echoed in his mind.

"You must take something."

The family's gratitude was unbounded. He could empty the pack that lay across Orania's spine and fill it with enough gold and jewels to buy his own kingdom. Well, perhaps not a kingdom, but a private compound that would make the merchant Kakran-mul's look like an outhouse by comparison. The scroll he was charged with delivering—it was just a scroll. A simple message. When it failed to arrive, another might be sent, carried by another courier as callow and innocent as himself—though he was less innocent now than he had been when first he had set out from Harup-taw-shet.

Except ... except ... growing up poor and without family there had been little to call his own. His prize possessions had been his pup, his pony, and his honor. What would the first two think of him if he so impetuously discarded the third?

They would think nothing of it, he told himself. Dog and horse now, they would be happy with his company and with food and water. Honor was an abstract concept of human invention. It meant nothing to a dog or a horse. Wasn't that right? Was that not what any scholar or wise man would tell him if he posed them the question?

Abandon his mission and take the fortune, he told himself. You can easily look into the eyes of Bit and Orania afterward and not look away. Just as you will be able to look into a mirror and do the same. Won't you? Can't you?

"You are wrong," he told the waiting Elenna. "I am not nearly as mature and experienced as you believe. As proof of it, I will take only the memento you suggest, to remind me of a family that I helped but to which I do not belong."

She responded with a maternal smile, the edges of which seemed to coil and twist upward independent of the rest of her mouth. Then she came forward, wrapped her arms around him, and hugged him tight, the side of her face pressing into his chest. When she stepped back he had to bite his lower lip to hold in the tears that threatened to seriously interfere with the warrior image he had so recently propounded.

"*We* can be your family," she told him. "Even at a distance, even if you never see us again. Then you can say to any who ask that you have a family."

His throat hurt. "A poor family that has lost nearly everything, yes."

The look on her face warmed his soul more than could any fire. That was not surprising, arising as it did from a smoke sprite.

"So now you have a family, Madrenga." She indicated the luminous mass of ballast. "Is that not worth more than any quantity of cut rock and forged metal?"

"No. Yes." He was confused, and knowing how frequently confusion led to one making bad decisions, he bent forward and reached for one of the open bins. As promised, he took only a single memento to remind him of his encounter with the family Col. That it happened to be a bright pink diamond the size of plum was merely coincidental. After all, he told himself as he straightened and pocketed the gem, he had promised to pick *something*.

He rode with the family of sprites a while longer, until finally their course diverged from his. The time spent with them allowed him the continued company of Bieracol, from whom he learned something of other lands and cultures; of Elenna, from whom he learned about valuable metals and stones; and of Elenacol, from whom he learned everything she could teach him whenever they could escape the notice of her parents.

Eventually, however, their route took them westward once again while his mission (if not his destiny) demanded that he ride east. Daria, as Chief Counselor Natoum had informed him, lay across the Sea of Shadows. To reach it he would have to take ship, which meant presenting himself at a suitable harbor. This would not be as simple as booking travel for one passenger since Bit and, more awkwardly, Orania would also be accompanying him. Having thus far spent little of the Council's money, he was certain that with time and the proper inquiries he would be able to secure transportation both for him and for his companions.

Though the ride from where he said farewell to his adopted family on down through the last of the mountains to the coast was long and hard, memories of Elenacol helped to shorten the journey in spirit as well as in distance.

Charrush was the biggest city he had ever seen, perhaps even larger than Harup-taw-shet. It was impossible to accurately compare the two because the harbor metropolis spread out in both directions along the coastline and disappeared to the north and south. Whether the outlying population considered themselves part of the urban area he did not know and could not tell. Unlike Harup-taw-shet, no great defensive wall encircled the metropolis. One minute he was descending the mountain road through forested hills and the next he found himself riding past extensive farms and through small villages. The structures that comprised the latter grew gradually taller and more dense until he was no longer in town but in a city.

The larger structures, some towering as high as the great astronomical observatory in the palace complex of Harup-taw-shet, loomed over the streets much as the fabled needle trees of distant Haxun overshadowed the apple and narfruit orchards of that northern land. Slowing Orania to a walk, he gave her the lead and relaxed, letting his mount go where she wished while he took in his new surroundings. There was more activity here, more stress and bustle, than could be found back home even on market day. Charrush was a conurbation founded on commerce rather than dynasty. Of the city's elite he knew nothing. Doubtless any passing citizen or visiting tradesman could fill him in on the local politics, but he was reluctant to display his ignorance.

Then Orania came to a halt and he forgot all about commerce and cliques, kings and crossroads. She had stopped because she had run out of land.

They had emerged onto the flat paved surface of a small triangular bastion. Protruding out into the harbor, its face was revetted with cut stone and slanted landward. An ancient fortification, it stood now devoid of armament because the harbor had been greatly extended and expanded by the addition of a vast breakwater that paralleled the shore. The city's defenses were now located much farther out, at the entrance to the expanded harbor.

So this is the sea, he thought as he stared eastward toward the flattest horizon he had ever seen. It was bigger than he had anticipated. Ships rigged lateen and square made their way in and out of the wide harbor mouth, bound for destinations whose names he did not know and whose languages he could not speak. Only one he knew: Daria. His destination was all he needed to know. But someday, another day, perhaps ...

Orania shook her head and snorted.

"I know I'm dreaming, girl. And I know you're hungry. For that matter, so am I. I need to arrange passage, but first things first. Let's see if we can find you a nice stable and something to eat."

It developed that there were many such facilities, built more to service supply wagons and carts than individual visitors. That did not mean their proprietors were unwilling to take money from a traveler who was not bent on trade. Leaving Orania in the care of a stablemaster who struck Madrenga as less disposed to larceny than the first two he had encountered, he started walking north up the main street that fronted the docks in search of an establishment that could provide him and Bit with suitable sustenance. Tongue lolling, the dog trotted alongside. The canine's ebullient manner notwithstanding, other pedestrians gave them both a wide berth. Madrenga would have been surprised and uncomfortable to learn that his own appearance had been altered to the point where it too was beginning to intimidate passersby.

As he worked his way up the avenue, ships and boats to his left and a solid line of shops to his right, it rapidly became clear to him that while Harup-taw-shet had its share of antisocial elements and individuals of low mien, Charrush was a much tougher place. Men and women of every shape and shade jostled with swarthy Harunds and slender Selndars from over the sea. He had heard tales of such semi-human folk but until now had never set eyes on such.

Harunds, he saw, walked with a distinctive side-to-side motion, throwing left or right hip forward at an angle with each step of their lurching gait. Rough as horsehair, their flowing manes and beards swallowed much of their faces. Broad, flattened nostrils were hidden deep within their facial hair while the smaller third eye in their foreheads invariably peered straight ahead. They were a muscular people, short of leg and short of words, with powerful arms and broad chests. A noteworthy assortment of weaponry was visible dangling from wide leather belts. Axes, clubs, maces hinted at a fighting style devoid of subtlety. Not a people to cross, Madrenga told himself as he walked on.

In contrast, the Selndars appeared to flow rather than walk along the street. Their clothing was elegant; fine-spun and soft, and they carried rapiers rather than axes or broadswords. They were as hairless as the Harund were hirsute, their skulls gleaming with polish and painted design. Their eyes were wide and narrow, the faces of male and female alike elongated and feminine. High-pitched conversation hinted at sarcasm and contempt though he could not understand the words they spoke in their own tongues. Of the latter there was a pair, each capable of joint or independent movement. No wonder their language was so complex and capable of such a variety of sound. There were other sentients present, but in addition to his own kind it was Harund and Selndar who stood out among the crowd.

Working the waterfront was a vast and varied hodgepodge of tricksters, vendors, fraudsters, accountants, recruiters, touts, and whores. The bewildering babble found him prone to distraction, especially by some of the females (and the occasional male) who leaned out of the upper floor windows of certain establishments. Flaunting their goods, these individuals were engaged in the purveyance of merchandise as transitory as it was pleasurable. The various appendages and protuberances they were making available for public purview put him in mind of similar neighborhoods in Harup-taw-shet. When younger he had frequently passed through them, though without awareness of what such sights represented.

Now that he understood, he was old enough to be almost as interested in them as in food.

Forcing himself to look away, he resumed scanning the line of shop fronts for one offering the simple food to which his innards were accustomed. While he would have liked to sample local cuisine, it would not do to fall ill his first day in town. Insofar as was possible, where his stomach was concerned, he would stick to the familiar.

He finally settled on one of the smaller establishments fronting the harbor. Not because it looked particularly inviting, or famous, or cheap, but because the flow of customers coming and going was steady, and those who were coming out looked more content than those who were going in.

Once inside he found himself in an exceptionally narrow, long room. Off to his right was a bar, on his left a line of tables, and a single passageway between. The bar stopped before it reached the front of the business, allowing for half a dozen tables to be positioned in front of the large window that looked out on the busy street and the harbor. Finding one unoccupied he sat himself down, pushed the tip of his sword's scabbard to the rear and out of the way, and waited. Mistakenly judging his age by his size, the attractive young woman who arrived to take his order eyed him with more than casual interest. Flattered and trying not to blush beneath her uncompromisingly direct stare, he did nothing to disabuse her of her misconception.

"What's on for today?" he asked, doing his best to lower his voice.

She was not put off by the artificiality of his effort. "What would you like to be on the menu?"

Having little experience at this sort of gender-denominated badinage, he hastened to get out of the semantic hole that was threatening to expand beneath him. "Something to eat," he told her, adding nervously, "fish would be nice. Do you have fish?"

She stared at him uncertainly, with great deliberation turned to look at the ships docked in the harbor just across the street, then returned her gaze to his.

"I mean," he explained as quickly as he could, "that I come from far inland and fresh fish is something I don't get too often." *Or at all,* he mused uneasily.

She was standing close enough for him to smell her perfume. Then he realized she wasn't wearing any perfume. She finally decided that despite his striking appearance this traveler was a bit too odd to pursue comfortably.

"We have cod baked in rice paper, some fresh tuna with lemon and lime, and I think there might be a piece of steamed gorelfin. Potato with it, if you wish."

Struggling in search of an urbane reply, he found only a vast and indifferent blankness. "How—how does your cook prepare the potato?"

"Baked." She had plainly lost interest. He didn't know whether to be insulted or relieved. "Or you can have it baked. Or if you prefer, baked."

He nodded. "Gorelfin. With—potato." Of the three fish she had described, gorelfin was the only name known to him.

"Excellent choice." Leaning slightly to her left she looked behind him. Bit lay there on his right side, front legs fully extended, his back pressed up against the wall. "If your dog makes noise you'll have to leave."

"I promise he'll be quiet. He's as tired as I am, and he'll nap while I eat. He won't bother anyone."

"That's good." She turned away, blue skirt flouncing, cleavage rippling. "Because if he was any bigger the owner would demand that you stable him."

Madrenga was as good as his word and Bit as quiet as his master's claim. When it arrived on a wooden plank, the pink-fleshed fish smelled of butter and onions and spices the youth did not recognize. Studying the steaming, unexpectedly elaborate repast, Madrenga wondered if he had been sensible in his choice of dining establishments. The exterior of the one in which he now sat had given no hint of the gourmand's delight to be found within.

Unused to such rich food, he ate slowly and carefully. With every third or fourth bite he glanced up to see if the serving wench was looking in his direction. As near as he could tell, she never did. After a while, he gave up checking in favor of devoting his full attention to the consumption of every bit of the excellent gorelfin. Choice morsels like the fins and head he passed to an eager Bit.

He was more than halfway through the meal when the two men approached. Swallowing, he sat back and dabbed at his lips with the heavy cloth napkin that had accompanied the food. It was the first time in his life he had utilized such a piece of sanitary dining fabric, whose purpose he had divined from observing his fellow diners.

He was rescued from any further uncertainties regarding local custom when the smaller of the two men started speaking. It struck Madrenga that the speaker was not looking at him but past him.

"That's quite an animal you've got there, young gentleman."

Madrenga glanced reflexively down at Bit. "You're half right, sir. I'm no gentleman."

"You eat like one," commented the other. "Utensils instead of fingers."

The youth smiled. "I always try to imitate the best of what's around me. If you're wondering about Bit, he's not for sale."

"Oh no, lad, no!" The smaller, older man raised his hands. "Wouldn't think of it. Probably couldn't afford it. Just wanted to compliment you on what a fine figure of a dog you got."

Noting that his master had ceased eating or, more importantly, sharing food, Bit yawned and rolled over on his back.

"Fine dog, yes." The other man was staring at Bit and nodding to himself.

His companion leaned forward and winked. "Want to make some easy money, lad?"

Effecting an urbanity that was alien to him, Madrenga

shrugged. "I'm always ready to make some easy money. How, exactly, might that worthy end be achieved?"

Straightening, the speaker jerked his head toward the rear of the establishment. "There's something of a beauty contest taking place out back o' Jorklin's place. Critter culture, one might call it. Your animal there would win by simply showing up."

A man of few words, his companion chimed in. "Win prize for biggest dog, anyway. For surely so!"

Madrenga pondered. What did he have to lose? Unless there was some sort of outrageous entry fee. On the other hand, if these two apparently stalwart, upstanding, but perhaps none-too-bright citizens were telling the truth, there might indeed be easy money to be made. Certainly there was no harm in checking out their story.

He desired to leave a little extra money for she who had served him. It did not occur to him to leave it on the table, of course. Doing so would invite its instant disappearance at the hands of fellow diners. He didn't see her as his helpful guides led him through the establishment and toward an opening at the back. Perhaps she was presently in the kitchen collecting food for other hungry diners, he told himself. He would do better to try and catch her on the way out.

The narrow dining area opened into a large rectangular yard walled in by high wooden planks set close together. There were indeed other dogs present, but they seemed even to Madrenga's unpracticed eye ill-suited to a canine beauty contest of any kind. Moreover, the yard was filled to claustrophobia with a surging, excited, loud mob of mostly men among which was sprinkled a few women. Harunds were also present in number, though Madrenga saw no Selndars. What he did see, as his guides alternately pushed and pulled him forward, was a deep circular depression that had been excavated in the center of the treeless yard. The bottom of the depression was filled with sand doubtless hauled in from a nearby beach. Suggesting the presence of a high water table, a third of the sand was stained dark from ...

It wasn't from seeping water. The small hairs on the back of his neck began to prickle. A contest was indeed in progress here, but it had nothing to do with beauty—unless one allowed that the two locals urging him to participate had a definition of the term very different from his own. He supposed there were mental types who might find a kind of perverse beauty in what took place below. As for himself, he saw only the opposite. Uncosmopolitan though he might be, Madrenga could recognize a fighting pit when he saw one.

Just as he could recognize stains that had been made by blood.

CHAPTER SEVEN

"Listen, this isn't what I had in mind when you ..." Madrenga stopped himself. The men who had escorted him through the dining establishment and to the killing field out back were nowhere to be seen. In their place was a wall of enthusiastic bettors and spectators who kept pushing him forward. Delighted by the crowd of excited strangers and rush of new smells, Bit leaped and barked with pleasure.

He doesn't know, a concerned Madrenga thought. *How could he? It's not like it was at Kakran-mul's compound. No one is threatening me, everyone is happy.*

The danger this time wasn't to him but to his dog. As he was jostled forward the air was filled with the shouts and demands of onlookers placing bets and debating the merits of the stranger's animal versus—versus what? It didn't matter, the youth told himself. He had come to Charrush to book passage on a ship going to Daria: not to fight his dog. Nor would he. Bit was his oldest and dearest friend. Despite his enhanced stature and the martial abilities he had shown during the clash days ago, Madrenga had no intention of risking injury to his friend for money he really did not need.

The mob, however, had other ideas. Pushing and shoving, they were packed so tightly behind him that Madrenga could not find or force a path back the way he had come. He could have drawn his sword and issued a threat, but that would likely have provoked problems of another kind with the crowd. There were at least a hundred people packed into the makeshift arena; maybe two hundred. Battling a dozen of the undead in Kakran-mul's spacious dining hall had been dodgy enough. Struggling with a hundred or more angry townsfolk in such close quarters as he now faced could prove fatal.

Maybe he could talk his way out of this. He had always been a good talker. Young and slight as he had once been, fast talking had been his salvation on more than one occasion.

"Listen to me!" he shouted to anyone who would do so. "This is a mistake! I thought this was something else and my dog and I are not going to …!"

It didn't matter what he said or how insistent his tone: those near enough to overhear either ignored the substance of what he was saying or took it for a joke. The laughter of the latter was even more frustrating than those who ignored him. One spectator, a florid-faced fellow with mutton-chop whiskers and the most garish red-and-gold hat Madrenga had ever seen on a man, was chortling with delight even as he offered to place a substantial side bet on the incipient fight on the youth's behalf.

"I don't *want* any side bet!" Madrenga found himself protesting angrily as the toque master sidled away and pressed coins into the waiting hand of the neutral Harund who was taking bets and holding the spectators' money. A muscular bodyguard stood watching over him. "I don't need any money!"

Eventually the crowd began to shift. But the open area they created appeared in front of and not behind Madrenga. Space was made not for him to leave but for the competition to enter.

The arriving fight master was himself massive; a huge lumbering splatter of silk-clad flesh with a grin as wide as a stirring spoon. Red ringlets slick with pomade had been plastered to his forehead in a pattern that suggested the close attention of a careful gardener more than it did a hairdresser. His eyebrows had been plucked almost to obscurity and his nose struggled to reach as far forward as his upper lip. Flesh hung from the underside of his upper arms like sacks of damp cotton hung out to dry while his huge feet would have shamed a steer. His dog …

His dog was enormous. If it *was* wholly dog, a startled Madrenga wondered, and not some brutal crossbreed. The barrel-shaped body must have weighed as much as two good-sized men. All of the teeth in the lionesque jaws had been filed to points. Flexible leather armor fashioned from the skin of the gray creotel covered its entire body, including a protective mask for the face. Insinuations of bear were visible in the animal's feet, which boasted long sharp claws the likes of which were decidedly un-doglike. Catching sight of the fighting pit it growled once and the energized spectators close to its path pushed harder against their neighbors to give the creature more room to pass.

Through means still unexplained, Madrenga and Orania had grown and changed a good deal since their departure from Harup-taw-shet. As had Bit. But increased size and dragon-like teeth notwithstanding, Madrenga did not see how his dog could be a match for what was plainly a carefully raised and professionally trained canine killing machine. Indeed, the animal whose lumbering handler was now leading it into the pit would be a good match for a tiger or a gryphon. Putting it up against another dog was not a fight—it was murder.

Seeing that Bit had taken notice of the other animal, the youth bent to hug his friend. "Easy boy; nothing's going to happen here. Everything's going to be fine. I'm going to get us both out of this."

An instant after Bit recognized the presence of another dog, that creature caught sight and smell of Madrenga's companion. A second, deeper growl issued from its throat, which was so thick and muscular that Madrenga could not have put his arms around it. Though he could not speak dog, it was not difficult to put an interpretation on that ominous sound.

Fresh meat, it was saying.

"Look, this is all a mistake!" Since a general appeal had failed to generate any interest or support, Madrenga tried speaking more quietly and directly to those in his immediate vicinity. "I didn't come back here to fight. We're not *going* to fight. I'm sorry if there was some misunderstanding, but I'm sure once everyone realizes ..." He struggled to find the words that would allow him and Bit to get away from this place of death. One hand gestured across the small arena. "It wouldn't be fair anyway. That *thing* is no dog. Even if it could somehow be a fair fight I still wouldn't ..."

While he concentrated on trying to sway those pressed close, to make them understand, several men joined together behind Bit and gave a quick, hard, coordinated shove. Madrenga's eyes grew wide and an agonized cry of despair left his lips.

"NO!"

Heedless of the finger-length steel spikes that formed spokes around it, he reached for Bit's collar. Fingers scraped on leather, slid off, and his friend and companion tumbled awkwardly into the excavation that served as the fighting pit. A roar went up from the crowd. Though this was not Harup-taw-shet, Madrenga knew that sound all too well. It was a sound that crossed all boundaries and cultures and needed no interpretation.

Blood lust.

Letting go of his animal's thick collar, the owner of the dog-thing stepped back. Helpful hands aided him in raising his bulk out of the arena. The noise of the maddened crowd rose to a deafening pitch.

Though no cat, Bit had still managed to land on his feet. Some of the human and Harund screaming faded as individuals scattered throughout the crowd now caught their collective breath. Expectation filled the air like the sharp stink of ammonia. When Madrenga moved as if to jump into the pit to recover his dog, multiple hands held him back in the belief that he was only endangering himself. Slowly he slid his hand down his right side until his fingers were wrapped around the handle of his sword. Once the fight started, he reasoned, excitement would loosen the helpful hands restraining him and he would be able to break free and leap into the arena. He might perish himself there at the hands of a furious, frustrated crowd, but he would not let Bit go down alone.

Massive head lowered, eyes focused on its intended victim, a rumble like a distant storm coming from its throat, the dog-thing took a couple of steps toward its target. Seeing it advancing toward him Bit responded, though not in kind. Sitting down on the sand he raised his right front paw and began cleaning it with long, steady licks of his wet red tongue.

It was not the reaction the dog-monster had expected. Sometimes its opponents, frequently overstimulated or otherwise artificially emboldened through the application of drugs and repetitive training, simply charged, in which case the fight was over quickly. More often, upon catching sight of the canine outrage that was bearing down on them, they backed up until they could retreat no further, laid down, and thrust their legs submissively into the air. In such instances the "fight" might last a little longer, though the outcome was always the same.

They did not, under any circumstances, sit down and start cleaning themselves.

Bit's uncharacteristic response did not unsettle the dog-thing, but it did confuse him. A deeper growl issued from the broad throat. Bit continued cleaning. The monster paced back and forth in front of the black newcomer. Bit's slurping grew louder as he started on the back of his foot. Having had enough of this and given full warning, the monster charged, halting close enough to his opponent to kick dirt and dust over the visitor's feet. Switching from one foot to the other, Bit continued with his hygiene.

No matter what the bigger animal tried, in gesture or in sound, it was ignored. Not only did Bit refuse to fight, his every action appeared to suggest that he was all but unaware of the other animal's presence.

Initially enthusiastic, the boisterous, bloodthirsty crowd had switched to hurling insults: not only at the new dog but at its owner. Madrenga hardly heard them. Let the locals call him anything they wished. His sole interest lay in extricating himself and Bit from the potentially deadly situation in which they had inadvertently found themselves.

Realizing that only blood would sate the mob's passion and seeing that the choice of opponent for his animal had been misconceived, the owner of the dog-monster relinquished all hope of seeing an actual contest. At least, he knew, the crowd would see some blood, even if butchery was a poor substitute for combat. Taking a step forward, he employed his mass as a bellows to ensure that the order to kill could be heard above the roar of the crowd.

Whether it was the sound of the kill command or a shift in the posture of the dog-monster, Bit's demeanor underwent a sudden change. Madrenga was less shocked than the rest of the mob because he had been witness to similar transformations before. But in speed and scale this far exceeded anything yet seen.

Bit did not so much grow as escalate. His body stretched and expanded far beyond anything that could be said to resemble canine proportions. As it did so the crowd grew progressively more and more silent. Unrestrained cries calling for disembowelment and murder were subsumed in a stunned murmur that reflected first shock, then uncertainty, and finally among a few of the more perceptive spectators, a growing fear.

Bit grew to the size of steer, then a water horse, his growth only ceasing when he had reached what could only be called near-elephantine proportions. His wagon-sized head hovered not just over the crowd but a couple of the surrounding structures as well. Had the buildings facing the waterfront not been several stories in height the upper portion of Madrenga's transmogrified puppy would have been visible from the harbor. From the lower jaw scimitar-like teeth thrust upward like tusks while those in the upper jaw curved downward and slightly forward, giving Bit's enormously enlarged head a crocodilian visage. Eyes the size of wagon wheels burned as if piles of brimstone had been lit behind the lenses. Wagging back and forth, the cable-like tail terminated in a sharp-pointed trident.

Having already begun its death charge the dog-monster, by comparison now reduced considerably in stature, could not stop. Dipping his head, Bit emitted a low snarl that reminded several of the sailors in attendance of the sound a ship makes when a storm runs it aground on the rocks. There was a loud *crunch* as Bit proceeded to bite the attacking dog-thing cleanly in half. The audience that had been howling for blood found its wish fulfilled as those in front found themselves splattered with a gush of carmine. This was accompanied by a healthy helping of flying guts and associated gore. Fountaining blood, the rear half of the dog monster fell back on its hindquarters, its insides as cleanly exposed as if by a surgeon's blade. The screams that followed this display did not exclusively emerge from feminine throats.

Panicking, the crowd rushed as one for the exit. As this consisted solely of the single door and passageway that led back through the dining area and out to the waterfront, there was a good deal of trampling and breaking of bones. Driven now by terror instead of anticipation, a few of the more athletic and enterprising onlookers managed to scramble over the high wooden wall that enclosed the arena and fighting pit. This did not include the erstwhile owner of the dead dog-thing, who found himself unceremoniously and seriously trodden underfoot by those whom only moments earlier had been eager to place bets on his behalf. The remainder of the dog-fighting crowd cleared the area with remarkable alacrity.

Would they summon the local equivalent of Hamuldar's nightwatch? Madrenga doubted the authorities in a free-wheeling seaport city like Charrush would care one way or another if an animal-baiting "sport" like dog-fighting took place within their jurisdiction. The presence of the present colossal iteration of Bit, however, might occasion somewhat more interest. It was therefore imperative that it be removed. But how? Having no comprehension of what had been happening to him or his animals, the bewildered youth similarly had no understanding of how to modify or otherwise affect it.

Worry often inspires actions that in less stressful circumstances and beneath the clear lens of logic might give rise to laughter rather than thoughtful contemplation.

"Bit, get down here!" Thrusting the index finger of his right hand at the ground, Madrenga repeated the command. It was good that he failed to think it through or he might not even have tried it. *"Now!*

From the height to which he had ascended, his dog gazed down at the determined figure standing almost directly below its greatly enlarged jaws. Then the immense fanged head dipped low, lower, the mouth yawned wide—and Bit proceeded to lick his master affectionately. Since the animal's tongue was now longer than Madrenga was tall, this resulted in him quickly being drenched in dog spit from head to toe.

"Stop that, stop it … yes, I love you too … but stop it! And *get down here!*"

It is a never-ending source of astonishment to those familiar with the workings of words just how much power even simple ones, when properly proffered and enunciated, can have. Before Madrenga's eyes his dog proceeded to shrink at the same speed with which it had reacted to the dog-monster's attack. Shrink until Bit was, if not again the puppy the youth had known so well in Harup-taw-shet, at least no bigger than he had been before the dog fight had commenced. Which was still, Madrenga reflected as he took his friend's head in his arms and let him nuzzle hands and face, an impressive four-legged dragon-toothed proposition.

Wait, he thought abruptly. Bit had *reacted to the dog-monster's attack.* The assault, the charge, was what had motivated his pet's sudden and unprecedented growth. Thinking back, it struck him that every time he and his animals had increased in strength and stature it had been in response to a direct threat of some kind. Fording the dangerously cold and swift river, responding to Langan of Jithros's assault in Hamuldar, dealing with the undead in the compound of Kakran-mul—each time he and his companions had faced attack, their bodies had responded with enhanced size and power.

That he and his pets were journeying under the protection of some kind of spell had been obvious from the first simple enhancing transformation. But who had placed the protective enchantment upon them? If Chief Counselor Natoum, why had he not so informed Madrenga before sending him on his way? Surely Natoum or anyone else leveling such thaumaturgy would know that its manifestations would be likely to unsettle the recipient: even more so if the one benefiting was but a youth of the streets uneducated in such wizardly ways.

But if not Natoum, then whom? he asked himself. An unmet sorcerer of the royal court, mayhap, engaged by Natoum for just such a purpose? An unknown onlooker protecting interests and assets of their own? Would the Queen order up such a spell without informing her Chief Counselor? The who was as much a mystery to Madrenga as the what.

Don't agonize, he told himself firmly. Don't exasperate yourself over that which you cannot understand. Perhaps all will be explained upon the successful delivery of the scroll to Daria. Desiring that explanation would motivate him even more to carry out his mission. Perhaps that was part of the reason for keeping from him the details of the sorcery and the sorcerer who had affected him. He would receive no explanation without the successful completion of his mission.

While the crowd of spectators had long since fled save for the dead or injured who had been trampled in the rush to escape, they had left something behind. Transformed or not, ensorcelled or not, Madrenga was still true to his roots. Therefore he could not possibly leave without scooping up and pocketing some of the betting pot that had been left behind. His purse now overflowing to the point where if he did not remain constantly aware of its presence and correspondingly careful he risked listing to port while he walked, he and Bit left behind the now blood and gore-splattered arena.

In choosing to depart by way of the nearest fence in order to avoid the attention of any soldiers who might have gathered outside the entrance to the dining establishment, he hesitated briefly. Could Bit manage the jump? Leaping and grabbing hold of the top of the wooden barrier Madrenga did not have time to call out to his dog because Bit leaped up beside him without having to be urged. Like a cat, the dog balanced effortlessly atop the narrow platform as he smiled at his master.

"I suppose I shouldn't have wondered." A straining Madrenga pulled his legs up and over and dropped down on the other side. He was pleased to see that a large crowd had gathered in front of the building. All eyes were trained on the entrance, thus allowing him and Bit to slip away along the waterfront walk without being noticed.

No one in the crowd retreated from his presence. Once he was sure they were not being followed he began to ask questions of his fellow strollers. Their replies were uniform in their discouragement. Where he sought to travel, no ship was going. With each negative reply he grew increasingly disheartened.

He had posed his query many times when a hand reached out to clamp down on his shoulder.

Drawing his sword and whirling about in the same motion, the youth took a defensive step backward. Bit growled softly while Madrenga held the blade out in front of him. Somehow he was not surprised that the hitherto unadorned steel was now inscribed with elaborate whorls and symbols, none of which he could recognize at a casual glance.

With the appearance of the sword and Bit's concurrent growl, the clutching hand had slid off his shoulder. Having retreated a similar distance, its owner now starfished both palms to show that he held no weapon of his own. Nor, insofar as Madrenga could tell, was animosity writ on the stranger's face.

It was a worn face, but the expression was kindly enough. A short beard flecked with white hid some of the flesh that appeared no less tanned than the skin of Madrenga's scabbard. The eyes were deep-set and orange. They were not reddened from too much sun or pink from a trace of albinism, but a bright, fruity orange. Never before had Madrenga seen eyes of such color. Furthermore, the man's ears lay flat against his skull, as if in constant fear of a punishing wind. Whether his hair matched his beard the youth could not tell, since his head was covered with a combination scarf and tri-corner cap of unknown material. Shirt and pants were fashioned of material as basic and tough as their appearance was simple. Their owner looked to be about forty.

"Back off there, boyo." The man's voice was thick and gummy, as if he was trying to chew and speak at the same time. But his mouth was empty of anything but words. "I mean you no harm." He nodded in Bit's direction. "I only wanted to compliment you on your dog. Tell me: was that infernal transformation real, or only an accomplished mystic's mindfuck?"

Madrenga considered. "The blood and guts were real enough. Does that answer your question?"

"In a roundabout fashion, I suppose. But then I'm not one to question an explanation of the impossible even if it comes to me in a roundabout manner, much as Miss Polly Peg of the Jounce House likes to do her own work. Where did you ever find such a —malleable creature?"

"I found him abandoned in the street. He's been with me ever since." Without realizing it the youth had resumed walking, the stranger by his side.

"Ah, piss then," the man murmured, clearly disappointed. "No way for me to acquire such a pet." Displaying more than uncommon bravery he reached out, laid a hand on Bit's massive head, and began stroking it gently. The dog raised no objection.

"He likes you," Madrenga observed. "That means he trusts you, too. A pity you don't own a ship."

"You'll find no one on the Charrush-na-tarad coast who agrees more with you on that, boyo. I'd near kill to have my own vessel.

Though standing on a decent one as first mate is not a bad way to live, nor to see the world."

Heedless of the crush of the crowd around and behind them, Madrenga stopped right there. "You're a mate on a ship? A first mate?"

The man chuckled and extended a hand. "Kapator Quilpit, at your service. Why so surprised? Do I look like a clerk, then, or perhaps a money-changer?"

"No, it's just that ... I wouldn't know what a sailor looks like." Madrenga indicated their surroundings; the bustling crowd, the harbor crowded with ships coming, going, loading, being rehabilitated. "Before today I didn't even know what the sea looked like. Except from drawings and paintings, of course."

"And having now set eyes upon it, what do you think of the mother of all worries and wonders?"

"She's—big," the youth told him.

"You've no idea. A wondrous wench is she, the sea. Much of my life have I spent in her company; enough to think I know her moods as well as anyone. She's beautiful, capricious, flirtatious, deadly, and will as soon drown as seduce you if you misjudge her mood. Sometimes I love her dearly and sometimes I hate her runny guts." He winked at Madrenga. "In other words, it's a typical marriage. But by the looks of you, despite your size you're too young to know much about such things."

"Where marriage is concerned, I readily confess my ignorance," the younger man said. "I have only the vaguest notions of the details and from all that I have observed from a distance would prefer to retain my unawareness for as long as possible. Your ship: what kind is she?"

"A fine vessel, the *Thranskirr*. Not as big as many nor as some, but her bottom is as solid as that of any girl at Boryn's Pleasure Place and she can roll as smoothly. I've seen her pop out of a swale that would swallow many a larger ship and challenge waves higher than her bowsprit. When she strains in storm her timbers laugh where those of other ships groan, and her rigging sings in the wind. I wouldn't trade my position on her for a captaincy on any boat plying the Shadows." His tone shifted slightly. "Make me the owner of another decent craft, though, and that's another kettle o' codlings entirely."

While the mate's affection for his ship was unrestrained, it did not answer Madrenga's question.

"I meant, is she a passenger vessel or cargo, the private transport of some rich nobleman or lord, or one seconded to a city or territory's defense? It is as to her purpose that I inquire."

"Ah, I see now. Clarification comes in like the tide. She is engaged in the movement of cargo, boyo. Whatever needs be transported, the *Thranskirr* can ship, usually by weight."

"Would that include me?"

Quilpit eyed the much younger man evenly. "Did you not understand what I said, boyo? She's a cargo vessel. Wherever you seek to go, there are cleaner and more pleasant options available for a paying passenger."

"Except that according to every one of whom I have made inquiry, right now no one is going where I need to go: across the sea of Shadows."

The mate nodded sympathetically. "What makes you think the *Thranskirr*'s course will be any different?"

"I don't know that it will be. I do know that I can't sit here and wait forever for a ship's factotum to stand up and announce passage to where I want to go. I'll take a chance that yours, which you compliment so highly, is at least sailing closer to my destination."

"Where might that be, boy?" The mate paused. "If you feel free to tell me, that is."

Madrenga didn't hesitate. "If I'm going to ship with you I can hardly forebear from telling you where I need to go. I have to get to Daria."

It wasn't a sudden gust of wind that lifted the mate's eyebrows. "Daria! I know of the place though I've never been that far inland myself. Get me too far away from the sea and both my skin and my soul start to shrivel from lack of salt air and moisture." He turned thoughtful. "Fastest way would be to find passage to Yordd. From there would be the shortest, though not necessarily the easiest, way inland to the country you seek. But it doesn't matter. Though I have not yet been told our future course I would wager a bag of elephant nuts it does not include sailing across the Shadows. Even if it did, the *Thranskirr* does not take passengers. There are no facilities aboard to provide for the comfort of guests."

"I'd happily eat and sleep with the crew," Madrenga countered. "If you knew the circumstances in which I grew up you would not worry about my 'comfort'."

Quilpit shook his head dolefully. "You are a stubborn youth, boyo. You remind me of myself, except that I am so much better looking." When Madrenga nodded easy agreement, the mate smiled. "Smart, too. I wonder—the *Thranskirr* can always use an extra strong back. Lack of brains and common sense aside, that's a position you could fill. Have you any experience on the water?"

Though from an early age he had practiced prevarication as a means of survival, Madrenga decided not to lie now. For one thing, he had come to think of this sailor as a friend as well as a possible mentor. For another, he suspected that the knowledgeable Quilpit would see through any lies as easily as he would thread a spike through a loop of rope.

"I have spent some time sailing on the Lake of Sighs, which is near to where I come from."

"A lake!" The mate treated this as the four-letter word it was. Quilpit calmed himself. "We will say you have limited sailing experience, and hope the Captain does not press for details. There is something else in your favor." He pointed to Madrenga's left.

"What—Bit? I don't understand."

"Your dog is magicked; that's for certain. I can readily describe to the Captain what I saw with my own eyes. A fighting animal is always welcome as another layer of defense on a ship carrying cargo."

Bending down, the youth hugged his now massive pet. "Bit's

not a fighting animal. He just seems, somehow, to respond proportionately to whatever happens to threaten him, or me."

"Even better." Quilpit was more than satisfied by the younger man's explanation. "If the spell that works within him only activates when a threat is present, he'll require a corresponding minimum of space and food."

Madrenga straightened. "Are you certain your Captain will believe such a thing? I was there and scarce believe it myself."

The mate considered, then nodded once. "Captain Hammaghiri has crossed many waters and seen much, despite which he has thus far avoided crossing Death's course. If I offer blood to attest to the truth of what I saw, he will believe it. Believing it, he will welcome your dog if not you." Quilpit's grin returned. "Taking the dog will compel him to take also the dog's handler. No over young bumbling handler, no enchanted killer dog. Keep out of the way, don't offer advice on matters you know nothing about, and the Captain will warm to you." He shrugged. "Or throw you overboard. He's stern, is Hammaghiri, but not capricious. He won't have you drowned without a reason."

"I am much reassured," Madrenga replied drily. He nodded toward the harbor, pleased that he was now tall enough to see over the heads of most of the crowd. "Which is the *Thranskirr*?"

"You'll see her tomorrow." Quilpit squinted at the sky. "The sunset is fine from the third floor of the Seaman's Snuggery." Lowering his gaze, he gestured up the harborfront street. "I'll take you there and introduce you to the owner, who is a friend of mine. The food is solid and cheap, if uninspiring. You'll get a good room, and at a discount."

Madrenga gazed down at him. "With a commission for you?"

Quilpit chuckled. "As I said—smart. Not this time, no. I don't make commissions off children."

Verbally sparring while employing a notably modest number of imprecations, the two men resumed making their way up the street through the teeming throng of townsfolk, tradesmen, sailors, vendors, pickpockets, wealthy merchants and impecunious riff-raff.

Quilpit was as good as his word. The room Madrenga rented at the Snuggery was complete and cozy, with the promised view over the crowded street to the harbor beyond. He watched the sun set behind masts and breakwater, then went downstairs to stuff himself on meat and bread (for who knew when he might next again enjoy such a selection of fresh food) and retired to a bed that was, surprisingly, long enough to accommodate his mysteriously drawn-out frame.

That did not mean he slept comfortably. Bit took up much of the bed. Furthermore, from time to time the great mass of dog would whine and kick in his sleep, dreaming of rabbits pursued and dark canine nightmares to be avoided. Madrenga would no more shove his pet out of the bed than he would have a wife, had he been old or mature enough to have such a companion. Perhaps someday, he told himself as he fell back to sleep after one flailing paw briefly jolted him awake in the dark. A wife—it seemed an unnecessary encumbrance. Yet nearly every adult man seemed to have one. Where, he wondered, was the attraction? Clearly he was missing something that he was not yet old enough to understand.

Then he thought of the smoke sprite Elenacol, and something of the mystery of long-term relationships slipped away from his almost-dream, with the remainder of it nearly making a confused semi-adult kind of sense. With Bit pressing close and aromatic against his back, Madrenga fell back to sleep on the edge of the bed. This circumstance did not distress him.

He had been living on the edge ever since leaving Harup-taw-shet.

CHAPTER EIGHT

THE WET ALARM OF BIT'S TONGUE WOKE HIM. HIS ALTERED, larger form requiring more fuel than the slender adolescent body that had left Harup-taw-shet, Madrenga downed not one but two breakfasts before walking back to the stable where he had left Orania. It was while he was settling the bill that Quilpit arrived, looking more awake and alive than anyone his age ought to at that early hour of the morning.

"You're sure now you want to try this, boyo? If the Captain agrees to take you, you'll find the accommodations plain, the food simple, and the language rough."

"I grew up on the street," Madrenga reminded him. "I've plenty of experience with all three."

The mate smiled. "So you may think. Right then. Let's to it."

They left from the stable area, Orania plodding along behind Madrenga, his saddle pack slung over her lower back and Bit trotting excitedly alongside. While the dog had shown himself capable of greater and greater feats of transformation, at heart he remained very much a puppy. He could not understand why strangers started in his presence or shied away from his innocent offers of friendliness. In his canine mind he was still small and weak, a conviction that persisted despite his greatly augmented mass, muscle, and dentition.

It was a strange sky that greeted them as Quilpit led the small procession from the waterfront boulevard out onto one of the many quays that protruded into the harbor like the steel spikes on Bit's collar. It was not a fog but rather a lowing gray sky, less damp than a proper fog. The air pressed down on the town like a moist blanket into which the masts of the bigger ships poked like wooden needles. The heavy atmosphere muffled sounds and there was an utter absence of wind, as if the weather itself had yet to wake from a long night's sleep. Other early risers spoke in whispers, as if by speaking loudly they might shatter the perspective and cause pieces of overcast to fall on their heads.

Halting near the end of the pier Quilpit eyed a knot of small boats that floated motionless in the water, pieces of a nautical puzzle tied to the quay and to each other.

"I see only one left from the *Thranskirr.*" Raising his gaze, he studied the crowded harbor. "The rest of the crew must already be back aboard and preparing to set sail. An unusually punctual shore leave, by my experience." He started down the stone steps that led to, and into, the water. "Come on then, boyo."

Madrenga hesitated. "What about Orania?"

Halfway down the steps the mate looked back. "I said I'd try to help you and your dog gain passage. Nothing was discussed about a horse."

The youth drew himself up. "I've only two true friends in this world. I'm not going anywhere without her."

Quilpit shrugged. "It's your choice, boyo." He pondered. "Best we can do is try this by degrees. Let's see if we can persuade the Captain to take you and your monster. Then you can make whatever decision you think best about the horse."

For a long moment Madrenga considered thanking the mate for his aid and friendship and then moving on in search of a more accommodating vessel. But if what Quilpit had been telling him about travel across the Shadows was the truth, finding such transportation was likely to prove difficult if not impossible. Why not, then, take his advice? If the *Thranskirr's* Captain refused him passage, the question of transporting Orania would be rendered moot and he would have to start all over with another ship anyway. If Hammaghiri consented to let him and Bit come aboard, then Madrenga could plead that the horse had to accompany him as well.

One step at a time. It had been ever so since the day he had walked through the outer gates of Harup-taw-shet and left the city behind.

Having never been on a body of water larger than a lake and even though they were safely within the protected harbor, he was still thankful that his first encounter with the sea found her in a quiet mood. In truth, Madrenga thought as the mate rowed away from the quay, he had encountered rougher water in the public fountains where he and his fellow urchins had bathed and played. Peering over the side he found he could see a goodly distance into the depths. Several times schools of small fish wriggled by beneath the keel, shining like so many drops of mercury. Later something yellow and tentacled arrowed past in pursuit of one such school, paused on the other side to look up at him out of a single contoured eye, and promptly did its best to spit in his face. It missed, hitting Bit instead. Front feet propped on the gunwale, Bit unleashed a succession of frantic barks at the water, which troubled the spitting cephalopod not at all.

The *Thranskirr* might not have been the grandest ship on the Sea of Shadows, but to Madrenga's inexperienced eye the big brig was most impressive. Her stout wooden flanks curved slightly upward near the top and her two masts seemed taller than the trees of the sacred grove that dominated the hills west of his home. Milled from pigo blackwood immune to insects, corrosion, or the debilitating effects of salt air and spray, the masts and the yards they supported needed neither paint nor varnish. Subjected to the effects of time and storm the rest of the ship might disintegrate, but her black masts, yards, and bowsprit would float on forever.

The hull was flanked by a pair of sturdy outriggers, one on either side of the ship proper. Each of these was attached to the main hull by means of a pair of pigo arches, four in all. The much smaller outrigger hulls, Quilpit explained, held additional stores for the journey ahead, from spare spars and rigging to barrels of salt meat and dried biscuit. In a dire emergency—for example an irreparable hulling of the *Thranskirr*—the outriggers could be detached, the single small sails stowed in each one raised, and the resulting configurations utilized as lifeboats.

As the mate continued to declaim on the virtues of his vessel, Madrenga struggled to memorize the seemingly endless list of descriptions and terminology. All the boats he had sailed previously had consisted of small, hand-made toys deployed in lakes, ponds, or fountains. They had been constructed for amusement. There was nothing amusing about the *Thranskirr*. Not just reaching Daria by way of Yordd but his very life depended on her staying sound and stable. So he paid attention to everything Quilpit was saying in the event his future might depend on him remembering a word, a term, a depiction.

Passing beneath the aft arch of the portside outrigger, the small boat drew up alongside the main hull. Securing a line from her bow to a bolt in the *Thranskirr*'s side, Quilpit started up a series of wooden steps that had been cut into the ship's port flank. Following the mate, Madrenga soon found himself on deck. A seaman's panorama greeted his willing gaze. Everything here was new, everything different, from what he had known in Harup-taw-shet. From the knots in the ropes to the packing of the cargo stacked on deck, at every turn strangeness and wonder greeted his inquisitive stare.

"Your animal?" Quilpit was standing nearby, watching his new protégé watch the crew finish final preparations for getting under way. "Can he climb the stairs?"

"I don't think so." Moving back to the railing the youth leaned over the side. Bit was standing in the small boat, gazing upward, panting excitedly. Quilpit joined the frowning youth.

"We could hoist him up in a cargo net," the mate suggested. "He'll be fine if he doesn't struggle too much."

"Let me try something first."

The mate's gaze narrowed. "More sorcery? Magic words?"

"I think they're only magic when spoken by a boy to his dog." Leaning over the side again, Madrenga extended his arms and called out. "Here, boy! Here, boy! Come on, boy!"

Bit drew in his tongue, crouched, and sprang. Legs that had long since ceased to belong to an ordinary canine contracted, and in one leap the dog had cleared the railing and landed in his master's outstretched arms. That was Madrenga's only miscalculation. Despite his own enhanced stature Bit's weight was now too much for him to handle. Both master and dog went down in a heap, with Bit coming out on top frantically licking Madrenga's face. Quilpit observed the affectionate goings-on with equanimity.

"I shouldn't be surprised, I suppose. If you'd been standing atop the highest yard and made the same request, I imagine he would have made the jump to that height as well."

Extricating himself from beneath his happily slobbering companion, Madrenga wiped at his sodden face. "I don't know, sir. I don't know what's happened to me or to my animals, or how, or why, but I would be a blind fool if I didn't think it had something to do with the carrying out of my mission."

Quilpit shrugged. "In a world where nothing can be predicted or explained with overmuch certainty, boyo, I would not be hasty in my conclusions."

Madrenga stared at him. "Are you saying you think there might be other reasons for what has happened—for what is happening—to me and my animals?"

The mate looked at him from the vantage point of many years spent voyaging the world's seas. "I'm saying that I *think*. I think—I don't try to predict. Except maybe the prospects for decent fishing and good weather. In a wooly world, boyo, certainty is the first casualty of assumption. Keep your mind open as to your options and you'll live longer." He grinned. "Something to keep in mind as we present you to the Captain." Gesturing, he turned and started toward the stern. Pondering the mate's wise words, Madrenga followed. As they passed by, members of the crew intent on their work eyed the tall, powerfully-built young man with interest, and his dog with something nearer to apprehension.

In the spacious main cabin at the rear of the ship, Madrenga stood silently while Quilpit related what he had seen and heard the previous day in the dog fighting arena. Seated behind his gimbaled desk, Captain Hammaghiri listened politely. Madrenga thought one could fairly smell the skepticism seeping off him.

While the same age as his first mate, the Captain looked younger. A little taller and a little wider, with a perfectly trimmed full beard and a full head of hair that flashed hardly any gray, his experience and profession were more forcefully represented by the look in his eyes. Deep-set and violet, they regarded both mate and visitor unblinkingly. So persistent and unwavering was that commanding stare that Madrenga found himself frequently turning away when it was aimed in his direction. There was about Captain Hammaghiri an air of repressed rage. Uplifting, encouraging rage, to be sure, but rage nonetheless. All but standing at attention, the youth did not think he would care to be the object of the Captain's anger, should he have occasion to lose it.

Where another man might have interrupted querulously, or with derisive laughter, Hammaghiri sat quietly throughout the whole of Quilpit's declamation. Expecting the Captain to question, or make rude noises, or respond in some patently negative fashion, Madrenga was surprised to hear not a word uttered in rebuttal to the mate's story. It was only when Quilpit finished and stepped aside that Hammaghiri turned his full attention to the mate's youthful protégé.

"So. You are a warlock." His gaze ran his visitor up and down. "Stature notwithstanding, to me you look to be a prime example of a sorceral virgin."

Having no idea how to respond to this demeaning observation, Madrenga stood silently while he tried to think of something not-stupid to say. A sideways glance showed Quilpit making barely perceptible motions with his right hand and considerably more agitated ones with his eyes. His meaning was clear enough even to one as artless as Madrenga.

Say something, boyo.

"I am no warlock, sir. I am but a student of a hard life who has been given a chance at something better. To this opportunity I have dedicated myself body and soul." He spread his hands and adopted an expression of helplessness. "It has been made plain to me that someone or something else, some other power, has been manipulating both. Thus far, to my apparent advantage."

Hammaghiri pushed out his lower lip (revealing a surprising abstract tattoo) and grunted. "And from what my hitherto trusted first mate tells me, to that of your animals as well." He nodded toward Bit, who was sitting quietly by his master's side. "Prove it, then. Confirm even a tiny amount of what Quilpit says. Show me something. I await with interest your effort to dispel common sense."

Madrenga swallowed. While he doubted Bit would respond to a transmuting command of any kind, he knew he had to try. Hammaghiri was clearly not the sort to give a supplicant a second chance.

"Bit." The dog looked up at him with characteristic wide-eyed eagerness. "Grow. Come on, boy, *grow*! Stand tall! Grow for the Captain!"

His canine companion responded immediately—by lying down, rolling over, and thrusting all four feet into the air. The tip of his lolling tongue made a damp spot on the wooden deck. Madrenga turned to plead with the Captain.

"He only responds—I only respond—defensively. That much I have learned about whatever transformative force clings to the both of us. Unless one of us is threatened, nothing changes."

The Captain nodded thoughtfully. "So *you* transmogrify as well?" When Madrenga nodded affirmatively, albeit reluctantly, Hammaghiri turned to his mate. "You saw this also?"

"No, Captain. Only the dog. Believe me, sir, anyone who was witness to what happened to the dog had eyes only for it. The youth here could have changed into an owl and no one would have noticed."

Again Hammaghiri nodded. "Perhaps another member or two of the crew noticed how much you had to drink in the hours before this supposed transmogrification took place?"

"Captain—sir!" Quilpit took a step toward the desk, then remembered himself and stopped short. "For once I was not drunk. I know what I saw. If needs be, I can go ashore and find several, or several dozen, others who saw what I saw and will attest to it even without having to be bribed."

Hammaghiri grunted. "We raise anchor in less than an hour. In contrast to my happy, carefree crew, I am compelled to concern myself with such unimportant details as making deliveries on time and hewing to a set schedule."

Seeing that he was losing both the argument and time, an anxious Madrenga stepped forward. "If I may make bold, if the Captain has on his desk something edible …?"

Hammaghiri frowned. Then he opened a small, exquisitely inlaid wooden box and removed a handful of nuts. Of these Madrenga recognized only half. Would they appeal to Bit? It was his experience that the dog would eat anything. But they were in strange surroundings, and he with nothing to offer but unknown foodstuffs. He could only try. He held the handful out toward his companion.

"Bit! Look! *Food!*" He tossed the handful into the air.

How the dog went from a semi-sleeping position on his back to flying through the air not even Madrenga could tell, such were the permanent changes that had come over his friend. One moment Bit had all four feet thrust skyward in a posture imitating death and the next he was soaring through the still air of the cabin to snatch up the handful of thrown treats. Quilpit leaned back out of the way while Captain Hammaghiri, his ingrained fortitude aside, practically fell out of his chair. Landing on all fours, Bit promptly sat down and chewed contentedly. But to catch the flung filberts the dog had been compelled to open his mouth, and in opening his mouth …

Trying not to show how much the dog's leap had unsettled him, Hammaghiri collected himself and looked over at his mate.

"I have never seen teeth like that in a dog, Quilpit. I have never seen teeth like that in the jaws of *any* living creature."

"I think they are akin to dragon teeth myself, sir," Madrenga put in helpfully.

Instantly the Captain was himself again. "Have you ever seen a dragon, boy?"

Madrenga tensed. "No sir, but I have heard.…"

"Speculation is for the story-spinner, young man. Sailors have no time for it. Not those who wish to live." He nodded to where Bit was contentedly swallowing the last of his unexpected treat. "I grant you that the dog, even if he cannot magically change size, would be a valuable asset in a fight. But I have confidence in my crew, each of whom knows the way of sword and spear. While I admit I would value your animal's presence onboard and the deterrence value he embodies, I fear it is not enough to grant the both of you passage."

"I can offer payment in addition." At this Quilpit's eyebrows rose, but the mate said nothing.

Stepping forward, Madrenga removed the purse from his belt, trying to keep both men from getting a good look at the corium container that held the scroll. Unsealing the sack, he measured out approximately half the coin Counselor Natoum had provided for his expenses. The glittering bauble Elenna and Bieracol had given him he kept hidden, knowing that its value was sufficient to buy several boats the size of the *Thranskirr*. He would part with it only in an emergency.

Hammaghiri did not have to pick up the coins to estimate their worth. Quilpit eyed his young friend with new respect. The Captain was silent for a long moment before he nodded.

"I grant you and your dog passage. What is your name, young man?"

"I am called Madrenga." He waited for what seemed to be the inevitable reaction to the pronouncing of his name. But neither Quilpit nor Hammaghiri batted an eye.

"Welcome aboard the *Thranskirr*, young Madrenga. She's no pleasure barge, but she'll smack a storm quick as you would a pickpocket and get you to wherever you be going. Quilpit here will show you a berth." He looked at the mate. "He and his animal can have the third mate's cabin. The gods of Pelskran knows he's paid enough for it."

Madrenga blinked. "Where will the third mate sleep?"

Quilpit spoke up. "In the throat of the flying shark, which is where last we saw him. The vacancy he left has not yet been filled. His belongings have been sent ashore without him. Of course, if you find the quarters too inflected with recent morbidity for your liking you can always sleep belowdecks with the crew."

"I've seen my share of death and managed to avoid it," the youth replied. *So far*, he added silently. "I cannot regret the passing of one I did not know."

"Spoken like a man." Hammaghiri nodded approvingly as he scooped the pile of coins into a desk drawer. "A practical man. As the rare paying guest, you are welcome to time with myself, my two mates, and the ship's doctor. I cannot vouch for the company, but the food will be better than what you would receive below."

"The Captain is too modest." Quilpit grinned. "A healthy ship survives on good weather, good seamanship, good commanders—and good food. Another Captain would let his men go without in order to pocket the provisioning money. Captain Hammaghiri feeds his crew well."

"And drives them hard," the Captain added tetchily. "There are times when an officer must ask from a man everything he can give, and you can't ask everything of a man when he's hungry." So saying, he returned his attention to the pair of charts on his desk, one open and spread and the other still rolled. A moment passed.

Seeing that both his first mate and young passenger were still present, an irritated Hammaghiri looked up and allowed his gaze to pass from older man to the younger.

"Well, was there something else?" One thick finger tapped the open chart. "The *Thranskirr* is a fine and willing ship, but she will not plot her own course."

Madrenga licked his lips, glanced at Quilpit, back at the Captain. "Bit is not my only animal, sir."

"Ah. You have another fighting dog. So much the better. Bring him aboard." Hammaghiri returned his attention to his work.

"Not another dog sir. It's—she's—a horse."

"A horse." Looking up anew, Hammaghiri folded his hands atop his desk. "You want to bring a horse on the *Thranskirr*."

Madrenga nodded, his voice eager and more boyish than he wished. "She's very good, sir. She won't be any trouble and I think I've paid enough to cover what feed she will eat. Please, sir—she's been with me since I was a child. I can't—I won't—leave her behind."

"A horse." The Captain echoed himself. "As cargo I have carried horses. Paid for and delivered. Accounting one as a passenger would be something unique."

Thinking desperately, Madrenga gestured at Bit. "You've agreed to take along my dog as a fighter. Orania can fight, too."

Hammaghiri was less than convinced. "I don't know what experience you have in war, young Madrenga, but I can tell you from my own that there is little opportunity to employ cavalry in a battle at sea."

"She could do other things, sir." Madrenga spoke as fast and earnestly as he dared. "She could—she could do work."

Hammaghiri's face screwed up behind his elegant beard. "Work? On a ship? What kind of work?"

"She could," the youth thought fast, "she could raise and lower the anchor."

The Captain let out another grunt. "The crew would like that, for sure. Though it's hardly necessary to spoil them with less work."

"I wager she can do it faster than the crew, sir." Madrenga rushed on. "Haven't there been occasions when you wished to raise anchor more swiftly than is normal?"

"There is truth enough in that statement." Hammaghiri's thoughts drifted back to an earlier moment in time. "There was that evening in the Foresworn Isles where we had to ..." He broke off. "I'll give your animal one chance, young Madrenga. *If* you can get her aboard. None of our boats is large enough to bring over a horse, and I'll not take the time to weigh anchor and joust for an empty spot among the docks. If you can get her aboard, we'll see what she can do."

"Thank you, sir! Thank you!" Without waiting to be dismissed, he whirled and bolted for the door, Bit galumphing at his heels. Hammaghiri watched him leave.

"Odd young man, that."

"I conjecture he is no odder than his dog, Captain."

Hammaghiri sighed. "The things an honest seaman does for money." He waved absently. "Go and see what transpires. If he gets the horse aboard, we'll deal with it. If he falls overboard in the attempt, let him swim back to shore."

Focused on the space above the Captain's head, Quilpit's gaze was impassive. "And if the latter, sir, what of his money paid?"

"Recompense for my patience and forbearance. Now leave me. I have real work to do."

Back on deck the first mate searched for his young friend. He found him standing at the rail on the port side.

"What will you do, boyo? Hire a larger boat to bring your animal over?"

"Not unless I have no choice. But I think she can swim it." Madrenga nodded at the mainmast. "You have crane and net for bringing large cargo aboard?" Smiling understandingly, Quilpit nodded. "She may struggle, but if need be I'll get in the water with her. I think I can calm her enough to get a net around her."

"We'll try, anyway, boyo. Shall I have someone row you back ashore?"

"No need."

Stepping up onto the railing and balancing himself by holding onto the rigging, Madrenga put fingers to lips and whistled. It took a couple of tries until the horse waiting patiently on the end of the nearest quay responded by looking up in his direction. Her master whistled again and then a fourth time, trying to put as much urgency into the call as possible. Without hesitation Orania took a couple of steps forward and, to the astonishment of a couple of elderly townsfolk who were fishing off the dock, plunged into the harbor.

Madrenga caught his breath when she vanished beneath the surface, only to relax when she popped up again a moment later. Did more than pop up, actually. As expected, she was swimming toward the ship. What was unexpected was the speed at which she was moving. All horses could swim: he knew that from childhood. But Orania appeared not only to be moving at excessive velocity, but to be gaining speed with each equine stroke.

Taking note of her approach, first one sailor and then another put aside what they were doing to watch. Soon many of the crew were crowding the rail or looking on from their positions athwart yards or in the rigging. As they kept a running commentary on her approach, an uneasy murmuring began to suffuse the air on the *Thranskirr's* main deck.

"No horse swims like that." Grizzled as a mummy and lean as a piece of piraya jerky from the ship's commissary, the second mate squinted through the lingering mist as the high head in the water drew nearer. "No normal horse."

Leaning close, the cook whispered to his old friend. "I think mayhap her owner no normal man, either. Look at him standing there and calling to his animal: he has the body and build of a warrior but the face of a youth: a callow one at that. One would not think such a sword as swings from his waist would belong to him."

"Or he to it." The second mate coughed. Though older than either the Captain or first mate, Korufh was content with his status, having by dint of sheer hard work raised himself up from common seaman to a position of responsibility. There was little about a ship with which he was not familiar, and the rest of the crew respected him unreservedly. To him the sea and all who sailed upon it were a well-thumbed book.

But this strange young man and his stranger animals—they were something new to him. He was not averse to newness. New things carried with them the promise of profit or an easing of hard work. But they could also bring danger. The youth looked innocent enough—indeed, his face was open and devoid of guile. But there was something about him that was not natural. No magus he: that was plain for anyone to see. That did not mean he was to be trusted; not yet. Quilpit was comfortable with him. That much was apparent. But just because a man kept coin in his purse and goodness in his heart did not perforce exclude him from carrying a curse on his back.

"A net!" someone shouted. The horse's owner was not the only one who divined what needed to be readied. "Swing over a crane!"

Breaking away from the railing, several of the crew set about preparing the equipment that would be necessary to hoist the swimming horse aboard. They did not have to wait for formal orders from the Captain. Hammaghiri had always encouraged initiative on the part of his crew.

As it turned out, neither net nor crane would prove necessary.

CHAPTER NINE

ORANIA'S SPEED INCREASED TO THE POINT WHERE A DISTINCT bow wave was breaking before her neck and chest. Staring at her, Madrenga wondered how she could move so fast in the water. He could not, of course, see her feet. Her tail and mane, however, had adopted a peculiar flatness, as if the hairs had somehow been welding together. Both were now moving from side to side so fast that they were a blur. From behind her water rose and fell in an arc, looking like the tail of a rooster. Driven by more than mere equine muscle, the upper portion of her body began to rise out of the water. The fascinated murmuring on deck gave rise to uncertain queries, then to a few exclamations of alarm. Those who had not gone to help with the cargo net and hoist began retreating, moving away from the railing. Even Madrenga stepped off the rail and down onto to the deck, though he did not back away.

The wake generated by the oncoming horse grew large enough to capsize a rowboat carrying a trio of fishermen. Madrenga was relieved to see that none of them suffered any injury from the encounter. As soon as they were dumped into the harbor, they surfaced with fists waving and foul language flying.

Like a bird reconnoitering a landing on a small, steep-sided island, Orania raced in a circle around the *Thranskirr*. Astounded sailors rushed from port to starboard and back again as they tried to keep track of the horse's progress. Lost in their continuing fascination they ignored the water she kicked up on deck.

Coming around one more time to port she backed off, braced herself, and then headed straight on amidships. Someone cried out that she was going to break herself on the solid pigo. Putting on a burst of speed that made it appear as if she had previously been doing little more than treading water, she exploded from the sea on the outside of the outrigger. As she descended, her feet touched down on its slightly rounded upper surface and kicked off with the precision of an acrobat. Jaws dropped and eyes widened as horse, saddle, and backpack soared through the air to land with a solid *bang* on the deck.

As she stood shaking herself off, Bit trotted over and began licking salt water from her legs, starting at the fetlocks and working his way upwards. Turning her head, she started to do the same to her neck and torso.

Seeing that a number of the sailors were looking at her and muttering darkly to themselves, Madrenga hurried over to his mount and began to stroke her neck.

"She's—she's very comfortable in the water," he explained lamely.

"Ay, and in the air too, it would seem," commented one man.

"In what other realms is she welcome?" asked another, his eyes narrowing as he stared at the horse.

To Madrenga's relief Quilpit arrived and reached up to put a hand on the youth's shoulder.

"This fine young man, Madrenga by name, will be traveling with us as a passenger until we reach his intended destination. For company he travels with some unusual animals. I grant you their appearance and abilities may be disconcerting to some, but there is no harm in them. His horse causes no trouble and his dog is a fighter." The first mate's gaze flicked from one uncertain seaman to the next. "I know the lot of you are fighters as well, so you should understand that one person we do not fight with, either with deed or word, is a paying passenger. Those of you who know the Captain also know he would sooner throw any one of you overboard than a stranger who has more than paid his way."

"Sorcery," mumbled one man from within the security of the crowd.

It did not provide the anonymity the speaker had sought. "And what business is it of yours, Baycrake?" the first mate challenged him. "Were I you, I would be looking to seek out the talents of a sorcerer, in the hope that he might, through his powers, negate the vengeance that was called down on you by the woman you entrapped in Poruu Valence."

"That would require the powers of a god, not a mere wizard," asserted another of the assembled sailors. At this observation the entire group roared, while the accused looked abashed.

Mollified for the moment if not entirely put at ease, the crewmen dispersed to their assigned tasks, still chuckling among themselves. Quilpit smiled reassuringly at the new passenger.

"Don't mind them, boy. Men at sea have little to do in their spare time but complain. In your absence they would concoct a conspiracy of shrimp. Best get used to the sidelong glances and hushed comments. Their paranoia will do you no harm." Reaching out, he tentatively patted Orania's still dripping flank. "Let's settle your horse on deck astern. She's not the first piece of four-legged cargo the *Thranskirr* has seen. We've carried cattle, shreep, and hogs. As the only livestock on board she'll have space and feed and fresh air all to herself, and you'll see her whenever you're on deck." He glanced down at Bit. "Your dog, I suppose, you'll want to keep with you."

"He's always slept near me," Madrenga admitted. "For warmth and for his safety."

"And now his presence will assure your own safety. That's how it is with dogs, boyo."

"Captain on deck!" someone yelled. The members of the crew abruptly became busier than they had been since Madrenga had stepped aboard.

126

Joining mate and visitor, Hammaghiri stared long and hard at the dog that was drying the horse and the horse that was drying herself. "You said that your animal alone might be able to raise the anchor. As I commented, while I dislike unnecessarily easing the burden of my crew, turning the capstan is an activity that in the past has occasionally resulted in a sprained leg or pulled ligament. Any opportunity to avoid such injuries is to be welcomed." Stepping past them he headed for the bow. "Bring her."

"Sir," Madrenga began uneasily, "she's just had a hard swim out to the ship and ..."

"What can I say? Life is harder for men than for horses. Bring her." Hammaghiri gestured toward the quay. "Or you can return her to shore and pick her up whenever you return. The choice is yours."

Exhaling deeply, Madrenga took his mount by the dripping reins. "Come on, girl." Leaning close, he whispered into one ear. "I hope you can do this. You know I won't go anywhere without you, even if it means delaying the directives of counselors and queens."

She responded with a short, sharp, snort. Or maybe she was just sneezing out some sawdust the wind had blown over from where the ship's carpenter was repairing a sea chest.

A good-sized ship, the *Thranskirr* required an anchor of proportionate dimensions. Normally she would have been secured to a fixed mooring, but when Hammaghiri had brought her into port the harbor had been packed with other ships and every mooring taken. As with any other captain in his position, time was more important than convenience. To get his cargo off quickly he had simply dropped anchor in a suitable spot. Safely behind Churrash's formidable breakwater, he did not even have to worry about ensuring that the anchor acquired a secure hold. Since the huge double-iron bar had been dropped over the side, the *Thranskirr* had not budged.

New cargo had been brought aboard and stowed, supplies loaded, and the last of the ship's drunken and debauched crew winched aboard. It was time to leave. Anticipating the call to the capstan, the members of the crew responsible for raising the anchor had begun to report for the duty, only to find themselves held back by their first mate.

"Rest awhile, boyos, while we see what the passenger's animal can do besides swim like a dolphin."

Biggest of a burly lot, the seaman called Kurron-bey folded huge arms and frowned. "It takes eight of us pushing hard on the four arms to bring up the weight, Quilpit. What makes you think one horse can do the same?"

"Eyewrath's truth, Kurron speaks." Hairiest of the hirsute, Ornym the Harund gazed with all three eyes on the horse and men who had reached the capstan. "If boy not careful, horse will maybe pull chain halfway up. Gets heavier the nearer it gets to deck. Horse strains, runs out of pull, *boom!*" He clapped thick, hairy hands together. "Anchor falls back in water, pulls horse with it, horse hits anchor channel, horse breaks neck." A huge grin appeared in the center of the fulsome beard. "Is not necessarily bad ending. Crew eats horse steak for next few days, has horse jerky for rest of voyage."

By this time everyone not busy at another assigned task had turned to watch what they believed to be an incipient failure. Hammaghiri and Quilpit stood off to one side. Three backup ropes, each as thick as a man's upper arm, were fastened to the iron anchor chain. In the event the chain broke, they would hold the anchor and keep it from being lost. Removing the sturdy saddle, Madrenga positioned it over the armored breastplate and perpendicular to the ground. He then drew one of the backup anchor ropes to Orania's left side, a second to her right, and bound them securely together over the saddle. The armor would protect her skin from harm while the leather would provide a groove through which the attached ropes could slide, making make it easier for her to push against the weight.

When he had done all he felt that he could, he stepped back, gave her an encouraging slap on the rump, and hollered, "Go, girl—go!"

Orania put one foot forward, followed it with the other, leaned her weight into it, dug in, and—nothing happened. Neither she nor the anchor chain moved. Guffaws began to rise from those members of the crew who had assembled to watch.

"Maybe a team of mulers would be a better idea, boy!"

"Or a team of bears," quipped another. "Thought for certain you were older than your animal. Now I ain't so sure!"

Madrenga bit his lip and did not respond. Orania was a slow riser in the morning. Maybe it was going to take some time for her to get her footing.

"Come on, girl. Press it!"

Hooves moved anew. Orania lowered her head until her muzzle nearly scraped the deck. Slowly but perceptibly, she began to move forward, one step at a time. The chain's thick iron links snapped straight. On the port side near the bow the open iron-lined channel where the chain vanished over the side and into the dark green water below began to squeal as first one link, then another, then a third, rose onto the deck.

"Three damns and a fool's fart, she's doing it!" exclaimed one of the other seamen.

"But slowly, slowly," argued another. "At this rate she'll tire out before she's halfway done." He chuckled. "Will be interesting to see which body part comes off first when the anchor falls back and pulls her with it."

As had Bit and her owner, ever since they had left Harup-taw-shet Orania had changed greatly under circumstances Madrenga could not explain. But he did not think, and he had seen nothing to indicate, that her transformation included a newfound ability to understand human language. The fact that she had looked over sharply at the last speaker was confirmation of nothing. She heard speech: that was all. But he knew from experience that she could be just as susceptible as Bit to the sounds of mockery and scorn. All animals were sensitive to such comments. None of the sailors would have dared taken that tone with Bit, he knew. Whether they or anyone else could safely do so with Orania was something he did not wish to find out. Taking a couple of steps toward the assembled, smirking onlookers, he raised both hands warningly and pleaded for understanding.

"Caution, if you will! You're making her angry!"

It was too late. That smoke seemed to emerge from the horse's nostrils could have been put down to the collision of equine exhalation with colder sea air. Harder to explain were the testimonies of two members of the crew who swore the smoke was accompanied by sparks.

Leaning even more sharply into the heavy ropes Orania began to pick up speed. As the rattle of the rising anchor chain changed from a metallic squeal to a steady hum of links sliding onto the deck, derisive laughter turned to cheers, which in turn soon surrendered to awe. By the time Orania had become a piebald blur around the capstan, this gave way to concern.

Smoke began to rise from the horse's hooves as friction threatened to set a circle of the foredeck on fire. Sparks flew from the iron brace where the anchor chain was now streaking onto the deck. So swiftly were the links winding tight around the capstan that it too had begun smoking. A moment later the first flames could be seen spurting from between iron and the black pigo cylinder.

"That's enough." Hammaghiri too had retreated. "Slow her down, boy, before she sets the whole ship afire!"

Stepping forward, Madrenga tried to do exactly that. Driven to excess by the taunts of the crew, Orania was moving so fast it was doubtful she could hear her master's commands—or anything else. Just as the capstan and the wooden decking beneath her hooves threatened to burst into full flame, a dark metal V-shape came flying over the side of the ship. Even though few of them were within the danger zone, every one of the watching sailors scrambled for cover.

The twin-barred anchor of solid, rusting iron flew through the air to land with a crash between railing and capstan. Even the strong decking of the *Thranskirr* could not resist such an impact.

Though slowed by the tough, weathered planks, the anchor crashed through to the lower deck beneath. It was only through good fortune that no one was working beneath the spot.

Advancing cautiously, Hammaghiri and Quilpit moved to the edge of the hole. Madrenga did not join them, having chosen to attend to Orania. Having finally come to a complete stop, the horse was perspiring profusely.

"She needs a blanket," he called to them.

The Captain made a rude noise as he examined the gap. "Here's work for the ship's carpenter." He looked over at the horse's master. "You're lucky, paying passenger, that she didn't hull the ship. Were that the case we'd all be in the water shortly, with me pressing down hard on your head."

Ever a voice of common sense at such moments, Quilpit spoke softly. "The crew teased her to it, sir. She was only responding to their goading."

Hammaghiri hated it when his first mate was logical, and even more so when he was right. "Since she has so much energy, the first port we come to we'll harness her to the loading crane. The two of them, man and horse, will work off this damage." Turning, he raised his voice so that the men now slowly emerging from the places where they had sought hasty refuge would be sure to hear him.

"New ship's order!" he bellowed, his voice carrying from bow to stern and well out over the water as well. "From now on, as long as she's on this ship, nobody dares the mare!"

He did not have explain what he meant.

Having taken shelter with the others when the anchor had come flying onto the deck, second mate Korufh did not linger to discuss the remarkable incident with his fellows. Quietly he retired to his cabin, there to contemplate a newly uncertain future. It was all beginning to make a certain perverted sort of sense now: the passenger with the body of a soldier and a face still redolent of adolescence, the dog-monster and the story Quilpit had told of it, and now this cursed horse-creature. As he laid down on his bunk and stared at the old wood overhead, he closed his eyes. One of the first things anyone who makes their life at sea learns is to take advantage of a sound sleep whenever the opportunity presents itself. Korufh did so now, a last thought loitering as he embarked on his nap.

Demons, the lot of them, he had decided firmly.

Bolted securely to the aft deck, the three concentric circles of the ship's wheel gleamed brightly, their stark whiteness visible from nearly anywhere on deck or in the rigging. Fashioned from the lashed-and-glued-together rib bones of a calianc sea serpent, the bones had been inscribed with symbols and sayings recognizable to any mariner. All five points of the compass, the directions taken by the known winds, safe harbors, dangerous shoals, famous ports—even the legendary lands of lost Nalduu, all had been inscribed on the bone by the *Thranskirr*'s shipbuilder's master artist. The same man had carved the masts whose tops terminated in birds of prey, and the figurehead of an atypically buxom fairy princess.

Standing behind the great wheel, Bolandri, the *Thranskirr*'s navigator, seemed a part of the ship itself, as much a fixture as rudder or ram. Every time Madrenga had come on deck since they had left Charrush behind, the helmsman was to be found at his station. It would not have surprised the youth to learn that the man slept there, his long arms embracing the wheel bones and his large spatulate hands gripping them like a necrophilic lover. His eyes fixed straight ahead, Bolandri did not glance in the passenger's direction, though a slight nod indicated that he was aware of Madrenga's presence.

Orania had been settled in forward where she had been provided with a makeshift bed of hay and straw. As she munched contentedly through her bedding, new fodder-filling was brought up from below. Bit, as always, trotted along happily by his master's side. By now every member of the crew had been subject to Quilpit's retelling of what had taken place at the animal fighting arena. While their reactions to the first mate's narrative ranged from dubious to apprehensive, each of them nonetheless continued to give the dog a wide berth. Bit found this standoffishness unutterably depressing, as he was naturally friendly and inquisitive. In his still puppyish innocence he was unable to understand that his recently acquired body armor, spiked collar, and dragon's teeth had a tendency to make even hardened seamen wary of becoming too friendly.

Hammaghiri stood at the very rear of the aft deck, behind his helmsman. From where he was relaxing in the elevated chair that was reached by a series of short steps he could see all of the deck, from bowsprit to topmast. The pair of special seaman's glasses he wore had been made in Charrush. Darkened to shield eyes from the sun, they also prevented each member of the crew from telling if their captain was watching them, studying the sea, or sleeping.

As Madrenga approached the captain's seat, a school of boomers broke from the water off to starboard. Inflating the sacs at the tips of their fins, they rose into the air and began to drift eastward with the wind. If only he could travel due east with such ease, the youth thought. Attached to their gills, sacs filled with water would allow the boomers to breathe while staying aloft for some time.

The reason for their eruption from the surface showed itself a moment after the last member of the school had risen from the water. Bursting upward, the pipe dragon opened its wide, bulging jaws. Connected by an expandable membrane, they formed a perfectly circular, fang-lined mouth. Late in inflating, the last of the boomers hung low over the water an instant too long. The pipe dragon's mouth closed around it as neatly as a pelican's and snapped shut.

A distant, low boom sounded as the dragon arced back into the sea and disappeared in a gout of water and foam.

"Sleep well, Mr. Madrenga?" The Captain was not asleep behind his dark lenses.

"Better than I have a right to expect, sir. I confess I was uncertain as to how I would fare once we left Charrush and found ourselves out on the open ocean, but having been many times forced to catch my sleep in far more trying conditions, I find the rocking of the ship greatly to my liking."

Hammaghiri was clearly pleased. "Perhaps we'll make a sailor of you, Mr. Madrenga, and you'll have no need to return to your dry, desolate, depressing landsman home."

"Three negatives you cast on my choice of residence, sir, none of which apply. But however misguided, I appreciate your concern for my welfare." He paused awhile to study the now quiet surface of the sea before continuing. "Much as I would appreciate finalizing the matter of my destination. Isn't it time to do so?"

"Oh, that." Hammaghiri grinned. "A small matter. You have paid enough to be set ashore anywhere along our transit. Where would you and your animals like to land?"

While far more confident in body, in mind Madrenga was still the inexperienced youth who had barely escaped an ordinary mugging in Harup-taw-shet. He was street smart enough to know that in an argument he was no match for the widely-traveled Hammaghiri. So, as he spoke, he kept his gaze aimed out to sea and avoided meeting the older man's eyes. As they had for days, mountains and canyons framed the coast, their presence interrupted only by the occasional broad river valley flush with forest and fishing villages.

"Ever since leaving Charrush we've not sailed out of sight of the coast."

The Captain nodded. "Time is cheaper than life. Safer to follow the shore than risk the dangers of the open ocean. In case of emergency the *Thranskirr*, like any mouse, likes to have handy a ready bolthole."

"But you and your ship have made ocean crossings before." Its four leathery green wings catching the wind, a male peurlu soared low over the topmast, forcing the lookout stationed there to briefly duck back into his protective cage. Indifference rather than curses caused the aerial predator to continue on a course that took it away from the ship and toward the coast, there to seek out potential prey that was more vulnerable and less voluble.

"Truth. Which exact line the ship takes depends on many factors. The weather, the time of year, reports of piratical activity, stories of encounters with or sightings of the more fearsome seabeasts, and of course where we are contracted to pick up and drop off cargo." He looked evenly at the youth. "So tell me, cargo; it sounds like you have decided where you would like to be put ashore."

"Yes." He took a deep breath. "Daria."

"Daria? You did say Daria, my young friend?" Madrenga nodded; the Captain considered. "First of all, Daria lies well inland from the coast. Having neither legs nor wings, the *Thranskirr* cannot get you there."

"I will settle for being set down as close as possible," Madrenga responded.

Hammaghiri pursed his lips. "That would be the seaport of Yordd, where much of the cargo that travels the waters of the world and is bound for Daria is landed. Yordd, Mr. Madrenga, lies almost directly across the Sea of Shadows from where you and I now converse. I can certainly land you there—in several months' time."

Madrenga pondered the Captain's response. Did he have months? While neither Counselor Natoum nor the Queen herself had given him a specific date by which the scroll had to be delivered, among Natoum's last words to him prior to their parting was the unmistakable implication that its contents were time-sensitive. He therefore did not think that a delay of several months would be acceptable.

He could ask to be put ashore at the next seaport of size and there hope to book more direct transport. But if Hammaghiri was reluctant at this time to make a direct crossing of the Shadows, none of his shipmastering counterparts were likely to be more bold. Besides, Madrenga told himself, he knew Hammaghiri now.

Knew his ship, and most if not all of the crew by sight if not always by name. By leaving the *Thranskirr* in a new port he would be abandoning a familiarity as comforting as it was useful—and he would have to start all over again.

Having come up behind them and listened silently to the exchange, Quilpit now ventured a suggestion.

"We have two more stops to make on the western coast, Captain: Colankka and Bis-on-Brevay. Then we face the long tack to Florask-ah."

Hammaghiri nodded. "Which we shall reach by following the southern coast before making the quick dash across the Straits of Berembrean."

"The Straits fertilize ambuscades, sir." The first mate glanced at an increasingly hopeful Madrenga. "We could avoid them by heading direct across the sea from Bis-on-Brevay to Florask-ah." He paused briefly. "Yordd lies on the eastern coast of the Shadows —and is but a short detour through Nazbay on the way to Florask-ah."

Hammaghiri harrumphed. "Yes, we could do that—and risk whatever greater perils the Shadows might choose to cast our way."

Quilpit smiled. "Every day of a life at sea is a gamble, sir. I know you." He gestured toward the main deck. "I know the crew. Offer them the chance to cut a few months sea time from their contract with the promise of the same pay at the end, and there would be few among them who would not jump at the opportunity. They'll take the risk."

"They'd only be risking their lives," Hammaghiri countered. "While I am responsible for the ship."

The first mate stared back at his superior. "Less time at sea, less wear on the ship as well as the men."

"Don't tell me my business, Mr. Quilpit."

"Never, sir—I wouldn't presume to …!"

"Calm yourself. Let me think."

It was all a matter of balancing risk versus savings. The months that would not be spent rounding the southern reaches could be used to extend the voyage. The additional potential income that could materialize from such a decision was substantial. He would certainly prefer to avoid having to cross the Straits of Berembrean.

But the dangers of the open sea, far away from land …

Those were always unknown, he reminded himself firmly. On this voyage, at least, perhaps it was time to put aside the fear of the unknown. Respect for it he would retain. Anyway, there was a girl in Florask-ah who would not wait forever and …

Turning, he cupped his hands to his mouth and bellowed in the direction of the *Thranskirr*'s helmsman. "Mr. Bolandri! Change of heading! Set us due northeast!"

"Yes sir!" In the helmsman's limber hands the great triple bone wheel began to spin to starboard. Stepping down from his seat and moving to the railing that lined the aft deck, Hammaghiri sought out the second mate. "Mr. Korufh! We're changing course." He pointed aloft. "Blocks and braces—we're coming around to starboard!"

"Yes Captain!" Even as he began giving orders to the men Korufh wondered at the sudden change of course. It was plain to see they were heading out to sea and leaving behind the safety and protection of the coast. To what purpose? Like every other member of the crew who had enjoyed shore leave in Charrush he had heard the stories of ships recently gone missing in the middle of the Shadows. He trusted Hammaghiri, both as an individual and a Captain, but knowing him as he did it was unlike the man to order such a change in plans while not in port and …

The passenger! Whirling, Korufh gazed at the aft deck where the strange young man could be seen deep in conversation with the Captain and first mate. What unknown words had this Madrenga whispered into Hammaghiri's ear to persuade him to alter course? For surely that was the reason for the unusual decision. Korufh could think of no other suitable explanation for the abrupt change. Had the youth somehow magicked both men?

Near the foredeck the passenger's deviant steed dozed content-edly on its edible bedding. As Korufh stared, the animal raised its head and looked directly at him. Eyes widening in fear, the second mate turned away, only to nearly stumble over the blocky shape of the passenger's shovel-mouthed dog. Panting agreeably, it licked his leg. While the gesture was nominally one of affection, the fact that the dog's red tongue extended outward the length of a man's arm only further flustered an already unsettled Korufh. He fled toward the open hatch that beckoned between the masts, badly in need of some privacy for his jangled thoughts.

Meanwhile the *Thranskirr* wheeled smartly about and struck a course across an increasingly deep line of olive-green swells.

CHAPTER TEN

Though prior to stepping on board the *Thranskirr* Madrenga had never spent time on a body of water larger than Mopoun Lake west of Harup-taw-shet, he adapted to the ship's rolling, heaving motion without distress. With each passing day he grew more comfortable with the ship, if not her crew. When he happened to encounter any of them they accorded him the respect due his unique position both as a paying passenger and an apparent favorite of the Captain. Most of the men were polite, if not particularly friendly. The youth's cheery "Good morning" was usually met by a polite "Sir" or "Sor," depending on the sailor's homeland. Or in the case of a Harund, the rising throaty grunt that was their equivalent of courteous acknowledgement.

Several crewmen did their best to avoid him altogether. Not even the most cordial of the lot would go near Bit. Expressions tended to tense whenever the dog was eating, as the sound of bones cracking between Bit's powerful jaws had a disquieting effect on the human soul as well as the ear. As for Orania, there were those who were tempted to approach so beautiful an animal. Yet among the several who tried there was universal agreement that the closer one got to the horse, the more persistent was the flicker of red in her eye. Whether this optical persistence was due to an illusion, a trick of the light, an imperfection in the lens of the animal's eye, or something deeper and possibly malevolent, none of the crew could say. It was a puzzle that defied resolution, as no man dared draw near enough to see clearly.

Occasional flocks of blue-feathered amrayads flew by overhead, heading west in contravention of the *Thranskirr's* course. The largest female led the way, her billowing wings creating a slipstream ridden effortlessly by those following behind. One evening a vomolak breached against the setting sun, momentarily blotting out the descending fiery disc before all three of its connected body parts crashed back into the water. It took such leaps, Quilpit explained, in the hopes of dislodging the vampire cod attached to its body.

It was in the third week that the strange vessel appeared on the northern horizon.

Alerted by the mainmast lookout, Hammaghiri had moved to the rear deck's starboard railing and was peering at the oncoming vessel through an intricately engraved spyglass. Occasionally he would murmur a comforting word to it, causing the device's integrated spell to juggle the multiple lenses mounted within. As words altered alignment, the high-masted newcomer came into increasingly sharp focus. After a number of minutes spent staring through the eyepiece the Captain was able to resolve the other craft's identity.

"They fly no flag." His tone was grim as he passed the spyglass to Quilpit while Madrenga looked on anxiously. "Men and other things who fly no flag stand only for themselves."

"Pirates." Quilpit was more solemn than Madrenga had ever seen the first mate.

When the Captain turned to his young passenger he spoke without rancor, but Madrenga could tell that Hammaghiri was rethinking his decision to leave the safety of the western coast and make a run straight across the Sea of Shadows. Realizing this, Madrenga struggled to decide whether to offer an apology or condolences.

"Don't say anything." The Captain spoke calmly, pre-empting his passenger. "This is not your fault. I knew the choices, and I made one."

The younger man was looking past him, trying to make out the shape of the ship that was closing fast on their course. Sensing his master's unease, Bit paced edgily back and forth behind the three men. Even Madrenga could tell that the oncoming vessel was larger than the *Thranskirr*.

"What do we do, sir? What's our course of action?" He looked over at the older man. "Do we fight?"

"Time and shrinking distance will give the answer to that, Mr. Madrenga. First we must see how big she is, try to get a sense of the size of her crew, and evaluate her visible armament. My men are experienced and know what is expected of them. We have drilled for such eventualities. If the odds are reasonable, certainly we will fight. If not, we will negotiate. Contrary to what landsfolk think, all pirates prefer negotiation to battle. Endless booty is useless to a dead man."

Madrenga studied the deck of the *Thranskirr*. Having not yet been informed of the approaching threat, the unconcerned crew continued with their daily tasks.

"What do you carry that they might want, sir?" He hastened to add, "Of course, such knowledge may be privileged and not mine to know."

"There are no cases of corium or barrels of jewels, if that's what you're thinking, boyo." Though already mentally preoccupied with preparations for a possible physical confrontation, Quilpit remained engaged in the conversation. "Another common misconception of landsmen. Pirates may prefer gold and gems: who would not? But they are perfectly content to take whatever is stealable and saleable. Furniture, food, medicines, tools—anything useful that can be converted to profit is grist for their efforts." He grinned at the broad-shouldered young man with the youthful face. "They will take your pants, if they feel them worth a coin or two."

The scroll, Madrenga thought with alarm. *They will take the royal scroll.* Perhaps not for what was written on it, but surely for the fine metalwork of which it and its container were made. Could he hide it somewhere? The notion did not linger. Surely professional brigands were accustomed to such ploys on the part of the passengers and crew of ships they accosted, and were adept at winkling out any valuables that might be secreted on board.

"I'd rather fight."

Had he said that? Inoffensive Madrenga, with his discrete street-wise friends a haunter of the holes and hiding places of old Harup-taw-shet? Except he was no longer that same youth. In mind perhaps, but not in body. Or in experience. Had not he and Bit fought off the monstrous cabinet of curiosities of the malicious merchant in Hamuldar in order to rescue the beauteous smoke sprite Elenacol?

Elenacol. In truth her beauty had been inhuman. What would she advise if confronted with such a situation as he now faced? Tell him to surrender all that belonged to him, or to fight to preserve it? Certainly Counselor Natoum would order him to protect the royal scroll with every resource at his command. Including if need be his life. But the decision was not up to him. Despite his mysteriously enhanced abilities he could hardly mount a defense on his own. If Hammaghiri decided to surrender the ship, some other option besides a suicidal resistance would have to be considered.

Not only was the strange vessel bent on interception bigger than the *Thranskirr*, it was faster as well. Finally alerted by the mates to the oncoming danger, the crew erupted in a frenzy of activity. Weapons were passed out from the ship's armory. Men were stationed along the starboard railing or sent scrambling aloft, there to rain down arrows and crossbow bolts from the yards and rigging. Of course, the pirates would position their own people similarly. In the forthcoming battle success was more likely to derive from weight of numbers than from strategy.

The lack of a flag on the oncoming ship was matched by the absence of a name. Unidentified, independent, and impudent, the three-masted fore-rigged threat pulled alongside the *Thranskirr* as easily as a sycophant beside a powerful politician. Built for speed instead of carrying capacity, she had more the look of a large racing yacht than a cargo vessel or warship; a piratical ferret alongside the *Thranskirr*'s squirrel. No wonder that from first sight Hammaghiri had given up any thought of trying to outrun her. More than a hundred armed men and Harunds, possibly twice that number, lined the railing in show of force. There were also, an agitated Madrenga saw, a trio of Golgox giants: the first he had ever seen in person. Wide of ear and flat of head, they towered over their fellow fighters. Each gripped and intimidatingly waved a double-bladed war axe with a steel head the size of a wagon wheel. If the intent was to frighten an opponent into surrender, the sight of three armed and armored Golgox constituted a significant beginning.

Holding a short sword in each hand, Quilpit appraised the threat dispassionately. "We are at an unmistakable disadvantage. Yet standing." He looked to Hammaghiri. The Captain had armed himself with the most ornately decorated sword Madrenga had ever seen. Encased in chased gold and speckled with semi-precious gems, it belonged more in a parade than in battle. But in combat, symbols were important. If a clash reached the point where the Captain of a ship had to defend himself in hand-to-hand combat then that fight was likely as good as over anyway.

"What does the Captain wish?" the first mate asked tightly.

Madrenga never got the chance to hear what Hammaghiri had decided. Before the Captain could reply, three port covers were raised on the side of the pirate craft to expose three dark muzzles. A knowing cry interspersed with a few pointed laughs rose from the enemy crew. Hammaghiri's expression fell.

"Cannon. They have cannon. Six, most likely."

There was uncharacteristic resignation in Quilpit's voice. "That explains why they hove to parallel to our course instead of immediately closing and trying to board." As Madrenga looked on, the first mate set his swords down on the deck. On the main deck below, men were mumbling and muttering and turning away from what had been furious preparations for battle. Bewildered by what looked like abject surrender in the face of not a single arrow being shot, the youth looked from Captain to mate.

"I don't understand. What's a 'cannon'? In truth, of engines of war I know only a little. I know catapults and arbalests, swords and siege towers. But of this cannon this is the first I have heard."

Hammaghiri had moved to resume his seat in his elevated chair, from which vantage point he could more easily send his deep voice coursing over the intervening waters. Though he would attempt to broker a deal with the captain of the brigands' vessel that would not leave empty and destitute the *Thranskirr* and its crew, both men knew which cards each held and that the game-playing to come was little more than a prelude to the cargo vessel's surrender.

"Cannons are those round metal cylinders with the open mouths that you see pointing at us. Through the employment of an explosive powder they are able to throw large iron balls with great force wherever their muzzles are aimed. Sometimes handfuls of broken metal and old nails are used, to bloody effect. If that fails to deliver the intended prize, hot coals from the ship's galley may be substituted." He gestured aloft. "Masts, rigging, sails, and decks are all too easily set afire."

A solemn Madrenga quietly digested this radical new notion. "Can nothing be done to counter such an evil spell?"

"No spell is involved, lad. No more so than a spell is required to fling a spear or snap a bowstring. It is all to do with something called chemistry and chemicals, which I'm told is akin to alchemy." He shook his head. "I account myself no fool, but I am a sailor. I know the sea. I know her moods, her citizens, her weather. Of these chemical things I know only what I have heard." Turning, he looked back across the intervening patch of ocean toward the pirate ship that was now paralleling the *Thranskirr*. "Cannon I know because I have seen them before. It is not pretty work."

Shouting from the Captain's chair, Hammaghiri began to

argue with his counterpart on the other vessel. He did not plead or ask after mercy, knowing that these were commodities which the occupants of the other craft held in short supply. As the two ships plowed on side by side, both full of sail and one of bluster, it became apparent that the commander of the threatening vessel was starting to lose patience with his quarry. The longer their activities and emotions are kept pent up, men intent on plunder tend to grow edgy.

The pirate captain finally signaled his displeasure at Hammaghiri's stalling by ordering the foremost of his three loaded cannons to fire. Rather than hole the *Thranskirr*, it was a demonstration intended to clear her decks of any remaining notions of resistance as well as to put an end to delaying tactics. There was an explosion of a kind Madrenga had never before heard. A great gout of white smoke haloed the barrel of the weapon that had been fired. Then time seemed to slow down.

He was perfectly aware of everything around him. Of Hammaghiri abruptly breaking off his ongoing discourse, Quilpit uttering a violent curse and throwing himself onto the deck, other members of the crew struggling to take cover behind tough pigo masts or diving for open hatchways. All this was normal—except they were moving so slowly that it looked like they were swimming in aspic. Why, Madrenga thought, he could have ducked beneath the flying first mate, tickled his belly, and emerged standing on the other side of him before he was likely to hit the deck.

As his gaze turned outward toward the attacking vessel, he saw the smoke from the explosion dissipating like oil in water and saw a round iron ball the size of a melon coming directly toward him. It was spinning through the air with infinite slowness as it crossed the space separating the two ships. Fascinated, he found that he could make out the imperfections in the metal, could discern small ridges and bumps on its otherwise smooth curved sides.

Reaching the *Thranskirr* after what seemed like an eternity in flight, it crossed over the railing on a path to sever the aft mast.

Without thinking, he reached out with his right hand and grabbed it, plucking it from the air through which it was traveling as easily as he would have picked a ripe fruit from the low branch of an orange or apple tree. The iron sphere was cool to his touch and virtually weightless.

Time abruptly returned to normal. It was the only thing that did. Picking himself off the deck, Quilpit stared at his young friend. For the first time since they had met following the incident at the dog fighting arena, Madrenga saw something in the first mate's eyes that had not been there previously.

Fear.

Realizing that their ship had not been struck, crew were picking themselves off the deck and emerging from hiding places. One by one they became aware of the current location of the deadly ordnance that had been directed at them. A few cheers started to ring out across the deck. Interspersed with these were expressions of awe and murmurs of uncertainty.

All three emotions raced through Captain Hammaghiri as he looked down at where his unfathomable young passenger stood holding the cannon ball, gripping it in one hand as if it weighed no more than a loaf of bread. One did not rise to his position by being afflicted with slow reactions, however, no matter how outrageous the circumstances in which he might find himself. Gesturing toward the other vessel, he spoke in a calm but firm voice.

"Good catch, Mr. Madrenga. Now give it back."

The youth hesitated, then understood. Still wondering how he was able to do such things but at the moment more occupied with simply doing them, he drew back his right arm and flung that which he had snatched out of the air. As fast as it had been fired from the other ship, the cannon ball sped back across the intervening water. Having taken only the most indifferent aim, Madrenga was relieved to see the sphere smash into the hull of the other vessel—below her waterline.

The pandemonium that broke out on the pirate craft reminded him of the chaos that had ensued at the dog fighting arena following Bit's transformation. Come to think of it, Madrenga thought with a start, where was Bit? His dog had been at his side all day, but now he was missing. Had the sound of the cannon firing frightened him and driven him to seek a hiding place below deck?

"There! Look there!" Quilpit had rushed to the railing and was pointing in disbelief. Madrenga gaped, then shouted.

"Bit! Bad dog! Get back here!"

In truth, Madrenga had properly described his animal. Expanding in size even as they watched, the dog was making his way toward the pirate vessel. Though Quilpit had witnessed a similar manifestation once before, it astonished him anew. That was nothing compared to the reactions of the *Thranskirr*'s crew. Their reactions were decidedly mixed. Observing Bit's sudden growth only confirmed every suspicion they'd held regarding the animal since it had come aboard. On the other hand, the increasingly frightening dog was swimming away from the *Thranskirr* and toward the attacking vessel.

As Madrenga yelled frantically in a futile attempt to persuade his pet to return, arrows and spears began to rain down on the water in the vicinity of the preternaturally fast canine swimmer. None struck him. Or perhaps some did and bounced off. Neither those around Madrenga or on the pirate craft could tell one way or the other. Then the powerful swimming shape disappeared beneath the waves. Gleeful cries rang out from the deck of the attacking ship. Stunned, Madrenga could hardly believe it. He kept watching the water where his old friend had gone under, unable to believe that after all they had been through together he would lose Bit now to the ocean they had greeted as strangers.

His eyes sharper than most, it was again Quilpit who pointed to the dog's reappearance. "There he is, boyo! There, at the stern of the other ship!"

Madrenga's heart jumped as a familiar black shape became visible. Bit had not drowned, nor had he been skewered. He had merely continued swimming underwater. His master had seen dogs do such a thing in the lakes around Harup-taw-shet, but never had he seen one stay under for so long.

He was still reflecting on the welcome surprise when Bit opened jaws that had expanded to the size of wagon seats and bit off the other ship's rudder.

Chaos ensued on the attacking craft. Steered now only by the wind, the pirate vessel slewed wildly to the south. Yards snapped and one sail came crashing to the deck. Men ran to help the helmsman, but with their rudder gone there was little they could do. Additionally, she was taking on water where Madrenga's returned cannon ball had hulled her. Out of control she swung around, heading south at an angle that would send her crashing into the *Thranskirr*. Hammaghiri saw the danger immediately.

"Hard a-port!" he howled at his helmsman. The bone wheel spun and the *Thranskirr* started to come about. Quilpit picked up his swords and with Madrenga at his side rushed to the starboard rail. The men on the main deck did not have to be told what to do. The battle would be decided in a matter of moments. With their own vessel now damaged and taking on water, the pirates would fight even more furiously to try and take their prize.

Arrows and crossbow bolts began to fly between the two ships. Heavily armed pirates massed near her port bow awaiting the moment of impact. They would come swarming over in a mass, would have to be stopped from boarding and driven back onto their own craft. The men of the *Thranskirr* crowded forward to meet them.

Both ships were very close now: the course-changing *Thranskirr* and the out-of-control pirate craft. Seeking protection behind stout planks and masts, fighters on both sides readied for the coming impact. The space between the two ships continued to shrink, closing, closing. One of the Golgox giants climbed up onto the railing of his ship, which groaned beneath his weight, and readied his massive axe. Bolandri strained to pull the *Thranskirr*'s wheel over even harder in a desperate attempt to keep the two vessels from colliding.

Everyone waited, waited—for an impact that did not come. Rudderless, the pirate vessel continued to sail where the wind drove her while the *Thranskirr* continued to turn away from her attacker. The space between them shrank further, further—and stabilized.

Grappling hooks soared from the attacker in a final desperate attempt to bind the two vessels together. Sailors on the merchant vessel frantically started hacking at the thick ropes in an attempt to free her from the unwanted lashings. To stop them, the crew of the pirate craft charged forward, intending by sheer weight of arms and numbers to overwhelm the *Thranskirr*'s forward defenders. The Golgox was first across.

Only to be sent flying back, to land halfway down the deck of his wounded ship.

Only slightly less stunned, the seamen on the *Thranskirr* gave ground to the heavy horse that had come up among them. Orania was showing the enemy her hindquarters, but not in defeat. Every time one of the attackers tried to board the merchant vessel he was met by a pair of flying hooves that sent him airborne. Harund, Golgox, human—Orania did not discriminate. Bodies fell on the deck of the attacking ship, were caught in its high rigging, were smashed into the hull, or flew completely over the craft to land in the water beyond. While they had cheered Bit's efforts, this time the *Thranskirr*'s crew was too stunned to do more than watch.

Even more impressive than the mare's strength was the speed of her reactions. No matter how many pirates tried to cross between the two ships, she was there to meet them. Sailors recalled the blur she had become when raising the ship's anchor. That quickness was duplicated now as she darted back and forth, back and forth along the *Thranskirr*'s railing.

Working furiously, other sailors finally succeeded in cutting the ship free from the last of the grappling hook lines. Gradually the two vessels began to drift apart; the *Thranskirr* under control, her assailant running wildly before the wind. Some of the pirates tried to steer her using their fore-rigged sails, but in the absence of a rudder their efforts were largely stymied. As their courses diverged, the *Thranskirr* began to pull away.

With no enemy left to launch, Orania let out a satisfied snort, retraced her steps between lines of staring seamen, and returned to her bed near the stern. It was left to Madrenga to break the ensuing silence.

"Bit. *Where's Bit?*" Rushing to the railing he anxiously scanned the surrounding, heaving sea for any sign of his friend.

The dog appeared moments later, swimming parallel to the ship. But for all his enhanced size and strength, he could not climb the merchant vessel's fast-moving wooden flanks. Orders were given and a cargo net lowered over the starboard side. Bit did not so much climb into it as get himself thoroughly entangled.

"Haul away!" Quilpit yelled. Muscles strained as the men brought the net up and over the deck. There it was upended and its sodden canine cargo unceremoniously dumped. A relieved Madrenga rushed toward his rescued dog.

"Bit! Next time come when I call you!"

Having shrank in size from enormous to merely huge, the dog ran to meet him. Just before they embraced, he paused and shook. By the time he stopped, his master was as well and truly drenched as if he had accompanied his pet over the side. The picture presented by the drenched passenger broke the remaining tension and a fair proportion of the greatly relieved sailors broke out in good-natured laughter. Cloths were brought up from below and thrown in Madrenga's direction until he was all but buried beneath the onslaught of woven cotton.

But not every member of the crew joined in the spontaneous celebration.

CHAPTER ELEVEN

LIE TO A SHIP'S OFFICER AND HAMMAGHIRI WOULD DOCK your pay. Steal from a fellow sailor and he'd likely have you keel-hauled. Other than that, as long as a man did his job, life on the *Thranskirr* was good compared to the often miserable conditions to be found on similar merchant vessels. That did not mean it was considered an easy ship: Hammaghiri worked his men too hard for it to be so designated. But it was a relatively free ship. After completing his assigned tasks, what a man did on his free time was his own business, so long as it did not interfere with ongoing operations.

Therefore no one thought it unusual or worthy of comment or notice when half a dozen members of the crew assembled on the foredeck on an evening that was clear, moonlit, and warm. It was a beautiful place to be on a calm night, listening to the melodious percussion of the bow crashing through the nephrite-green water as the moon silvered the crest of each successive swell and drifting durugonds burped drum-like mating calls across the surface.

Their joviality was false and their relaxation a pretext, however. They had assembled not to drink in the delights of an amenable night but to listen to old Korufh. About himself he had gathered those he deemed most sympathetic to his views. They were attentive. Glancing skyward, the second mate saw that the mainmast sentry was at ease in his basket-like lookout. There was no one else in view. In any event, this far forward the sound of the bow's wave-cutting would keep cautious voices from being carried to other parts of the ship. Counting his audience at the ready, he began without preamble.

"They're demons. I suspected so from the first. That dog—unnatural a sight to any man's eyes, even without Quilpit's telling of the tale that took place at the arena in Charrush. The horse: far too alert to human speech. As for their master, one moment he play-acts the perfect fool of an adolescent, the next he fights like a mystic warrior out of legend. No, the proof of it lies in their very appearance. Not to mention in their actions."

His audience was amenable, yes—but some still remained to be fully convinced.

"What proof have we that they represent a danger?" asked one of the attentive seamen. "Did they not save us from the sea brigands?"

Having anticipated the most obvious of objections, Korufh was ready with a response. "They were in danger as much as any of the rest of us. Who is to say but that they acted to save themselves, and that our consequent salvation was but coincidental?"

Murmuring among the assembled showed that this argument held weight, as Korufh had suspected it would. He was quick to follow up on the advantage.

"If this seeming youth is a good sorcerer honest and true, and not putting forth some kind of innocent act for our benefit, why would he not declare himself such when he first came aboard? Why a need to disguise himself and his abilities if not in the service of some devious plan? Only the piratical attack compelled him to reveal his skills. Otherwise we would know nothing of them or of him save one story told by the first mate, to which no one else on this ship was witness."

"Just so," muttered another of the group. "Honest men are

open and up-front about their true intentions. Those who hide them are usually up to no good."

"Then," Korufh continued, "there is this business of us abruptly changing course near the beginning of a voyage." He lowered his voice further. "The Captain is a strong man, but even a strong man can be taken in by the intrigues of a wizard. I would not put it past this Madrenga to have bewitched him."

"I was told the amount the young stranger paid to secure his passage," a third sailor said. "He can bewitch me thus anytime!"

There was laughter, which was not the response the second mate sought. He hurried to counter it.

"I will not dispute that it was money that paid for transport. But the coin had been handed over *before* the Captain ordered the change of course that sends us across the Sea of Shadows. You all know him. Would he have done such a thing had he not been placed under some kind of disorienting spell? What one fears in chancing such a crossing is exactly what has happened already. The sorcerer sends us into danger, then tries to gain our gratitude by countering it." He sat back. "I do not believe for a moment that he was in any personal danger. You saw how he dealt with the enemy's cannon. By such measures and demonstrations he attempts to gain our trust, perhaps also our admiration. Are such efforts expended for nothing? He has something in mind for us, this demon Madrenga. I, for one, do not look forward to what it might be, and would strive mightily to avoid it."

The youngest of the group gave voice to his own feelings. "That's what sorcerers and witches do, they do. Bind you to them through gratitude, or spell, or obligation, and then use you up like an old deck rag. Cast you aside alive or dead when they've done with you."

"Is that a chance we want to take?" Korufh gave the assembled time for the thought to sink in. "Do we take control of our own destiny, or do we let this necromancer of a landsman determine it for us?"

"Hush," whispered one of the men tersely. "The night watch comes."

Conversation shifted to the main topics of interest among seamen; namely, the weather and women. It changed back only when the bored but alert night watchman completed his circuit of the foredeck and resumed his repetitive march sternward.

The discussion lasted well on into the night, until Korufh decided to call an end to it. Off-duty crew enjoying the night air was normal. Extending such relaxation into the wee hours of morning at the expense of necessary sleep might occasion comment. Korufh was not yet ready to act. At this point in his plans, scrutiny was a streetwalker seriously to be avoided.

While the *Thranskirr*'s cook had one full-time galley assistant, the remaining necessary food preparation and serving help was shared by several members of the crew. The one Korufh took into his closest confidence would be responsible for carrying out the most delicate, if not necessarily the most dangerous, part of his plan. Another week passed before the second mate felt sufficient confidence in his design and in his co-conspirators to put his plan into effect.

Drugging the monster dog and the deviant horse were simple enough matters, but ultimately useless and possibly even dangerous unless their master could be similarly incapacitated. It was given to a willing Molt Reddan, an innocuous but cold-hearted seaman, to insert the premeasured dose of seproth extract into the iniquitous young man's potatoes. Korufh had chosen the dinner carefully. The slightly bitter taste of the seproth would be more than adequately masked by the thick gravy that inundated the boiled spuds.

Still, no one, least of all Korufh himself, knew whether the extract would have its desired effect. Ordinarily, the dose measured out by the second mate and surreptitiously administered by the sailor Reddan should be sufficient to knock a big man flat cold. But someone who could catch cannon balls with one hand and then throw them back at the ship from which they were fired was, if naught else, no ordinary personage. All the conspirators could do was shovel down their own nightly meal—and wait.

The second mate knew his men as well as he knew his ship. Holding off until the night watch was assigned to members of his cabal ensured that they could go about the disreputable work confident they would not be disturbed.

At the appointed hour he joined a dozen of his fellows in slipping quietly from their bunks and hammocks. So as not to arouse suspicion among the rest of the crew they exited quarters one at a time. Assembling on deck, they awaited further instructions from the second mate.

While he and a chosen group slipped quietly into the main rear cabin, the rest set about the business of preparing the passenger's mount. Animal fat was used to over-grease the block and tackle of the cargo crane to render it as silent as possible. By the time six of the men had succeeded in silently manhandling the anesthetized heavy animal onto one of the ship's large wooden cargo platforms, the others had returned hauling dog, master, and the passenger's possessions. As final preparations were being made to conclude the business some objections were raised concerning the disposition of the passenger's clothing and gear.

"There may be valuables," one sailor murmured hopefully. "Why should we not keep them?"

"Truth," concurred another. "See this finely-wrought scroll case that is fastened to his belt? I reckon it would bring a double handful of silver in the main market at Yordd."

Korufh growled softly at the hopeful thieves. "By all means, take everything. Our story is to be that this creature took his leave of us voluntarily, for reasons no ordinary man can fathom. Would he do so and leave his possessions behind? Were the Captain to discover any of them in your sea chest, what do you think his reaction would be?" The mate spat over the side. "Your miserable carcass would join this Madrenga in the water, only without a platform on which to float. No—everything that belongs to him, everything he owns, goes with him." Korufh's expression turned wolfish. "Or would you chance waking in bed to find that a ring or scroll holder or sword had taken demonic possession of *you*. Turned you into a salamander, or worse, slithered up your bunghole."

"Or shriveled your genitals," added another of the crew whose thoughts and emotions were wholly in tune with those of the second mate. "Or worse, banished them."

"I once heard tell of a demon who switched a soldier's face with his nether workings," added another sailor. Nervous laughter greeted this revelation. Every man bent to his work with redoubled effort, and no more was heard of keeping anything that belonged to the demon or his animals.

The two newly arrived bodies; one human, the other canine, were dumped unceremoniously beside the horse. Clothing, weapons, and the double pack that on land was slung over Orania's hindquarters was piled atop them. As an anxious Korufh whispered orders, men strained to manipulate the fat-silenced crane.

Emitting a barely perceptible creak, the thick loading platform rose off the deck and into the air. Under the second mate's direction it was winched over the starboard side and then lowered into the water. At a signal the metal latches at each of the platform's four corners were released. Ropes were withdrawn and the crane's boom swung back over the deck.

Korufh joined several of his fellow conspirators in rushing to the railing. With a steady breeze behind her, the *Thranskirr* was making excellent progress to the northeast. The current, on the other hand, was flowing in the opposite direction. Within moments, the platform drifting on the swells was almost out of sight. By morning ... Korufh allowed himself a tight-lipped smile of satisfaction. By morning it and its insensible passengers would be one with the vast open expanse of the Shadows. That is, if by then they had not already slid off the slick platform and drowned: something he dared not risk in the immediate vicinity of the ship itself lest the cold water revive the trio prematurely. As for the cargo platform, there were more than a dozen such on the *Thranskirr*. No one, including a captain busy with other matters, would think to look for a missing piece of wood until the business of the missing passengers had receded into memory.

He felt no remorse. Better for men to have no truck with demons than to rely on the whims of supernatural beings to remain friendly. Such creatures might save a ship from attack one day only to consign it to an even worse fate the next. The second mate had confidence in his own skills, in the crew, and in the seamanship of Captain Hammaghiri. But even the best man, when presented with coin piled high, can see his judgment impaired. Korufh felt he had done nothing more than polish the Captain's glasses so that he could see things clearly. As he would, the mate was confident, on the morrow when the sun shone down on a ship that had been cleansed of unnatural presences.

One by one the conspirators retired to their sleeping quarters. Korufh had a last word with the two men of the night watch to rehearse one final time the sentences they should speak if they should be questioned on the night's happenings. Then, content in conscience and secure in spirit, he too allowed himself the pleasure of returning to bed.

Neither member of the evening watch glanced in Korufh's direction as they exited the Captain's cabin. This was according to plan. Not that such eye contact would have imperiled any of them, but the perceptive Quilpit might have taken notice. So the crewmen ignored the mates as the two senior members of the ship's staff waited their turn to be interviewed.

Korufh was pleased that there was more puzzlement than

anger in Hammaghiri's voice when he ordered them to enter. The Captain was seated in the usual place aft of his desk, charts and navigation tools and items of a personal nature illuminated by the morning sun that poured in through the rank of windows behind. He was clearly troubled, but not panicked. A good sign, Korufh felt. Interlacing his fingers and holding them up before his chin, the older man regarded his officers.

"You were both at breakfast. You know that when our passenger—our *guest*—the young Mr. Madrenga, did not appear, it was assumed that he was sleeping in. You know that subsequently I sent a man to check on him, only to be told that he was not to be found in his cabin. You know that I then ordered a search of the entire ship, only to find that there was no sign of him or of his animals. Even more strange, all of his possessions appear to have vanished with him."

"It certainly is strange," Korufh agreed helpfully.

Hammaghiri was visibly conflicted. "What sort of man commits suicide by taking his possessions with him? He was anxious to fulfill a mission that had been entrusted to him. Why would he abandon it, and life itself, when he was set determinedly and successfully on such a course?"

"It makes no sense to me, sir." Quilpit was distraught. "It's true I didn't know the young man well, but I thought I knew him well enough." He shook his head dolefully. "It's plain I did not."

To Korufh the moment seemed right. "Perhaps he was not a man. Perhaps he was not even young. Both aspects may be utilized by other beings as easily as a man changes his shirt."

Hammaghiri and Quilpit were staring hard at him now. This did not bother the second mate. He had expected such a reaction and had prepared for it.

"Consider, my friends. This young fellow arrives seeking passage not around the Sea of Shadows but straight across it. His dog swallows fighting animals whole and bites rudders off ships. His horse, if that is what it is, runs 'round a ship's capstan fast enough to set it ablaze and fends off an entire boarding party all

by itself. And their master—their master affects a youthful innocence that belies hidden motives and abilities. Such as playing
catch with a cannonball as if it was a child's toy. Who can
imagine the reasonings of such a creature?" He straightened.
"While I hope he has come to no harm I, for one, am not
entirely displeased to believe that he has for reasons of his own
decided to take leave of the *Thranskirr* and proceed onward
toward his goal in a fashion and by means of which no normal
man can imagine. In that I wish him good speed and a fair wind.
Having seen what we have seen of him, I believe no honest sailor
can do more."

A troubled Quilpit was wrestling with his thoughts. "It *would*
explain why all of his possessions and all of his gear have gone
missing with him. But how could he travel across the water laden
with such possessions? Not to mention the armor all three of them
wore."

Korufh shrugged. "Perhaps he can swim as well as his dog. Or
his horse. Remember how back in Charrush the tail and mane of
the latter seemed to propel it through the water from quay to ship
as if they had become fins. Or maybe if sorcerally called upon, his
animals can grow wings." His voice fell conspiratorially. "Or even
he himself."

"If that were the case," Hammaghiri interjected, "then he
would not have needed to book passage on a ship like the *Thranskirr* in the first place." He was staring evenly at Korufh, as if the
second mate might know something he was not saying. But
Korufh had been around too long and seen too much to be rattled
by a hard gaze, even one as penetrating and forceful as that
mustered by the venerable Captain.

"I wouldn't know, sir. I know the minds of men, but not those
of wizards and warlocks. Ignorant as I am of their reasons and
motivations, I cannot begin to give an explanation for what to we
mere mortals appears incomprehensible. Possibly he simply grew
impatient with our progress and decided, by methods unguessable,
to proceed ahead on his own."

It was quiet in the cabin for a long moment before Quilpit broke the silence.

"We have to go back."

"What?" In their simultaneous exclamation of surprise and disbelief, Hammaghiri and Korufh were in agreement.

"We have to look for him. I don't know what happened to him. No one can know that, unless he can be asked. I don't know why he chose to disappear together with all his worldly goods without venturing so much as a by-your-leave to me, or to either of you, or to anyone aboard ship. I do know that if he suffered some sort of accident, or mental derangement, or believed himself misplaced in time or space, that he may even now be floating in the current behind us, treading water while scanning the eastern horizon and hoping for the reappearance of the ship he abandoned."

Korufh wanted to argue against the first mate's suggestion but knew he dare not protest too vehemently. Thus far suspicion had avoided casting its noisome eye on him, and he devoutly wished it to continue so. He was therefore much relieved when instead of asking for his opinion, Hammaghiri himself responded.

"One must be realistic, Quilpit. I myself developed a fondness for the young man. It existed before he saved our ship and ourselves from brigandage, and only grew thereafter. But the sea is vast and unpredictable. Were we to come about, we would have the current beneath our keel but the wind would be in our faces. It freshens, and gives promise of continuing to do so. We would risk having to sail all the way back across the Shadows, with all the dangers that presents, while missing our delivery dates on the eastern shore. Our contracts would be voided and the ship's reputation irreparably besmirched. All in the hope of finding in the great expanse of the sea a man, a dog, and a horse—who may even as we speak be traveling by means safe and sorceral to the same protected harbor we seek." Unlocking his fingers, he pressed his open palms down on his desk and rose.

"While I feel a deep concern for our missing passenger, my

first responsibility is to this ship, to the men who serve on her, and to her owners. We will offer to the sea gods our prayers for the continued good health of our honorable young friend, his horse, and his ugly dog, in the hope that by whatever means at their disposal they may arrive safely at their intended destination. I hope, thusly, no less for them than for ourselves."

"So we will sail on?" Discouraged but realistic, Quilpit had as much as conceded to the Captain's logic.

Hammaghiri nodded somberly. "If the gods wish it, it may be that we may meet up with our young passenger again. Who knows? Perhaps we might encounter him in the markets or streets of Yordd."

Knowing the truth of the situation, this was not a likelihood that concerned a now completely at ease Korufh. But he felt bound to embrace it, if only to show that he was unafraid of the possibility.

"What would you do if we did, sir?"

The Captain looked surprised. "Why, I would inquire as to his means of travel without us, of course—and offer him a prorated refund of that portion of the journey he chose to conclude in lieu of our assistance.

"Gentlemen, you are dismissed. Return to your duties, as I shall to mine."

Though cold and wet go together as naturally as coffee and chocolate, they constitute a much less pleasing combination. From a sound sleep Madrenga awoke to a decidedly discomfiting evening. Snugged tight against him, Bit was snuffling and kicking in his sleep. Across the platform, Orania was kicking her legs as she sought to stand.

Platform?

He sat up quickly. His possessions, including his knife become sword and all of his clothing, lay in a heap at his feet. Orania's saddle and tack were present, too, and Bit's spiked collar. Like the rest of him, all were soaked with salt water.

Of the *Thranskirr* there was no sign.

Rising, he was thankful that the wood they were standing on was at least strong and stable enough to support all of them. It rocked but did not tip over even when Orania gained her footing. Of course such stability might be due, he knew, to the fact that the wooden platform was slowly becoming saturated, in which case they could look forward to the inevitability of their present refuge sinking beneath their feet.

Turning a slow circle, he scanned every horizon. There was no sign of sails or mast, much less an entire ship. He did not shout for help because there was no one to shout at. How had this happened to him? An evening meal had been shared, in good company. Then he had retired, with Bit curling himself beside the bunk, and both had fallen into a deep sleep. A very deep sleep, he told himself.

Perhaps his dinner company had not been such good company as he thought.

But why would anyone on board do this to him? Hurriedly he checked his pile of possessions for one particular item, only to heave a sigh of relief when he found the scroll container where he had left it last, fastened to his belt. Even his half full purse was there, with its heavy coin and sprites' memento. Not robbery, then. But what? Try as he might, he could not conceive of a motive, could not think of why anyone he had met on the *Thranskirr* would wish such a fate on a traveler cast in their care.

It didn't matter now. Reconnoitering his gear brought the welcome discovery that a set of clothing within one of Orania's backpacks had remained untouched. Stripping off his wet shorts, he let the fading sun dry his bare flesh before he donned fresh attire. While he might not need the covering for warmth, he knew it was important to keep himself protected from the naked sun lest his skin broil and peel. Such sores were to be avoided as long as was possible. Also, he felt better with the precious scroll container and the belt to which it was fastened once more securely buckled around his waist.

As night fell and the only illumination came from the moon and the stars he reflected more fully on his desperate situation. Gazing down at his companions he found himself envying them their ability to sleep regardless of the circumstances. Never before had he regarded sentience as a curse: he did so now. How much easier it would be, how much simpler all of life, if one had only to react to matters of the moment. Forethought brought with it worry, contemplation fear, while the offspring of analysis was confusion.

Lying down against Orania's side kept most of him out of the water that sloshed over the wooden platform. A single strong swell, a sufficient gust of wind, would tumble all three of them into the water. Then his mission would be well and truly come to an end, along with his own life. Whatever mysterious enchantment had empowered and saved him up to now could not turn him into a fish. For all the size and strength he had acquired since leaving Harup-taw-shet, if dumped into the open ocean he would drown as miserably as a chick in a cow bucket.

What a sad, strange way for a lifelong landsman to die, he thought. Especially for one who had not lived much of a life at all, and with a royal assignment wasted to boot. Reaching down, he felt once again at his waist. Knowing the scroll was still there, safe in its tightly sealed cylindrical container, provided reassurance all out of proportion to its unknown contents.

I've failed, he told himself remorsefully. Failed Chief Counselor Natoum, who had shown confidence in him. Failed the Queen, who had done likewise. Failed himself and his trusting companions.

He started to cry. While Orania slept on, the noise awakened Bit. Yawning, the dog stared at his master for a moment. Then he crawled over, advancing through the water on his belly and all fours, to lay his head against his master's legs. Strange, Madrenga mused, how the simple act of petting a dog can mute the most monstrous of fears. He fell asleep like that; lying on his horse, his hand resting on his dog's head, with a dense fog closing in around them. The thickening mist shut out the rest of the world like a benign acid bent on dissolving reality.

He awoke to the mournful aria of Bit's howling and sat up. With Orania stirring beneath him he had no choice but to move anyway. The world was still swathed in mist. So deep and thick it was that he was unable to tell if it was night or day. He could see only a short distance in any direction. It was as if gauze had been draped over his face. Of one thing there was no doubt: they were still drifting at sea. Ominously, the water that pulsed as if from a great heartbeat was now deeper where it swept across the platform. The process by which the wood was becoming more and more waterlogged was increasing. The platform, like the rest of his life, was steadily sinking away.

Nothing penetrated the fog save Bit's despondent howling. How far the sound carried Madrenga could not estimate. He had no more reference points for sound than he did for sight. But the yowling was heard, and drew listeners. Or mayhap it was merely coincidence.

After all, the vast expanse of water was not called the Sea of Shadows for no reason.

Though it showed no sail, the ship that parted the veil of damp vapor came toward him nonetheless. Her naked hull and masts were the same shade of gray as the air itself, as if they were formed of big chunks of fog that had been shaped and turned and sawed on mystical lathes. Here and there a touch of dark green could be seen: signals and signposts suggesting that the angular vessel was as much a part of the sea as a traveler upon it. As he sat regarding the ghostly apparition Madrenga could hardly move. It would not have mattered if his muscles *had* been able to respond. He had nowhere to go anyway.

Shapes appeared near the bow. So bright was the anatomical whiteness of their bones that their skeletons were visible through their ragged attire. Here were the shades and shadows of men and women who had been lost at sea. While most journeyed onward to whatever land the dead inhabited, these ship-lost souls found themselves still traveling, for whatever reason, on a vessel with no course and no destination. No safe, warm, welcoming harbor awaited them as they sailed interminably on a heading toward a distant Hell.

Regaining his presence of mind, Madrenga considered sliding off the platform and ordering Orania and Bit to come with him. It was their trusting expressions and attitudes as much as his own indecision that prevented him from doing so. While he continued to debate, the shadow ship slid alongside. Nets deployed like spider silk. He was saved the trouble of trying to make up his mind.

Lifted onto a murky deck into which his feet sank up to the ankles, he rose without trembling. It was not confidence or self-possession that saw him stand so, but rather the fact that his body had done so much shivering during the chill damp night that it could shake no more. Orania shook her head, sending water flying toward and through several of the attentive watchers. Ever affable, Bit padded over to the nearest shadow and tried to lick its hand. Though his tongue passed through the miasmatic digits, the tall shade of a long dead seaman drew his skeletal hand back with a moan of disgust.

"A long while it has been since one of the animate has come among us." The shadow woman who spoke had hair that fell to her waist and was still tinged with blond, though half her face was missing.

"This one burns with life." Reaching out, a fat gloominess put a hand on Madrenga's arm. He felt only a slight tickling sensation as the sausage-like fingers passed through him. A clammy tingle, as if the blood in his limb had ever so briefly been replaced with sea water.

Like milk with tea, curiosity began to blend with fear. "Who are you?" he asked. He thought he knew the answer, but the question was all he could think of to say anyway, and some sort of response seemed to be wanting.

"Sailors overboard." The Harund who spoke was a ghost of a beard mounted on a pair of stick-legs. "Passengers storm-tossed. Sea-soldiers slain in battle. Brigands who did not live long enough to collect. We are flesh made flotsam, condemned by chance or curse to sail this sea until a time unknown and unappointed. In all that time we have no company save our own—and that of the occasional guests or guest we may chance upon."

"Am I your guest, then?" Madrenga spoke boldly. There was no point in begging or pleading, he knew. For one thing, he had no boat upon which to be set free. For another, there is no charity among the dead.

His query stimulated some conversation among the shadows. Their words, like their discorporeal selves, were difficult to discern. From what he could make out, opinion seemed divided between enjoining him to stay for story-time, throwing him back overboard, or stretching his limbs between the masts until the sway and twist of the sea and sky tore him apart. All these words were whispered, the various vocalizations as faint as the throats from which they sprang.

"It is the Mark of the Moon's Month," one shade said from deep within half-collapsed shadow armor. "For a day and a night, revelry reigns on the water. See first how he dances and sings, and then we will decide."

"Yes! ... Truth! ... Let it be so!" A chorus of ghostly attitude stirred the damp air on a deck of gray splinters held together by heartache.

Madrenga swallowed. He had no reason to think that whatever enchantment had rendered him progressively bigger and stronger had done anything to improve his voice. As for dancing, he had seen more graceful puppets performing in a booth. But he would give it his all. He would have to.

And then what? Become a passenger on this ship of post-death? Destined to sail to and fro across a great sea until he, too, perished from want of food, or water, or human companionship? Looking down at the worshipful Bit, he tried to view his peculiar circumstances through the eyes of a dog. One day at a time, Bit would tell him if he had the power of speech. Life is to be taken one day, one moment, one bone at a time. Could he, Madrenga wondered, do less?

So he smiled at the circle of shadows that now surrounded him and lied most efficaciously. "I'm happy to participate in your celebration, though this is the first I have ever heard of the Mark of the Moon's Month."

While no louder than the barking of frogs, the sounds that rose from the assembled shades were unmistakably expressions of delight. He was careful to conceal his own lack of enthusiasm. After the celebration, of which he truthfully knew nothing, then what?

One bone at a time, he reminded himself. Surrounded as he was by a multitude of bones, or at the very least the specter of them, he could hardly forget.

Where once had been day, now there was night. Madrenga knew this, not because the fog had lifted or the sun had shown through, but because it was told to him, and he had no reason to doubt it. Certainly it had grown darker on the deck of shadows. Just when he was concerned that vision was to be denied him for the duration of the celebration, the looming darkness was split by the lighting of first one, two, a dozen torches. They blazed high, the flames glittering off dew-laden masts and spars, deck and cabins. Fashioned no less of shadow-stuff than was the rest of his surroundings, he was left to wonder how fire could spurt from fog.

He was still wondering when the Mark of the Moon's Month celebration was to begin when he found himself in the midst of it.

They came pouring out of shattered ports and rotting hatchways, fell like phantom flowers from the branches of yardarms, waltzed onto the main deck from the main stern cabin. Each was dressed in his or her finery, though given a steady degradation of spirit that sometimes stretched back for millennia it was sometimes difficult to tell male from female. More recent shadows were better intact. Some retained sufficient aspect of flesh to almost be appealing.

He was grateful that the one who approached him first was definable of gender. Breasts that had not yet begun to degrade bulged from the lip of a low-cut gown the color of blood-infused sputum, and her black eyes were not so far sunk into her skull that he had to strain to see them. She paused before him; contemplating, assessing, deciding. Finally she extended both arms. Her fingers were long and so supple as to be almost cephalopodan.

The music started. It arose not from a band or an orchestra but from the depths of the shadow ship itself. The entire hull expanded and contracted like a bellows, generating a sound akin to a full pipe organ. Echoes of ghostly woodwinds piped from groaning spars while the ragged rigging strummed and plucked. Last to make itself heard was the percussion caused by the slap of the sea against the hull itself. He was not listening to music, he realized as his deathly consort began to spin him around the deck: he was inside it.

He could feel his own bones vibrating in time to the music and his organs pumping in identifying rhythm with the hull. Where there ought to be dread was joy. Faster and faster the ship played itself while everywhere on board the shadows of those stuck in a seaward limbo pirouetted and spun about one another.

Rising from the deep, a brace of whales joined in, their sonorous singing causing the last unaffected bits of the spectral vessel to quiver with delight. Squid of monstrous size and bejeweled flesh rose to flank the vessel to starboard and port, refulgent patterns of colored light racing in perfect tandem along their cylindrical flanks while eyes the size of dinner plates glowed like irised suns. Sonophores sparkled everywhere and comb jellies paraded rainbows within the mist. From the deep dark depths rose all manner of bioluminescent monstrosities and serpents to bathe the ship and its celebrants in an explosion of heatless, heartless light.

As the dancing grew wilder and more uncontrolled, Madrenga's mistress for the evening began to sing. Despite recognizing neither melody nor language he did his best to emulate her words. He could be accused, tried, and convicted of tunelessness, but not a lack of enthusiasm.

Dizziness assailed him. The enveloping fog had become a voluptuous cape, wrapping him in an embrace that was at once damp and comforting. No one and nothing within reach of the music was immune to its rhythmic blandishments. Out of the corner of an eye he saw Bit dancing with half a child. While she hopped grotesquely on one foot in perfect time to the music, the dog bounced and spun on his hind legs. Madrenga had seen him stand thus before, but only for a minute or two before being compelled to drop again down onto all fours. As it was with his master, the evening was summoning forth unexpected talents.

From Orania, too. She did not rear up on her hind legs and presume to waltz. On all fours she pranced partnerless in the center of the deck and dashed around the fore and main masts, teased by giggling sights and tempted by promises of the sharing of shadow food. In truth, Madrenga thought she looked a little drunk. As he no doubt did, letting himself be spun about by a feminine apparition formed of fog and mystic miasma.

Then a most wondrous thing happened.

The fog broke. For an instant, or maybe two. A full moon shown unimpeded down on the deck. The music and dancing stopped as all aboard halted whatever they were doing and tilted back their heads to look upward. Conversation ceased abruptly, as did all singing.

For that brief, argent interlude the ship of shadows was whole again. Sturdy and gleaming with fresh paint, she slipped over the swells as cleanly as any fast cutter. It was no less with her passengers and crew. Men and women, Harund and even one or two Selndar, stood on her deck dressed in the finery of many lands. Gilt armor gleamed on stalwart soldiers while jewels of every cut and description adorned the flesh of women whose skin shaded from pure white to obsidian black. None of the men were less than handsome, none of the women wanting in beauty. The revealed moon having drawn his gaze as powerfully as the others, Madrenga now lowered it. Had he found the wind, he would have gasped.

The woman standing opposite looked but a few years older than himself. Such beauty he had never before beheld: not in paintings idealized, not in sculpture venerated, and most certainly not in the flesh. Her eyes were jewels of the night, her body a mathematician's wet dream, her lips formed from the juice of the ripest pomegranates.

"Only at this time," she told him in a voice of vanilla and honey, "do we become briefly again what we once were." She gestured skyward with fingers that unfolded like the petals of an orchid. "At the Mark of the Moon's Month." Her sadness was epic. "We who loved the light now have none."

It was not within him to ask by what curse she and her companions had been condemned to the shadows. He had neither the experience nor the knowledge to understand anyway. He could only be sad with her, could only draw her close and feel the delicious curves of a body that was momentarily once again radiant with life.

Then the fog closed back in. The moon disappeared, banished somewhere above, and once more all was mist and gloom. The dancing slowed, the music went away like a scream in the night, and he found himself again surrounded by the decaying shades of the dead. With the light and the moment of the moon went all joy, all pleasure, all compassion.

"He cannot sing," a raggedness of a sailor croaked, "and he dances only when a woman leads. Kill him."

"And his animals, too," hissed a shape who a moment earlier

had been an image of beauty and font of desire. "Feed them to the fishes and the water serpents."

Stunned, Madrenga turned to the enthralling vision who had been his companion for the celebration. But she was gone. Standing in her place was a hellspawn harridan with barnacles where her ears should have been and hollow eye sockets crawling with eels. The cackle that came from where lips had once promised chilled his blood.

"Save me the finest piece, for I would try to taste what I cannot kiss."

Orania held her ground as the crowd closed in. Drawing his sword, Madrenga backed up against her. He was under no illusion concerning his weapon's effectiveness against the spectral horde, but he felt bound to try and defend himself. Standing at his feet, Bit charged forward and snapped powerful jaws. They came away with a leg, whose owner simply laughed at the osteal excision. A moment later the dog was spitting out water.

A thunderous bellow halted the advance of the whispery circle.

"What's all this? Why was I not awakened for the celebration? By Balatho's lightning, I'll wrap the lot of you around the main-mast and knot you there for eternity! I, Admiral Baros Soen Dailanceon, swear this!"

Shadows parted to make way for a shade twice the height of any other present. It was the echo of a Golgox giant, clad in the tattered uniform of a senior naval officer. Torn epaulettes hung from shoulders better suited to the body of a bear. Earlobes that had once been stretched by weights hung low while eyes were shaded by a shelf of solid bone from which thick hairs thrust and curled.

A nervous tittering arose from the assembled. One shade, serving as supplicant on behalf of his fellows, took a daring step forward and pointed at the grim-faced Madrenga. Beside him, Bit whimpered and Orania whinnied nervously.

The figure continued to advance until it was looming over the castaway. It would have blocked out the moon, had the moon stayed to observe. Huge glowing eyes glared down at the youth as a hand big enough to fit completely around Madrenga's waist reached for him. He started to raise his sword. Young man and primeval shade locked eyes. The ancient admiral snarled like a mad thing.

Then his glowing eyes blinked. He halted, drew back his reaching hand, and fell backward, throwing up his arms to shield his face.

"Fools of the dead! Can none of you see what you so blindly have brought aboard? Are you as devoid of perception as you are of life? Unclean, unclean! Tainted even to the deceased!" By now he was back on his massive feet and scrambling in the direction of the stern cabin from whence he had emerged.

"Cast it off! Give it and its creatures a boat lest by trying to drown it you only make it enraged. Even a shadow may feel pain from something capable of inflicting it. Send it away before it thinks through all things and realizes itself!"

Bewildered by the reaction of their fearsome commander, the shadows of the ship hastened to comply. A small boat was lowered into the water. Though itself composed of nothing but fog, it floated as buoyantly on the swells as did the larger vessel. Full of questions but not daring to say anything that might delay or inhibit his departure, Madrenga allowed himself and his companions to be placed in the small boat by the same means that had brought them aboard. His possessions were thrown over the side and he had to strain to catch them before they landed in the water. Standing in the front of the boat, his feet poised on the bow, Bit was barking furiously as the shadows on board.

"Make haste, make sail!" Even in his confusion Madrenga recognized the deep voice of the Admiral. "Away from this contamination and out to the safety of the middlemass!"

No less confused by the unexpected turn of events than the shadow ship's compliment, Madrenga sat on the hard watery bench at the center of the boat and watched until the ship faded from view. Or faded into it—he could not be certain if it had sailed away or simply become one with the mist that surrounded it. Something had frightened the Admiral. Something menacing enough to scare even the dead. *Him.* The Admiral of ancient specters had been frightened of *him.* Madrenga brooded on this. But not for long.

Because the more he pondered what had just happened, the more he began to frighten himself.

CHAPTER TWELVE

THOUGH THE SHIP OF SHADOWS VANISHED INTO THE SAME mist that had given it birth, the fog itself hung around like an old acquaintance with a big smile and an empty purse. Composed of scarcely sterner stuff, the small gray boat that was all that lay between Madrenga, his companions, and the ocean beneath somehow held its shape.

In the bottom of the craft he found a mast made of mist and a silvery sail so feathery light it seemed that the mere act of raising it would cause it to be torn to bits by the slightest of breezes. With low expectations but determined to strike back against inertia, he raised the mast and set the sail. To his surprise it filled with the same east-blowing wind that had propelled the *Thranskirr*. Scudding along more swiftly than he had any right to expect, he was soon dashing forward in the wake of the ship that had deserted him. He had no illusions about overtaking the much larger and more substantial vessel. Staying afloat would be satisfaction enough.

How long he sailed thus he did not know. Lost within the persistent fog and in the absence of clearly defined day or night he could judge neither time nor speed. Though his muscles and joints grew stiff from inactivity, no such hardship afflicted his companions. Threatening many times to upset the little boat, Orania would scramble over the side and into the sea whenever Madrenga deemed it calm enough to be safe to do so. As he watched her swim lazy circles around their insubstantial refuge, he found himself envying her the opportunity to exercise. He dared not join her lest the untended boat, even with its sail furled, drift out of reach. As she swam, she munched on drifting seaweed and other aquatic plant life. Whether it was to her taste or not he could not tell, but the dark green water plants sustained her.

Fishing gear would have been welcomed. In its absence he had to rely on Bit, whose proficiency at snatching passing fish proved something of a revelation. With no fire to cook with and no means of starting one, he joined his dog in eating the canine's catch raw. When he is grown sufficiently hungry, a man will do away with fire, condiments, even salt, and revert to consumption of the most basal nature.

Cold and damp, he ought to have welcomed the sun on the morning when it finally began to burn through the seemingly never-ending fog. He did not because in addition to dissolving the mist that had surrounded him for an unknown number of days, it also commenced the slow but steady evaporation of his boat. Frantically he prepared for the moment when it should give way completely beneath him; stowing smaller bits of gear as tightly as he could within his clothing, securing the double pack across Orania's lower back, then strapping on her saddle and the rest of her tack.

He was preparing to bring down the mast and sail in the hope they would lend another few moments of stability to his improbable craft when a silhouette appeared out of the mist and directly ahead. At first he thought it must surely be a mirage. He had heard of such things but never seen one. The more the mist around him lifted, the more substantial seemed the vision forward. From what he could remember, mirages tended to ripple and flow from the heat that produced them. This one did not. He hardly dared believe.

It was an island.

Settling himself at the increasingly soggy tiller, he steered straight for the apparition. Even if it turned out to be a mirage it was the only destination in sight. Soon he was near enough to see trees: coconut and morefruit, screwbark and laplate. The composition of the dense green and lavender understory was less familiar to him, but an equally welcome sight.

As it started to come apart beneath him the boat began to ripple like a fading dream. Straining to see as far ahead as possible he detected no hint of breaking waves. According to one more piece of knowledge he had picked up by listening to sailors' conversations while on the *Thranskirr*, that suggested the absence of a murderous reef, or at least one that was situated too deep to present a threat to a struggling small boat. Rising rapidly in the sky now, the sun blazed down on him and his barely intact craft. Though he had not seen the sun in many days he did not welcome it now.

Orania's greater weight sent her plunging through the disintegrating bottom of the boat first. She sank swiftly—and stopped. Lowering her head and neighing excitedly at the prospect of something green yet dry to eat, she trotted right through the dissolving bow and onto the shore. A moment later the boat, now a shadow of a shade, ran the rest of the way up onto the beach. There it collapsed, leaving Madrenga sitting on the sand and a barking Bit running off to join the mare in exploring the fringing jungle. Too relieved at having made it safely ashore to let out even the mildest of triumphal shouts, Madrenga clasped his arms around his knees and watched his companions. Orania was already nibbling at something like purple spice cane while Bit ran back and forth along the line of vegetation barking at everything in sight.

When finally he rose and brushed the grit off his backside, a downward glance showed a damp but fading outline in the sand where the boat had landed. It was the final indication that there had ever been a boat, much less one formed from fog. The last remnant evaporated even as he stared at it. Then he was pushing his aching leg muscles to carry him up the beach and toward the line of vegetation, calling to his companions as he went.

The jungle in which he found himself was utterly different from anything he had experienced in his short life. Here heat and humidity worked a kind of green and purple magic that was new to him. Save for the trees he had recognized from his boat, the remaining growths were pulpy of bole and soft of branch. Having subsisted on raw fish for days on end he was sorely tempted to try some of the vast variety of fruits he saw hanging around him. He resisted the temptation. In food as in life, surface beauty often concealed internal poison.

He saw no animals, but the land was full of birds and the smallest dragonets he had ever imagined. When they competed for some of the same fruit the brightly colored dragonets invariably won, as the beaks and claws of even the largest birds could not compete with the pipe-sized puffs of flame emitted by the bat-winged reptiles. Listening to them fuss and fume as he walked beneath overhanging palm leaves and branches reminded him of the workplace sounds in the metalworkers' quarter of Harup-taw-shet's main marketplace.

Some of the smaller trees twisted about one another to form intricate puzzle shapes. A quintet of metallic green and black spiders the size of his palm had constructed a huge communal web in the shape of a star. Giving it plenty of space, he saw that the weavers had caught a spitting salamander in their trap. Each time a spider approached, the snared salamander spat corrosive poison in their direction. The poison was dissolving the web around the reptile, but slowly. Having already spent too much time in Death's company it was not a drama Madrenga paused to see played out. He kept moving deeper into the tangle of weird and wonderful vegetation that pressed ever closer around him.

So obscured by branches and leaves was his vision that he nearly tripped over the Felf.

Standing no taller than the young man's knee, the creature was fully grown. The hand-woven wide-brimmed brown hat he wore was decorated with an exquisite spray of small flowers. His bare chest was as bronzed and solid as one of the coco palms that lined the beach where Madrenga had come ashore. Loose pantaloons covered his nether regions. Being a fishing Felf he carried a trident and net, both slung over his back. His intention could be readily divined: he was on his way to fish from the shore where the enormous person had just arrived.

It was difficult to say who was the more shocked. Man and Felf stared at each other for something between a contemplative moment and a split second. Stepping forward, a panting Bit extended his tongue to greet the diminutive fisherman. Believing he was about to be not tested but tasted, the latter let out a horrified squeak, whirled, and fled into the understory.

"Wait!" Madrenga raised an arm as he cried out. "I mean you no harm! I only want to—Bit, get back here!"

Having decided through natural application of dog logic that by running in the other direction the tiny man was indicating that he wanted to play, Bit had taken off after him. Having a giant, partially armored, spike-collared black dog pursuing him did nothing to assuage the Felf's already elevated level of anxiety. With a muttered curse Madrenga swung himself up into the still damp saddle on Orania's back and urged her forward. She responded without hesitation, elated to be once again given the command to run.

His fear now doubled, the Felf put on such a burst of speed that he and his pursuers arrived on the other side of the island at nearly the same time. Halting Orania, Madrenga stared in amazement at the neat village of thatched longhouses, the double-outrigged fishing boats pulled up on the beach, the wooden racks full of drying fish, and the fleeing families of Felfs. Standing tall between buildings and shore was a carved wooden figure that was half Felf and half fish. Scaly arms upraised, it appeared to be blessing the boats and, presumably, their catch. Similar finely carved totems formed the support posts for many of the longhouses. While he was unable to attest to their skill as fisherfolk,

Madrenga could see that this community was home to some master woodcarvers.

They might be fearful of the stranger, but they were not intimidated. As he fought to control the excited Orania, the flight through the village was soon reversed. Determined men and some women began to gather on the outskirts facing the much larger intruder. Armed with tridents, spears, and nets, they spread out as they came toward him. Though no military strategist, it was what he would have done had he been in their place. Surround the interloper, restrain him and his animals with nets, take them down, and run them through. Still hoping to play, Bit awaited the advancing fighters with lolling tongue and an excess of spittle.

His master had no intention of fighting. If the Felfs would not listen to reason he would turn and disappear back into the jungle. He desperately did not want to do that. He needed food and water, he needed to rest. These past weeks had seen him unwillingly involved in enough fighting. Ignorant of their language, he hoped the trade tongue common to all who passed through the markets of Harup-taw-shet would suffice for communication.

"My name is Madrenga. I mean you no harm. I have been washed ashore on your island after having been cast adrift by those whom I thought my friends." He pleaded unashamedly. "I need real friends, not more enemies."

The advance halted. Realizing that sitting atop Orania must make him an even more threatening figure, he promptly dismounted and then knelt on the sand. He kept his sword handy, though. Experience had shown him that despite harboring the best of intentions, in the course of argument, reason and logic did not always prevail.

"You can kill me if you wish. Without your help I am lost here. I will not resist." *Two lies bracketing a truth,* he thought. If they charged, he would have no choice but to defend himself.

At which point the long days at sea spent living on raw fish and the lack of fresh water combined with his complete exhaustion to render any further discussion moot. Thinking himself well prepared, his eyelids fluttered and he fell forward unconscious, face first into the sand.

🐚

"We don't much like fullmen."

The first words he heard upon reawakening were not encouraging. Neither were they voiced in an especially hostile tone of voice. It was simply a—statement of fact. He found it hard to swallow. Tall for a Felf, the figure who had spoken turned to several others standing nearby.

"He looks like he needs water. Give him water."

Aware that he was lying prone, Madrenga reflexively reached for a container. It was not handed to him. Instead, several Felfs upended a large wooden basin over his face. Choking, gasping, he managed to swallow enough to momentarily assuage his thirst before the rest ran away down his cheeks and chin.

He was lying on his back on sand beneath a peaked thatched roof. The contents of the open-sided meeting hall had been removed to make space for him. Near his feet, a wide groove in the sand showed where he had been dragged from the place where he had collapsed. Remembrance flashed across his mind like torchlight.

He had collapsed. They could have killed him where he had fallen—though Bit and Orania might have had something to say about that. Instead of being harmed he had been brought to a place of shelter and given water. He was not bound. All positive signs.

Additional hopeful indicators greeted his eyes as he rolled to his right. Close to where he had dismounted, Orania was standing and quietly cropping the strange foliage. Laughter came from farther down, toward the beach. Raising himself up on his elbow he saw Bit splashing and chasing Felf children. An initial surge of alarm at the sight of his now immense dog cavorting with much smaller Felf offspring fell away as he observed the children's agility in the water. They swam like seals, darting in among the giant dog's legs and competing to see who could pull his tail. Both Bit and the local brood seemed to be having a delightful time.

Turning back to his left, Madrenga regarded the adult Felf arraigned before him. Besides the bearers of water, who had departed in search of a refill, there were several elders clad in finely woven shorts and embroidered vests. All wore a version of the sensible wide-brimmed hat sported by the fisherman the youth had surprised deep in the jungle. While the design was the same, each differed in color and decoration. Only the senior Felf standing close at hand wore a different kind of headdress; a tall conical fabric hat around whose crown spiraled a row of shark teeth.

"I am not a fullman," Madrenga responded. "I am from Harup-taw-shet."

The chief, if that was indeed the rank of the owner of the conical chapeau, glanced back at his council, or advisors, or whatever they were, and then back at Madrenga.

"All men who are not Felf, Gelf, or Skelf are fullmen."

Madrenga realized that the chief was referring to his physical size, not his place of origin. Though his mind was clearing, fog of kind different from that of the ship of shadows lingered. "Why don't you like fullmen?"

"They look down on us, in every way." In the manner of all elven families his face was neither lined nor worn, but his voice was. "There was a time when the family of elves was regarded with admiration, sometimes with fear, but always with honor. With the continuing development of practical things, the esteem reserved for elder beings as well as elder ways is being abandoned. Where once they sought improvement, now men seek only profit, and darknesses of all manner and kind stalk the land." Behind him, the row of advisors nodded ready concurrence.

"These days we of the Felf keep to our islands, the Gelf to their caverns, the Skelf to their mountain aeries. Men multiply and infect the land, and in response, the land infects them."

Madrenga was not sure what the chief meant by this, but it sounded like a condition devoutly to be avoided.

"When we travel across the Strait of Chanchindd to sell our fish, our mussels and clams and limpets, and the fruit and nuts we collect from the forest, even those with whom we regularly do business make jokes behind our backs. Is it any reason we trust no fullmen?" He did not exactly smile, but his expression and tone grew less harsh. "But we sensed that you were different from such as them. Even so, the decision whether to attack you or help you balanced for a moment on the point of a fishhook. In the end it was you yourself who provided the reason for not attacking."

"I did?" Madrenga was bemused. "What did I do?"

"You fell down. You abased yourself before us."

"I wish I could take credit for that, but I can't. I just passed out from exhaustion and weakness."

The chief shook his head and muttered under his breath. "Give a man an escape route and instead he runs into a wall." Raising his voice again, he continued with great certitude and volume. "You *abased* yourself. Do not linger too long on the details. It was on the basis of your self-evident helplessness that we decided to bring you here, out of the sun, and await your recovery." He gestured beyond the shelter. "Your animals have already proven their friendship."

Madrenga looked to his right again, toward the sea. "Aren't you afraid that Bit—my dog—will step on one of your children?"

Now the chief did smile. "In the sea nothing catches a young Felf by surprise. We are as at home there as on land and can do anything in the water a fish can do, except breathe."

Behind the chief an impatient elder could stand it no longer. Slamming the butt of his decorated ceremonial staff into the ground he growled the question that had been simmering within him ever since the visitor had returned to consciousness.

"The gold! Ask him straight out if he has come to steal our gold!"

"You have gold?" As soon as he said it, Madrenga realized it would have been better if he had not. But the chief seemed unconcerned.

"No. But that does not keep the occasional party of fullmen from crossing the Strait to hunt for it. When such invasions take place we pack up all our people and move deep into the forest. After the fullmen have satisfied themselves that our villages contain only fish, they leave. We repair the damage they have wrought and resume our lives." He shook his head sadly at the folly of it all. "A persistent rumor can be more damaging than a moment of truth."

"Well, I wouldn't want your gold even if you had any. I only want to complete my mission, which is to deliver this scroll," and he indicated the cylinder riding on his belt, "and return home."

Taking notice of the scroll container, the chief moved in for a closer look. His eyes widened slightly at the sight. "Corium. I had not noticed that before. Well-forged and wrought, too." His gaze rose once more to meet that of the visitor. "Maybe you don't *need* any gold, Madrenga."

"Every man needs gold," the youth replied automatically.

"Every *man*, I suppose." The chief studied the visitor. "You speak to us with respect and you do not smell of threat. You arrive here by yourself yet there is no sign of the craft that brought you to our shores. You say you wish only to conclude your journey. With these things we of Ool-lak-lan can sympathize."

The name of the island meant nothing to him, anymore than had the mention of a body of water called the Strait of Chanchindd. His knowledge of the Sea of Shadows and its surroundings was limited to what he had learned in his time on board the *Thranskirr*. The chief continued.

"You, with your great stomping feet, could have killed many of us when you arrived. By the same token, we could have killed you while you were insensible. That there has been no killing on either side is a tribute to both. What are you going to do now?"

Lying in the shade of the vacated meeting hall, with a warm breeze caressing his face and the sound of low surf lapping at his ears, Madrenga felt as if he had come to an end. But he could not come to any kind of end: not yet. Not until after he had delivered the scroll to the queen of Daria. Except that he had no idea where he was or how to get from where he was to anyplace else, far less his intended destination. He was lost and found and trapped all at once. His money was half gone and he was still, in a sense, at sea. For all he knew he might have drifted and sailed a thousand leagues off course.

Still, somehow, he had to go on. He could not retrace his steps and return to Harup-taw-shet a self-confessed failure.

Size and armor notwithstanding, inside he was still the youth who had been plucked from the streets of his home city by a royal counselor whose faith in him now seemed more than ever seriously misplaced. It was all too much. Turning his face to the sand, he did his best to muffle his sobs.

Shocked and not a little dumbfounded by the tall human's reaction, the chief conferred with his advisors. As soon as they reached a conclusion he turned back to the distraught visitor.

"As you have arrived here without the ill intent that is a component of most fullmen, and as you have shown your good feelings toward us while reserving your misery for yourself, it has been decided that you may stay. Without fear of having your throat cut in your sleep. I will not deny that there are some in the village who would prefer to see you dismembered for bait, but the council has made its decision and the discontented will abide by it. You are welcome to our island."

"But you must get your own food," declared one of the advisors loudly. "And that for your great animals as well."

"And make your own shelter," insisted another. "This is our meeting hall. It was not raised for the convenience of oversized strangers!"

Madrenga rolled onto his side. "I can take care of myself," he assured them. "I've been doing so all my life."

The chief nodded sagely. "There are many admirable qualities about you, young visitor. You could demonstrate your good faith by helping us later today."

An eager Madrenga started to sit up, remembered where he was and how low the roof, and remained on his side.

"I will gladly do anything you ask of me. Fight, fish, move rocks, cut trees. Just tell me: what can I do to help?"

"You can shoo chickens."

A pause proved that the chief was not being condescending, nor was he making a joke. He and his advisors were quite serious.

"Chickens?"

"Several escaped from their enclosure. We do not eat just fish and coconuts, young visitor. Not when a single egg can feed several Felf. But chickens are strong runners and single-minded of purpose. We ride the roosters, but these who have fled escaped before our wranglers could saddle up. With your long legs you could do much to help us herd them back to where they belong."

"Of course I'll help," he told them, salivating not only at the chance to prove his benign intentions but at the prospect of a possible omelet. "And wait until your runaway chickens get a look at Bit. You'll be picking up eggs all over the place."

CHAPTER THIRTEEN

HAVING ALWAYS ENVISIONED PARADISE AS ENCOMPASSING AN area somewhat greater in extent, the longer he remained on Ool-lak-lan, the more Madrenga found himself having to reconsider.

While he never learned the full extent of the island, he soon discovered that it was bigger than he could traverse in several days of trying, even while riding Orania. He had come ashore at the narrowest point. Coves to the north and south of the village were home to additional communities of Felfs. Gelfs dwelled in the limestone caves that riddled the island's mountains while several separate clans of Skelfs inhabited the higher peaks. From time to time they would visit their lowland cousins, leaving their saddled sea eagles perched on platforms secured to the tops of old coconut palms.

True to his word, Madrenga pitched in when and wherever he could, from helping to round up rogue chickens to pulling in the lines and nets by which the villagers made their livelihood. Skilled as sharks, they commonly caught far more than they could eat. Periodically they would convey their surplus to one of the human settlements on the other side of the Strait of Chanchindd. There, whether sold fresh or dried, their excess catch always fetched a good price.

As did the villagers, Madrenga supplemented a diet of fresh fish with the bounty of the land. Fish, fruit, nuts, wild vegetables, domesticated fowl: a man would have to be crazed or unutterably lazy to go hungry in such a place. A varying but reasonably constant sea breeze moderated the humidity. The longer he stayed, the less urgent seemed the need to deliver a foil scroll to a distant kingdom.

He became friends with several of the villagers. Eventually his presence was accepted to the point where they would let their children play with him in the lagoon, darting and dashing like elemental water sprites around his much larger form, teasing and splashing with him. The men came to count on riding Orania in front of and behind his saddle as they went to gather produce from more distant sites. Even Bit was no longer shunned, though when gazing at the dog's outlandishly toothy maw there was not a man or woman in the village who believed Madrenga when he insisted that his pet's bark was worse than his bite.

I could live here. The thought occurred to the youth on more than one occasion. The longer he remained, the more currency the notion gained.

Not every one of the Felf was as friendly as some. A few still avoided his unintentionally overbearing human frame. These individuals could be seen muttering and glancing in his direction when they thought he wasn't looking. He was prepared to be patient and overlook the occasional suspicious squint and unkind comment.

He had not broached the subject of his staying permanently with the chief or any of the senior villagers. But the island was extensive and there were numerous deserted beaches. He could establish himself separately, apart from his new friends without being truly isolated, and without intruding on anyone's territory. For a boy raised begging and stealing in the crowded, hostile streets of Harup-taw-shet the gorgeous beaches and fecund jungles of Ool-lak-lan were a tempting prospect, even in the absence of members of the opposite sex.

In regards to that, who could say what such a future might bring? Some day he might travel with the Felf as they journeyed across the Strait to sell their fish in the market of a human town, and there he might meet a comely lass of similar inclination. One willing to surrender all to live with a strange foreigner on a beautiful island populated by elven clans. Perhaps, if he was fortunate, a girl with black hair and dark eyes who …

If only the scroll didn't burn so fiercely against his body and his sense of responsibility so hot against his soul. Try as he might when contemplating his future options, he could not banish from his mind the kindly visage of Chief Counselor Natoum, who had invested much in an unknown quantity from the streets. True, that had been a tactical decision designed to ensure that the scroll reached its intended destination, but the counselor's cold calculation did nothing to mitigate the trust he had placed in Madrenga. While the youth could betray his own promises to himself, he found it far more difficult to do the same to someone else.

If only, he mused, he had not developed such a strong sense of ethics. Why couldn't he be as amoral as some of his friends? Was that what had attracted Natoum to him in the first place? If so, then the counselor was more perceptive than Madrenga had given him credit for.

Could he trade the paradise into which he had accidentally stumbled for the promise of an uncertain future? The rewards of Ool-lak-lan lay all around him, plain to see. Delivering the scroll promised only mental satisfaction, modest payment, and when he returned possible promotion to a position within the Queen's retinue. All assuming he survived to complete the mission.

On Ool-lak-lan he had found satisfaction. So long as he continued his mission, he retained his honor. Could he enjoy the former without the latter?

A lightly-clad figure appeared at his left side. With Madrenga sitting on the sloping beach and the chief of the village standing on the sand slightly above him, the leader of the local Felfs was able to regard the visitor almost eye to eye. The elder held his beautifully carved, mother-of-pearl inlaid staff of office in one hand. The top of the staff was pointed, in the event that while carrying out his duties of office he should happen to chance upon a particularly tasty fish. When he spoke, his voice was full of concern.

"Madrenga-man, your heart must be full up with unhappiness, because it overflows from your face." Reaching out, he put his free hand on the much bigger human's shoulder. "You brood like an unsuccessful hen."

"There is something that weighs heavily on my spirit, yes," the bigger but much younger man confessed.

The chief nodded knowingly. "Your task. It calls to you."

Madrenga looked surprised. "How did you know that's what it was?"

"You have shelter. You have plenty to eat and drink. You have never mentioned the name of a loved one. What else could it be but that which brought you this way?" Using the tip of the staff he pointed toward the engraved cylinder that never left its place of attachment on the visitor's belt. "You long to stay but your sense of duty pulls at you like a twice-moon tide."

Madrenga turned his gaze back out to a sea that was blue and beckoning. "I can't keep myself from thinking about it. I try, and fail."

The chief patted him on the shoulder. "I sensed you were a good man when first you came among us."

"No you didn't. You thought I'd come to steal your gold."

Shaking his head slowly, the chief made a tut-tutting sound. "Sometimes you are a difficult fullman to assist. I put it down to your youth. What is on this scroll you are charged with delivering?"

Madrenga pushed out his lower lip and shrugged. "I have no idea. It is a royal communication and not for eyes such as mine."

"And you must deliver it to …?"

"A land and city called Daria." With a bob of his head he

gestured seaward. "It lies somewhere to the east. Exactly where I am not sure."

The chief pondered this for awhile before speaking again. "When we cross the Strait of Chanchindd to sell our produce to the fullmen we are always traveling east. Sometimes southeast, sometimes more to the north, but always east. If you are bound to continue, we can take you that far. To the nearest point on the shore of the great eastern land." He was quite confident. "We can lash several of our largest boats together and atop them place a wooden platform large and strong enough to hold you and your animals."

Visibly touched, Madrenga stared at the chief. "You would do this for me?"

"You have killed no one, stolen nothing, and caught many chickens." The chief smiled. "You have also helped to catch many fish. It is small repayment, and the platform will in any case bring a good price in Yordd. We have sold cut timber there before and ..."

"Wait, wait." Madrenga's mind was whirling, his heart racing. "Did you say 'Yordd'?"

The chief nodded. "Yes. It is the nearest fullmen city of size to Ool-lak-lan and a place where we often do business."

Yordd, the younger man thought wildly. *Yordd.* What had Quilpit told him, lo these many days past in Charrush, when first Madrenga had inquired of the mate about a route to distant Daria?

"Fastest way would be to find passage to Yordd. From there would be the shortest, though not necessarily the easiest, way inland to the country you seek."

He didn't know whether to express his thanks to the chief or burst out laughing. Here he had sat, marooned and half come to grips with his accidental newfound station in life, when all the time he had been staring across the water at the very destination he had sought from the other side of the Sea of Shadows.

Yordd. The stepping-off point, the seacoast city that served as harbor gateway to Daria. How much time could he have saved had he learned of its presence weeks earlier? How much time had he wasted…?

No, he told himself firmly. No time had been wasted. He'd made friends, had regained his strength. No time can be called wasted that is used for making friends. But he could move on now. The chief's revelation had reinvigorated his determination. He would finish his mission and deliver the scroll. Then, if the fates and his own desires were so inclined, he might well choose to return to the blissful land of Ool-lak-lan rather than risk the long and dangerous journey all the way back to Harup-taw-shet. If naught else it was an option he would hold as close to him as the scroll itself.

Preparations were made in surprisingly short order. While the chief and a portion of the population would have been pleased to see the visitor remain among them, there were others who were happy to see the towering young fullman and his animals go. Construction of the platform atop the linked outriggers proceeded apace.

When it was completed Madrenga was surprised to see how little in the way of provisions were brought aboard. He could only muse and marvel. Yordd must lie even nearer than he thought. There was also a large quantity of salted and fresh fish to sell. The villagers were not about to embark on a crossing of the Strait simply to convey one visitor to the other side.

When all was in readiness, he bade farewell to the chief and to those others who had welcomed him into their community. Some he now knew by name, others only by sight. As he struggled to lead Orania onto the makeshift but sturdy craft, tears came to his eyes as the Felf women broke into an ululation of farewell. He could not understand all the words, but there was no mistaking the sentiment.

The weather being fine, sail was raised to supplement the muscles of the Felf rowers. Soon song and palms and village shrank into the distance, until at last they vanished entirely beneath the western horizon. When a patient Orania folded her legs beneath her, Madrenga sat down beside his horse. Bit curled up against his legs. Mindful of the dog's armored, spiked collar, Madrenga was careful where he placed an open palm against the animal's shoulders. As the improvised raft effortlessly bucked the gentle swells, he turned his head and his focus resolutely to the east.

Behind him, the farewell gathering was breaking up. Children returned to playing in the lagoon, the women to their work, and the men to gathering. Those responsible for the next day's fishing repaired to the greeting meeting house. It was empty now, devoid of its temporary fullman inhabitant. Bending to the sandy floor, the men soon exposed the storage lockers concealed beneath. Even those with whom the visitor had made friends had to admit there was benefit to be gained from his departure. At least now they could set out the longlines that had remained unused while he had lived among them.

From the buried equipment lockers, lines of braided gold cable were unspooled, from which hung more than a hundred large hooks fashioned of hardened, alloyed gold.

In the great harbor of Yordd, Felf fishermen arriving from the islands of the Strait to peddle their catch were not an uncommon sight. The appearance of a makeshift raft composed of a large wooden platform set atop multiple smaller outriggers, however, was something of a novelty. It drew enough curious onlookers to make Madrenga uncomfortable. He relaxed once the improvised transport docked and it became apparent that the bulk of the crowd's interest lay in what his Felf friends had to sell and not in their single fullman passenger.

There was no need for extended goodbyes, as these had been exchanged prior to the departure from Ool-lak-lan. There were no tears, no sobs. Those Felf who had been chatty enough during the crossing found themselves thrown into noisy negotiation with the

initial wave of fish buyers. Thus left to his own, Madrenga led
Orania off the craft and up the stone steps that led into the city
proper.

After his extended bucolic interlude on the island it felt
strange to be back among his own kind again. Pedestrian traffic
was more frenetic and the crowds even denser than they had been
in distant Charrush. The mix of people was familiar enough:
Harund, the occasional slender Selndar, plus clusters of a short,
squat folk whose appearance was new to him. Among the surging,
nattering multitude he saw not a single representative of the three
elven tribes. Their absence did not surprise him. While completely
at home on their islands, they would have been swamped by the
size and smells of the city.

Fashioned of finely quarried basalt and limestone, some of the
buildings in Yordd rose higher than even the lookout towers of
Harup-taw-shet. Everything was outsize here, from ships in the
harbor beside which the *Thranskirr* would have paled in size to the
fortifications that marked the entrance to the port. Only he and
his companions did not seem diminished in comparison. He stood
as tall as ever, while dogs both domesticated and wild shied away
from the hulking Bit and other horses eyed the now massive
Orania the way a refined hostess would a barbarian requesting
entrance to a tea party.

As he led his animals up a main street and deeper into the city
proper, Madrenga could hardly believe he had made it this far.
Yordd! Gateway to his final destination. Though changed, he was
alive and well, as were his companions. Despite all he had been
through he still retained the majority of his gear. Thanks to the
inexplicable transformations he had undergone he felt as if he was
in the best health of his young life. Possessed of physical strength
he had never known, much less imagined, he felt confident now of
completing his mission. He would return to Harup-taw-shet with
his head held high—nay, higher than when he had left. Amazement and gratitude would accompany his triumphant returning.

Calm yourself. Remember your place. You are delivering a

scroll, not winning a battle or rescuing a princess. You are a glorified delivery boy; nothing more. Still, what stories he would have to tell upon his return! His friends on the street, should he deign to meet with them again, would have the honor of basking in the aura surrounding his accomplishment.

Then he got his first good, clear look at the mountains behind the city, and pre-emptive self-glorification gave way to a reality check.

Snow-covered peaks gleamed in the morning sun; beautiful to look at but arduous to cross. He consoled himself with the thought that a city of commerce like Yordd would necessarily sit at a juncture of multiple trading routes, and that at least one or two of these must run through those same mountains. They were far higher than any he had ever seen. At least, he thought as he looked over at Orania, he would not have to hike through them. His erstwhile pony had become big and strong enough to carry three men, much less simply her master and if need be, his dog.

The presumed existence of a limited number of well-known, heavily-traveled routes into the interior meant it would be hard to get lost while making the crossing. His confidence returned full-blown. As for the time lost he had spent recuperating in Ool-lak-lan, with every step deeper into the teeming streets of Yordd that dream-like sojourn receded more and more into memory.

For some time now he had ceased to worry about sneak thieves and pickpockets. Anyone who drew too near or lingered too long became the recipient of a bark or two from Bit. Though he was only being friendly, the sight of those dagger-like teeth flashed in a smile was enough to deter even the most ambitious of cut-purses.

He still had nearly half his money left. When he had emptied it onto the desk of Captain Hammaghiri he had been careful not to be overly generous. Though he had no idea of local costs, he hoped what remained would be enough to get him all the way to Daria. He would begin the last stage of his journey with a late morning meal in this new city. The crossing from Ool-lak-lan had left him hungry for something besides fruit and fish and eggs.

Though most pedestrians accelerated alarmingly out of his way the instant he started to swerve in their direction, a few were sufficiently secure in their selves to allow him to ask a question or two. Eventually he found himself outside a tavern whose exterior hanging sign identified it as The Blunt Instrument. Belying its name, its clientele bordered on the sedate. There was an associated stable where he was able to leave Orania, and a choice of empty tables and booths for himself. It being mid-morning, the place was far from crowded despite its excellent location on a main street leading inland from the harbor. Feeling very good about things, he entered, he sat, he ordered.

Ordinarily he would have politely but firmly waved off the two men who approached his table and asked to join him. But one was the blondest fellow Madrenga had ever seen, with hair and brows the color and thickness of gold thread, and the other a rock-like Harund with, in an astounding first in Madrenga's experience, a beard that had actually been washed, combed, and trimmed. Such an unlikely pair he could not have turned away individually, far less in tandem.

He was not concerned about their possible motives in seeking out his company. The heavy wooden table at which the three of them now sat was near the front of the eatery, was well lit and exposed to the attentive gaze of the proprietor, and should anything go awry there were numerous potential witnesses seated at several other tables.

Besides, as much as they might want to talk to him, he equally needed to talk to some locals.

"Dariak?" The Harund's voice was characteristically deep and rough, the consonants rubbing together like rocks. "Never beenak there myselfk." He nodded at his lithe companion. "Bors, now he maybek, sa?"

The lean-muscled blonde shook his head. "No, I've never been there either. But I know of the way. It is straightforward enough. Many caravans ply the main route."

Between mouthfuls of plied pork and swallows of an excellent dark beer, Madrenga nodded and strove to sound more sophisticated than his age would suggest. "I'd heard there was considerable trade between Yordd and Daria. I was counting on that."

"It should be a simple matter for you to gain passage." The blonde hesitated. "If you can pay."

Madrenga's expression fell, the further to emphasize a necessary prevarication. He had no intention of informing these two strangers of the actual state of his finances.

"I hope so. I've come a long way and spent much of what little I have. I retain enough for this meal, food and fodder for my animals, and a room for the night. After that ..." His voice trailed away meaningfully before brightening once again. "I've hired myself and my animals out before. My horse can pull a wagon, and my dog," he glanced down at where Bit was dozing by his feet, "can fight and defend." Feeling bolder (or perhaps it was the beer), he placed his right hand firmly on the pommel of his sword. "I can fight as well."

Leaning back in his chair, the Harund eyed him appraisingly. "You big enough, sa. But no offense meaningk, I thinking maybe a little youngk for a warrior."

"You have no idea what I've been through," Madrenga responded. The beer was making him feel very good indeed. Truthfully, he was still hard pressed to believe the changes that had come over him and his companions in the course of his journey thus far. "But to be honest, though I've had to do my share of fighting, I'm not a professional soldier. I'm actually just a courier." Pulling aside his shirt and shifting his lightweight armor revealed the cylindrical scroll carrier attached to his belt. "This is why I have to get over the mountains. It's a communication from Queen Alyriata of Harup-taw-shet to her counterpart in Daria."

Two wisps of golden spider silk, the blonde's eyebrows rose slightly. "A royal communication! What does it say?"

Madrenga blinked, started to down another draught of beer, and now thought better of it. He'd had more than enough to ensure that he would sleep well tonight no matter where he bedded down.

"I have no idea. There is no reason for me to look at it. I know only that I am to deliver it."

"Of course. Pardon my natural curiosity." The blonde smiled. "You really do need to get to Daria, don't you?" Madrenga nodded. "I think mayhap we can help you." He glanced at the Harund, who nodded vigorously. "There is an acquaintance of ours, a local nobleman. His name is Hinga Cathore. Though not a merchant himself, he does deal in commercial matters. As such, he knows many of the traders who travel inland. A gracious and kindly man, he is always ready to assist those in need. If you ask, he might be willing to provide you with a personal contact who will take you over the mountains for a fair price. Especially since it involves so worthy a cause."

Madrenga immediately perked up. "Can you arrange an introduction?"

Slim human and squat Harund exchanged a glance. "I don't see why not," the blonde replied easily. "All he can do is refuse to see you. But if he accepts, and learns the truth of your situation, he may even offer to let you stay at his home until it is time for you to join a caravan. Cathore is famous for his hospitality!"

"Then I would not have to pay for a room for tonight." Madrenga was more than taken with the thought. "How soon can you speak to him on my behalf?"

"Time can be chop-up like a steak." Pushing back his chair, the Harund was already rising. "Best not to waste the pieces. We can go right nowk."

A grateful Madrenga gestured expansively. "Why not?"

He paid for the meal, but when he offered to also pay for his new friends' drinks they politely refused, insisting that he needed to conserve his funds. In Madrenga's eyes that further solidified their benign intentions. With Bit at his side he recovered Orania from where she had been quartered. In another surprise, the kindly stablemaster refused payment.

"She wasn't here long enough and didn't eat enough to matter," he told the horse's master. Truly, Madrenga thought, if Yordd boasted such an abundance of fine folk as he had already encountered then it was no wonder it had grown to assume such prominence as a place for gathering and trade.

The blonde had a horse of his own while the Harund preferred to ride tewkback. Madrenga had never seen a tewk. Looking like a cross between a mule and a chameleon, it was one mount that would never lose sight of a trail. Not with its bulging, independently swiveling eyes.

Relieved to be with friends who knew the way, Madrenga was able to relax and enjoy his surroundings. While Orania followed the mounts of the two guides, the youth on her back drank in the sights of bustling Yordd. It wasn't long before they left behind the commercial district that sprawled along the harborfront and entered a residential district comprised of small shops and neat homes. Exotic plants bloomed in flower boxes and the air was saturated with pleasant aromas. No palms here, but plenty of shade trees that overhung the entrances to homes of one and two stories.

As the road began to slope upwards, scattered larger dwellings took the place of packed-together smaller ones. The increasingly grand estates with their views of the port and the ocean reminded him of similar gracious structures in Harup-taw-shet. No views of the ocean there, he told himself. Only mountains and canyons and distant high plains.

Grander in its setting than in its shape was the House of Hinga Cathore. Not as large as some of the manors they had passed in the course of ascending from the harbor, the compound clung to a promontory that jutted out of the mountainside. A masterpiece of the stone mason's art, the multistory structure put Madrenga in mind of an eagle poised to take flight as it kept an eye on fish swimming below.

"Nice panorama," he commented admiringly.

Slowing until his own smaller horse was beside Orania, the

blonde nodded. "Cathore has mounted on a balcony a long lens that lets him see everything that is going on in the city. He is a most intensely curious person."

Madrenga smiled. "You mean a telescope."

The blonde frowned in confusion. "No. It is something else. I know what is a telescope. This is—different."

Madrenga left it at that. He was only making polite conversation. The nobleman's furnishings were of no particular interest to him. He was here in the hope that the man could help him reach his destination and for no other reason.

At the entry gate a servant took charge of their mounts and guided them toward an open stable area piled high with hay. As Madrenga waited, the blonde gestured toward his feet.

"Hinga Cathore is a particularly fastidious man. I'm afraid your dog will have to wait here."

"Not a problem. These two are used to being together." Kneeling, he gave Bit a good rub. "You go with Orania, boy. I'll be back soon." Straightening, he pointed as the footman led the two horses and one tewk toward the waiting area reserved for animals. "Go on."

Obediently, Bit turned and trotted off alongside Orania, dog and horse briefly touching noses. The Harund's tone was approving.

"Fine animals you have, bothk. I would like to have for myselfk."

Madrenga laughed. "Sorry. The three of us have been together too long. Even if I ever thought of doing such a thing they would never accede to it. If I gave them to you, you wouldn't be able to control them."

The deep voice emerged again from within the beard. "Seeing them so, I think samek thing."

Another servant conducted the three men through a modest ground floor entryway and up a twist of spiral stone stairs. They emerged into a surprisingly high-ceilinged room filled with cabinets and shelving on which were stacked innumerable books, jars, stuffed animals, and other arcane paraphernalia. A hunter, Madrenga mused. After noting that none of the examples of the taxidermist's art were particularly large or impressive, he revised his initial supposition. Merely a collector, then. A naturalist by hobby, perhaps.

Hinga Cathore was big, broad-chested, and gray of hair. In the absence of a beard, a brushy mustache hung down over his upper lip. His hands and head were outsized, his feet presumably likewise. He looked more like a retired drover or brewer than a nobleman. If you blended the talkative blonde with the bearded Harund, you might get a man who looked like Hinga Cathore.

The analogy was only a trick of the mind and the eye, Madrenga told himself. Had any familial relationship existed between the three men, surely one or the other of his new friends would have mentioned it by now. Nor did Cathore greet the two locals in the manner of a relative. Instead, they exchanged greetings that were so softly voiced Madrenga could not make out the words. But the nobleman's welcome was effusive enough.

"I am always delighted to meet someone from a far land, especially one I myself have not had the opportunity to visit!" Standing as tall as his visitor, Cathore was able to put a reassuring arm around Madrenga's shoulders as he guided him toward a quartet of chairs. Choosing one, he directed his guest to a seat opposite his own. Not invited to join them, the twosome from town remained standing nearby. A large table overflowing with books and devices stood to one side while an arched opening framed another balcony and a spectacular prospect of the city beyond. Madrenga ignored the view.

He was far more interested in the large pink-faced monkey that was sitting on the table perusing a book. Noticing his guest's captivated stare, Cathore let out a hearty laugh.

"Sobo can't read. But he likes to look at the pictures. And I think he also likes the smell of old books. One time he started to eat a valuable treatise on medicinal plants. I let him. He shit vellum streamers for a week. Now he just looks."

Torn between empathizing with the monkey's discomfort and laughing at the image thus described, Madrenga settled for a sympathetic smile. "To the best of my knowledge none of my companions has ever tried to eat a book. They don't look at them, either."

"Fine animals," the Harund put in. "Strongk horse, really big dogk. I admire very muchk, sa."

The master of the house nodded matter-of-factly. "So, what brings one so young all the way to Yordd from far-off Harup-taw-shet?"

Madrenga bridled slightly at the "so young" but by now had learned when to comment on the observations of others and when to hold his peace. "I am a courier, charged with conveying a communication from my Queen to her counterpart in Daria. I can pay for guidance but must find a reasonable way to get inland." He indicated the men who had brought him from town. "These good gentlemen suggested that you might be able to recommend to me a caravan or convoy traveling in that direction."

At this Cathore roared anew. "'Good gentlemen?' My young friend, you have a way with words as well as with travel." He wiped his nose, then his tearing eyes, then his nose again. Flinching slightly, Madrenga reminded himself that not all noblemen had noble manners. Still, he was surprised.

"What sort of communication?" Cathore was suddenly intent.

"I don't know. I was directed to deliver it. I have not looked at it."

"An honorable young man. I see why you were chosen. Maturity is not a function of age, my young friend. That is a constant across countries. Indeed, across worlds." Leaning forward, he extended a hand. "May I have the privilege of seeing this communication, my friend?"

"My name is Madrenga."

The nobleman seemed momentarily taken aback, though why this should be so his guest could not imagine. It was not the first time mention of his name had occasioned an inexplicable response. Madrenga had put it down to coincidence, deciding that he must share a name with someone famous, or perhaps infamous. No doubt one day the explanation would manifest itself.

"Very well—Madrenga." The hand gestured anew. "The communication: may I see it?" When his guest continued to hesitate, Cathore grew impatient. "Come, come, young man: how can I decide whether to help you unless I am allowed to determine if you're telling the truth?"

A sensible enough response, a wary Madrenga concluded. He noted that while the blonde and the Harund wore swords and knives at their belts, his noble host was unarmed and clad in plain embroidered silks. The servant who had led them upstairs was nowhere to be seen. No artfully positioned spray of spears or rank of axes decorated any of the room's walls. Meanwhile he still had his own sword and armor. Appraising the available weapons, an impartial observer would have concluded that his host had more to fear from his guest than the other way around.

Reaching down to his belt, he unfastened the protective travel container and passed it to his host. The engraved cylinder was still sealed as tightly as it had been when Counselor Natoum had handed it to his chosen courier. Cathore inspected it closely, turning it over and over in his fingers, noting the designs that had been incised into the metal.

"Corium. A valuable trinket, to be sure, but only a trinket." He held it up to the light and smiled. "As with any communication the value lies on what is written, not on what it is written upon." Without hesitation he slipped the cylinder into a wide pocket of his pants. "It has been a pleasure meeting you, young Madrenga of Harup-taw-shet. You may go now."

Shocked beyond words by the flippancy of the incipient larceny, Madrenga was reduced to gaping open-mouthed at his smiling host.

The moment that ensued following Hinga Cathore's pocketing of the precious scroll passed in an eternity of contemplation. Upon its conclusion Madrenga rose, wrapped the fingers of his right hand around the haft of his sword, and drew it halfway from its scabbard. Instead of responding with a challenge of their own the blonde and the Harund immediately retreated in the direction of the doorway. A seated Cathore cast them barely a glance and a derisive sniff before returning his attention to his visitor.

"What are you going to do with that, young Madrenga? Stab me to death, here in my own home?"

"My wish is to take neither your life nor violate the sanctity of your house, but only to have returned that which is mine." Now it was his turn to extend an open palm. "Give me back the scroll and I will leave quietly." His voice was taut. "I will find others to help me get over the mountains to Daria."

"Possibly you will." When Cathore rose, Madrenga stepped back and pulled more firmly on the sword. The blade was now most of the way out of its scabbard. His every sense was on edge. The nobleman made no effort to confront the threat that had been aimed his way, nor did he make any effort to remove the scroll cylinder from his pocket. Instead, he walked slowly to the over-flowing table. A hand gesture caused the child-sized monkey to drop the book it had been examining and drop to the floor. It stood there screeching, occasionally throwing its arms into the air to punctuate its fusillade of complaints.

"Or possibly," Cathore continued, "it is your destiny now to find your way elsewhere. Which I promise that you will if you do not leave quietly." Ominous portent gave way once more to an engaging smile as he tapped the pocket holding the cylinder. "Why so much fuss? This is just a communication. Not gold or jewels or some precious medicine. Your journey has been long and your traveling, I suspect, arduous. Return, go back home, say that the scroll was stolen by bandits or swallowed by a dragon. Be inventive. Be convincing. Few will doubt you. Those who might will be unable to prove otherwise."

Madrenga held his ground. "Give me back my property, or I will have to take it."

"Dear me. What are you, Madrenga? Of years spent alive,

seventeen? Eighteen? Your size may fool others, but I am a
connoisseur of truths. I see you for what you are, and what you are
is no threat to me." One hand fluttered in the direction of the
doorway that was presently occupied by the blonde and the
Harund. "Go now, while you can."

"I want his animals." The bearded one grinned expectantly.
"Good eatingk!"

The thought of the hairy deceiver and his friends feasting on
the roasted bodies of Bit and Orania was enough to decide
Madrenga. With a cry he rushed forward, intending as he did so to
draw his sword the rest of the way.

Hinga Cathore raised both hands and declaimed, in a voice
that shook the stones of the tower all the way to the bedrock
beneath, "*SAALAMAK!*"

Madrenga was stopped in his tracks. His body suddenly weakened to the point of collapse, his fingers relaxed on the sword hilt.
Freed from his grasp and drawn downward by its own weight the
blade slid slowly back into its scabbard.

The yellow embers that had replaced Cathore's dark pupils
were blazing bright, like burning sulphur. Previously brazen in
their lying, the blonde and the Harund now cowered in the doorway, at once too fascinated and too fearful to flee. The monkey was
going crazy; running back and forth, leaping onto shelves and
bouncing off the walls, throwing books and found objects in all
directions as it shrieked with an insane mixture of terror and
delight.

The embroidered inscriptions and designs on Cathore's
clothing now shone with an unwholesome green glow. Day fled
from the room, to be replaced by a darkness wholly independent
of the position of the sun outside. Far off in the distance
Madrenga believed he could hear Orania neighing frantically and
Bit barking and snarling like a mad dog. That was strange, he
thought. The courtyard where they were being attended to was not
that far away, and the large balcony opening close at hand. Why
then did they sound so far away?

Again he tried again to draw his sword, but his hand would not respond. Nothing was responding. He was paralyzed, frozen in place. A veil had been drawn over his head through which he could vaguely see shapes and hear sounds, but he could not move. When he tried to give voice to his outrage, his lips and tongue failed to respond.

Only one voice could be heard: that of Hinga Cathore. No nobleman he, the helpless and disconsolate youth now realized, but a warlock vile and true. If his sulphurous gaze was not enough to confirm it, his mastery of forbidden words was more than enough proof. Madrenga damned himself for a gullible fool. A stranger to good beer, he had allowed to much of it to dull his senses. Having said too much, having trusted too much, he had been led here like a sheep to the slaughter by the promise of friendship and help, only to be …

To be what? With nothing left to hide and his collector's desire fulfilled, what did Cathore have in mind for his naive young visitor? "Possibly it is your destiny to find yourself elsewhere", he had said enigmatically. Was the cryptic now to be made reality? Were the warlock's words promise or threat—or both? Through the darkness that hooded him he could hear his nemesis growling.

"I gave you your chance, young Madrenga. I offered you the opportunity to leave. You chose to challenge me, and you have lost. Now you must go. Having seen that your boldness and your foolishness are inextricably linked, I cannot believe that, given another chance, you would not try to return and retake that which you have lost. Therefore I must be rid of you permanently and for all time."

Moving to the heavily laden table he picked up a book. Though finely bound, it was smaller and less prepossessing than many of the larger, more impressive volumes that surrounded it. Opening it, the warlock searched until he found the page and the words he sought. One hand he raised high overhead. Straining, Madrenga could barely see what the mage was about.

"*SINATHAM REES KAHL-LETH*—I banish you to the first

place of death and disease upon which your body and spirit may impinge!"

At this a darkness constricted around him to fall whole and entire upon the hapless Madrenga, who did not even have time to shout out his fury and frustration at having been so wantonly and cruelly deceived.

Passed then a moment in time and space to which he could not give a name.

CHAPTER FOURTEEN

THE STRANGENESS IN WHICH HE FOUND HIMSELF EXTENDED to the very light. It came from within glass in the ceiling; small windows that channeled unseen lamps that gave off no familiar smell. Some kind of prism designed to convey the light from elsewhere, he decided. Hand on sword hilt, he struggled to make sense of his surroundings as his mind recovered. What the warlock Cathore had done to him and where he had been sent the youth did not know. But he felt alive and not dead. He *was* alive. From that much he would move forward.

Of the spacious chamber in the warlock's dwelling there was no trace. Nor was there any sign of his pair of lying, contemptible underlings. If Cathore was to be believed, Madrenga had been banished "to the first place of death and disease upon which your body and spirit may impinge". Mindful of the curse, his senses fully alert, he was careful to touch nothing.

Though the much smaller room in which he now found himself was adorned with many objects he did not recognize, others were instantly familiar. Its peculiar design notwithstanding, a chair was a still a chair. There were two in the room, upholstered with some woven green material. A pitcher and a glass sat on a small narrow table. Approaching warily, he sniffed of the pitcher's contents, then chanced a cautious sip. It was comforting to know that if this was some corner of the underworld, water was still water. He must be in a cold place, he reflected, because chunks of ice floated in the container.

Through the single large window he saw the lights of a city. They were unusually bright. As near as he could tell, the moon that hung over the nocturnal vista was the same moon he had always known. He was relieved to see that it was in three-quarter phase just like the one he had left behind.

Just as a chair was still a chair, just as water was still water, just as the moon was still the moon, the girl lying in the bed in front of him was nothing more than a girl.

A thin blanket of what looked like wool but was something else covered her to her shoulders. There was a sheet beneath. These appurtenances he understood on sight. What he did not recognize were the tubes of what felt like soft glass that ran from her body to bags and bottles and boxes that emitted lights of their own. Some of the latter displayed numbers, others lines and pictures. One made repetitive noises as if something might be living inside, though he could find no opening in which to look. The girl's eyes were closed.

There was a door. Opening it quietly he found himself looking out into a dimly lit corridor. He saw no one. Voices were few and distant. Closing it softly he returned to studying the sleeping girl in the bed. She was, he noted, extremely pretty, very thin, and with unblemished olive-hued skin. Her long red hair (dyed, he guessed from the intensity of the color) had been recently washed and bound into a single braid. She looked to be the same age as him, or close to it.

Her eyes opened. They were a pale shade of violet. She blinked and saw him and they widened perceptibly. When she spoke her voice was sweet but weak.

"This is the best dream I've ever had."

He hardly knew how to respond. Having just been cursed and banished by a warlock of considerable power, his reticence was understandable. If this girl felt she was dreaming, might not the same be true of him? Reaching down, he pinched his leg. If it was dream-pain he was feeling, it was exceptionally realistic.

"This is not a dream," he heard himself saying quite clearly.

"Of course it is." Unlike himself, the girl did not seem in the least bit nonplussed. "Each night I try to dream my favorite game. They don't let me play on the console all the time: the doctors say it wears me out too much. But they can't stop me from dreaming." She smiled, and even in her debilitated physical state it was a beautiful thing to see. "You're my dream hero, of course. Although you look different from how I've imagined you." A hand rose slowly to gesture at him. "Your clothing is different, too, and your armor. But you're acceptable."

Madrenga's fear and anxiety did not prevent him from feeling slighted. He replied stiffly. "I am glad I meet your requirements."

"What I don't understand is what you're doing in my hospital room." Even her frown was beautiful, Madrenga thought. "That's not part of the game. You're supposed to be rescuing me by slaying a dragon."

"I've never even seen a dragon," he muttered. "With luck, I never will."

The frown deepened and he saw that cheeks which were now sunken had once been dimpled. "That doesn't sound right. What an odd dream this is becoming."

He moved closer, until he was looming over the bed. "Listen to me, elsewhere woman. This is not a dream. Not yours or mine. My name is Madrenga, and no one has dreamed me. I was banished to this place by the warlock Cathore and I need to try and find a way back." Once again he examined his surroundings. "He said he was sending me to a place of death and disease. Where am I?"

"Stranger and stranger." Her luminous eyes were locked on him now. "Not that it matters in a dream, but this is St. Stephens Memorial Hospital, and you are in Pittsburg."

Madrenga considered. "I do not know that country. Is it near Daria?"

When she shook her head no he could see that even that simple gesture required a conscious effort on her part. "I've never heard of a country called Daria. I don't think I've ever dreamed of one, either."

"It's inland from Yordd," he explained impatiently.

"Yordd." The smile returned. "That's a funny name."

"All place names are funny to those who live elsewhere. 'Pittsburg' is a funny name."

"So is Madrenga. Not as funny as Rumpelstiltskin or Baba Yaga, but still funny. Mine is Maya Bhargava. Do you think that is a funny name?"

"No. It is kind to the ear. Cathore said a place of death and disease. You don't look well. Are you ill?"

"I'm dying."

She said it calmly, with the surety of someone who knows there is no hope and therefore has no reason to argue. Acceptance of the inevitable brings with it a peace that is beyond the understanding of the fit and healthy. Resigned to imminent termination, she could speak freely about it.

She looked weak but not on the verge of death, he thought. Wan but still beautiful. Death did not always announce its arrival through violence, however. In his short life he had seen it manifest itself both ways. Certainly he had no reason to doubt her disclosure.

"A truly wicked man has cursed me. Has someone also put a death spell on you?"

"I suppose you could call it that." She had to pause between sentences to gather enough strength and air to continue. "I have acute lymphocytic leukemia."

He shook his head. "That is an affliction that is unknown to me. Which means nothing. I am ignorant of many things." The words of the Felf chieftain came back to him. "Men multiply and infect the land, and in response, the land infects them." Perhaps this lymphocytic leukemia—such strange words!—arose from such an infection.

"I know boils, and fever, and many other sicknesses of the body. But yours is new to me. It sounds," he finished, "like a truly terrible death spell, though."

She tried to nod, failed, and gave up. In the absence of energy-draining gestures, words would have to suffice. Besides, who needed gestures in a dream?

"It is. My body bruises so easily, and my joints and bones hurt all the time. I don't understand all of it. That's what the doctors call it for short: ALL. Now you, you're lucky. When I play a game, I always play through a character who can't get sick. Killed maybe, or maimed, but never sick. I have enough sick in what's left of my life. I don't need it in my dreams."

Exasperation leavened his compassion. "Why do you keep saying that? This is not a dream; not from all that I can perceive. I am not something of your imagination—though I am beginning to wonder if you are something of mine."

Slightly alarmed, she looked to her right, toward the door. "Sssh—keep your voice down or the night nurse will hear." Having voiced the warning, she shook her head again. If she'd had the energy, she would have laughed. "What am I saying? Dreams don't make any noise. Unless I start shouting in my sleep, and I only do that when the pain gets too bad and I need my meds upped."

It was Madrenga's turn to frown. "What's a nurse? Some kind of servant?"

"Something like that," Maya told him, "only more powerful. Real. Not like you."

She was feverish, Madrenga realized. Hallucinating in her delirium. That would explain much. "My life is no one's 'game'," he growled. "I remember all of it. Being abandoned, losing my younger brother—who would be about your age now, had he lived. I remember growing up, the taste of certain foods, the chill of particular winters and the heat of certain summers. I remember dozens, hundreds of people, places, things. If I had the time, I would relate them all to you, each and every one, and by so doing refute your irrational and misguided foolishness!"

Her visage was not so beautiful that it could not make room for confusion. "I don't understand. I haven't had time to dream all that." Her expression brightened. "But I know what I've gamed you for. You're on a quest, aren't you? A noble quest?"

He sighed and shook his head. "I'm a courier, charged with delivering something." The emptiness at his belt where the precious scroll had been fastened burned hot against him.

She persisted. "Didn't you leave your home city and cross a dangerous lake?"

"No; a river," he corrected her.

"And then you had to fight and slay a grunting giant?"

Again he demurred. "He was just a big fighter, and perfectly articulate."

"You rescued a fair princess." She was staring at him intently, violet eyes flashing.

He shook his head again, more forcefully this time. "A smoke sprite, daughter of a smoke sprite and a mirror sprite." Memories came flooding back. "I do not recall the exact shade of her skin, but it was most certainly not fair."

"You slew a dragon."

"It was spitting salamander, it was trying to fight off some spiders, and I only watched it." He was growing tired of her assertions and of having to refute each one. "I told you: I've never even seen a dragon."

She took as much of a deep breath as she could manage. As she did so one of the strange illuminated boxes beeped loudly. "You—battled—an—evil—witch!"

"A warlock, not a witch. And I lost, which is why I am here in this incomprehensible place of disease and death, conversing with a crazy dying girl when I should be trying to find a way back to where I belong." He thought of Bit, barking frantically because he knew his master was in danger, and Orania, doubtless trying to reach him because she knew something was seriously amiss. Were they still in Cathore's stables, wondering and worrying at his absence? What would become of them if he failed to return in time? He remembered the Harund's hopeful request, and shuddered. Somehow, anyhow, he had to reverse the curse, had to get back, if only to save them. In his heart if not in his mind, the scroll had now become of secondary importance.

The words of the Felf chieftain had come to him earlier. Now it was the turn of some that had been spoken even longer ago. "And along the way, if you are true Madrenga, you will muster any help you need", Chief Counselor Natoum had assured him. Where in this outlandish, dark, foreign realm could he find the means to return him to his own place and time?

He had appeared before the sick girl—or else the sick girl had appeared before him. Precedence did not concern him. Was she the help he needed? If she was telling the truth, and he had no reason to doubt either her words or her appearance, then she was on the verge of death. What aid could a dying and deluded girl render to one who had been cursed by a warlock as powerful as Hinga Cathore? His gaze turned back to where she lay in her bed, unmoving and thinking furiously.

"This isn't right. Something isn't *right*. The game isn't going the way I dreamed it. Everything you said ..." she looked up at him. "Everything is similar, but not the same. Alike, but not identical. Just like you. You should be blonde and have blue eyes, and be not quite as tall, and slimmer. I should see light, and looking at you I see darkness. It's wrong, all wrong." She looked as if she was going to start to cry. "I'm losing my life, and now I'm losing my mind, too! It isn't right, it isn't fair!"

Instinctively he started to move toward her, to try and comfort her. But she recovered her equilibrium before he had taken more than a step. Her voice strengthened. She was staring up at the ceiling, as if he wasn't there.

"It doesn't matter anyway. Nothing matters anyway. A month, they give me. Maybe two. Then it won't matter at all. I just—I'd rather not die crazy. There are people I want to say goodbye to. My mom and dad, my friend Elena, my ..." Her voice trailed away, words shading into whispers.

He inhaled softly. "Can you help me?"

His words were like nothing she expected to hear, or to dream. Her eyes moved to meet his. "Can I help *you*? Didn't you just hear what I was saying? You're the wrong dream, just enough off center to make me doubt my own sanity, and I'm going to be dead soon. I can't help anyone or anything. All I can do is try to stay rational." She turned her head to the side, away from him. "I think it would help if you would go away now."

"Believe me, Maya, I would like nothing better. But I can't."

"Sure you can." With great effort, she raised her right hand and waved at the door. "Evaporate. Take a hike. Let me wake up." She closed her eyes.

When she opened them a moment later, he was still standing there, eying her with concern.

"Don't look at me like that. That's all I need now; a dream taking pity on me."

"Can you read?"

She blinked, stared hard at him. "Of course I can read. I read very well."

"I can't. Someone who can read may be the help I need. If not now, then eventually. Will you come with me?"

A laugh that had once been bold and ringing emerged now from her throat tired and tiny. "Sure, why not? I'm dying. Maybe the doctors were wrong and I don't have a month or two. Maybe you're Death and I won't get to say my goodbyes. What the hell; what difference does it make? What difference does anything make? Yeah, I'll go with you—what'd you say your name was again, dream?

"Madrenga."

"Okay, Madrenga, or whatever you are." She closed her eyes. "Take me. Or wake me."

Bending over the bed he pushed back the blanket and sheet.

Though ravaged by the curse that was consuming her, the outlines of what had once been a beautiful body were clearly visible beneath her white gown. When he slipped his hands beneath her, he was startled to find that the simple attire was open at the back. At his touch her eyes snapped open and she looked at him sharply.

"Hey! Oh, wait—it's only a dream. Only dream fingers." Her voice softened and her eyes half closed anew. "Strong hands, though—for a dream."

He lifted her up. She could feel herself rising, and the reality of it was striking.

"Let's go," he told her firmly.

"Go? Go where?"

"To where I belong." He looked down at the tubes and wires that were trailing from her body. "If I take you away from these, what will happen?"

She managed a nearly imperceptible shrug. "I'll die a little sooner, I suppose. It doesn't really matter. Even the last goodbyes don't matter if I'm not sane enough to say them. Go on, dream. Carry me away. To the afterlife, if it's Death who you are, or to wherever."

"I am hoping Yordd," he told her solemnly.

She sighed. She didn't care anymore. There was no reason to, really. Reaching up, she put her arms around his neck. "So strong, for a dream. Death would be strong, too, I guess."

If I'm dreaming now, she wondered, can I dream myself into another dream? Can you dream a dream within a dream? Is that what dying is about?

She shut her eyes and let her head loll against the dream armor that was covering a dream chest. A very nice chest, solid and muscular even if it did belong to Death. Turning away from the bed Madrenga started toward the window that overlooked the city. She thought she could hear voices out in the corridor, beyond the door, growing louder. The last voices you'll ever hear, she told herself. She wished they belonged to her mom and dad, but when one is dreaming, or dying, choices don't present themselves.

The figure holding her prepared to utter a short stream of words. The same words that had been used by the warlock Hinga Cathore to send him here. Would they work in reverse, and for him? Would taking this featherlight girl from her deathbed help to enhance them, inhibit them, help him to "find himself," or do nothing at all? He could only try. He had to. If not for himself, then for Bit and Orania.

The door opened to admit not one but two nurses. One sucked in her breath while the other said nothing. A sprawl of disconnected wires and tubes lay on the floor. One was dripping a solution of saline and medication, the other was spilling a blend of sucrose and nutrients held in suspension. A monitor was beeping, very loudly now. None of these registered immediately on the two women because their attention was focused elsewhere. The first thing they did was check the bathroom. The next thing they did was sound an alert.

The patient in room 3046 was gone.

CHAPTER FIFTEEN

WHAT SENT HIM BACK HE NEVER REALLY KNEW. HIS OWN wishfulness, perhaps. The fear he felt for the safety of his animals. The girl … the beautiful, dying girl falling asleep again, or perhaps the act of being ripped from her web of tubes and fires. Or maybe a combination of all working in tandem with the words he spoke, or a combination of none. What mattered was that he had returned to the world he knew. The only world, of course. The real world. It was exactly as he remembered it.

Except that there was a beautiful dying girl in his arms.

He was standing in the entry hall of the warlock Hinga Cathore's dwelling. It was dark, as it had been when he had been cursed, as it had been when he had been sent to Somewhere Else. As he stood wondering what to do next the sylph in his arms yawned and stretched. The boy who had left Harup-taw-shet could never have held her so long. The stalwart figure that boy had become supported the girl's attenuated weight effortlessly.

"Nurse, is that you? Maria, Annalee? Can you turn up the heat, I'm cold and …"

She opened her eyes. Even in the dim light he could see they were still violet. He could tell because they opened very wide.

"You …!" She started to look around. "My dream—what's

this? Another dream? I'm dreaming a dream inside a dream? I wondered about that. I guess it's possible because I'm doing it, right? Then why am I asking you? Dreams don't explain themselves, they just go on, like a movie without a pause button." Reaching up, she jabbed him in the chest and giggled. It was the uneasy laugh of someone in distress. "No pause button. Hey, I remember your name. Madrenga, right?" He nodded. "Madrenga, I'm getting really scared now. They say it's hard to scare somebody who's dying of cancer, but I guess it's not impossible, because it's happening to me."

He was looking around anxiously. "When the people where you come from are dying, do they all talk so much?"

"I don't know. I don't talk to other patients in the ward. Only to the living who come to visit me. My doctors and the nurses, and my friends from school, and my mom and dad...."

She started to hyperventilate, her chest heaving, and though he couldn't be certain he felt that the cause was rising panic and not her death curse. So he put a hand over her mouth to quiet her. She started to struggle then, flailing weakly at him, the panic moving from her breathing to her eyes. Slowly, he eased off his smothering hand.

"Be silent! Think what you will. You may be dying where you come from, you may be dying here, but I am not and do not wish to." His gaze rose to the winding stone stairs that led to the rooms above. "Something was taken from me. I need to get it back."

She swallowed. When she spoke again it was in a whisper. "I'm supposed to die from leukemia, not suffocation. I never knew a dream could kill you."

"Then maybe," he told her as he started up the tornado of stairs that were lit only by the last flickering embers of dying torches, "you might consider the possibility that this is not a dream."

"I—I don't think I can do that. I don't want to go crazy before I die." Realization struck. "That's it! It's the medication. It's affecting my mind. One of the nurses got the cocktail wrong. It's

all such powerful stuff, they tell me. I'm getting the wrong mix."
Turning in his arms as much as she was able, she checked her right
side, then her left. Where there had been tubes she found only
needle holes. "My feeds. Where are my feeds?"

"If you mean the things that were sticking out of you, I
pulled you free from all of them. You came with me. They did
not."

Thinking he heard footsteps, he paused until the faint noise
disappeared entirely before resuming his climb.

"What a great dream," the girl in his arms murmured. "A
knight errant …"

"I am a courier," he corrected her primly.

"A knight errant," she repeated insistently, "in realistic
surroundings. Really realistic. I know I'm not dead. The dead don't
dream, right? Right?" Letting go of his neck, she folded her arms
across her chest. "It's so realistic that I'm cold."

"You're wearing very little clothing," he pointed out.

"Oh, you noticed that, did you? It's a hospital gown. It's what
they give you so if you make a mess they can just throw it away,
and because it's easier to get at your body and all the stuff they
hook up to you." Her expression twisted. "I'm supposed to get my
meds constantly. I guess in a dream I don't need them. I don't need
nurses or doctors or friends or anyone."

"I do," he snapped. "I need Bit and Orania back."

She looked up at him. He was handsome enough, she decided,
though far from the rugged image she had invented for her
gaming. "Your friends?"

"My dog and my horse. They have been with me all the way
from Harup-taw-shet. They have been with me since I was a
child."

"You don't have a childhood. I dreamed you up fully grown.
And I never heard of this hup-two-three place. I *did* dream you a
horse. One with a long, flowing golden mane and tail, but his
name was Brucelus."

"It's Orania," he said again, "and he's a she."

She didn't seem to hear him. "And there was no dog. Of what use is a dog to a supreme warrior?"

"I'm not a supreme anything," he shot back, "much less a warrior. Strange things have happened to me since leaving home, it's true, but I am no warrior, supreme or otherwise."

She considered the young man who was carrying her as easily as if she was a leaf. Broad chest, wide shoulders, arms like tree branches, legs like pillars. A heavy sword slung at his waist, armor like steel but something else gleaming on his limbs and torso.

"You should take a closer look at yourself," she murmured. Her heart raced, which given her general physical condition was not a good thing. "Of *course* some 'strange things' have happened to you since you left home. They're all part of the game I invented, to keep from going crazy before I die. Tell me: with each challenge you faced do you get bigger and stronger?"

That brought him to a halt. He stared at her. "I did, yes."

She nodded knowingly. "It's because that's how I designed your character to react. With each enemy you defeat you gain power and stature."

"Then," he asked her after a long pause, "why didn't I get big and powerful enough to defeat Hinga Cathore? Why were a bunch of ordinary seamen able to maroon me on a wooden platform? I didn't fight my way out of that. I was just lucky that the shadows showed compassion toward me instead of filling my lungs with seawater. And if I acquired so much sway, how were a couple of ordinary minions able to trick me into coming here in the first place?"

She peered up at him. "I don't know. I don't know. Maybe I turned the wrong way in my sleep or something."

His voice was firm. "Or maybe there are just some coincidences here. Fate has a strange sense of humor. Maybe this world; now, here, in this stairwell, on these stones, is the real one. Maybe I'm dreaming *you*, and this netherworld of 'Pittsburg' is the invention." Seeing that he was frightening her, he softened his tone and his expression. "You're cold."

"Or I'm dreaming that I'm cold. Either way, it's uncomfortable." She looked around: at the stone stairwell, the stinking smoking remnants of wooden, oil-soaked torches, the occasional small colorful banner. "I think I want my nurses now. I think I want to wake up. I don't like this dream anymore." Her eyes met his once again. "I don't think I like you anymore."

"I am sorry for that. I didn't ask to go where you were. But you asked me to carry you, remember?"

"Only in my dream."

"You're shivering. We'd better find you some heavier clothing. Even though you're dying of this curse of which I know nothing I would not wish for you to perish first from the cold. Then I would feel myself responsible."

Growing colder, she continued to hug herself and press against him for warmth. When he stopped she assumed they must be near the top of the stairs because light was visible from above.

"Stay here and be quiet." He set her down and she had to lean against the cold mortared stone for support.

"Nasty dream man," she muttered. "Quit giving me orders or I'll dream you awa ..."

He'd put his hand over her mouth again. Remembering how uncomfortable it had been the last time he had done so, her eyes widened and she nodded slowly. Putting one finger to his lips he headed up the stairs, making nary a sound as he ascended. A moment later there was the muted noise of a scuffle. When he returned, he was carrying pants and shirt fashioned from a fabric like heavy silk. She did not need his gestures to tell her what should be done with them.

Though large for her slender form, she was able to make them work by folding back the sleeves and cuffs and tightening the included belt to the last notch. When she had finished slipping this new attire over her hospital gown and pulling the right sleeve down over her hospital bracelet, he showed her a short sword.

"Can you use one of these?" he whispered tightly.

She eyed the thick metal blade. "I don't even think I can lift it.

Where did you get …?" Before she could finish the question, he had swept her up in his arms again and was carrying her upward. She would have pursued the question and followed it with others, but the speed of the ascent was making her breathless and the tautness of the muscles in his arms was unaccountably distracting.

They reached the top of the stairs and burst into a high-ceilinged, moonlit room. Through an open portal in the far side she could see the lights of a distant city that was, even via a brief nocturnal glimpse, plainly not Pittsburg. Off to one side the source of her new clothing became apparent in the form of a prone, naked man. Still cradled in Madrenga's arms, she nodded in the figure's direction.

"I know it's all a dream, but in it isn't he going to be cold when he wakes up?"

"He's not going to wake up." Setting her down gently in one of four chairs, Madrenga began searching through the pile of books and artifacts that filled a large table to overflowing.

That was when she noticed the blood. Spending as much time as she had in hospitals she had become quite familiar with blood in all its many forms. Her particular incurable condition had made her intimate with its morphology, its chemical makeup, its moods and manifestations. What was leaking from the prone man's neck and forming a spreading pool on the stone floor was indisputably blood. As if her dream senses were not heightened enough, she could not only see but smell it.

To her surprise she found that despite all the dream running around, she felt a little better than usual. Pushing against the arms of the chair, she tried an experiment. When she found that she could actually stand on her own her joy was unbounded.

"Look. Look at me, Madrenga! I can stand! By myself. Of course, anything is possible in a dream."

He continued rummaging through the materials atop the desk. "Myself, I never believed that lying abed did anyone's health any good."

She turned a slow, hesitant circle. Once she nearly fell and had to steady herself by grabbing the back of the chair. Her fingers gripped graven images of fantastical animals and astronomical signs.

"Before I wake up, I'd like to know what you're looking for so desperately."

"A message. A scroll that I am sworn to deliver to its destination." Anxiety was writ large in his expression. "It's not here," he announced despairingly.

She gestured at his left hand. "Then what's that you're holding?"

"A book. A book of curses and spells. The words within were used against me. If naught else I can see to it that they are never used against anyone else ever again."

Walking tentatively toward him, conscious every moment of her precarious balance, she extended a hand. "Can I see it?"

He hesitated. "How do I know you will not use it against me?"

She almost laughed. "I'm a dying girl in a dream. What harm could I do to you that Fate hasn't already done to me?"

He passed her the book. Opening it, she flipped through the pages. In oddly skewed fashion some of the symbols and words made sense to her. She had once invented a book of spells for her game, but it was much bigger than this. Far heavier, with a different and thicker binding and gold fore-edging. The book she held was fully functional and unlike the one she had envisioned, not intended for purely ceremonial purposes. Like so much else she had discussed with this Madrenga it was close but not quite a match for what she had dreamed. It was just off enough to be … what? Real?

She could not ever remember dreaming a dream that had gone on for so long, not even when under sedation for extreme radiation or chemotherapy, not even in the course of surgery. She hefted the modest tome he had handed her.

"This must be the paperback version," she joked.

Her description held no meaning for him. "All books are made of paper, or something very similar. Come. Or do you need me to carry you again?"

I'd like you to carry me again was what she thought. "Let me try," was what she said. She had to lean against him for support and several times while descending the spiral staircase she nearly fell, but by the time they reached the last step and the hall where they had materialized she was, inexplicably, feeling stronger than ever. Seeing that she was able to walk by herself he did not pause in the hallway but continued onward toward the large arched doorway.

"Where are we going?"

"To find my friends," he told her without looking back.

The stables where Bit and Orania had been boarded were unchanged from when he had last seen them—if one discounted the iron bars that now formed an impenetrable cage around the mare's stall. He worried about Bit's reaction, fearing that the dog might start yapping uncontrollably and thereby draw attention, but his old friend was so pleased and relieved to see his master again that he forgot to bark. Pressing his face against the checkerboard of bars he licked Madrenga's proffered hand until the youth worried the skin would begin to come off. Standing nearby, Maya frowned as she studied the two animals.

"This isn't right. Again. The horse I dreamed for you was white and had a long, neatly combed golden mane and was slim as a thoroughbred. This creature's hair is mostly reddish brown, its mane is cut way too short, and it's built more like a rhino than a racehorse." Her eyes shifted to Bit. "Like I said, I didn't dream you a dog at all. I don't much like dogs. I prefer cats."

Turning away from his master's hand Bit moved to his right and growled at the girl. Dream-growl or not, Maya drew back hastily.

"See? He doesn't like me either."

If not for the seriousness of the situation Madrenga would have smiled. "You said you preferred cats. How would you expect him to react? Just ignore his teeth and give him a chance. He's really very friendly." Looking anxiously around the open court-yard, the youth urged her forward. "Let him get a whiff of you, see that you mean him no harm."

"Well, okay—why not?" Stepping forward, she boldly thrust her hand through the bars—and promptly got nipped.

"Bit!" Madrenga shook a finger at the dog. *"No!"*

Maya was holding her hand. Looking down at it revealed a tiny trickle of blood, dark-hued in the moonlight. "That *hurt.* It *still* hurts." She looked up at the tall young man who was eying her with concern. "It's not supposed to hurt, in a dream. I'm not supposed to keep bleeding in a dream. It's not ..." She broke off and looked around, clutching the small book he had entrusted to her. "I don't remember dreaming anything like this place."

Seeing that, at least for the moment, she was going to live, he started hunting for a key. First he would free his companions and then ...

"You there! *What are you doing!* Guards, an intruder!"

A gong sounded. Before it ceased reverberating the courtyard began to fill with armed men. They came from two directions; some fully equipped, others struggling to pull on the last of their clothing or armor. Both columns headed toward the stables. Uttering a curse that was beyond his years and caused Maya to blink in surprise, Madrenga drew his sword. In the dim light it gleamed brighter than the moon.

She found it prudent to set the dream vs. reality debate aside when the first severed limb came flying her way. She wished she had accepted the sword Madrenga had offered her upstairs even if she could do no more than plant it in front of her.

The battle that raged in the courtyard was devoid of the grace and gallantry she had often choreographed in her mind. There were no gracile lunges, no delicate pirouettes, no balletic spins and twirls. Spinning and twirling would have meant showing your back to your assailant; a stupid and likely fatal mistake. What she was witnessing was more akin to setting a time limit for a dozen *chefs de partie* armed with very large knives to butcher a steer. The blood that flew made that lost by the single guard in the tower behind them look like red spit in the ocean. There was also, thanks to Madrenga's enhanced size, strength, and skill, a great deal of active dismemberment. Behind her the dog and the horse were going crazy, but despite their own singular abilities were unable to break out of their stout prison. There was more to their cage, she suspected, than mere iron bars.

The one individual who knew by what means Madrenga's companions were kept penned parted the surviving guards like a lion through a herd of gazelles. Disbelief gave way to anger as Madrenga, bloody sword hanging from his hand, met the other man's burning gaze without flinching. Though panting hard from the fight the young visitor still found the words he needed.

"I've come back, Hinga Cathore."

"How …?" The warlock flicked the rest of the question aside. "You should not have come back, Madrenga. By what means and effort it matters not." Leaning slightly to his right he peered past the youth. "And brought something with you, it seems. Unfortunate for it."

So engrossed by the confrontation was Maya that she did not express outrage at being referred to as an 'it'. The night air was suffused, was saturated, with the smell of death of a kind very different from that to be found in the hospital.

Reaching down to his waist, the warlock removed a small metal cylinder from a pocket and shook it at Madrenga.

"This is what you came back for, isn't it? Not for me, nor to justify and restore your own miserable existence. For this!"

"You've read it." Madrenga spoke flatly, his fingers white-knuckled against the haft of the great dripping sword. "You know what it says."

"No. There was no hurry. I had dispensed with the courier. Why rush what promised to be an unexpected delight? Expectation is savoring. But I will read it just the same, this very night. Later, after I have had time to regret my previous compassion." He straightened, and Madrenga tensed. "I should have known better than to simply send you away." Again he glanced toward Maya who, though she believed him to be only a dream figure, found herself nonetheless cowering behind the tall young man. "I send you to a place of disease and death, and instead of having the grace to die there you return with both in tow."

How, she wondered in confusion, how did this creature know she was sick? How did he know she was dying?

Cathore slipped the corium cylinder back into his pocket. Raising both arms, holding his palms toward the ground, he aimed his fingertips at Madrenga.

"My store of mercy is small, youth, and you have used it up."

Echoing a battle cry he remembered from the fight on the *Thranskirr*, Madrenga raised the massive sword fully over his head and charged. He got exactly two steps before both he and Maya were englobed in a sphere of pale blue flame. Before he even had time to realize the nature of the rotund prison, it began to contract around them.

Raising his sword he swung it in a mighty arc at the curve of pulsating fire. The blade did not penetrate. Maya crowded close but this time he did not respond to her proximity. Bit and Orania were in a frenzy now, barking and neighing their alarm and frustration. He turned to the girl standing behind him. She looked dazed. With his free hand he reached down and shook her.

"You said you could read!" Releasing her shoulder, he indicated the book she held. "Then read! Find something!"

"Find—something? Find what?"

"Something to let us out of this infernal conflagration! Out of this trap!" His fingers tapped the book, hard. "A counterspell. Try!"

"I ..." She stared at him. The burning blue wall was closing in behind her and she could feel the rising heat. What burns first in a dream, she wondered? Clothing, or flesh? "I want to wake *up*!" she wailed.

There was no time for him to be angry at her. "Do as you wish but find something first. Find some *words*!"

"Words," she mumbled, "yes, words." To his immense relief, however transitory that might prove, she opened the book, lowered her gaze, and began skimming. As the ball of flame drew ever tighter around them and the heat continued to intensify, he silently urged her to read faster.

Using his hands he tried to bodily slow the fire globe's contraction. Though for reasons unknown his fingers did not burn, neither did he succeed in holding back the shrinking globe. As the flames used up the air inside he was finding it harder to breathe. Realizing the hopelessness of his efforts he drew his hands back lest they suddenly start to burn. A man with blisters cannot handle a sword—though it was beginning to look as if that opportunity was unlikely to ever again present itself.

As with the first time she had laid eyes on the book's contents, some of the symbols and images were familiar to Maya and some were not. It was the same with the words. It was only when she found a page that seemed as if it might be relevant and hesitantly began to chant its awful poetry that she felt reasonably sure she was pronouncing the words correctly. As she spoke into the night air and felt the end of her thick braid beginning to smolder she wondered if what she was doing in her semi-dazed state would have any consequences at all.

They did.

There came a great *whoosh* and gust of air as the fiery globe exploded and sent blue flame flying outward in every conceivable direction. Sheds, stable buildings, the remaining guards: anything and everything inside the high-walled stone courtyard that was combustible instantly burst into flame. Screaming men afire scattered in all directions until they fell, overwhelmed by the smoke and heat. They burned where they lay. Wasting no time in marveling at the overpowering effect of the countering spell, Madrenga sheathed his slickened sword and rushed to where Hinga Cathore had fallen. Her fingers touching her lips, a wide-eyed Maya followed haltingly.

The warlock's clothes were completely gone. So was most of his flesh, the remainder blackened and steaming. Empty eye sockets stared vacantly at the night sky. Madrenga did not blanch as he knelt to search the smoking corpse. Behind him, Maya turned and vomited. Along with the slight contents of her stomach went a good deal of the certainty she held about being lost in a dream. But not quite all.

Skull, bones, flesh, clothing—all had been burned away from the warlock's body. But the sealed corium container was fireproof as well as waterproof. An elated Madrenga picked it up—and promptly dropped it as the heat it retained threatened to set his own shirt afire. Only when the night air had cooled it sufficiently did he feel safe wrapping it in a fold of his shirt. Rising, he hurried toward the stable.

So intense had been the blast from the exploding blue sphere that it had partially melted some of the bars of the stable cage. At Madrenga's command Orania turned ass-forward and kicked out enough of the weakened barrier for her to duck through. While recovering from the shock of the eruptive blue conflagration Maya had formulated more than a few questions. She didn't get the chance to ask them.

Sweeping her off the ground Madrenga deposited her on the saddle between himself and the pommel while Bit leaped to his usual position atop the double backpack and took hold of the material with his claws.

"HUP—GO NOW!"

Snorting just a little bit of fire herself, Orania charged toward the gate. Several of the surviving guards had regrouped and prepared to bar the way. This proved an unwise decision, as those who were not decapitated by Madrenga's whirling sword went down beneath his mount's thundering hooves. One of those who perished thus was the Harund who had helped to deceive the youth into believing he had friends in Yordd. As he brought his sword straight down instead of swinging it in an arc, Madrenga neatly cleaved the stocky axe-wielder from the top of his skull all the way down to his sternum. Blood fountained and Maya, leaning forward, tried to throw up again. That her stomach was empty did not make the attempt any less raw.

They were forced to halt before a second, barred gate. From the parapet above, concealed guards sent arrows whistling toward the would-be escapees. While Madrenga warded them off with the blade of his sword Bit jumped down and began to gnaw through the heavy oak. When he had weakened it enough, Orania turned without having to be ordered and reduced the remaining wood to splinters.

As they fled down the hillside toward the city there was no indication of pursuit. Behind them jets of intense blue leaped from within Hinga Cathore's compound as if the flames wanted to set the clouds themselves on fire. Leaning back against Madrenga's solid bulk an exhausted Maya found her thoughts drifting.

"What a dream," she murmured. "What a dream. Even if everything really *hurts....*"

CHAPTER SIXTEEN

SOMETHING SMELLED SO WONDERFUL THAT MUCH AS SHE
wanted to, she could no longer keep her eyes closed. She did try,
but as soon as the first bit of sunlight struck her retinas, a second
Bit began licking her face. Warm and cloying, it caused her eyes to
snap open.

An absolutely enormous dog with wide dark eyes and bander-
snatch teeth was energetically cleaning her cheeks, her chin, and
her throat. Disgust overcame shock when he began cleaning her
ears.

"Pfagh, fu—get away!" Without thinking she began flailing
wildly at the unrequested attendant, still too asleep to realize that
the monstrous animal might take her blows the wrong way. That
he did not was a tribute as much to Bit's inherent good nature as
to any training supplied by his master.

"Yuck!" Sitting up, she rubbed furiously at her face in a frantic
attempt to wipe away the last vestiges of canine saliva as the
tongue-lolling perpetrator stepped back. Looking around, her eyes
fell on a pair of precisely folded pale yellow cloths hanging from a
wooden loop bolted to the nearby wall. Clutching at one, she
gratefully scrubbed her face with the dry fabric.

There was that smell again. That thick, wonderful, sweetish

smell. Breakfast today was something different. The cafeteria must …

The full foreignness of her surroundings finally registered with her. She was not in a hospital bed. She was not in a hospital room. Though she could not immediately prove it, she was not in a hospital of any kind.

Then—where was she?

The events of the night before came back to her in a rush. Swept from her meds and bed and monitors by a dream warrior who insisted he was anything but that. Thrown into a raging battle with sword-wielding soldiers and a flame-throwing warlock. Escaping into the night, the rocking motion of a heavy horse lulling her to sleep. Waking up to … to …

Could she dream she was waking up and wake up still in the dream?

The source of the delicious aromas entered, borne in the strong hands of the dream warrior. Or courier, or whatever he really was. Madrenga was carrying a tray crowded with small pots and bowls from which issued the wondrous fragrances she had been inhaling. Setting it down on the small wooden table beside her bed, he smiled encouragingly.

"How did you sleep, Maya Bhargava?"

"Sleep? Did I sleep?" In her mind all that was logical had tangled itself into a Gordian knot and she had no sword of reason with which to dice it. For now she could only stare at the tray and try not to drool. "My gods, what is all this?"

He took a step back and gestured. "A sound breakfast for one who looks like she could use a decent feed. Porridge with cinnamon sugar, eggs Matroush, ponno rolls with honey, lyster bacon, some fresh fruit, and colobead tea."

"Colobead, lyster …" The names didn't matter, she realized. Nothing that smelled so good could possibly be bad for you. Except … Her expression fell.

"What's wrong?" He was suddenly concerned. "Would you like some milk for the tea? I can get it for you."

"I—I'm not supposed to eat solids. Besides my drip I'm only allowed soft foods. Pudding, yogurt—that sort of thing."

He frowned. "I know what puddings are, but of this yoghurt I am ignorant. Try the porridge first. It's soft enough. The eggs are not hard. If you must, you can skip the rolls and fruit and bacon."

She did not. When the first couple of bites of ponno and honey went down and stayed down, she attacked the rest with a fury that made Bit think twice about trying to swipe an overlooked roll. Of one thing she was absolutely certain: wherever she was, she was not eating hospital food. It was not until she had pigged her way through most of what was on the tray that she thought to inquire if he would like to share.

He smiled politely. "I have already eaten, thank you."

She held up a last roll. "No dessert?"

"My dessert," he told her softly, "lies in watching you enjoy yourself."

She did not let the roll go to waste. Licking the honey from her fingers, she realized with a start that she had consumed the entire meal while sitting up in bed. It was the longest continuous period of time she could remember sitting up in bed in—in months.

"Why are you doing this, Madrenga? Why are you being so good to me?"

He shrugged. "You saved my life. I could not have read the counterspell that you found in the book of curses. I would not even have recognized it for what it was. When I took you from the strange room where I found you, I told you that I might need the help of someone who can read. That is why I brought you. My premonition proved to be true. Now mayhap I can help you."

The pleasure she had taken in the phenomenal breakfast fell away. "That's sweet of you, Madrenga, but no one can help me. My condition is terminal. All the doctors say so."

"Ah," he murmured. "Then, not being a doctor, I do not have to agree."

She had to smile at that. "You're a funny sort of warrior. You're big, but I get the feeling you're not that much older than me. Oh, wait, you said you're not a warrior." A broad grin creased her face. Had a mirror been handy she would have been startled to see that the reflection in it had begun to acquire a touch of color. "But you sure don't fight like a courier."

He looked self-conscious. "Strange things have been happening to me since I left Harup-taw-shet. To me and to my companions as well."

"I think maybe," she told him quietly, "the strangeness of my situation tops yours. At least, it does until I can figure out what's going on. *If* I can figure out what's going on." She smiled anew. "The easiest explanation is that the leukemia has gotten to my brain and I've gone completely mad. If the doctors are right, that would make you the offspring of raging endorphins."

"I did not know my parents," he responded stiffly.

She sighed, leaned back, and rested a hand on a stomach that, for the first time in memory, felt full. "Where did you say we are?"

"I did not say, but we are in the town of Allgoeon, which lies athwart the mountain pass of Fannetten, which leads to the lands controlled by Daria. We rode most of the night. Though it is late morning I persuaded the inn's cook to make you a breakfast. Are you tired?"

She pondered her condition and was amazed. "After what you put my body through last night I should be on the verge of death. But I'm only sore. From using muscles I haven't had to use in months." How could a dream strain her muscles, she wondered? Had she tossed that much in her sleep? Wait—wasn't she still asleep? She licked her lips. They were redolent of flavors so real that she had no choice but to wish them to be real.

And still the mountain of food she had just consumed stayed down, and her insides continued to offer no objection to its presence.

"This is the best dream I could possibly imagine. Even if I've gone crazy. Even if it makes me sore."

He rose so sharply from where he had been sitting that Bit had to scramble to get out of the way. "You saved my life. I would try my best to save yours. But a fool who wishes to remain forever a fool cannot be helped!" Approaching the bed he reached down, grabbed her shoulders, and squeezed hard enough so that they started to throb.

"You are not crazy, Maya Bhargava. You are not dreaming. The Chief Counselor to the Queen of Harup-taw-shet foretold that I would find help when I needed it. Did you 'dream' that as well? A now-dead warlock sent me to your realm. Now you are in my realm. Why can you not accept that? Why can you not believe what has happened to you?"

"Please," she whimpered, "my arms ..." He released her. One hand reached up to rub the red streaks where he had been gripping her right shoulder. "I—I don't know. Nothing makes sense anymore. I'm sorry, Madrenga. I suppose if I've gone insane I might as well stop trying to fight it." Her hand fell to touch her stomach again. "Everything that's happened: the place changing, the fighting, the food, even throwing up—it's all so real. But that's what madness is, I suppose. Making the insane real. Crazy is as crazy does." She hazarded a tentative smile. "It's not a bad way to die, thinking this is real. It sure as hell beats staring all day at a hospital room."

"It is a strange sort of acceptance you propound, but I suppose it must do for now. I have only enough money left, I hope, to pay for guidance and assistance in getting through these mountains. I cannot pay for another night in this inn. Can you ride?"

Her laugh tripped over a cough. When she could speak again, she nodded. "I'm not supposed to be able to stand or walk, and I did those, so I suppose I can ride, too."

"Good. Get dressed. We need to go before the last caravan leaves or I will have to wash dishes and chop wood to pay for this room; tasks I dislike in equal measure." He continued to peer down at her.

She gestured at the door. "If you don't mind, Madrenga? I may not have my mind, but I still have my modesty. And take that dog with you. He looks at me like I'm a piece of meat."

He snorted. "To Bit you are a piece of meat. Everyone is." Turning, he opened the heavy wooden door and exited.

Perhaps, she thought in a sly moment, she ought to have asked him to stay. Just to help her get dressed, of course. She had not dressed herself in quite a while. *One step at a time,* she told herself. Slide legs sideways out of the bed, bend knees, hands at your sides, now push down.

She stood. By herself.

The clothes taken from the man Madrenga had killed in the warlock's study lay neatly draped over a nearby chair. Walking over, she wondered how she might make them fit still better. If she could get hold of a needle and some thread—her grandmother had embroidered wedding blouses in the old country and had taught her how to sew. A dying art for a dying girl. She remembered watching as sequins and gold and bits of mirror had slipped like lozenges through the old woman's dexterous fingers.

She studied the man's shirt and trousers. Where to start? She had no proper undergarments and had to begin with …

The hospital gown. The sight of it could not have hit home any harder had someone snuck up behind her and whacked her across the face with a cricket bat. The white garment was cool to the touch, and clean. Someone had seen to it that it was washed during the night. Madrenga. Courier.

And what else had he seen? It didn't matter. Dream world, real world, another world. The cancer that was consuming her body would finish her in a month or two anyway.

She dressed, taking her time with and enjoying a process she had not engaged in for a long, long time. When finally she had finished there was only one item left on the chair. A small, tightly bound book. The book of curses and spells. Picking it up, she eyed it wonderingly before turning toward the door. He trusted her with something of such power. He trusted her that much.

She had no choice but to trust him.

So different from the sterile atmosphere of the hospital was the mountain air that hit her as soon as she stepped outside the inn, so cool and pure and refreshing, that she thought she was going to faint. She didn't have time, because Madrenga once more swept her up in his arms and set her down on the saddle in front of him. The caravan stretched out ahead and behind them; horses, mules, camels, some thickset sway-backed lizards piled high with canvas-covered goods, a trio of tewks and their armed riders, a brace of giant ostrich-like birds saddled by heavily-armed mercenaries, and one extraordinary creature that looked like a land octopus. A horn brayed near the front of the line, setting the entire menagerie of commerce and crankiness in motion.

On both sides of the narrow, winding dirt trail snow-slapped peaks scraped the undersides of scudding white clouds. From her seat in front of Madrenga she was able to lean back against him and enjoy the spectacular scenery. Before the leukemia had weakened her the point where she could no longer travel, her parents had bundled her up and taken her on a trip to the Rockies. The mountains through which she was now traveling looked more like pictures she had seen of the Himalayas. Everything was on a larger scale; higher, more massive, with the white tongues of healthy glaciers licking the mountainsides.

Off to the left of the well-used trade route the slope fell away into a canyon so steep and narrow it was easy to believe no one had ever plumbed its depths. Deep down, a river roared in frustration at being so tightly confined. Things with feathers of wings and things with wings of membranes circled in silence above the rushing white water, competing to kill brown splotches that scurried among the bare rocks and then fighting over the kills.

One of the ostrich-bird riders pulled up alongside Orania and slowed. The woman rider batted her eyes (Maya had never actually seen someone bat their eyes before) at Madrenga and smiled. Then she caught sight of the slender girl riding against his chest and between his arms and her expression fell. Spurring her mount with a double kick to its feathery flanks, she took off toward the front of the column in a clashing of metal bracelets and bells.

Not long thereafter an elderly man edged up beside them riding an ox. To Maya it looked like a perfectly normal ox so long as one discounted its six legs and the fact that it was dark maroon splotched with orange. There was also the matter of the broad bony shield that started just above its eyes and widened as it extended backward to halt just above the shoulder blades. On this natural ossified platform, a gilt samovar steamed merrily away. Surrounding it like horses on a miniature carousel were several cups of similar highly decorated metal.

"Tea?" Madrenga murmured into her ear as he leaned slightly forward.

"What?" His breath was warm mist in her ear, tickling and confusing. "Oh, okay." She caught herself. "You sure it's safe?" She kept her voice down as she indicated the bearded old man. "I mean, he's boiling it atop this cow-thing and there's no telling where the water's come from."

"What a land you must live in," he muttered, "where people can criticize tea." Reaching down, he fumbled with the purse at his waist. Each time he embarked on an expedition to its interior there was less and less to be found. But tea was cheap and he was thirsty too.

Accepting the small payment, the old man carefully poured out two cupfuls, working the heavy samovar like a sailor on a ship, timing his movements to the rolling gait of his plodding mount. He did not ask if they wanted sugar: it was integral to the brew and already present. As they drank he rode alongside, his beast maintaining the same pace as Orania. The aged vendor said nothing, though his professional politeness did not prevent him from stealing the occasional sideways glance at the exceedingly odd couple, their extraordinary horse, and the hideous but happy dog asleep on the mount's hindquarters.

When they finished they handed the exquisite cups back to

their owner. While so very different from where she had come, Maya mused, this place she was maybe-dreaming also had its similarities. In the country of her grandparents the old man would have been called a chaiwallah. How different from that country this place actually was the oldster demonstrated by removing from his waistband a small silver hammer. With this he proceeded, to Maya's small gasp of surprise, to rap the lumbering hexapod beneath him firmly on its head. Apparently, this was the best, or perhaps the only, way of getting the beast's attention through all that bone. It promptly accelerated from a steady plod to a lugubrious trot as its master sought to inveigle the next potential customer in line.

That evening, in response to Madrenga's polite inquiries, a couple of the caravan's hired escorts offered to share their large tent with their fellow travelers. As the three men sat swapping stories, the escorts would take turns casting looks in Maya's direction that were very different from that of the old tea vendor. By now she felt well enough for them to make her nervous. They did not inquire about her, however. While Madrenga was awake the two mercenaries could talk of nothing but combat and far places.

It was near the end of the first week on the trail that she awoke in the middle of the cold mountain night to feel a presence nearby. Blinking, she looked up to see one of the guards looming over her. As she tensed he put a finger to his lips.

"Sssh. There is no need to be afraid, pretty one. Never have I seen a beauty such as yours. Your hair, your eyes, the willow tree that is your body, have called to me since first we met."

"We haven't met," she snapped back nervously. A quick glance to her left revealed the silhouette of Madrenga. He was sound asleep. Would she have time to wake him before a hand went over her mouth, before pressing weight held her down? The guard saw the direction of her gaze and smiled in the near darkness.

"Tonight your large young man's dinner contained a condiment specially prepared. He will sleep exceedingly well." He started to drop toward her. "As will you, when we have finished …"

A low snarl ricocheted through the tent. It came from the deeper registers of a throat that was not human. It drew the immediate attention of Maya and the guard, both equally startled. From near her right shoulder rose a shape like a block of chiseled volcanic rock. Dim light flashed off teeth longer than her middle finger. Bit, it appeared, had been sleeping beside her ever since she and Madrenga had joined the caravan. So soundly had she been sleeping that she had never noted the dog's presence. She noticed it now.

So did the mercenary. Uttering a sharp exclamation, arms windmilling, he rose and fell backward in panic. This caused him to trip over his dozing colleague, who promptly woke up and struck his companion with both fist and slur. As the would-be paramour rushed to climb (and doubtless hide) within his own bedroll, a relieved Maya turned toward the massive black shape now standing fully alert beside her. From partially parted jaws a long wet tongue emerged to begin cleaning her face. Reaching up to scratch the dog and ruffle his ears, she let him finish.

He had earned it.

It was at the top of the highest pass that chaos descended upon the caravan.

To that point all had gone as smoothly as an insurer's wet dream. There had been no sign of the mountain bandits who infested these peaks and canyons. It was because the presence of roving parties of such mounted brigands that savvy travelers hired armed fighters to protect their lives and their goods. For such hazardous country the capricious weather had been more than amenable, with only one brief wall of sleet that had slammed into the front of the caravan and blown quickly on through. With everything in the universe being in balance, the powerful but short-lived storm had resulted in excellent sales for the elderly tea-vendor.

The peace of the perfectly ordinary morning was shattered by the sounds of commotion up near the front of the column. Soon figures both mounted and on foot came racing back toward its tail end. Instead of halting there they continued running down the trail—a bad sign. Frightened traders spurred their steeds to dangerous speeds as they crowded perilously close to the edge of the road and the drop beyond. Bird riders, including the one who days earlier had made eyes at Madrenga, passed the fearful retreating merchants at even greater speeds.

Most unsettling of all was the presence in the panic of members of the caravan's hired escort. Holding fast to their weapons they fled along with everyone else, leaving only expres-sions of fear in their wake. From the front of the line of heavily laden beasts of burden came a flurry of screams; most from animal throats, but some that belonged to people.

Thus aroused, Madrenga hastened to appraise this new state of affairs as best he could. Having been forced to deal with one threatening situation after another since leaving Harup-taw-shet, such analysis was something he had grown progressively better at with each succeeding confrontation. What could it be this time? The much feared but hitherto unseen mountain bandits? A violent dispute between rival merchants? Would either be enough to induce such panic among the caravan that it would extend even to its armed mercenaries? He spoke to the young woman seated in front of him.

"I need to find out what's going on. For all I know it may be Hinga Cathore come back from the dead to challenge us here."

Her face paled. "Do you really think that's possible?"

"Not really," he told her firmly. "But so many things have happened to me since I left my home that I no longer believe anything is impossible. You, for example, should be impossible."

ALAN DEAN FOSTER

Twisting around to look back up at him, she offered a wan smile. "That's what my cousins say to me. That I am impossible."

Not understanding what she meant, he added, "Then I have corroboration. We must find out what is happening before it finds us. Bit!"

At his command the dog jumped down from behind him and started forward. Spurring Orania to a gallop, Madrenga followed.

It was difficult going against the tide of people and animals that was pushing and shoving the other way, but Orania's broad, armored chest punched a path through the mob. As they neared the head of the column they began to encounter bodies. Dead pack animals, the contents of their baggage strewn about, were the first indication that whatever the nature of the force threatening the caravan it was not interested in plunder. Among the twisted and torn carcasses that bloodied the narrow road Madrenga and Maya saw enough body parts to make up two or perhaps three intact mercenaries. The remnants of their weapons lay scattered among them, as shattered as the bodies of their owners. Amid so much blood it was difficult to tell ropes from intestines. Equal parts ominous and mysterious, the dead men and their broken blades alike were coated in a fine layer of ice crystals.

A fresh scream caused both of them to look up. Firming his stance, Bit let out a horrific growl. Orania whinnied and reared despite Madrenga's attempts to calm her.

Bereft of its head, the body of a fourth mercenary came flying around the sharp bend in the road. It landed like a sack of soil, rolled over a couple of times, and came to rest with its limbs akimbo like an unwanted child's toy. Save for the ongoing panic among the people and animals of the caravan lined up behind Madrenga, there was silence for a moment.

Then, a hiss. A hiss that crackled. A long low cloud came around the rocky cliff that formed a corner on the trail. Almost immediately the white pall condensed, froze, and fell to the ground, shattering into long gleaming icicles.

The cloud was followed by a blunt snout from which smaller

242

clouds emerged in regular, steady puffs. These likewise froze and fell to the ground as soon as they contacted the warmer air. Behind the snout came a pair of snaggle-toothed jaws encased in blue scales so pale they were almost white. It was a mouth that looked capable of crushing rock. Or ice. Like pellucid pearls, bulging and reflective eyes attended the jaws. Slowly the massive head turned to peer around the corner and down the road. The first thing it saw were the unfortunate men already stilled. Then the cold, pumpkin-size eyes rose to fasten on dog, horse, and riders.

Bit made a noise like nothing Maya had ever heard before. An increasingly agitated Orania took a couple of steps backward until Madrenga was able to halt her. Maya simply stared. This was all wrong. This was not the animal she had imagined in her dream games, with its flowing whiskers and bright red eyes and splendid wide wings of iridescent carmine and gold. The creature before her was heavy-set and brutish, with a bestial expression and broken gray claws like splintered steel for climbing the glaciers where it lived. As she stared, unable to look away, a long dark blue tongue like a snake's licked out, wrapped itself around the most recently deposited headless corpse, and whipped it back into that yawning maw. When the jaws closed there was a conspicuous crunching sound as bits of shredded flesh and ripped organs oozed out between the ranked teeth. Her stomach turned right over.

"Frost dragon." Madrenga's tone was as cold as their surroundings. "Stay here. Bit, you too—stay!"

Then he was dismounting, leaving her alone in the saddle as he landed boots first on the ground. Drawing his sword and aiming the point toward the monster, he uttered a loud command and charged. Ordered to *stay*, a frantic Bit ran back and forth beside Orania, barking like a mad thing.

Wrong, she thought hysterically, her heart pounding. This was all wrong. He should have fought the dragon earlier, and it should have looked so different, and so many things were all *wrong*, and happening way too fast. It was almost as if *she* was in *his* dream and … and …

No one's dreams, she decided as she swayed slightly and fought to stay conscious and upright in the saddle, should have this much blood in them.

The great blunt reptilian head drew back. Pearlescent eyes focused on the small figure running towards it. Opening wide its crushing jaws, the frost dragon spat. No fire emerged from its mouth, no sharp stink of brimstone polluted the mountain air. Instead, a great gout of vapor issued from the depths of the dark maw. Utilizing more energy than she believed she possessed, Maya screamed.

The cloud slammed into Madrenga head on. It ought to have froze him solid on the spot, turned him into a bipedal ice sculpture, stopped his blood from flowing. It only made him mad. So mad that a faint glow enveloped him from head to foot, a refulgent pulsation like a translucent garment of yellow silk. A second blast from the dragon's mouth engulfed him—and fell away as it turned harmlessly to water.

Enraged, the dragon reared, seeking to smash the puny onrushing shape beneath its great weight. Madrenga did not wait for the massive body to fall on him. Drawing back both arms, he flung the sword with all his strength. Once, long ago in Haruptaw-shet, it had been little more than a knife. He had been quite good at knife-throwing. This was not so very different, he told himself. All that had changed was the size of the blade—and the body behind it.

The sword flew true, straight into the frost dragon's heart. The pearl eyes bulged as taloned forefeet clawed at the long blade that now pierced it halfway through. Knocked backward by the gush of dark blood, Madrenga hit the ground hard. So did the dragon. One madly scratching hind foot finally kicked out the sword, but too late. The wound was mortal. Hissing and howling the monster rolled to its right, as if by so doing it could somehow excise the damage the man had inflicted. It kept rolling until it disappeared right over the side of the cliff. So long was the drop that Madrenga was able to rise to his feet and make it to the edge in time to see the creature, already dead, hit bottom. It lay there, a mountain of flesh half in and half out of the river, as the white water flowed indifferently around it.

Limping slightly, he walked over to where his sword had fallen. Picking it up he sought to wipe the blade clean against the clothes of one of the dead mercenaries. He could not. A thin layer of the dragon's blood was frozen solid to the metal, fused to it by a cold beyond imagining. Red now instead of steel gray, he slipped it back into its scabbard.

"That was—that was incredible! I never dreamed …!" Having dismounted and run toward him, Maya now drew herself up short. Her tone turned reflective. "I never dreamed." A new thought struck her. She looked back to where Orania and Bit stood waiting, then turned again to Madrenga. One hand reached up to wipe blood from his face, then hesitated. "I—I just ran. Just now. To you. I *ran*. I'd forgotten what it was like to be able to run." Tears began to flow down her cheeks and drip off her chin.

He grinned down at her. "Aren't you supposed to be cleaning my face?"

She sniffled, laughed softly, smiled, and began to do so. Wiping his right hand against his side as best he could, he very gently proceeded to brush the already drying tears from her cheeks. Having come up beside them Bit sat down and watched, tongue lolling, his head cocked to one side as he struggled futilely to understand why the two humans were brushing each other's faces with their front paws.

CHAPTER SEVENTEEN

LIKE THE LAYERS OF AN ONION, PORTIONS OF THE CARAVAN began to peel off to go their separate ways as soon as the column reached the base of the eastern foothills. Some merchants set their course for the oasis of Halamanza, some for the cluster of hill towns called Pitriche, and one heavily-laden group of traders struck out for Ars-mak-malda, a country so distant that even to some of the businessfolk from Yordd it was little more than a fable. There was of course a group of merchants who had joined the caravan with the intention of selling their wares in Daria. But after talking with some local colobos herders they chose to join the line going to Pitriche instead. It developed that business was somewhat slow in Daria at the moment.

Lying under siege has that effect on commerce.

"What are you going to do now?" Sitting on the carpet inside the tent that were just two of the many gifts the grateful traders had bestowed on Madrenga for saving the caravan from the frost dragon, Maya studied the young man who was standing in the doorway. After a further moment's contemplation of the terrain outside he turned back to her. Bit lay asleep nearby while Orania browsed freely outside.

"I have no choice. Having come so far and being now so close,

I have to try to get into the city to deliver the scroll." When she started to comment but broke down in a fit of coughing his voice and expression became concerned. "How are you feeling?"

"Odd." She took a long drink from the nearby water vessel. "One moment I feel halfway normal and the next it's like I'm back in the hospital bed unable to move more than my hand. It makes no sense, Madrenga."

"Of course it doesn't. Nothing that has happened to me since leaving Harup-taw-shet has made any sense. Why should it be any different for you?"

Her brows drew together. "I'm not just an accessory to your mission, you know. I have a life of my own. We still haven't determined if you're just something I dreamed up."

"Or I you." He softened his tone. "The way you feel may be due to a tug on your existence. Part of you belongs back in your own realm while part of you now exists here. Your essence lies on the border between, neither fully here nor fully there."

She coughed again, but less roughly this time. "Why don't you just leave me here, with Bit for protection? If you're going to try and ride into a city that's under siege, I'd only slow you down."

He shook his head. "I can't leave you. Especially in the vicinity of a besieging army. Remember what almost happened to you that night on the road? And that involved a mercenary hired to protect you." He sounded considerably less young now. "To a renegade military force a girl alone would be no different from a sheep or a covey of fowl: just something else to scavenge."

"I'm willing to risk it." She smiled thinly. "I'm going to die soon anyway. I don't want you to fail in your mission because of me."

"I won't." He returned her hard smile. "I'm going to succeed in spite of you."

She took another sip of water. "That doesn't flatter me, Madrenga. Forget about me. If you succeed—*when* you succeed— you can come back and pick me up."

"No. We go together." He turned back toward the open tent flap. "I'll hear no more about it."

"Yes, master," she replied sarcastically.

"I am no one's master." One hand was gripping the side of the tent opening. "Not yours, not Bit's, not Orania's. Sometimes I think not even mine." Exhaling heavily he pulled the opening shut. "Get some rest. We'll wait until the sun sleeps and then head northeast toward the city. Moving at night we should encounter fewer patrols."

She spoke admiringly. "For someone raised in the streets you seem to know a lot about military tactics."

He smiled back as he moved toward his own resting place. "What do you think boys who live in the streets and have nothing to do play at?"

The night had turned pleasantly cool when they packed their belongings and started out. Among the small mountain of gifts the caravan merchants had bestowed on their young savior was a bogoln to carry them. The sturdy, stout dray animal looked like a mule that had been stepped on by a giant. Built low to the ground, sure footed and with two heads, it could carry a great weight a considerable distance without losing sight of the trail. If they had to make a run for it, however, they would have to leave it and its cargo behind. In flight there was no way it could keep up with Orania.

For most of the night they plodded onward through rounded, scrub-coated hills that grew lower and lower, like mocha ice cream melting into the sand. From the crest of a modest escarpment the scrubland and veldt stretched out before them. Shimmering like quicksilver in the distance, a river that was broad and deep was fringed with the checkerboard pattern of hundreds of small farms. On the far side of the watercourse the well-developed fields were dotted with small towns that reached to the horizon. On the near side the cultivated land broke like a green wave against the outer walls of Daria City.

Within the walls and the high buildings they protected, hundreds of lights were winking out as the city awoke to a new dawn. Between the last of the hills and the first reaches of the eastern wall, a ring of other lights was being similarly extinguished. Belonging to the forces of the besieging army, these formed a great arc that encircled the city from north to south and was interrupted only by the river.

Madrenga's spirits fell as he studied the terrain. How was he going to get through so many soldiers? Each light that flickered out as the sun rose represented the bivouac of an unknown number of men. The line appeared unbroken. He considered circling around the besiegers and approaching the city from the river. But surely the aggressors would have posted sentries on the far shore or even on boats to ensure that no supplies or reinforcements reached Daria from that direction. Somehow they would have to find a way through the besiegers' lines.

"Tonight," he told the girl seated in front of him. "We'll move back a ways, finding a good place to camp, and sneak into the city tonight."

She twisted her head around to look back at him. "Not a very original plan."

"You have a better idea?" he snapped.

"I could try to dream us inside."

"Yes," he replied dryly. "You do that. I think it will have as much effect as trying to dream away the man who tried to attack you, or dreaming away the frost dragon. While you are at it, why not dream us up dinner as well?"

She glared up at him. "I could also try to dream you up some manners."

"You see?" Pulling on the reins, he turned Orania and the little troupe started back the way they had come. "More proof that this is real."

"Your sarcasm certainly is."

Miffed, she said nothing until they found a small sheltered hollow among the rocks and scrub. Too weak to help, she could only sit and watch and fume as he set up the tent and unpacked carpet and utensils. While Bit went off exploring and Orania wandered in search of fresh fodder, the chunky bogoln hunkered down and promptly went to sleep.

CHAPTER EIGHTEEN

It was after sleeping away all of the morning and some of the afternoon that Madrenga awoke to the unsettling realization that neither his dog nor his horse were anywhere to be seen. Bending over Maya he shook her gently until she awoke. Rubbing sleepily at her eyes, she squinted at the half open tent flap.

"It's still daylight? I thought we were supposed to sleep until nightfall."

"I've been outside." He looked and sounded worried. "I can't find Bit, or Orania. I've called softly. It's not like either of them to roam so far."

She continued waking up. "Maybe food or interesting things are harder to find around here."

"Maybe." He straightened. "I'm going to risk shouting. We're far enough from the besiegers that I don't think I'll be heard." Turning, he exited the tent.

She heard him calling for his companions, his voice rising or falling depending on his distance from the tent. When he had been quiet for some time she started to grow nervous. Rising from the carpet she walked slowly to the entrance and pulled the flap fully aside.

"Madrenga, what is …?" The remaining words caught in her

throat as she put the back of her left hand to her open mouth.

The man standing guard outside the tent was not Madrenga.

After tying her hands they slung her over a horse: one more prize to convey back to camp along with the bogoln and its cargo. Only upon arrival did she see a disarmed Madrenga, securely bound in heavy chains. Despite their desperate circumstances she was unutterably relieved to see that he was alive and unharmed. Her relief was reciprocated.

"Maya! Are you all right? Did they hurt you?" He glared at the leather-armored warrior who was leading the horse on which she was bound. "Did they do—anything?"

Dismounting, the warrior grinned at him. "Not yet, outlier." He looked over at Maya. "Not much there, but a slim young duck is tastier than an old fat one. Myself, I'd rather take my share of the spoils from your beast's burden. But that will be up to the Colonel-Captain."

Roughly wrestled off her horse, Maya immediately collapsed to the ground. Madrenga strained futilely at his bonds. Astoundingly, one or two of the links that held him chained seemed to stretch slightly. But his unnatural strength gave out before the steel did.

"Don't touch her! She's under a curse. She's—dying."

"Oh, so?" With one hand the leader of the troop yanked the girl to a standing position. "I thank you for that information, outlier. Now I will be sure not to request her as part of my share."

Other warriors wrestled the bound Madrenga forward until he was standing beside Maya. Then the two of them were hustled ungently toward a beautifully decorated tent high and wide enough to hold dozens of devotees without crowding.

Despite hurting all over she managed to find her voice. "What happened, Madrenga? I watched you kill a dragon. How did you get yourself caught like this?"

The fury he expressed was directed entirely at himself. "I found Bit and Orania down by a waterhole. Beside them was a nearly consumed wild hog and much chewed vegetation. I thought they had simply eaten too much and had fallen into an overstuffed sleep. Thirsty from searching and calling for them I took a moment to drink before waking them. Before I knew what was happening I fell down among them." He indicated their captors. "The waterhole had been poisoned with a somnambulant. When I awoke it was to find myself bound too securely to break free." With a gesture of his head he indicated the area to their left. "Bit and Orania are over that way, still sleeping and tightly tied. It may be that when they awake they can break free. I don't know. Orania's legs are burdened with steel hobbles. Bit likewise, and muzzled as well." He licked his lips.

"We are in a bad way, Maya. I have been fortunate thus far. Several times my companions and I have fought our way out of difficult situations, but each time we were free to use arms and legs and teeth to do so. This time …" His voice trailed away.

They were almost to the oversize tent. Resting their hands on the hilts of their swords, a pair of leather-clad Golgox flanked the entrance. Their blades were as long as Maya was tall and nearly as broad. Other than a deep-browed glower they offered no comment as the two bound prisoners were marched past them and inside.

The interior of the tent was, in essence, a portable palace. All the trappings of barbaric royalty were present, from the gilded and bejeweled throne that could be quickly disassembled for transport on horseback to the heraldic banners that hung from the ceiling supports. Consorts and commanders chattered away like crickets on a sultry summer evening, their attire a mix of the warlike and decorative. None wore metal save in the form of blades long and small. To a man their armor consisted of the most exquisitely embossed and incised leather. Some of this had been dyed in bright colors the better to highlight each individual display of artwork.

Seated on the throne, the middle-aged man with the narrow black beard had eyes only for the prisoners. Neither the casual conversation nor the presence of a number of beautiful women distracted him from the new arrivals. His eyes were like little obsidian beads, shiny and still. Being of medium height and build, he was notably less imposing than some of the physical specimens in the tent. A snake among dogs, Madrenga decided. The dogs looked far more impressive, but it was the snake that was deadly.

The warrior who had escorted them in gave them a rough shove forward but did not command them to kneel. Madrenga would have resisted such an order while Maya quite simply could not have complied. Her health had improved miraculously, but not to the point where she was capable of dropping to her knees with her hands tied behind her back.

"The spies, Colonel-Captain."

The setter of the siege eyed the two youths for a long moment. Then he rose, stepped down off the low dais on which the portable throne had been placed, and walked toward them. Conversation in the tent ceased as everyone turned to watch.

Slowly he walked back and forth in front of Maya, studying her intently. When his rough hands moved across her she trembled but held her ground. Looking on, Madrenga ground his teeth but said nothing. This was not the time and place to put one's life into the pot. Better to wait and hope for a higher card.

Satisfied, the Colonel-Captain grunted and shifted his attention to Madrenga, looking him up and down.

"Quite a specimen. This one might make a fine slave, once he's been castrated." He peered deep into the younger man's eyes. "You are a spy, then—boy?"

"We're not spies. We're only travelers who hoped to visit Daria."

The Colonel-Captain nodded. "And visit Daria you shall, in our company, once we have surmounted the city's walls, smashed its gates, or accepted their formal offer of surrender. Being a merciful man, I am content to let you live and accept you as slaves, but in order for me to do this you must prove you are not spies."

"You can't prove a negative."

"What?" Moving as quick as the serpent Madrenga had imagined him to be, the Colonel-Captain shifted to his left to once more confront Maya. "Are you correcting me? Don't correct me, girl. I don't like being corrected. Spy or not, I've mind to give you to the lower ranks. When they're done with you, they'll cook you. Or maybe they'll cook you first." His smirk was most unpleasant. "It depends what they are most hungry for. With warriors in the field one never knows."

She did not reply. It was far and away the most sensible thing she could have done.

He waited for a minute, just in case she was stupid enough to challenge him again, and then returned his attention to her companion.

"You say you're only travelers hoping to visit the accursed city. For what purpose? To visit relatives? To see the sights? You do not look like merchants to me. In any event the stock of goods that was found with you, while of notable quality and variety, is too slight to mark you as traders. Nor do you have the smell of commerce about you." He took a step closer and his voice tightened. "If none of those identifies your purpose in coming here, then why should I not mark you as spies?"

As Madrenga thought furiously for a reason, any reason, that would satisfy the remorseless Colonel-Captain, he wished Haruptaw-shet's Chief Counselor was present. Natoum would know what to say, would know how to disarm with words this leader of brutes. But Natoum wasn't here. Maya had spoken up once and nearly gotten herself disposed of on the spot. It was left up to him, then.

Try as he might he could not think of anything to say that might successfully challenge this barbarian's thesis. Like his warrior, the Colonel-Captain had made up his mind that the two younger interlopers were spies, and were to be treated as such.

About to release them to be disposed of as he saw fit by the burly warrior who had brought them in, the Colonel-Captain hesitated. Something had caught his attention, and it was not Maya. His eyes dropping to Madrenga's waist, he nodded, then raised his gaze anew.

"There is a transfer cylinder at your belt, soon-to-be-slave.

What is it?"

Madrenga stared past him lest the man read his eyes. "Nothing, merciful sir. Just another piece of my personal kit."

"Really?" The Colonel-Captain stepped forward. "May I see it?" Without waiting for an answer he reached out and unfastened it from the young man's belt. Madrenga squirmed mentally but there was nothing, absolutely nothing he could do except continue to pretend that the cylinder was worthless.

The Colonel-Captain turned the silvery container over in his fingers. "This is corium, isn't it? Yes, I'm sure it is." He smiled. "I pride myself on a small knowledge of precious metals." He held the container up to the light of a nearby oil lamp. "Expertly worked, too. You say it is nothing more than a part of your personal effects?" Madrenga nodded assent, hoping he was not doing so too vigorously. "You have expensive taste, young man. Either that," he concluded shrewdly, "or you are delivering it to someone else on behalf of someone else. Someone in the city you say you desire to visit, perhaps?"

"It is only part of my ..."

"Of your personal kit; yes, yes, so you insist. An excess of insistence, if you ask me." Taking his time, he broke the outer wax seal and began to unscrew the top of the cylinder. "Now what might one suppose a container of this quality could contain? Personal revelations? Potentially valuable. Commercial knowledge? More valuable still. Diplomatic secrets?" He was watching Madrenga very closely now. "Who can say? But we will see."

Damn the artisans of Harup-taw-shet, a despondent Madrenga thought to himself! If only they had made the scroll container out of plain, unadorned wood. But then neither the container nor its precious contents would have survived this long. As the Colonel-Captain drew out the tightly rolled length of ribbon-bound gold foil, Maya unexpectedly lurched forward.

"Kill me, if you must, but let my friend and his possessions go untouched and unharmed."

Surprised, the Colonel-Captain paused with the scroll half out of its container. If the barbarian was surprised, Madrenga was genuinely shocked.

"Maya! Don't go crazy on me, not now! Don't say such a thing!"

When she looked over at him she was smiling thinly. "Why, what's wrong? I'm going to die anyway. What's the difference if it happens sooner or later?" She turned resolutely back to the leader of the besieging forces. "Give my friend back his property and let him go, and you can do what you want with me."

The uncomprehending Colonel-Captain responded with a mixture of sorrow and admiration. "Girl, you started dying the moment you came into the possession of my officer and his men. You are quite correct when you say that you're going to die anyway. But it will be in a manner and time of my choosing or theirs." He looked her up and down in the most insulting manner possible. "Something already owned cannot be offered as a gift."

Swallowing, she lowered her eyes. "I'll do whatever you want —voluntarily."

"Your boldness surely does you credit. But it doesn't buy you any." Again he flashed that dreadful, dehumanizing smile. "What you do not understand is that willingness among captives is not something my men particularly value. They will do what they wish to do. Whether you cooperate in the fulfillment of their desires or not is immaterial to them, and to me."

Maya subsided and lowered her eyes. It was bad enough this horrible man was going to allow her to be abused and killed before her time. In addition, he had taken a moment to deliberately diminish and devalue her first. She felt cheaper than dirt; all the more so because her most valiant effort had done nothing to help Madrenga.

Removing the contents of the battered but still intact corium cylinder, the Colonel-Captain undid the formal ribbon that held them closed, unrolled the scroll, and began to read. Madrenga closed his eyes. On several occasions previously he believed he had failed in his mission. Now he could be certain of it. He could only hope with all his heart that the information that was contained on the scroll and was now about to be revealed contained within it nothing that could bring harm to Harup-taw-shet itself.

A few of the onlookers murmured expectantly. One pair of senior officers nudged each other. The only other sound in the tent was Maya's quiet weeping, which was universally ignored. The Colonel-Captain read, his eyes moving down the scroll. He reached the bottom.

Then he began to laugh.

Starting small, it soon became a great roaring bellowing succession of guffaws. His whole body shook with delight. Ever alert to an opportunity to flatter, everyone else inside the tent except the two prisoners soon joined in. Though they guffawed and squalled and howled at they knew not what, none could match the sheer, overpowering degree of the Colonel-Captain's amusement. Meanwhile Maya continued to sob helplessly while the chain-bound Madrenga could only gaze at the carpet underfoot and silently bemoan his failure.

The riot of unconstrained hilarity continued until the Colonel-Captain abruptly stopped in mid-chortle. What he was staring at no one could say because he did not hold his gaze long enough for anyone to track his line of sight. For an instant he stood swaying ever so slightly before finally falling over backwards to slam into the carpet. When he hit the ground his right hand snapped open and the scroll spilled from his fingers.

Within the tent, no one moved. For a moment it seemed that no one breathed. Even Maya was shocked into silence. Finally a senior clansman hesitantly approached and knelt beside his fallen leader. With one hand he lifted the Colonel-Captain's right hand. The arm, Madrenga noted, was completely limp. Bending forward, the clansman turned his head sideways and placed his right ear against his leader's chest. He remained like that for several moments before straightening. When he finally spoke, his words were suffused with disbelief.

"The Colonel-Captain Vashak-Len of the Southern Horde is

dead."

Under her breath, so low that not even Madrenga could hear, Maya whispered, "Heart attack. He laughed so hard for so long he …" Even her whisper trailed away to nothingness.

One of the armed ladies present had moved to pick up the dropped scroll. Now she retreated quickly. Cries of *"cursed! … foul content! … the words are cursed!…"* and worse began to be muttered.

Expressions of general bewilderment accompanied by murmurs of confusion began to make the rounds of the gathering. Then one leather-and-fur clad warrior moved toward the prisoners, drawing a long curved blade as he did so. As Madrenga's heart missed a beat the fighter placed the scythe-like edge of his long knife against Maya's neck. With his free hand he grabbed her long braid and pulled her head back to more fully expose her throat. He glared unforgivingly at the other prisoner.

"The scourging written words have slain our beloved Colonel-Captain Vashak!" As the knife edge pressed a little more firmly against Maya's skin she whimpered in fear. "*You* read the words now—or I will let out her blood where she stands!"

What a cruel bitch was Fate, Madrenga thought to himself as he inhaled his own agony. His response flowed out of him in a great, gasping moan of helplessness.

"Don't! I'll do whatever you want, you can do whatever you want to me, but leave her alone. She's no part of this, she doesn't even belong here, and I …" he hung his head anew, "I cannot read."

The clansman holding the knife to Maya's throat stared at him a moment. He did not laugh. Not because he feared sharing the Colonel-Captain's fate, but because he could not read either. The same was true of many of those present. Bearing in mind the Colonel-Captain's shocking fate, those few who could read chose not to volunteer the information.

The clansman hesitated. Was this tall, powerful youth nothing more than he claimed to be? A bold but ignorant fighter like the clansman himself? Or was he lying? Grimacing at the prisoner he held he edged the blade inward ever so slightly, just enough to draw blood. Maya let out a cry, Madrenga a moan of helplessness. A small drop of blood from the girl's neck dribbled out onto the clansman's thumb—and sank in, absorbed as if by a sponge.

The warrior gaped at his hand. There was no sign of the blood that had leaked from the tiny wound on the girl's neck. A moment passed. Then, without any warning, blood began to pour from his gums and nose. The lymph nodes around his neck, stomach, groin, and beneath his arms swelled suddenly and alarmingly. His skin turned from a healthy sunburned beige to white and his breath came in increasingly short gasps. As he stumbled in circles his colleagues and comrades hastened to move away from him. Before he reached the wall of the tent he was down and dying.

Madrenga was no less taken aback by what he had seen than everyone else in the tent. Preoccupied with one of their own who was presently dying a death as inexplicable as it was horrible, no one moved to stop him when he shuffled over to stand closer to Maya.

"What just happened? What did you do to that fighter's poor murderous soul?"

"I-I don't know." Maya looked as bewildered as everyone else. A trickle of blood from her throat continued to run down her neck and pool against the top of her shirt. "His symptoms, what he's exhibiting, they're those of a kind of leukemia. Like the disease I have, but not exactly."

Madrenga's eyes grew very wide. "Some of your blood got on him. He contracted your sickness. Only instead of months it went through him in minutes."

She looked up at him. What he said made no sense. And why should that, she reflected, be any different from everything else that had happened to her recently? That was happening even as she spoke? Could it be that for reasons unknown, that even while tightly bound she was not entirely helpless? Could she, after all, do something in her own defense?

Bending her head forward she slurped up some of her own blood, turned, and with all the force she could muster spat the salty fluid at the nearest cluster of besiegers. Her aim was nonspecific and the bloody spray she expectorated trifling in volume, but her effort was forceful enough to ever so slightly dampen the neck of one woman and the left forearm of the man standing next to her.

Before they could turn completely to identify the source of the vermillion spittle, both had begun to bleed at the mouth and nose and turn pale. The woman collapsed in the warrior's arms a moment before he too fell to the floor. Maya was already reloading before they hit the ground. Having backed away from his bound companion a stunned Madrenga was careful to give her room lest some of her blood accidentally land on him.

As the bound prisoner's puffed-out cheeks turned toward them, utter panic descended on the interior of the tent. Huge muscular men screamed like children as they fled through the single opening. Trampled or flung aside, concubines and warrior women alike were among the last to flee. Brave in the face of an enemy, fearless when under attack, they understood instinctively that swords and spears were of no use against the inexplicable malady that had in short order struck down three of their number. In less time than it would have taken a warlock to lay a curse, the last of them had fled from the presence of the two prisoners. Their panic spread to the pair of Golgox guards, who joined their lesser brethren in flight.

They would not forsake the command tent forever, Madrenga knew. Eventually one or two would gather up enough courage to explain to their countrymen what had taken place. With bowmen in tow they would return to finish off the prisoners from a distance beyond which Maya could not spit. The slight wound the now dead warrior had inflicted on her neck was already beginning to seal itself. Soon the trickle of blood would halt completely. He did not want to be the one to have to start it flowing again.

Hurriedly searching through the vacated surroundings, he

spotted one abandoned battle axe and shuffled over to it as fast as his chained ankles would allow. Some hasty but adept maneuvering with his feet enabled him to jam the handle beneath a heavy wooden settee. Sitting down facing away from the weapon he presented his bound wrists to the steel blade. As he sawed away he praised the unknown blacksmith who had ground so fine an edge. Whether it would stay sharp enough only time and effort would tell.

His arms and shoulders were beginning to cramp when the chain that linked together the bands on his wrists finally separated. With his hands now free he made short work of the chains around his legs and ankles. Then he turned his attention and efforts to releasing Maya from her bonds. Made of leather instead of metal these quickly succumbed to the blandishments of the axe. Her neck, he noted with profound relief, had stopped bleeding completely. While it turned out to be a fortuitous twist of fate that her tormentor had cut her, they were even more fortunate he had cut no deeper.

As the two of them moved cautiously toward the tent entrance Madrenga reflected on the wisdom of old Natoum. The Chief Counselor had picked out a courier who was inherently immune to whatever embedded curse or magicked words had brought low the Colonel-Captain because he had chosen one who could not read the scroll's contents even if someone tried to force him to do it.

A glance outside revealed that none of their captors were lingering in the immediate vicinity. Ducking back within, Madrenga quickly recovered the scroll where Vashak-Len had dropped it, carefully rerolled and retied it, and slipped it back into its corium container. After screwing on the cap and clipping the metal cylinder back onto his belt he rejoined Maya near the front of the tent.

No one appeared to confront them. As they looked in astonishment, tents and other equipment were being broken down, gear and supplies loaded onto wagons, torches extinguished, siege engines taken in tow or abandoned. Word of what had happened to the Colonel-Captain and then three of his most respected fighters had spread through the encampments like wildfire. By nature a suspicious people, the besieging clans wanted nothing to do with those whose weapons included written curses and lethal blood.

"Why don't they shoot at us from a distance instead of just running away?" a stunned Maya wondered aloud.

Madrenga considered. "Those who witnessed what happened saw their commander die of words and laughter. Then a warrior and two more killed by a completely different means. Perhaps a few did think of loosing some arrows and crossbow bolts in our direction. To one unnatural means of execution such brutal folk as these could respond. Encountering two different ones has left them confused and uncertain. I believe that no archer or anyone else could be found who would be willing to chance sacrificing themselves to yet a third method." He put a hand on her right shoulder (though not before ensuring that it was free of her blood).

"Come. Let's find and free Orania and Bit. If these people assume you and I are cursed, or masters of the dark arts, they will not risk that my companions are free of such association, and will therefore not chance taking them with them."

Sure enough, horse and dog had been abandoned as completely as the late Colonel-Captains' tent. A joyful Madrenga saw that his sword was there too, tossed casually atop the pack on Orania's back. Recovering the weapon to which he had grown more than a little attached he proceeded to free his friends. After an ecstatic Bit had done his best to lick Madrenga's skin from his face, the three mounted the armored horse and headed downslope toward the walls of Daria as fast as Orania could carry them.

So preoccupied were they with their own unexpected and unlikely escape that they did not pause to consider the rather remarkable fact that by themselves the two of them had inadvertently raised the siege of the city.

CHAPTER NINETEEN

ANOTHER TIME, ANOTHER DAY, MADRENGA WOULD HAVE
marveled at Daria. At the stone towers sheathed in colored gran-
ites, the fountains of polished marble, the broad streets with their
elegant shopfronts that were busy with well-dressed citizens.

Hesitant, frightened, well-dressed citizens, he told himself.
Peering out from half-open doors and the windows of living quarters above; men, women, and finger-pointing children followed
the progress of the young warrior, his female companion, and his
hulking animals as they made their way toward the palace. Word
had spread quickly through the walled metropolis of the youth
who had arrived at the main gate claiming to have single-handedly
put an end to the barbarian siege. Admiration for his having
managed to reach the gate without getting killed was followed by
disbelief at the sight of the besieging army packing up and quietly
departing. Once the flight of the enemy was confirmed by outrid-
ers, it was a brave Darian defender indeed who dared to so much
as approach the stranger to thank him. Clearly powerful forces
were at work of which only the most sophisticated and knowledgeable scholars might make sense.

Had they really wrought death by laughing and spitting?
Madrenga asked himself. Having as a child on several occasions

seen the use to which nobles put the intangible, invisible aura of power, he had no intention of voluntarily surrendering that which had apparently attached itself to him and Maya.

Maya. Another time, another day, he would have enjoyed the sights of the grand city at the edge of the desert. But not at this time and not on this day. Not while she was growing weaker as he watched. Bringing her back with him from the place of the warlock's banishment had given her a burst of unexpected strength. That was now clearly beginning to fade. She did not have to tell him it was so and he did not have to ask. He could see the increasing tiredness in her face, perceive its consequences in her slowing pace and heavier breathing. Dying in her own realm, she was now dying in his. Soon now, very soon, he would be able to devote all his time and energy toward helping her. But first there was one thing he must do.

In a little while now, he would fulfill his obligation.

Though he had willingly, even gladly, taken on the mission, with each passing day and each subsequent near-fatal incident, failure had come to seem a greater and greater likelihood. Now he was here, in Daria, on the verge of completing the task. It scarce seemed possible.

The palace of Zhelerasjju, Queen of Daria and all the dry lands and green rivers to the eastern horizon, gleamed beneath the afternoon sun like a mirage of the ghost lands it echoed. The royal guard that formed up around him as he dismounted maintained a respectful distance. Though trained to present a defiant and indifferent face to any visitors consigned to their care, individual soldiers could not keep from casting sideways looks at the imposing young warrior who had raised the siege of the city. Despite their curious glances they concealed their nervousness well, save for those who were left behind to look after the visitors' horse and, especially, his monstrous dog.

There were many steps. Too many for Maya, who had to stop several times to catch her breath. If anything, Madrenga thought worriedly as he watched her, whatever benefit she had gained from accompanying him was wearing off faster with each passing day. If nothing could be done, if nothing *was* done, the dark understanding in his mind and the cold knot in the pit of his stomach told him she would be dead within the week. That realization had begun to bother him more than he cared to admit.

So many shields decorated with different emblems and insignia lined the walls of the reception room that little of the stone of which the palace was made showed between them. It was as if the chamber had been paneled in shields. The throne on which Queen Zhelerasjju sat was unexpected, fashioned not of gold or bejeweled metals but of the finest bits of marquetry Madrenga had ever seen. There must have been tens of thousands of pieces of exotic wood in the high-backed chair of office, flashing more than a dozen different unstained colors. As an exemplar of royal workmanship it was impressive without being overbearing. Portrayed in wood, entire histories marched in miniature across the arms, legs, back, and seat, ever-present reminders to whoever sat on the throne of the considerable legacy to which Daria and its lands were heir.

Queen Zhelerasjju herself was about the same age as Alyriata of Harup-taw-shet. Perhaps a little older but no less imbued with inherent beauty and nobility of countenance, Madrenga thought to himself as he and Maya approached. In the presence of royalty Maya had summoned her reserves, struggling to look alert and presentable even if within she was feeling very different.

Halting a short distance from the seated queen, Madrenga bowed slightly. Striving to curtsey, Maya nearly fell and had to be steadied by her much larger companion. Though she said nothing, the look on Zhelerasjju's face denoted her sympathy.

Taking a deep breath, Madrenga removed the corium cylinder from his belt, dropped to one knee, and offered it to the dignified, regally dressed woman seated before him.

"I am honored to present this scroll to Queen Zhelerasjju of Daria on behalf of Queen Alyriata of Harup-taw-shet, with all goodwill and greetings."

She nodded once, took the cylinder, and started to open it.

Done, Madrenga thought to himself as he straightened beside Maya. It was unbelievable how much joy and relief could come from the saying to oneself of a single short four-letter word. Then, with a start, he remembered what had happened to the Colonel-Captain of the besieging army. He had been so focused on finally delivering the scroll that that extraordinary incident had entirely escaped his mind. As anxiety flooded through him he moved to hastily inform her majesty of what had taken place in the enemy encampment—only to end up maintaining his silence. It was too late.

She was reading the scroll. Attentively, closely, but without a hint of a smile crossing her lips. The reading provoked no amusement, no violent hilarity, no heart-stopping laughter: not so much as a hesitant giggle. When she had finished, Queen Zhelerasjju neatly rerolled the scroll and slipped it back into its container. Madrenga and Maya could only stare.

"Thank you for bringing me this, young sir. It is most welcome. I assure you that in the course of your return journey home you will have the additional pleasure of carrying my reply back to your Queen."

Madrenga's spirits fell and he tried not to slump. Really, ought he to have expected anything else? He told himself that he had to return home anyway, and with the still-unexplained changes he and his animals had undergone and the knowledge he had gained, it should prove less of a near-fatal experience than had the journey outward.

"I will of course be honored to convey Daria's response, your majesty," he managed to mumble.

"Now then," she said briskly as she handed the cylinder to the heretofore unmoving albino Harund who had been standing silently at attention to the left of the throne, "I know this must have been an arduous and difficult journey for you." Before Madrenga could even begin to relate the harrowing details of his trip she added, "in addition to which you have apparently managed to somehow persuade our ruthless assailants to peacefully depart our borders. While the first achievement merits our admiration, the second demands a reward. Though I dislike dealing with magicians and the mysterious, I have no choice but to recognize the results of your efforts. It is undeniable that you have saved many lives and much property. Name your reward, young sir."

Though he had expected nothing of the sort, Madrenga was quick to take advantage of the offer. With a nod he indicated the now pale and drawn young woman standing beside him.

"My friend is from a land far, far away. Inconceivably far away. As she was suffering there beneath a curse that promised death inevitable, I brought her here in hopes that help might be found for her condition. For a while she bettered from the change itself. That has now begun to seep away from her as does water down a steep slope. Is there anything your majesty might suggest? Perhaps your court physicians and mystics have access to medical knowledge unknown in Daria."

The look on her face indicated that the Queen was giving the visitor's emotional request her full attention. Eventually she turned and beckoned to an elderly couple who had been standing in a doorway off to one side. Approaching the visitors they commenced a close examination of a hesitant Maya; running their hands over her body, feeling of her hair, staring into her eyes, sniffing her torso, and generally acting like the doctors they were not.

Upon concluding this idiosyncratic but thorough examination they shuffled over to the queen and bent their elderly bodies toward her the better to hear what their liege might have to say about the matter. While Madrenga and Maya looked on intently, the three important personages conversed softly among themselves. When finally they concluded their conversation, Madrenga felt he already knew what their response would be. He had seen both the old man and woman shaking their heads one time too many for him to be optimistic.

He was right, and yet he was wrong.

"What you ask is beyond our modest curative powers," the old man explained in an aged but strong voice. "Truly the girl lies under a lethal curse of considerable dimensions. It lies not within our ability to drive it from her body, whose farthest recesses it has already penetrated."

A barely articulate sound escape Maya's half-closed lips.

"But," added the old woman, "there is one who might possess the power to do so." Her husband, or partner, or paramour, nodded agreement as she spoke. "The Witch of Si'abayoon."

The strange sibilant name meant nothing to Madrenga and less to the downcast Maya, but mere mention of it was enough to trigger a rush of nervous murmuring among those in attendance. Such reactions did not bode well for contacting the individual in question, Madrenga felt. Even the Queen seemed nonplussed as she regarded her most senior advisors.

"How can you propose such a thing? These who stand here before us are undeniably brave, and perhaps special in ways we cannot conceive, but to suggest that ones so young deliberately seek out the Si'abayoon is effectively to send them to their deaths."

The old man shrugged ever so slightly. "The girl is already doomed by the curse that lies upon her body. We sense that the boy-man has avoided death many times to reach Daria. They asked for a solution to their problem. We have provided one. The only possible one. What next to do is his choice and her choice. We make no recommendation one way or the other." His partner added her concurrence.

Maya coughed. She was coughing more each day, Madrenga knew. When she had regained control of her breathing she turned to him and peered up into his dark eyes.

"You don't have to do this. I'm ready to die. I was ready to die when you took me from my hospital bed and brought me—here. You risked your life to carry out your mission. It would be wrong of you to risk it again for me. Especially when there's no guarantee of success."

Ignoring the fact that a queen, her advisors, and her immediate royal court were watching, he replied without hesitation. "If I've learned one thing in life it's that there are no promises. There is only hope. The advisor is right: in coming here I've had to face death several times. I think I know him now, a little. Death. He's no longer a stranger to me and—I'm not afraid of strangers. If you're willing to chance this, I'll go with you. We all die some time."

"Some sooner than others," she murmured. Then she threw herself at him. When he embraced her back she all but vanished within his enveloping arms.

"Brave and foolish." The Queen did not smile. "I can do no more and no less than wish you good fortune."

Releasing Maya, who remained close to him, Madrenga turned back to the Queen. "If this witch has so much power, why did the court of Daria not seek her help in fighting those who besieged your city?"

The old man spoke up. "The Witch of Si'abayoon fights for no one but herself. She keeps to her own counsel and her own ways. Try, and she may deign to speak with you—or as readily turn you into food for worms."

"In any event," added the old woman, "she is not free to help anyone, including herself. For the past thirty years she has been held captive by the Woaralins of Mount Murrl. They alternately tempt and torture her in vain attempts to convince her to reveal her secrets. She refuses all and broods alone in the cave that is her prison."

Madrenga blinked in confusion. "I have heard of many peoples, but never of the Woaralin."

The elder continued, her tone grim. "They are degenerate Selndar, debased offspring of their dignified progenitors. Long ago they were forced from the Selndar tribe to congregate in the caves and tunnels of Mount Murrl. There they have remained ever since, interbreeding prolifically while garnering powers dark and decadent. Any who stray near are in danger." She paused. "Any who attempt to enter never come out."

It was quiet for a moment until Maya spoke. "If this witch is as powerful as you say yet cannot free herself from these creatures, how can we hope to do so?"

"We can only try." Though it required a conscious effort Madrenga mustered his most encouraging smile. "If we don't try, you'll die. As for me, I'm not afraid of death. Not anymore. The boy who left Harup-taw-shet was frightened of many things. The man I have become (and he said it with confidence) is frightened of far less."

Cocking her head to one side, the old woman eyed him curiously. "Then tell us a thing you are still afraid of, boy-man."

Drawing himself up to his full height, Madrenga met her wizened stare without flinching. "Failure, for one thing. It is a great motivator." He smiled a second time down at Maya. "So are you." Returning his attention to the Queen and her advisors, he posited the next question firmly and without hesitation.

"Now, how do we get to this Mount Murrl?"

As had the caravan merchants when he had saved them from the frost dragon, so the grateful citizens of Daria pressed gold and jewels and other precious objects on the mysterious stranger who had somehow raised the siege of their city. One portly merchant even attempted to make a gift of his exceedingly comely daughter to the solitary warrior in the hope that he might remain among them. For some unknown reason Maya viewed this offering with uncharacteristic disdain. Noting her reaction Madrenga thought he might question her about it, but they had no time. Accepting a few of the finest offerings more to convince himself that he was going to have a chance to make use of them in the future than out of any greed or need, he stowed them away in Orania's pack as they left the clusters of cheering, grateful citizens behind. Ahead lay the heavily eroded Anandar Escarpment and at its rugged heart, the broken mass of limestone known as Mount Murrl.

With each passing day he urged Orania to greater and greater speed, because with each passing day Maya grew weaker and weaker. The curse that was killing her was spreading rapidly through her body. Now she responded with a wince when he touched certain parts of her, and tiny red spots had begun to appear just under her skin. In addition to her increasing fatigue she started to complain of pain in her bones and joints. It was plain to see that if they could not free the witch and convince her to render assistance, then Maya would be dead within a week or two.

Of course, a brooding Madrenga told himself, even if they succeeded in freeing the Si'abayoon from her captors there was no guarantee that she would do anything to help them. According to everything they had been told by Queen Zhelerasjju and her advisors, once loosed from her bonds the witch was as likely to strike out furiously in every direction as to listen to those who had rescued her.

No distinct or signposted trail wended its way up the mountainside to the lair of the Woaralin, but the two travelers had no difficulty finding it. All that was necessary was to follow the uneven line of dismembered skeletons and decomposing corpses of animals, men, Harund, and yes, even Selndar. A mound of bodies further marked the way into the bowels of Mount Murrl. High, arched, and black as a socket where a diseased tooth had been removed, the stalactite-festooned cave ceiling loomed above them. To Maya it looked like an open mouth just waiting to swallow.

"You'll stay here," he told her. "I'll move faster without you."

Somehow she mustered enough strength to speak in a normal voice. "I'll *not* stay here. If you don't come back, I'll die terribly alone. If you succeed, I should be with you."

His teeth clenched. "You'll get in the way. And you can't fight. In your present condition you shouldn't even bleed."

"All true," she argued, "but I'm the one seeking the witch's help, and I should be the one to ask for it. If she kills me in a fit of rage, or pique, or whatever, I'll be no worse off than if I didn't try, and while she's dealing with me it might give you a chance to escape."

As always when they were riding he could feel her weight leaning back against him. It seemed so much less now. Just as there was no time to waste in seeking out this last possibility of help, so there was no time to waste in arguing.

Also, it was exceedingly irritating when she was right.

"Come then, and we will triumph or fail together."

She pushed back against him a little harder than usual. "That's all I'm asking for, Madrenga."

While she waited atop Orania he scavenged enough dry brush to make several torches. Putting a pair in reserve, he used flint and striker from his supply pack to set two others alight. Thus illuminated and armed he chucked his mount's reins and set a course for the dark unknown.

The charnel house road they had followed outside was not replicated within the mountain. Bones and bodies had been cleaned up, or else they had never been brought inside. Only occasionally did they encounter the corpse of some unlucky traveler.

"Wait!" Maya shouted.

"What?" An alarmed Madrenga pulled back on Orania's reins. "What's wrong?"

"Nothing." Leaning to her left, she pointed. "What's that, there?"

He peered in the direction she was indicating. "Yet another who strayed too far and too deep and suffered for his boldness. I see no difference between his bones and the many we have already saluted."

"Not the skeleton. What lies by its hips."

Squinting, Madrenga made out the gleam of metal. Some small weapon that had been unable to preserve the life of its owner. From the lie of it, he thought, it had never been drawn.

"A war axe of some kind," was his appraisal. "A small one at that. What of it?"

Her tone was one of hushed amazement. "It looks like a farsa. A legendary weapon."

He shook his head. "Never heard of it."

She looked back at him. "It's not from your legends. It's from mine. From my people. I remember my grandfather mentioning it in stories he told to me of an ancient time, in the country of my ancestors."

"A very small legend, then," he concluded dismissively. "Would you like to have it?"

"It can't be real." She was murmuring as much to herself as to her companion. "Especially not here, in this place. But it *looks* like a farsa." She nodded. "Can I?"

"You haven't the strength to dismount by yourself yet you want a battle axe." He sighed. "Well, it's small enough that you can cradle it. Wait."

Dismounting, he walked over to the finely dressed corpse and took possession of the unused weapon. Returning to where Orania waited patiently, he handed it up to Maya. She studied it reverently as he remounted.

"It can't be." She kept repeating the denial as they resumed their advance. "It just can't be."

Twenty minutes riding brought them to spacious rooms and corridors that shone with the light of thousands of tiny insect larvae and fields of luminescent fungi that rendered the need for torches superfluous. Save for the occasional bell-like ping of dripping water it was a deceptively peaceful place.

Rounding a corner, they nearly ran over a browsing Woaralin.

Down on all fours grazing a hillside of moss, it hardly looked like a person. It was only when, startled by their sudden and unexpected appearance, it stood up on its hind legs that it became recognizable as something whose forbearers had once walked among men. A short length of cloth barely covered its loins while a vest of crude woven material hung from its shoulders. From a rope around its waist an assortment of small utensils hung from shorter cords. Letting out a reptilian hiss, it drew a knife and bolted.

"Orania, *go!*" Madrenga yelled.

The Woaralin was fast and agile, but Bit ran him down before he could scramble up a chosen slope and disappear into the crevice at its apex. As the slender biped tried to use his blade to strike at the snarling, barking dog, Orania arrived and Madrenga slid from his saddle. So thin were the Woaralin's wrists that the youth was able to pin them behind the creature with one hand. The other he placed on the grazer's neck.

"Now you'll hold still and listen," Madrenga growled at his prisoner, "or I'll break your neck!"

Grinning, the repulsive creature turned his head around to look at his much taller, heavier captor. "Weel yee now, brave cheeld? Go ahead and breek eet, then. I've no gold, no geems, I've nothing to geeve yee anywees."

"On the contrary, creature, you carry something of great value to us: information."

Bugging out of their too-small sockets, huge eyes stared back at him. "Knowleedge weel do yee no good heere, feellow. Ask awee, theen. I'll not refuse yee. There's no need. Yee deaths are alreedy foredained."

Having been the recipient of far worse threats these preceding months, Madrenga ignored the warning and maintained his unyielding grip on the Woaralin's wrists and neck.

"We've come for the Witch of Si'abayoon. Tell us where she is being held."

For the first time since his capture the Woaralin looked unsure. "Yee've come heere, to the caveerns of Murrl—to reescue a weetch?" When Maya nodded solemnly, the debased creature burst out in a demented cackle that ceased only when Madrenga tightened his grip still further.

"What reemarkable creetures yee two bee! A meesion feet for the Keeng of Fools heemself!" Had Madrenga's grip permitted it the prisoner would have shaken his head in disbelief. "Weel theen, who bee I to stand in the way of such an admirable goal? Ride on as yee go and yeel come to a treeo of tunneels. Take the right-hand fork. Eet narrows queek. At the end are the ruins of olden Murrl, where first the Woaralin seetled theese mountains. Eet is a place of collapse and ruin. There weel yee find the witch, impreesoned as she has been for decades thrice. If the Woaralin do not keel yee, then by all meens free her and shee surely will." Once more his inhuman screeching filled the cave. It stopped only when Madrenga, with a single powerful twist, wrenched the grinning head around until it was facing completely backward. Letting the now limp body drop from his hands, it collapsed in a rubbery pile at his feet.

"Did you have to do that?" Though she had seen her share of violence over the past days, Maya was still taken aback by the cold abruptness of her companion's action.

Madrenga mounted up behind her, chucked the reins, and sent Orania onward again. "I had no choice, Maya. If I had left him be he might well have raised an alarm. I made him no promises. Besides, the thing did not much seem to care if he lived or died. I, on the other hand, do."

She nodded knowingly, if not entirely understandingly, and went quiet as she solemnly returned her attention to the small battle axe cradled in her hands. There was no rust on it. In the deviant fungal light that suffused the cave through which they were riding it shimmered as if with an unholy glow of its own.

Behind them all was still and silent. Long moments passed. Then the crumpled body of the Woaralin lifted itself up and straightened. Reaching up, one bony hand took hold of the protruding chin while the other wrapped itself spiderlike around the back of the head. A quick wrench, a sharp cracking sound, and the grinning skull was once more facing forward. Gathering itself, the sinister figure scrambled up the steep slope off to its right and disappeared into the fissure at the top.

The ruins the two youths encountered as they turned down the indicated corridor were extensive if not especially imposing. At the age of thirteen Maya had seen far more impressive ones in the course of the trip her family had taken to the old country. Here, as many structures were hewn out of the solid rock as had been constructed with block and boulder. The architecture was as alien to her experience as the rest of this world.

The roof and sides of the cavern continued to contract until they felt sure they must be approaching the end of the corridor and the prison that lay at its terminus. They did not reach it, however, because a line of Woaralin emerged from the rubble to block their progress. Taller and broader than the rest but equally bulging of eye and with a small additional one set too close to the right orb, a figure clad in rags stepped forward to greet them.

"I am Urathu, Chief of the Woaralin. You are weelcome heere, bold strangeers."

Madrenga's hand dropped to the hilt of his sword while Bit growled and showed enormous teeth. "That's not what we were led to believe, Urathu."

Thick-boned shoulders lifted and fell. "Theen yee were meesin-formed. The Woaralin are always weelcoming to a meel." Where-upon he raised the hatchet he was holding, let out an echoing hiss, and charged.

The chaotic cacophony in the corridor was magnified as the sounds of fighting bounced off the enclosing walls. Orania reared and plunged, kicked and twisted, her heavy hooves smashing one attacker after another into a pile of broken bone or sending them flying to smash into the surrounding stone. Darting to and fro among the army of hissing assailants, Bit snapped off arms and legs and flung them in the faces of their stricken owners. Madrenga's great sword rose and fell or whirled in sweeping arcs that sliced through several attackers at once. And still the horde came on; relentless, replenished, and undead, determined to bring down the young and careless life force that had dared to intrude upon their misery.

Seated in front of Madrenga, the enfeebled Maya desperately wished to help but lacked the strength to do more than yell and wave her hands. It was only when one smirking foe slipped in beneath Madrenga's all-devouring blade that she instinctively, reflexively, struck at it with the small battle axe she was holding. Though she could put little force behind the blow, a remarkable thing happened.

Pulsing a bright red, the axe flew out of her hands, propelled by a power unknown and unidentifiable. True to its nature it cut vertically through the skull of the knife-wielding Woaralin. And it did not stop there. Describing a wide arc, it flew completely around the corridor, loping off heads and limbs as it soared. One assailant after another went down beneath the red-tinged blade as it sliced through the oncoming ranks, until at last it returned to nestle soft as a baby's kiss in her open hand.

She gaped at it for a long moment. Madrenga would have joined her in staring save he was too busy. So she released it again.

Another twenty Woaralin went down beneath the flying axe, then another. Their defensive exertions thus unexpectedly reinforced, Madrenga and his companions bore down more forcefully than ever on the depraved multitude. Blood and body parts piled high around Orania's hooves until at last, beset by blades both in front and behind, the remaining Woaralin broke. Hissing and screaming their outrage and frustration they vanished into holes and cracks in the corridor walls as swiftly as if they had been sucked from sight by a plethora of unseen throats. On the goresplashed ground in their wake they left nearly two hundred of their number, among whom was the inhumanly inhospitable Urathu.

As he gasped for breath it took Madrenga a moment to realize that the bloodthirsty denizens of Mount Murrl had been well and truly vanquished. Then he threw back his head and let out a howl of triumph. It reverberated off the walls and echoed up the corridor and penetrated the length and breadth of the three caverns. Turning in the saddle Maya looked at him in shock. So did Bit. Orania whinnied and reared uncertainly.

By the time her hooves once more hit the ground no one was more shaken than Madrenga himself. He gaped at Maya.

"Did—that sound come out of *me*?"

"You and no one else." She was eyeing at him uncertainly. "What I'd like to know is where else it came from."

"I ..." He swallowed. "What do you mean?"

"I mean that didn't sound human, Madrenga. Look." She gestured downward to where Bit was staring up at them. "Even your dog doesn't recognize you."

"No. No," he repeated firmly. "It was a cry of exultation. Nothing more." He closed his eyes and shook his head violently. "I am much changed in body and form from the person I was when I left Harup-taw-shet. A similar change in voice should not surprise."

She nodded slowly, unconvinced, and regarded him a moment longer before returning her attention ahead and past Orania's mane. Picking their way through body parts that oozed and stank, they resumed their measured advance ever deeper into the narrowing corridor. Each lost in his or her thoughts, neither said anything.

At the very end of the long tunnel they halted before a wall of solid rock. Within it was cut a small round window. Closer examination revealed the faint outlines of a door, so perfectly set in the surrounding stone as to nearly be invisible. Dismounting and approaching the barrier Madrenga sought a handle, a pull, a lock. Of these there was none.

"How can it be opened?" he wondered aloud. "There is no place to get a grip, not even a crack in which to squeeze a blade. There is no lock in which to insert a key."

Standing beside him and swaying slightly as she fought to remain upright, a sallow Maya contemplated the door that wasn't there. "I would never have dreamed of trying something like this." A smile creased her wan but still beautiful face. "'Dreamed of.' That's funny. Step back."

Puzzled, he complied as she moved up alongside him. Taking careful aim with the undersized battle axe she let it fly in the direction of the etched stone, putting as much of her remaining strength into the throw as she could muster. Erupting out of her hand, the farsa struck the exact center of the doorway directly below the small circular opening. The two of them had to throw up their hands and turn their heads away from flying shards and splinters of shattered stone.

Before the last of the rock dust had settled they were rushing forward. Where the impenetrable door had been was now an opening in the rock wide enough to admit Madrenga without bending. Beyond lay a cell of modest size. His gaze swept rapidly over a table on which rested a pitcher and bowl. Beyond lay an unkempt bed, a pair of mirrors, an open wardrobe, a chair, a lounge on which reposed …

A handsome older woman, white of hair and fine of feature, who when erect would stand no taller than Maya. As snowy as her hair, her eyes flashed pupils of gray so faded as to almost disappear. Coughing into one hand because of the still swirling dust, she braced herself with the other as she sat up on the lounge.

"We've come to rescue you," Maya blurted, not knowing what else to say.

The Witch of Si'abayoon finally raised her nearly pupil-less eyes in the direction of her enthralled young saviors. Still choking she nodded at Maya and at the same time took note of the unnaturally large black dog that was standing panting beside her. Finally her gaze fell upon the tall, powerful figure who was warily gripping the handle of his sword. Her eyes widened.

Then she screamed.

"Madrenga!"

CHAPTER TWENTY

Scrambling backward on the lounge the witch tried to press herself into the rock behind it. One finger shook uncontrollably as it pointed accusingly in the direction of the bewildered, wide-eyed youth. "Get back, stay away, refute, refute, *refute!*"

Though a stupefied Madrenga could think of nothing to say in response to this utterly unexpected and wholly astounding reaction, Maya's outrage more than compensated for her companion's stunned silence. Weak as she was, her voice rang out clearly in the enclosed space.

"What are you doing, woman? Where's your gratitude? Madrenga has risked his life to save you and you react like this? You should be kissing his feet, not screaming and waving fingers at him!"

"Maya, please." Madrenga was more than a little embarrassed at the ferocity of her response.

Slowly the witch eased away from the wall, her gaze shifting back and forth between the two oddly-matched young people standing before her. A glance behind them revealed no sign of the horrid beings who had for the past thirty years kept her imprisoned in the cell at the end of the long corridor.

"You've really come to rescue me? The Woaralin have not sent a demon to kill me and chew the flesh from my bones?"

"Of course not!" He was still trying to make some sense of her reaction. "How did you know my name?"

"Know your name? Know your name?" Now kneeling on the lounge, the witch stared at him. Stared so long that he began to grow nervous. But she was not trying to cast a spell; only to understand. "You really don't know your own name, do you?"

Concern gave way to exasperation. There was no telling when or if the Woaralin who had fled might recover their courage and return with reinforcements.

"My name is Madrenga. It has always been Madrenga. I have had no other name but Madrenga. What I want to know is how *you* know it. I heard you shout it, no mistake."

"What was the name of your mother?" The witch was studying him intently.

His eyes lowered. "I never knew my mother."

"The name of your father?"

"The same. I remember growing up on the streets of Harup-taw-shet with others like me." When he raised his gaze again his expression was tormented. Seeing it, Maya's heart went out to him as never before. Over the course of the preceding days they had discussed many things, but for some reason never his background, his childhood.

"No." The witch of Si'abayoon spoke decisively. "The others with whom you played were not like you." Knowledge wrapped around her like a dark shawl. "It happens, but rarely. Circumstance sometimes precludes demons from raising their own."

His lower jaw dropped. "What gibberish is this, old woman?"

Her eyes never left him. "In the language of Enar-set, which has not been spoken for a thousand years but which retains its power, 'madrenga' means 'demon.'"

"No." He was shaking his head in disbelief. "No, that's not possible. I'm just another street boy from Harup-taw-shet." He looked down at himself, back up at her, over at a wide-eyed Maya. "I'm no demon!"

The witch spoke slowly, almost comfortingly. "In coming all this way, you must have encountered many dangers, must have dealt with many threats. Surviving such challenges changes men. Unless I am very wrong I suspect it has changed you more than most. More, even, than is natural. Tell me, Madrenga: when I speak thus am I right or wrong?"

He felt faint. His mind was whirling. There was no truth to what the old woman was saying, no truth at all. There couldn't be! And yet, and yet ... it would explain so much. The changes that had overcome him as he faced each new challenge. How he was able to defeat Langan of Jithros and the ravening cabinet of Kakran-mul. How he could catch cannonballs with his bare hand and slay a frost dragon. How he could invite and survive the attentions of smoke sprites and shadow folk and be asked to join in the celebration that was the Mark of the Moon's Month.

How he could survive banishment by the warlock Hinga Cathore and despite that, return safely to his own realm—bearing with him an innocent from elsewhere. But he was only a street youth from Harup-taw-shet. The last thing he felt was demonic.

"Look at your dog." The voice of the witch was firm but gentle. "A demon's famulus if ever I saw one. I sense also the presence of another in the cavern beyond. Who travels with two famuli but a demon or a sorcerer? Having neither the experience nor the aspect of the latter confirms you as the former. Madrenga indeed!" Coming forward she slid off the lounge and drew herself up to her full height. That was not impressive, but the rest of the Witch of Si'abayoon certainly was. "Accept who and what you are, youth. Be not afraid of being!"

He sat down where he had been standing. "Demon. I still—I cannot ..." Confused, a whimpering Bit lay down beside his master.

Natoum, a dazed Madrenga thought. Chief Counselor he was for a reason. Chose a courier who will not be noticed indeed. Who better to carry out such a mission than a demon? A demon unaware of his own self. A demon who, furthermore, could not read.

The witch walked over to stare down at him. Her eyes were like ice. "This ill girl who accompanies you. There is about her an aura that is not of this realm but of another. How come you by her?"

Distraught, he looked over at Maya. The shock had begun to fade from her face, but neither did she rush to console him. Hesitation clung to her like sweat.

"I fought with a warlock," Madrenga mumbled. "A true warlock. His name was Hinga Cathore and I had to fight him because he tried to steal from me the reason for my mission and ..."

He remembered now. Remembered the expression on the warlock's face when Madrenga had provided his name. What had that been? A look of recognition? Comprehension? His throat was dry but he finally found his voice again.

"'I banish you to the first place of death and disease upon which your body and spirit may impinge.' That was what he said when he flung me out of this realm and into ..." he turned imploring eyes to Maya. "Into her realm."

The old woman nodded, deep in thought. "There is more here, I think, than meets the ear or the eye. A 'place of death and disease,' you say. Certainly the girl looks sickly enough."

Maya spread her hands. "I'm dying," she said simply. "Of acute lymphocytic leukemia." She glanced at the unhappy Madrenga. "He called it a curse. He thought by coming here and helping you ..." Her words trailed away. "He thought you might be able to help me."

Turning her head to one side the witch spat an unladylike glob of mucus onto the floor. "Curse or disease, I know not the name you speak. To me they are all one and the same anyway. It certainly resounds with the syllables of death. As to helping you, I am but a poor old woman past her prime, past her time. The paltry few bits and pieces of knowing that I retain may not come near to being able to deal with a misery from another realm. Yet, one may try, one may try."

For the first time since they had entered the benighted underground realm Madrenga brightened. "Then you'll help her?"

"Try, I said. For a demon, your comprehension is slow." The witch returned her attention to the shaky, unsteady Maya. "While I know not the name or nature of your affliction," she said solicitously, "even an indifferent simpleton can see how severely it has diminished you. Do you know anything about it, my dear? Its characteristics, its causation, the manner in which it wracks your body?"

Maya swallowed. She was feeling faint. "It's a disease of the blood."

"Ah! Strange in name but not so strange in essence, then. Blood is blood, wherever it is found. Its color may change but never its purpose." Her voice fell as she nodded to herself. "Yes, maybe, perhaps." When she looked up anew both her posture and tone had strengthened. "I will share my blood with yours, my dear. I will give of myself something to you. That and the right words may with resolve and good fortune affect a change for the better."

An alarmed Madrenga rose to his feet. "Share blood with a witch? How do we know that is for Maya's benefit and not for yours?" His hand hovered near the hilt of his sword and his gaze narrowed. "Are you playing at some game here, woman? Because if you are, and if anything happens to her ..."

The Witch of Si'abayoon peered up at him, her pupils almost invisible against the remaining whites of her eyes. "If I do nothing, I intuit that she will be dead in days. You have nothing to fear, Madrenga, but your caution. Think, boy. Would I risk a freedom so recently regained?" Her eyes dropped to meet Maya's. "Trust me, child. There is danger in this for me too."

Maya smiled thinly. "Have I a choice?"

"None. Live to die, or at least die trying to live. Now then; we need a sharp blade."

Madrenga automatically reached for where his knife had once hung before remembering it was now a sword nearly as tall as Maya. He smiled sheepishly. His altered weapon: another transformation brought about by his travels. Another demonic transformation?

The witch noted the movement of his hand. "Too much blade, I think. Perhaps you have something smaller?"

"Wait." Turning, Maya stumbled to where she had set the small battle axe aside and retrieved it. As soon as the witch took possession of it the faintest of red glows enveloped both blade and handle. The old woman eyed it admiringly.

"How interesting. I do not know this weapon, but I do know it partakes of more than mere metal. Where did you find it?"

Madrenga cast a glance back the way they had come. "It lay in the grasp of a man of bones. It did him no good but served Maya well."

The witch nodded again. "There is about it the air of that which is more than mortal. Not just everyone may wield such a weapon." She squinted at the girl standing before her. "He says it served *you* well. You were the one who wielded it?"

"I didn't exactly wield it." Maya's tone was deferential. "I just sort of aimed it in a general direction and it flew off on its own."

"More interesting still. I believe, my dear, you may have a little of the demoness in you as well."

She blinked, manifestly confused. "What? I'm no demon. I'm a student, that's all. My mother and father are …"

"This is not about them, my dear. It is about you. All about you. About your ability to make use of a weapon that is more than metal." She gestured in Madrenga's direction. "Think, child. The young demon is banished from his realm to yours. To whence does his spirit fly? To what is it attracted? Why you and not another out of millions and billions? Why you?"

Maya tried to formulate a sensible reply but she was too weak. Having enfeebled her body, the leukemia was beginning to work on her mind. Reality and unreality and dream began to swirl together, forming a fog of incomprehension around her. The witch moved closer.

"Turn your left side to me, my dear."

Maya had barely enough sense left to obey. Reaching out, the witch rolled up the sleeve of the guard's uniform the girl was wearing, then that of the hospital gown that served as a crude undergarment. After studying the exposed flesh for a moment she promptly brought the blade of the small axe down in a quick, slashing motion. Bit sat up and barked sharply while Madrenga reached for his sword before catching himself. It was only to be expected that to treat a curse of the blood, some blood would be required.

What the old woman did next, however, surprised him even more.

Rolling up the sleeve of her own garment she drew the blade slowly along her own upper arm. Following the slow, methodical pace of the cut, Madrenga winced. Bit whimpered anew and hid behind his master. So dark red as to be almost black, the witch's blood oozed out not in a steady stream as did Maya's, but more like hot tar. As it contacted the cool air of the cave it gave off occasional wisps of smoke that smelled like broiling fungi.

"Now then," the witch said tightly, "hold still and no matter what, don't move!" Whereupon she pressed her open wound against the one she had just inflicted on the girl.

Maya let out a gasp. Her half-closed eyes snapped wide open. As she exhaled and closed them again, the witch inhaled and opened hers. A curious vapor arose from the point where their flesh met. While this new smell merely caused Madrenga's nose to wrinkle it sent Bit into a perfect frenzy, whirling and jumping, barking and snapping at the air. In the corridor nearby, Orania could be heard stomping the ground and whinnying loudly.

The witch began to speak. Softly at first, then with increasing energy. Madrenga recognized not one of the words. Indeed, many of the sounds that issued from the old woman's mouth were unknown to him. Eyes shut tight, she moaned and gibbered and howled as if in a trance. At the end, the thamaturgical litany collapsed into song.

The blood smoke and conjoined vapor faded. As the last of it vanished into the still air of the cave, Maya collapsed. Madrenga reacted just quickly enough to catch her. She lay limp in his arms, unconscious, head lolling, eyes closed. Grief-stricken he looked over the witch, who stood swaying and fighting for balance.

"You killed her. It didn't work. You killed her!"

Licking her lips noisily the old woman straightened. Except— something was different, he saw. There had indeed been a change —but in the witch, not in Maya.

"You lied to us! You did something to her; you took something from her." He was almost in tears. "*What did you do to her? What did you take?* Tell me before I kill you!"

Maddeningly, the Witch of Si'abayoon looked amused. Her smile was a blaze across her face. "You should see yourself, demon. Eyes searing. Muscles tensed. As simple a thing as a mirror would confirm for you all that I have said. Yes, I took something from her. A little of her youthfulness. A little of her life force." With a sweep of her hand she indicated their surroundings. "I was dying fast here, in this cold, sterile place. I was drying out, going stale. She has rejuvenated me! I am most grateful."

The deed was done. There was nothing he could do. Nothing but mourn and then slay. Though he had the anger, for the latter he had no heart. His was too broken.

"She is dead, then?"

"No, leaper to childish conclusions. She sleeps. My blood and my magic will work within her." She paused. "But not here."

A coldness ran through him. "What do you mean, 'not here'?"

"Her disease is not of this place. Her curse is not of this realm. For what has just transpired to be of any lasting effect it must work on her in her own dominion. She must be sent back." Her gaze met his evenly. "You must do it."

"Me?" Madrenga shook his head. "I don't even remember the

words I used to bring her here. How can I go back? How can I find my way?"

"It is within you, Madrenga. Such things, once learned, are never forgotten. Look within yourself. You are a geography. Everything you have ever done, every place you have ever been, lies there waiting. Exercise yourself. Be what you are. Take her back."

He inhaled deeply. "Tell me I can stay there with her."

The Witch of Si'abayoon laughed. It was deep and scratchy and scarcely feminine and it echoed off every wall and rock.

"This is your home, Madrenga. This is your realm. You are of it and not of hers. You ask a thing that cannot be. Accept it, as you are slowly coming to accept yourself for what you are."

"No." Mouth tight, he shook his head. "No, I won't do that. But I do accept that I have to take her back now or she'll die. If what you say is truth then she may die anyway."

This time the old woman did not laugh. "There are no guarantees in either blood or magic. But we can both live knowing that we tried our best."

He nodded, understanding now. Understanding at last. "If you can't do it then I'll find another way to save her. If you can't do it, then perhaps there is another who can."

She shrugged. "I am five and fifty, but it is true there are those who know ways with which I am not familiar. I do not know all. I am not omnipotent."

He frowned. "You look younger than fifty-five. Has Maya's blood already wrought such a change in you?"

"Somewhat, to be sure." The beautifully crooked smile returned. "I am five hundred and fifty years old, young Madrenga. Old enough to know that I do not know everything. It is called wisdom. Now go. Remember the words and the way. Return her to whence she came. There are some things that must be. There are some things that cannot be changed."

Now it was his turn to nod somberly, and smile. "We'll see."

And then he went.

It was exactly 3:50 AM when the duty nurse on the eleventh floor of St. Stephens Memorial Hospital passed room 6120, glanced automatically inside, and paused. She checked her duty pad, looked again. According to this evening's update room 6120 was vacant. Only it was not vacant. It contained a patient. Entering, she switched on the night light. Except for the patient in the bed, the room was abnormally empty. There was no active equipment, no glowing monitors, not even the omnipresent jug of ice water on the rolling table beside the bed. But there was most definitely someone *in* the bed.

Closer inspection revealed it to be a young woman, sound asleep. Puzzled, the nurse checked the girl's right wrist. The appropriate identification band was in place, though it was far dirtier than it should be. Someone would be taken to task for that, the nurse knew. Entering the hospital identification number into her pad quickly brought up the patient's name and vitals. As the nurse studied them, she frowned. Slowly her frown turned to a little 'O' of amazement. As she continued reading her hand went to her mouth and stayed there. She checked the wristband again, compared it once more with the information now displayed on the glowing pad.

Then she was running from the room, running down the hall and shouting, not caring who she awoke or how many official protocols she was breaking.

Where had she been, her parents and doctors wanted to know? She couldn't remember, she told them. How had she survived so many days out of her bed and disconnected from her support system? She didn't know and couldn't say. How had she ended up in room 6120 on the hospital's top, largely unused floor? She didn't know and couldn't explain.

Sleepwalking with eyes open, one doctor hypothesized. Dazed and moving, but with no memory of what she was doing. Obvious temporary brain disconnection, surmised another. Such conditions were rare but not unknown. Taken together they at least partially sufficed as possible explanations for the implausible. In the crowded corridors she had simply been overlooked, had been regarded as another patient out for exercise. Existing in such a state of suspended reality a person could act perfectly normal and engage in all manner of normal activities, from eating to sleeping. She must have moved from room to room and thereby avoided notice. She might still be doing so, another doctor declared, had not the night duty nurse discovered her.

Yes, bizarre as it was, it was all explicable. Even her parents accepted it. Just as they accepted the one revelation that none of the doctors could fully explain.

"Your leukemia has gone into spontaneous full remission." Standing beside the bed Maya's principal physician, Dr. Handler, had difficulty taking his eyes from the chart readout. "In a couple of days I think we can release you to home care." A huge smile split his round, closely shaven face. "How about that, Maya? Here not long ago we were giving you a few weeks to live and now you're going to go home. It's days like this that not only make me proud of what I do, but make me feel good about it."

Lying in the bed, unattached to any machines or cables or feeding tubes, she smiled back up at him. She looked radiant, he thought. Positively radiant. It made no sense. Her leukemia had been beyond advanced. Now it was almost gone, and in a matter of days. He did not understand it any more than he understood how she had been able to wander the hospital for days upon end without being noticed or questioned, but he was willing to accept the one on behalf of the other. As in life, not everything in medicine was quantifiable. When this was the result, he didn't care. Even her voice sounded healthy.

"Do you think my remission has anything to do with my

being lost in the hospital unaware of where I was or what I was doing?" she asked him.

He shook his head. "I wouldn't think so, but who can say? Maybe you ate something that had just the right combination of vitamins and minerals and trace elements that in your particular body, in your particular case, induced a constructive chemical reaction that's never been documented or studied before. Maybe unconsciously you improvised your own successful chemotherapy, as it were. If that's what happened, I'd give a year of my life to know what it was that you ingested."

"I do feel that I ate some strange things," she murmured.

"What?" He frowned at her.

"Nothing, Dr. Handler, nothing. I do remember that one treatment for the kind of leukemia I have—that I had—is blood transfusions. Isn't that right?" He nodded and she added, stretching as she did so, "I feel so much better."

He laughed softly. "The differences between living and dying are noticeable. You must be excited about going home."

She nodded, contemplating her future. There were her parents, who were beside themselves with joy. And her friends at school, and her extended family, all in a frenzy of excitement over her astonishing recovery. And yet ... and yet ...

One day she would find him, she knew. One day Madrenga would come back for her. It might be this evening, it might be tomorrow. Or next week, or next year. But he would come for her. She was sure of it. As sure as she was of what was dream and what was reality. And she wasn't afraid, not afraid at all.

He might be a demon—but he was *her* demon.

ABOUT THE AUTHOR

Alan Dean Foster is the author of 138 books, hundreds of pieces of short fiction, essays, columns, reviews, the occasional op-ed for the *NY Times*, and the story for the first *Star Trek* movie. Having visited more than 100 countries, he is still bemused by the human condition. He lives with his wife JoAnn and  numerous dogs, cats, coyotes, hawks, and a resident family of bobcats in Prescott, Arizona.

IF YOU LIKED ...

IF YOU LIKED *MADRENGA*, YOU MIGHT ALSO ENJOY:

The Dragon Business
by Kevin J. Anderson

Knight of Flame
by Scott Eder

Gamearth
by Kevin J. Anderson

OTHER WORDFIRE PRESS TITLES BY
ALAN DEAN FOSTER

Oshenerth

The Taste of Different Dimensions

The Flavors of Other Worlds

Mad Amos Malone

Our list of other WordFire Press authors and titles is always growing. To find out more and to see our selection of titles, visit us at:
wordfirepress.com

 facebook.com/WordfireIncWordfirePress

 twitter.com/WordFirePress

 bookbub.com/profile/4109784512